"A woman has got to love a bad m
to be thankful for a good one." – Mae West

THE HUNTING

By Kerry Peresta

To Jane!
Happy Hunting!
Kerry Peresta ♡

Pen-L Publishing

12 West Dickson #4455
Fayetteville, AR 72702

Pen-L.com

P

This book is dedicated to single moms, the bravest women I know. Your perseverance is to be applauded, and will be rewarded.

PROLOGUE

There is just one man at the bar, sitting in the darkest, most lonely corner of it, nursing a drink. I gaze around the room, looking for the mystery man I'd arranged to meet. I order a glass of wine as I wait and move toward the empty stools. Maybe he's running late.

The bartender works his way over, stops in front of me and smiles.

"What'll it be tonight, Izzy?"

"A pinot, I think. Do you have Bearboat?"

"Yep." He plucks a bottle from the shelves behind the bar, deftly uncorks, and pours. "Give it a sec, Izzy."

I nod, wait impatiently for the wine to breathe. Turning the stool around, I scan the bar in case the man appears. After a few minutes, I swirl and sniff, then sip. Heaven in a glass.

The man who had been sitting alone at the far end of the bar pushes off his stool and walks toward me. My eyes lock on his face as he emerges from the dark. The scene unfolds eerily, like something from an old Hitchcock movie.

I clutch the stem of the wine glass like a security blanket and lift it to my mouth. The disgust I feel spikes as he pulls out a stool and sits beside me. The stench of cheap cologne curls up my nose. He must have freshened it since our meeting at the office. I still feel the sting of his words.

"Understandable that you are upset, Izzy. We need to clear the air, I think."

I turn my head toward him, my lips a firm line. "I agree," I spit out. "But this is not the time. I'm meeting someone in a few minutes. So can we talk about this at the office tomorrow?"

Twin rows of perfectly straight, white teeth blaze through the dim lighting. "Nope. We're gonna talk about it right now. Who you waiting for, by the way?"

"My business. We've had this discussion."

His grin does not diminish by a single kilowatt. "Yeah. We have. However, the discussion is ongoing." A beat of silence, then he continues.

"Dreamsicle."

The dread starts at my toes and slithers the entire vertical length of my body. My brain, a hiccup or two behind the dread, snags the realization I've been had. An impromptu prayer pops into my head before I can argue with myself that it never works

I turn to him, my tongue finally loosed, mad as hell. "You? *You?* What are you thinking? This breaks every privacy law ever legislated, for Pete's sake! This is . . . this is . . . *unspeakable!"*

The smile falters, then disappears. His eyes, in the murky light, are unblinking. Reptilian.

"Izzy, you and I have some business to process together." His lips press close to my ear and he whispers, "For Chrissakes, you treat me like a leper. It's going to stop. *Now."*

My hand reaches instinctively to cover my ear and he backs away. The moistness of the whispered words lingers. I rub my ear and put my hand back in my lap.

My hand still clenches the stem of the wine glass. I am afraid I will break it, so I unwrap my fingers, nestle the globe instead, and drink. The glass makes a soft clink when I set it down. I focus my eyes behind the bar. My mind spins furiously. Doesn't this fall under the realm of predatory? How does one go about proving it?

CHAPTER 1

Izzy

I tell myself the late night had been worth it. The date had turned out to be a disaster, I'd missed my alarm this morning and my kids had been upset and snarky before they'd left for school, but let's look at the bright side. I can cross one more guy off the list.

Dabbing concealer on the dark half-moons under my eyes in morning rush hour traffic, I strive, but fail, to keep my Honda in the lane. I ignore the angry honks of startled motorists, and correct my course with one knee. I screech into the *Sentinel's* parking lot a few minutes late, swipe on tinted lip gloss as a final nod to looking presentable, grab my purse and speed-walk into the building, hoping my hair is not sticking out in all directions.

The ancient elevator in the lobby, a dubious attempt at historic preservation in the heart of downtown Chatbrook Springs, creaks from the third floor to the first when I push the button. The doors take a full four seconds to open. I wonder, as I step in, why I don't just run up the stairs to save time. Leaping out of the elevator before the doors fully open, I toss my purse on my desk conveniently located exactly two steps away, and thread my way through the maze of cubicles to the corner conference room.

"Hey, Iz!" My assistant yells at me across 20,000 square feet of industrial carpeting divided into two workspaces by a wide strip of ugly linoleum. I spin around on one foot. He lifts a fresh ad proof he has retrieved from the production department, unfurls, and points to it.

I squint at it, and him, nod vigorously, then lift my hand in the classic thumb-and-forefinger circle, which translates as *Go ahead and clear it.*

The other assistants sprinkled throughout the room smile at the exchange, glancing at each other and the moon-faced clock on the wall. I huff an exasperated sigh. Single parents have a little more to do in the mornings than some people.

A recently hired young assistant with a shocking splash of orange in her hair approaches, her hand motioning me closer. "Just so you know, Phil hasn't made it in yet," she whispers. She smiles, winks, and continues to lay piles of advertising proofs on the desks of appropriate sales staff.

I smile at her. "Thanks, um . . . ."

"Amy," she finishes. She tilts her head in the direction of the conference room door. "Better go on in before he gets here. Most everyone else is already in there."

I enter the conference room quietly, thinking the world needs more Amys. I leave the door ajar for Phil, and look for a seat.

"Izzy!" I squint at the back row where a hand is waggling to alert me to an available spot above the heads of the twenty-five-ish salespeople already seated. Heads bob up, note my arrival, shout out a few *heys* and *good mornings*. The room smells of freshly starched shirts, coffee, aftershave, intermingled perfumes.

The door abruptly opens, and Phil, the Advertising Director of the *Chatbrook Springs Sentinel*, strides into the room, a laptop under one arm. I scurry toward the hand that is still waggling at me and plop down. "Barely made it this time, Izzy," she murmurs, grinning.

"Yeah, whatever. Didn't even have time to get coffee."

"Why would you want to?" she says, acknowledging the consensus that the *Sentinel's* coffee – though free – is completely disgusting.

"Right," I say. "You're absolutely right. Habit, I guess."

Phil scans the room with managerial eyes, quickly digesting who is in attendance and who is not. Woe be to those who are not, his eyes say. His mouth is a tight line, which tells me the sales meeting is probably not going to be a pleasant experience. He punches his laptop to life, and a PowerPoint slide appears. He nods to one of the front-row sitters to turn off the lights, then turns toward us.

"Good morning, people!" We respond with the obligatory pleasantries. He continues, "Got some trending information and some demographic research fresh from the statistics department." He walks around the conference table at the front of the room to stand before us, his wide-legged, hands-clasped-behind-his-back stance familiar. He wears the manager's uniform: heavily starched, expensive white shirt, fashion-forward tie, suit trousers. His suit jacket, I know, has been carefully placed on a hanger in his office closet. Office casual is not tolerated at the *Chatbrook Springs Sentinel*, a respected and award-winning newspaper.

The conference room holds forty standard vinyl and metal chairs, eight around a wood-veneered conference table reserved for senior sales team members or visiting associates from different departments. The remaining chairs are pushed together in four tidy rows of eight each, facing the conference table.

I'm glad I am in the back row, because I am having trouble keeping my eyes open. Maybe I can slouch down and get a nap since Phil has doused the lights. My stomach is queasy, compliments of the two large glasses of wine I'd had last night, and I am not in the best mood.

Phil turns, retrieves a pile of booklets, and passes them to a couple of salespeople in the front row, indicating everyone is to receive a copy. With a flick of his index finger, charts appear on the dry erase board attached to the wall which doubles as a handy presentation screen. Phil pulls a laser pointer out of his shirt pocket and a green dot hovers uncertainly over a series of brightly colored, vertical rectangles.

"This is where we were last year." The green dot slides to its neighbor rectangle, a shorter vertical. "*This* is where we are this year. The booklets you've just received are filled with statistics and results of demographic studies of our primary circulation area."

He pauses as we leaf through our booklets. "Use it on sales calls when you reach out to your clients, or develop new relationships." His face flits through several expressions, none of them encouraging, and he continues, "*Don't* let your clients tell you their advertising budgets are going to online media, *prove* to them that print is doing just fine! Yes, our circulation is dropping, but we're still the best bang for the buck! Talk about our credibility. Focus on the integrity and reputation of printed media. An online presence is cheap for a reason! In order to work, it must be augmented with print." He slides his laser pointer back into his pocket, turns toward us, and assumes the commander-in-chief stance.

"Augment, people. Augment! That's the word of the day."

I open one eye and try to ignore the strings of saliva that punctuate his more aggressive assertions.

"Look, people, the newspaper is not going away," he continues. "We are experiencing a hit from all the web options out there, and maybe we have to adapt to a changing marketplace, but we can't just *roll over*. Our web packages are an excellent value. Sell your customers into our online product and the print product. He grazes each face, his expression somber. "Comments? Suggestions? Questions?"

I fidget in my chair, uncomfortable with the pressure I feel in these blasted sales meetings. I glance around the room at the white cinderblock walls bearing posters that supposedly motivate: *Every no gets you closer to a YES!* and *Successful people never quit. They make mistakes, but they keep moving!* I can't help but grin every time I read them. In light of three failed marriages, I have adopted them as personal mantras. Like last night. The guy was a huge *no*. However, every *no* gets me closer to the big *Yes*.

My neighbor pokes me in the ribs. "Izzy, pay attention!" she whispers. "Phil is looking straight at you!"

I sit up, force my eyelids fully open, and stare back. He gives me his patented hairy eyeball, then continues an energetic narrative, the green dot whizzing over several pie charts depicting missed sales goals by month. They are super-sized on the screen, as if his words have been spat out in bright colors and shapes. I glance at the associate sitting next to me. She stifles a giggle. The sales team is nearly immune to Phil's haranguing, and we simply hang on until the bitter end. I smile back at her and roll my eyes.

Phil concludes the meeting with a litany of barely-disguised threats if we are unable to meet our monthly quotas and attractive monetary incentives if we do. I perk up a little at the 'monetary incentives' part, and glance at a large, wooden plaque on the wall beside the posters.

Across the top, *Salesperson of the Year* is engraved in gold, and underneath are twelve slots reserved for names of team members that have won monthly quota sales contests. Eight of them are engraved, four are not. Two slots, January and June, bear my name, Isabelle Lewis. If I win one more month, I might be in the running for the biggest monetary incentive of the year.

I'm not ashamed to admit it. I am all about monetary incentives.

After the sales meeting, we single-file out, chat briefly, and within ten minutes are in our cubes perusing the newspapers folded neatly and laid on our desks each morning by our assistants. I am eyeing my grungy coffee mug and thinking about filling it when my landline rings. I do not recognize the number. It is a little early for clients to start calling.

"Izzy, *Sentinel*." I am curt, perturbed that my morning newspaper-and-coffee-time has been interrupted.

"Hey, gorgeous!" a breathy voice whispers.

My body tenses. It's the man I met last night, I think. "Umm, hey there . . . aaah . . . ." I try to remember his name, already forgotten. It had been quite the forgettable experience.

"Jacob!" he asserts.

"*Jacob*, yes, how are you today? Thanks again for last night, and don't worry about the little . . . thing – "

"Yeah, that was weird, so terribly sorry about that, really, I thought I had paid that ticket, and oops!" His laughter creaks like a rusty hinge. "Figured I'd make it up to you. When are you free again?"

"Listen, um, Jacob . . . I am pretty busy right now with kid activities and the job, and I don't think, um, that I should – "

"Hold on a minute!" Jacob said, his voice becoming louder. "Already deciding not to get to know me because of one incident? You are not serious! I thought you were different, Izzy. I *explained* to you what happened." He is nearly shouting by the end of this little rant.

"Your face went white as a sheet after you read the note, or ticket, or whatever it was," I respond, my mind clutching at phrases that will placate. "I thought you might be addressing some, um, issues, and that it may not be the best time for us, to, ahh, go forward." I cover my face with my hand, and hope no one is listening.

"It must be really great to be able to figure a person out in one meeting! I am sick of arrogant witches like you!"

I hold the phone away from my ear and stare at it, like it's the phone that is crazy instead of the man. Who talks to a woman this way after one really lousy, ill-fated, date? After his car being towed, the grimy cab transport home at an ungodly hour, and a mystery note at the curb, did he really think I'd be overjoyed to go out with him again?

My cubicle-mate, Winston, eases into his desk beside mine in our pod, his hand holding a fresh mug of coffee. He notes my expression with raised eyebrows. I glance at him, and put the receiver back to my ear.

I take a minute to gather my thoughts, and listen to Jacob's agitated breathing on the other end of the line. How do I manage to get myself in these situations?

"Well, maybe I'm *not* so different from the other arrogant witches you have met," I say. "Good thing you won't need to be seeing me again." I quietly put down the receiver as he hurls further invective, his voice receding until there is blessed silence.

I force the call off my radar and focus my attention to the top of my desk where a pristine, freshly printed newspaper awaits my scrutiny. I unfold it, smooth the pages, and open to "Main News." The pungent scent of ink on newsprint blooms.

I think for the thousandth time how great it is to have a job that actually *pays* me to drink coffee and read the paper every morning before I go out on sales calls to see my clients. Ostensibly, the paper is there so that I can make sure my ads have printed correctly, that no typos have slipped through and that they are placed in the correct section. Unostensibly, seasoned sales reps like me mainly drink coffee and enjoy scanning headlines and catching up on local news.

Winston bids me a chirpy good morning over the eight-inch pod-divide. He then places his reading glasses on his nose, smoothes his tie, licks his thumb, and neatly turns the page of his newspaper.

I adore my pod-mate on several levels. For starters, he convinced the *Sentinel* to hire me when I was a desperate, newly divorced, broke, single mother of three young children eleven years ago when my first marriage died. He convinced upper management to hire me on sheer gut instinct, because at that time I had very little sales experience. I will *always* love him for that.

Winston has clear blue eyes, a closely trimmed white goatee that matches closely trimmed white hair, a penchant for bursting into songs he has written, and a light-hearted disdain for management.

"And how are we this fine day?" he asks.

"I'm fine, Winston. What's happening in your world today?" I take in the pert bow tie that matches both his sport coat and the lanyard around his neck that holds his reading glasses. A driving beret hangs from a corner of his cubicle.

Winston turns another page, sips coffee, flips his glasses off his nose, and graces me with a distinctive knowing smile. I find Winston's expressions entertaining. This one is vintage Sean Connery. He leans toward me on one elbow.

"Have you heard?" he whispers.

Winston's voice tends to get hushed when he has juicy information. Must be really juicy this morning, I can barely hear him. "No! What?"

"Phil hired a new Retail Advertising Manager. He starts next week." He leans back in his chair and crosses his arms.

"No kidding!" My mind careens through best- and worst-case scenarios around the implications, and I am silent a few beats.

"It'll be okay." Winston has an eerie ability to read my mind.

"Yeah, whatever," I say, disgusted. "Last time this happened, look what we got!" I nod toward one of the manager's offices that line an exterior wall.

Winston shrugs. "In God's hands." Winston is a Baptist, and his references to God always perk me up.

"Right. Okay. Well, who is it? Do you know anything about this guy? I'm assuming it's a guy. . . ?"

"I do. Matter of fact, I used to handle his account many moons ago." He pauses to let this sink in and strokes his chin dramatically. I cross my arms over my chest and give him a *c'mon, c'mon. c'mon*, stare.

"The man of the hour is none other than the infamous Birdie Costanza. Used to be one of our biggest clients, and a pain in the butt. His advertising budget was huge, though, so management put up with him. Then he left Georgia to open his own business, but it apparently didn't work out. He needed a job, we needed a retail sales manager." Winston shrugs, elbows bent and tucked to each side, palms upward. "*C'est la vie*," he says.

I think a minute. "Wasn't he in manufacturing or something?" Winston nods. The smile remains on his face, his eyes glued to mine. He sips more coffee. "Then he has *no* advertising experience?"

"Bingo."

I shake my head in dismay, thinking about the tenacious and multi-tentacled *good ole' boy* network the *Sentinel* routinely taps into. Not an excuse for hiring a manager with no advertising experience.

"What's he like?"

Winston cocks his head, then wags it side to side. "You don't want to know."

"Oh, great! You're kidding, right?"

"I could be wrong. People change." He stretches both arms out, then pulls them behind his head, entwines his fingers, and stares at the ceiling.

Having achieved twin goals of dropping a bomb *and* planting unsavory gossip-nuggets, Winston resumes reading his paper and sipping his coffee. His face is implacable. I give him my best consternation look, stew for a minute or two, decide to drop the subject.

As I try to pull up my calendar on my desktop to review scheduled client meetings, I hit all the wrong keys, and have to start over.

CHAPTER 2

A familiar anticipation tingles through my chest. I am rewarded with a couple of winks and three messages. The attention I'm getting online is doing amazing things for my self-esteem. It's a lot cheaper and more effective than counseling ever had been, that's for sure.

My last divorce had taken me completely by surprise. Though we'd been struggling with intimacy and communication issues, I had not been overly concerned. All marriages struggle a little in the first few years, right? Apparently, in my overly optimistic view of the world, I'd thought our problems were normal. Well, they weren't. In fact, *disturbing* was the word the therapist had used to describe my husband's behavior as each crisis fed into another.

I read the carefully composed messages slowly, savoring every word.

One is intriguing. I quickly click on his profile, which reads: "Lover of life seeks adventurous, attractive woman between the age of 35 and 45. Must be young at heart, fun, and ready for romance. Kids okay. I am setting sail for my perfect match; could you be the one? I am ready for love! I am a fit, handsome (or so I am told), mature, non-smoker. I'm ready to settle down. I love long walks, handholding, hugs, dancing, 90s rock, and sailing. I like a woman who works out regularly and takes pride in her appearance. I hope she will have a flexible schedule so we can travel sometimes." I scan the rest of his information, which includes career, age, religious preferences, favorite movies, quotes, and more. His photo is not great, but good enough.

I sit back in my chair and begin composing my response in my mind. I scan his message again. *Mature man* means he is probably around sixty. At least fifty. I am nearing forty, so fifty might work, but sixty is definitely out, and I don't care how much money the guy makes. I have rules about this stuff.

Ready for love and romance means he expects sex while dating, which for me, is a no-no. Call me old-fashioned, but I'm not sleeping with a guy until he commits.

Works out regularly or *takes pride in her appearance* means plus-size women need not respond. *Likes to travel* means he probably makes a good living, has some money stashed, or is retired. This particular profile, on a scale of one to ten, is about a seven-and-a-half, but I am going to respond anyway. Never know.

I finish composing a response and hit *reply*. I like the sites because they are entirely anonymous. I am careful to get to know someone before an in-person connection, but sometimes – maybe too often lately – I throw caution to the wind. The romantic rush is kind of, well, glorious.

I click on my profile and study my head shot.

Dusky blonde, highlighted, straight, shoulder-length hair. Huge blue eyes. Full, pouty lips I'd bought from a dermatologist that had convinced me of the virtues of Radiesse. I click on the full-length shot, which portrays a confident, fun woman in business attire with mischief in her eyes. Locked, loaded, and ready for love.

Or something like that.

I cock my head and squint at the photos, trying to figure out what a man would think, shrug and move on. I had long ago given up trying to figure men out.

Two Years Ago

After six confusing months of marriage counseling, I'd attended the final session surrounded by supportive friends in the therapist's office. I felt we were in the home stretch of a long and difficult separation. He had just returned from a ten-day stint at a celebrated rehabilitation facility for sex addicts, and I thought he would finally apologize for his actions, sweep me theatrically into his arms, and declare his re-commitment to our marriage. I'd not given up, not once, on my third marriage.

My husband had been seated centrally in the room, and everyone around the perimeter clutched their hands, leaned forward eagerly. The counselor probed for indications of repentance, remorse, or reconciliation. My husband had simply gazed vacantly at the counselor and around the room and uttered these words: "I am not going back. Ever. I want a divorce."

The Present

My sons' gentle snores behind their bedroom doors make me smile. I shake the tears off my cheeks. An invitation to chat appears on the screen. My response is quick.

CHAPTER 3

"Mom! Where is my basketball?" my oldest son, the rule-abiding, responsible one, yells up the stairs.

"In the garage!" I yell back, trying to finish my makeup in the small bath off my bedroom. "On the top shelf with Mimi's volleyball!" I tap the makeup brush free of excess, then brush on blush. Do a last-minute once-over in the mirror, stare at the unmade bed, decide against making it up, and run downstairs.

Mimi, my twelve-year-old, is slurping up the last of the milk in her Cheerios, and mumbles in my direction. Irritated by cabinet doors that have been left open in the daily stampede for breakfast, I slam them shut harder than necessary. My mind rambles ahead, taking in our typical morning chaos, planning the next move to speed things along so everyone will get out the door on time.

As I pull out the orange juice and the toaster, I scan the kids' ensembles. Mimi – brunette, hazel-eyed, and within spitting distance of being a teenager – has managed to match. Chad, my introverted blond and brooding middle son, has chosen black, black, and black. No surprise there, I just hope the private school they attend doesn't ask him to go home to change. I sigh. No time to fight with him about his clothes.

My eyes quickly slide to Peter, who is texting on his phone, backpack already slung over one shoulder, ready to walk out the door. I know his dishes are rinsed and put in the dishwasher. His attire, of course, is perfect. I smile as I pour my juice and pop bread in the toaster. At least I have one kid I don't need to worry about.

"Ready to go, guys?" Peter asks, shrugging his backpack into a more comfortable position and sliding his phone in a pocket. "Lookin' sharp, Mom," he adds. "You may want to, um, iron that skirt, though."

"Thanks honey." I turn and address the gang, leaning against the kitchen counter. Sunlight streams through the window behind me, its warmth enveloping us in a gold halo. "Got everything? Mimi, did you get your homework done? And Chad, how about yours?" They chorus assents. "What's going on after school today?" A jumble of information is tossed at me as they trot down the stairs from kitchen to garage to car.

My toast pops up and I smooth on butter and jam over it with a knife, shove it into my mouth and chew as fast as possible. I only have about five more minutes before I am absolutely assured of being late again. I force the toast down my throat, throw back the rest of the orange juice, and walk to the front door to wave to my kids as their car disappears down the street, thumping a bass line that I'll probably get complaints about from my neighbors.

Ahh, the life of a single mom.

I trot upstairs for jewelry and a final tweak of makeup and hair, which takes longer than necessary. I decide to forget about ironing the skirt.

"So I'm late again," I announce to an empty house as I gather purse, keys and tote before I head to the garage. "Nobody's perfect." My Honda purrs smoothly out of the drive, and I wait until the garage door closes before I floor the accelerator.

As I pull into the *Sentinel's* parking lot twenty minutes later, I carefully avoid running into people streaming by in chatty groups, heedless to the cars nosing by them, sniffing out a parking space. The morning sun creates dappled patterns on the sidewalk. Chilly autumn evenings have turned the leaves of the trees surrounding the parking lot the color of gold coins. A breeze ruffles them, tiny golden hands applauding my efforts to locate a parking spot. The breeze feels delicious on my face as I exit.

After a few steps, a familiar form approaches. His hair hangs in graying, oily, clumps around his face and his form is puffy with layers of threadbare clothing. His hand is outstretched. I search my purse, find no cash in my wallet, but scrounge the bottom, and triumphantly produce a quarter and a dime.

"Here you go. Sorry I don't have any other cash." I place the coins in his hand. His dirty fingers curl around the money. Then he leans back, winds up like a baseball pitcher, and throws them back at me, an angry scowl on his face. He mumbles and leaves to approach more likely candidates.

I stare after him, my brow wrinkled. What was that all about? Inflation?

As I bend to scrape up the coins from the chipped cracks in the parking lot concrete, I suddenly remember what day this is. My heart, like a slug covered in salt, withers.

This is the day Birdie Costanza is handed the reins to the retail sales team. How many new ad managers had whizzed through the Retail Advertising Department in the past few years? Four? Three? For some reason I cannot not put my finger on, a new manager tends to regard me as a bit of a challenge. It takes them a while to warm up to me. And *this one* – a product of cozy business relationships instead of a killer resume – should be trouble times ten. Which could ultimately affect my bottom line. I straighten, throw the coins back into my purse, and walk toward the entrance to the *Sentinel* with a sigh.

I brighten, however, at the plethora of opportunities around his name.

Winston is going to go crazy with puns. He might even write a song.

I hop up the three stairs to the ponderous double doors that lead to the lobby and administration floor, then three more to the elevator. Change my mind and decide to take the stairs. What if I meet Birdie on the elevator? What would I say? I would be trapped with him on that godforsaken slow elevator.

As I move toward the stairs, I collide with a tall, overly tanned man perched at the top of the stairs a few steps from the elevator. He nearly falls backward. His ice-blue eyes flash daggers of irritation as he regains his composure.

"Oh gosh! Sorry, I just – "

"No problem, honey." He smiles, adjusts his navy sport coat, smoothes his tie, and scans my face. The rest of me too, I notice. He has a kerchief tucked into his sport coat pocket. Who wears pocket kerchiefs?

"In a hurry, sweetheart?" His hair is wavy and blonde, slicked straight back with something shiny. His hand flutters around it, patting here and there.

"I guess so," I say and laugh a half-hearted laugh. "Really sorry. Have a good one." Then I turn and trot up the stairs, not bothering to introduce myself, still smarting from being referred to as *sweetheart*. And *honey*. Really?

I have the sinking feeling I have just run into our new sales manager.

So much for first impressions.

I burst out the second-floor door from the stairs well in advance of the elevator, toss my purse on my desk, grab my mug, and hurry toward the back to get coffee.

A megawatt smile greets me. "Hey, Iz, good morninck! How are you today?" Darlene is stirring creamer into her cup. The smell of the *Sentinel's* coffee is mildly noxious. I grab the carafe, check my mug for residue, decide a little residue won't hurt, and pour.

"Awesome, actually. Had a good morning. We all got out of the house pretty much on time for once."

Darlene glances at her watch. "Ja, I see that! Good for you!"

Darlene, a petite personality-powerhouse of German descent, is my staunch ally and best friend. Married to one of the top sales reps, she works in billing and has an inside track on much of what is going on.

"So what's the latest conquest story, Iz?" she asks, teasing.

I shrug. "Not a conquest, more like a nightmare." I give her a quick recap of the weekend, which had yielded a couple of *absolutely nots*.

Darlene laughs and throws one arm out to the side. Fortunately, it is not the one holding the coffee. "Why do you waste so much time hunting for guys online? You know, there's only about a fifty percent chance one will live up to his profile, right?"

I shrug a bigger shrug, defensive when she lectures me, but okay with it because best friends get a pass. "Whatever. Every no gets me closer to –"

"A YES," she finishes for me. "Got it. But be careful, okay? Maybe you should send me their profiles before you agree to meet."

I give her a mean look. I am too tired to argue with her.

She looks at my face and laughs. "I know you've got a meeting, Iz, so I'll catch you later. Get a drink after work this week, maybe?"

"That'd be great," I say, nodding my assent. "Okay. Gotta go meet the new retail sales manager." I stifle a gag reflex before I swallow a sip of coffee.

"Oh that's right!" she says. "My husband told me somezhink about him, but I just can't remember. . ." She pauses, thinking, cradling her mug in both hands. Steam spirals from the coffee in a slow arc. Her short, blonde curls bob in frustration. "I just can't remember! I guess since he works in the classified department, and you work in retail, I didn't think it vas important. I'll try to remember."

"Well, maybe it wasn't that important. Let me know." I give her a two-finger salute, walk toward the meeting, high heels clicking briskly on the linoleum, then muffling as I step onto the carpet leading to the conference room. My online dating venture feels exactly like a second job, and I'm sick and tired of being tired.

Eighteen Months Ago

I'd completed a six-week Divorce Care program in lieu of therapy after the shock of a third divorce had worn off, and it had been very helpful. Our graduating class of freshly encouraged divorcees had bonded around shared emotional pain, participated in the requisite celebratory potluck at the end, and hugged each other good-bye. I was ready to get back out there and spread my healed little wings.

I eventually cruised a few dating websites and stumbled upon that impossible-to-resist free trial period. A veritable sea of men! Anonymously! Seven days at no charge! It had been as if someone had told me I could have all the chocolate crème brulee I wanted and not gain weight. I was addicted immediately.

The next day at the office I'd mentioned casually to Darlene that I was giving online dating a whirl. I'd spoken in guarded tones, glancing down the hallway in each direction, obviously uncomfortable with the admission. She had listened attentively, smiling, stirring her coffee. I'd waited with the tiniest bit of anguish while she chewed on her lower lip.

"Well, lots of people are doing that nowadays," she'd responded, which gave me no indication whatever of her opinion.

"Thought I might give it a try," I'd said casually, shrugging my nonchalance. She'd chosen her words carefully, unwilling to douse my enthusiasm, but hesitant to embrace it.

"Hey, try it and if you like it, great!" she'd said. "Maybe you'll meet someone. But I have heard horror stories. Haven't you heard the horror stories?" She'd tilted her head, squinted her eyes, and looked at me sideways.

I'd shot back to my desk feeling like an idiot. Chewed on her remark like a dog with a bone the entire afternoon, and finally decided to go forward. How bad could it be?

CHAPTER 4

The Present

Phil and the guy I nearly knocked down the stairs break from the gaggle of managers around the glass-walled corner offices and walk in my direction. The sinking feeling on the stairs had been correct. I jerk open the door and scan seating opportunities.

My co-workers are spiffed up in honor of the occasion. I look down at my own ensemble and sigh. In the morning scramble to get out the door, I rarely have time to make sure everything matches, much less ironed. Sometimes I slide into my cubicle and under the fluorescents see that the hue of the brown jacket and brown skirt I've thrown on go together about as well as peaches and ketchup. Today, I've managed to look rather presentable. Rumpled, but presentable.

I smooth my skirt self-consciously and slide into the back row.

We hear Phil's jocular commentary a few seconds before he steps through the door. Glances and smiles are exchanged all around, because this is typical Phil-behavior with a new person. *Jocular* is not the adjective one would use to describe our advertising director's personality.

Phil and Birdie enter, manager-Twinkies in navy sport coats and crisp, starched, white shirts. Phil indicates that Birdie sit at the conference table and glances meaningfully at the salespeople already seated there. One of them hastily vacates his seat and finds a spot in the back row. Phil stands in front of the table, clasps his hands behind his back, and scans the faces he knows so well. We understand the look. It means, "Don't embarrass me in front of the new guy or you will regret it."

We all straighten to full attention.

"As you know," he begins, "we have been looking for a new retail advertising manager for some time."

Heads nod.

He crosses his arms over his chest. "Obviously," he looks toward Birdie, "we have selected that person."

Pause.

We wait silently. I cross my legs and wonder if applause is expected. Phil continues, but seems a little disappointed.

"Birdie is going to take over the responsibilities I have been handling since the position was vacated." We sneak glances at each other. None of us knows exactly what happened to the last retail manager, whom we had liked and respected. One day he was there, the next he was not. The general consensus was that he didn't fit in with the upper tier.

The advertising director, retail advertising manager, and classified advertising manager are as tight as Moe, Curly, and Larry. You rarely see one without the other. If someone doesn't fit, they are history. The reason why is always obscure and mumbled and accompanied by glares, so we quit asking. As sales reps for a major daily newspaper – which, due to the mammoth strides internet has made, is bleeding ink all over the place and a dying breed – we know better than to push things. So we keep our heads down and hope we still have a job each week.

Phil continues, "As some of you may know, Birdie was the advertising decision-maker for one of our biggest clients few years ago. He has been around advertising a long time, and we feel he is going to make a *great* sales manager."

Another pause.

No applause.

Phil stares at us with steely eyes. Turns to Birdie. "Birdie? Say a few words?"

Phil and Birdie exchange places. Birdie clasps his hands behind his back just like Phil, but manages to look more like Hitler than a new guy in need of the staff's respect. I know from experience that Phil is soft, cream filling underneath his crunchy exterior, but I figure if I give Birdie a little Pillsbury Doughboy poke my finger might not remain attached.

Just a hunch.

Winston catches my eye and shrugs. This is not good. If Winston has signed on to the guy, I would see the knowing smile. Not only is Winston shrugging, he is gripping his lanyard, a sure sign of emotional distress. Which in turn, causes *me* distress. I have learned to trust Winston's instincts. *Man up*, I tell myself. Then I absurdly wonder why there isn't a *Girl up* or a *Woman up*. If there were, that is what I would tell myself.

"First of all, I'd like to say howdy to all of ya'll!" He grins, but his light blue eyes remain cold, like glacial ice. He moves to the front of the conference table, sits on it, one leg swinging from the table, the other perched on the floor. Phil frowns in disapproval.

"Now, I know some of you are thinking, who *is* this guy? What does he know about advertising? Is he going to try to tell us what to do without even coming from our industry?" He grins and scans our faces. He pauses a few seconds on mine, trying to place me. Recognition hits his eyes briefly. I uncross my arms and look at the floor. "Well, I want to let ya'll know that I have been very successful at leading a team so I think that part'll work out good. But I am trusting Phil here," Birdie dips his head in acknowledgment of Phil's advertising prowess, I suppose, "to get me up to speed."

He reveals strikingly white teeth. I wonder if they are false. "O'course, I am going to learn from all of you, too. I'll be going out with you on calls, meeting the clients, for a while. I want to be up close and personal with the front end *and* the back end." He gazes earnestly at each of us. We are all suppressing outward displays of inward groans that accompany the suggestion of *ride-a-longs*.

Birdie is unfazed, however, and proceeds, oblivious to the depressing bomb he has just dropped.

"I'll be scheduling one-on-one meetings with all of ya'll this week and next. We can work out a schedule for the ride-a-long, and get to know each other. I look forward to it."

His hair does not move at all and I suspect is sprayed to the consistency of concrete to hold its gale-force, windblown look. His appearance, while impeccable, shouts *mobster* instead of *professional*.

Phil gives a few half-hearted, positive strokes about recent sales, bludgeons us about sales goals, and dismisses the meeting. Winston and I join the single-file line forming to go back to our desks.

"Just what we need, a day or two of ride-a-longs," he whispers.

I shoot an eye-roll at him. "I know, right? Like the clients don't have enough to do? This is going to kill my schedule for the next two weeks."

"And mine," he murmurs and shrugs.

CHAPTER 5

Darlene watches the mass exit with interest. Her desk is surrounded by metal file cabinets and sandwiched between the coffee break area and the sales floor, which makes it relatively private. This allows her to participate in all manner of hushed conversations with disgruntled employees.

I make a beeline for her desk.

Darlene is a mom and big sister all rolled up into one lovable package, and I adore her. She has no children of her own, which probably accounts for all the time she spends chatting with needy employees, myself included, in the break room or at her desk. Plus, she has a German accent, which makes her fun to talk to. If one lives in Chatbrook Springs, Georgia; population 232,504 if you include surrounding communities, one finds entertainment where one can.

I stand at her desk. Her eyes regard me attentively.

"How vas it?" she asks.

"Let's just say, I am in need of . . . a little encouragement right now. Not liking the way things are going. *Another* new manager? Seriously?" I lift my right hand to my left shoulder and massage the area that tends to knot when stress is involved.

She nods, and says, "*Jede dunkle Wolke hat einen Silberstreifen am Horizont.*"

Only Darlene can encourage me in German. I have no idea what she is saying, but I feel encouraged anyway.

"Every dark cloud has a silver lining," she translates. "It will work itself out. You'll see. You might even grow to like him!"

I stand there, thinking.

Darlene says, "Don't take on a lot of vorry before it's time, Izzy. A day at a time." She is right. I unclench my fists and look her full in the face, and notice circles under her eyes and an unhealthy pallor. I wonder about her. She never complains about anything, doesn't seem to have problems.

"So did you remember what it was your husband said about Birdie?"

"Ja! I did." Her expression imperceptibly shifts. "He said he was very successful in St. Louis with his company, but that somezhink happened. Somezhink that caused his company to shut down very quickly." She pulls her eyebrows together, looks at me quizzically. "Too quickly, I zhink." Her eyebrows unfurrow, she cocks her head and lifts her hands. "All I know," she says. "A mystery."

I nod, contemplating. "Whatever. Who knows? Businesses open and close all the time. I'm just wondering how he is to work with."

She shakes her head. "Can't answer that one. Time vill tell." She turns to her computer. "Better get started on these invoices, I guess," she says, smiling at me. Her eyes, typically bright blue, are a washed-out gray today.

"You okay? I mean, you seem tired, that's all. Is everything all right?"

"Ja. Ja. Oh, things are fine, I mean . . ." she sighs. "Things *will* be fine. I believe that."

Alarm bells clang ever so distantly. "*Will* be fine? So what is not fine?

Tension passes briefly through her petite features. She pauses, then nods to herself as if she has made up her mind, her eyes suddenly liquid.

"Can you go out for a drink after work? Just for an hour or so?" I reply in the affirmative. Stress eases off her face.

I, however, am now carrying more of it on mine.

As I walk back to my desk, I notice Birdie, Phil and the classified manager, Milton, enjoying animated conversation in Phil's office seated around his corner table. Winston is not back in the pod yet. I am slightly disappointed. I have become used to bouncing depressing thoughts off him, and usually feel either vindicated or hopeful afterward. Either is preferable to what I feel right now.

I allow myself a small, exasperated sigh before I plunge into the tasks ahead of me. I pick up the phone, start dialing. Client after client responds to my confirmation calls that yes, a meeting is good, yes I'll be glad to talk to you about that opportunity, blah blah. After using up all my conversational sales skills, I shoot out a chatty group email with appropriate propaganda-laden advertising rhetoric.

My assistant, Lonnie, thumps into his chair with a stack of proofs from the production department. I give him a quick thumbs-up.

I notice out of the corner of my eye that Winston is heading toward our pod. Too late to participate in a marathon dissection of the sales meeting. I locate a *Sentinel* tote bag and dump in some promotional materials. My clients are unfailingly grateful for any small gift I bring, which is a pretty funny, because, well, think about it. How many newspaper-shaped stress balls, cheap insignia pens and key rings does one need?

I grab my purse and wait for the cursed elevator, the consummate sales professional, jumping into the fray with unparalleled zeal to rack up more advertising dollars. Winston gives me a knowing smile from his seat in the cube. I widen my eyes at him and cross them, which is a cool trick I learned years ago and routinely pull out to indicate the ridiculousness of a given situation. He nods in understanding. As the elevator doors open, he waves, smiles, and begins to thoughtfully caress his lanyard.

When I plunk all my paraphernalia down in the passenger seat of my Basque Pearl Red Honda Accord, I feel motivation leaking out of me like a helium-filled balloon at life's end, wafting lazily to the ground.

Lazily wafting sales reps, of course, are absolutely worthless. Somehow I must re-inflate myself.

Twenty minutes later I arrive at my house. Five minutes after that, my laptop is plucked from its charging station at the desk upstairs and in my lap in the downstairs den. Two minutes after that, a few deft strokes reveal several blinking "You have a message!" icons. My insides flutter, and all thoughts of Birdie and sales goals and ride-a-longs and mysterious business revelations vanish into thin air.

I would have to fake my sales report today. I need to be right here, of course, as I am in serious need of re-inflation. It's all about priorities.

CHAPTER 6

I am still at the computer, rapidly typing responses to various potential online matches, when my kids, Mimi, Peter, and Chad, arrive home in a cloud of exhaust fumes and thumping bass. I figure I'd better wrap up, as they are increasingly voicing concern over mom's obsession with dating sites. I tap out a few more comments as I hear the thuds of each car door closing, the tread of three pairs of feet on the stairs and the clunk of backpacks on the kitchen table. I quickly minimize the screen, set my laptop aside and trot to the kitchen.

Mimi smiles at me through a mouthful of Oreo cookie. Black crumblies polka-dot her smile. "Hi, mom. Yes, I'm gonna do homework."

I nod at her, say "Yep, good, Mimi. You know homework starts right after snacks. Agreed, everyone?" Chad and Peter groan. The boys start making excuses at the same time and I hold up my hand to signal that they should shut up and listen.

"Let's talk about that when I get home from work later, guys. Right now, all I am interested in is that you get your homework done. I want to see it, and go over it with you tonight. After that, we'll talk about what else is going on. Got it?" They shrug and reluctantly dig around in their backpacks and pull out notebooks.

I plant a kiss on top of each head, or whatever I can reach, gather my bag full of client goodies and my purse and head back to the office to complete the sales report that is required by close of business. Must buy an alternative to the *Sentinel's* coffee on the way, of course.

Starbucks is nearly deserted mid-afternoon. I pull up and order my standard Grande Breve Latte with two pumps of raspberry, extra hot. My favorite barista, Lydia, knows to add one packet of raw sugar, stir and top with lots of nutmeg. She extends it to me from the drive-by window and smiles. I clutch it gratefully and zoom off.

After ingesting half, a combination of guilt and caffeine zips through my bloodstream to my brain and the resultant fervor incites me to aim the Honda toward a couple of my recently assigned automotive clients nearby. I pull up in front of the showroom, pleased as punch with myself that I am actually making a cold call, grab my bag and start for the door. Thoughtful preparation is not a strong suit, but my impulsivity is boundless.

A salesman on the lot runs to open the door for me. It is obvious by his manner that he thinks I am an "up" (an interested potential car buyer) and when I identify myself, his disappointed expression tells me he regrets the courtesy.

I ask if the general Manager is available, and the salesman runs off to check. He returns, a pie-faced, eager, young man displaying good manners and a tie that does not match his wrinkled yellow shirt. He asks me to follow him to the general manager's office.

A hint of delicious men's cologne tickles my nose as I enter a room paneled in dark wood. The office is carpeted with the indoor-outdoor stuff that plagues most offices. I notice that he, or maybe his wife, has brought in an expensive Oriental rug to anchor desk, credenza and two matching, brown leather chairs. The man seated at the desk turns from his computer screen toward the young salesperson and waves him off. He rises, smoothes his tie and extends a hand, his scent sailing my way on the wings of his smile.

Wings of his smile? The caffeine is definitely working.

I extend my hand. "Isabelle Lewis. Izzy for short. Thanks for seeing me on the fly like this!" My lips form themselves into the winsome smile I have practiced in the mirror.

"Tom Burke. You're welcome." His eyes linger on my face.

"I'm kind of confused . . . we already have a sales rep from the *Sentinel*. Jon Hoyt."

I am expecting this. "Yes, I understand. Jon is your classified rep. I represent retail, the front sections of the paper like Main News, Local News . . . and Sports. Also the Society section. Different marketing approach. Different demographic, typically."

Tom sighs. "Too many reps to keep up with. Whatcha got for me?"

I like his directness, quickly sit and share a few retail advertising opportunities that might fit his market. We hit it off immediately, and set a date to meet to discuss the opportunities in depth. We shake hands again, and I leave, feeling, as always, the thrill of the *Yes*.

Now if I could just experience the same success in my personal life, I'd be set.

Greatly encouraged, I point the Honda to another new client. Maybe I won't have to fake my sales report after all.

CHAPTER 7

The restaurant Darlene and I had agreed upon is just beginning to fill with the happy hour crowd, and I ease in front of a parking meter. The popular River's Edge District, which had arisen practically overnight on the heels of the city's decision to develop the riverfront, is alive with activity. A red and green trolley rumbles by, and groups of laughing people make their way to River's Edge restaurants. A street musician pounds a trio of trash cans hoping his efforts on the makeshift drum set will entice a few dollars into the upturned hat by his feet. Multiple frothy wakes from barges churn the Savannah River in the background. I trot up the stairs to Raphael's looking forward to girl talk, a glass of wine, and light jazz from the piano bar.

Her hand waves at me from a table in the back. I catch the eye of my favorite server, who gestures that he will bring a glass of the La Crema Pinot I typically order. I drop into the chair by Darlene, study her face, lean forward, and cross my arms on the table. "So what's up?"

Darlene lowers her eyes and fiddles with her martini glass. "I'm sure it's nozhink. I am just a little paranoid, probably." Delicately raises her martini to her lips. Darlene's accent presents itself more noticeably when she is under stress.

"Yeah. *Nothing*. Right. Darlene, you are the most trusting woman I know. If *you* have noticed something, it probably really *is* something. So, what has happened that is upsetting you?"

My wine arrives. I wink at the young server, swirl the wine, hold it aloft, push my nose into the glass for a bouquet-sniff. Yum. I swallow with closed eyes, relishing the first taste. Nod to the server that the wine is satisfactory. He gives me a seductive, slow grin – that I return – and disappears.

Darlene pushes her glass around the table, which wears a white starched tablecloth, a one-quarter-inch-thick slab of edge-beveled glass, and a small centerpiece of white and yellow real daisies. She pushes her shoulders back and sits up straighter in her chair. "I think Richard is havink an affair."

I almost choke on the wine, and spend a few seconds attempting to force the liquid down my throat instead of spurting it out my nose. "The only thing you could've said that would have shocked me more is that you're moving back to Germany! You are not serious!" I grab a starched, white napkin and blot my nose.

Darlene's face reddens, and she squinches her eyes, holding back tears. Takes a long swallow of her martini, then looks past me, out the window. My gaze follows hers. A few bold strokes of Cirrus arc across a hard, blue sky. She leans forward, places an elbow on the table and puts her chin in her hand. She spears an olive with the other and pops it into her mouth.

The jazz pianist arrives and slides onto the bench at the gleaming, black grand piano in the corner, easing into "That Satin Doll." A few people get up and move to stools circling the piano.

I am speechless. Darlene's marriage is the last one I would have thought to have problems. I continue, as delicately as a locomotive on a nature trail, "What are you going to do? Are you *sure* this is happening? Have you approached him about it?"

Tact has never been one of my strong suits.

Darlene's expression indicates that she has not yet approached her husband about her concerns. Happy hour revelers are congregating in earnest now. The River's Edge District is a wildly popular after-work destination. By nine p.m. on weekdays it is silent as a tomb, but from five p.m. until then, it's a huge party.

"I don't know, Izzy. I am kind of, how would you say it . . . shell-shocked. I am hopink you might give me some thoughts."

"Yeah. I'll give you some thoughts. Just kill the bastard." I gulp my wine. I do not normally gulp wine, but I am truly dismayed. Anyway, it seems to help those people in the movies who kick back booze when a severe problem arises, so I figure it might help me, too. I order another glass.

Darlene smiles glumly. "Well, I *have* worked through the anger part of it somewhat, and now I am hoping to find an online group or something – people who have *experienced* this. Because I have no idea what to do. I know I have to talk to him, but I am not sure how to approach it."

She reaches for the new martini that has just arrived. The handsome server winks at me, obviously flirting, which I, of course, encourage on a regular basis.

"I have done a lot of research online and there are pros and cons. Some women have forgiven and worked it out, and others have simply left. And then, I think, maybe I am paranoid." Tears spring to her eyes. "I love him, Izzy." She wipes them away quickly.

My heart turns over in my chest. Germans don't cry easily, she has told me many times. I am unsure how to respond, so I reach for my wine glass. At times like this, I wish I had a better relationship with God. Then, at least, I could offer to pray for her. As it is, I feel helpless. Moronic. And my tension quotient is now off the charts.

Darlene tactfully changes the subject.

"So I noticed you came from the direction of the office, did you go back in? I figured you were gone for the day when you left."

"No, actually I made some calls and came back in to fill out the daily call report. I *hate* those things."

"Richard does too," Darlene laughs, then stops.

I jump back in to distract her.

"All the sales reps do! Plus, I figure half of the stuff they put on there isn't even true. I guess management spot checks them. But as long as we're meeting our quotas, I don't understand those stupid call reports." I shrug, reluctant to go back to her monumental issue and content to talk about tiny-molehill issues that I have a bit of control over. We lapse into comfortable silence, each aware of our need to get home soon, and that this time, *her* problem looms larger than my chronic single-parenthood-multiple-divorce-problem.

This is significant, because in all the years I have known Darlene, she has not seemed to have any problems. At least none to sprout tears over. I reach out for her tiny hand. Darlene is only five feet tall, but because of her outgoing nature, seems taller.

"Honey, you know I am here for you. Whatever you need. I would just open up to him and see where the conversation goes. Maybe it's just a friend. Maybe he has something going on that is completely different from what you think! But whatever it is, you can count on me to help you through it."

I look meaningfully into her eyes, hoping to convey comfort and assurance. I think, though, that I am mainly conveying inebriation creep and watery eyes. I am getting really tired from my late date the previous night, and I still need a little energy for the kids when I get home. With a start, I realize it's nearly eight p.m. and I haven't checked in. I release her hand and pull out my phone, which has been on silent, and see several missed calls.

Darlene says, "I know you have to get goink. I don't much want to go home lately." She smiles tiredly. "But I know that's not the right attitude and I have to come at it head-on. And I vill. I just wanted someone else to know."

I get up, hug her, murmur more reassurances, and run to my car. When I call home I am relieved to find everybody accounted for. As a bonus, it appears they have actually done their homework. I point the car toward my two-story, brick contemporary in west Chatbrook.

I have to admit, I am wondering about the responses from the interesting and not-at-all-bad-looking men I had answered on the dating sites earlier. For once, I berate myself, I should go to bed without scouring the internet for single men. Right. A snowball's chance in hell *that* will happen.

CHAPTER 8

The caller on the other end of the phone disconnects. I continue holding the phone to my ear in a hazy rush of romance, unwilling to let go of his voice. Online dating is so incredibly delicious, I can hardly describe it. People just don't understand.

Another possibility. Meeting him for coffee tonight. I quickly assess the kids' plans for this evening. Chad has the car because he has a date tonight, Peter has a late basketball game and has a ride home, and Mimi . . . hm. Have to think about Mimi. Her homework is done, and her laptop, as usual, is melded to her as she Facebooks her friends. When I walk into the den to talk, her fingers are flesh-colored sausage links flying across the keyboard.

"Hey, sweetie, do you have any plans tonight? Study for a test, go to a friend's house . . . ?" Mimi's body language indicates that mothers should never, under any circumstances, interrupt Facebooking.

"Mimi . . . I want to go out and meet a friend tonight, so . . ."

"Mom!" Mimi suddenly shifts focus. "Not again! You just went out last night!" Mimi snaps her laptop shut, hoists it to her side with one hand, jumps from the chair and runs to her room. The door slams shut with a loud bang that reverberates through the house.

My stunned silence lasts a few seconds, then I follow her up the stairs and open the door, which fortunately, is not locked. She is splayed face down on her bed. I gingerly sit beside her, and stroke her hair. She reaches up and pushes my hands away.

"Honey, it's just for a couple of hours. Why is this such a big deal? You have stayed alone before! You are almost thirteen! And Peter should be home by ten o'clock or so, even if I am not." Mimi's face is buried in a pillow and her voice comes out muffled.

"Whatever, Mom. Whatever." She rolls over and stares at the ceiling. "Is this another one of your internet guys?" Her hazel eyes bore accusingly into mine. Mimi's eyes are that rare, perfect hazel: sometimes green, sometimes chestnut brown, depending. Right now, they are shooting bright green spikes of adolescent wrath.

"Oh no, no sweetie! It's just a friend I haven't seen in a while, who wants to get together to catch up!" I lie, and am a little surprised how easily it rolls off my tongue. Rationalization says this tiny lie is necessary, because finding *the yes* trumps honesty with one's children, always.

Besides, it's only a couple hours.

Mimi searches my face, doesn't seem satisfied, but the wrath seems to have gone out of her, replaced by a kind of slumped resignation.

"It'll be all right, honey. I won't be gone long. Done your homework, right? Want me to fix you a treat before I go?" I am really good at bribery. She shrugs. I take that as an affirmative and trot downstairs to throw stuff together. I quickly grab butter, honey and vanilla into a small saucepan and turn the heat to low. Stir. Add oats, a little whole wheat flour, a few carob chips and a teaspoon of peanut butter. After five minutes of stirring, I pour the healthy concoction into a bowl, stick a spoon in it, pour a glass of milk and run to Mimi's room. I hand her the bowl, but she ignores me. I sit the bowl and glass of milk on the table beside her bed.

I leave and go to my bedroom to change clothes.

After the weirdo I met a couple of nights ago, I am in semi-chastise mode, but I am confident that every meeting gets me closer to an appropriate, responsible, decent, fun guy that will carry me off in his late-model BMW (or something equally capitalistic) to fulfillment. Also, he will be a good stepdad and role model to my kids, dress well, be romantic, and possess various other attributes that are on my list.

I slap aside one top after another hanging in my closet and land on a rhinestone-accented tunic that I will belt and wear over skinny jeans. Next, I add a pair of open-toed platforms. A quick re-touch of makeup, a comb-drag through my hair, liberal douse of Flower Bomb, my latest fragrance, and I'm good to go. *Still pretty hot,* I mouth to my reflection.

After scooping up car keys and purse and carefully setting the security alarm and locking the door, I realize I have forgotten to tell Mimi good-bye. I lurch out of the car back into the house, high heels making speedy progress questionable. I teeter up to her room and find her still messaging simultaneously her 1657 Facebook friends. Notice the treat and milk have been consumed. Her eyes make a vertical sweep of me and she resists rolling her eyes.

"Bye," she says, and resumes her quest to connect with as many of her peers as possible in one night. I run over and hug her, dangly jewelry clanking, and dash off into the night.

My trusty Honda pulls into Starbucks ten minutes later. I glance at my watch and give myself a firm hour and a half with this man. I want to keep my word to Mimi. Nervous anticipation zings through me like electricity. When I pick up my purse, I notice my hands are trembling.

I approach the Starbucks with careless ease. In case he has arrived first, I strike a pose at the door, which I have practiced in the mirror a hundred times. The pose, which I have invented by watching old movies, is based on combined observations of old Marilyn Monroe and Lauren Bacall movies, with a touch of Charlize Theron. It includes a hesitant pause at the door, one hand gracefully placed on the doorframe, the other sliding seductively across a pelvic bone. Thus posed, I then search the room with wide eyes, pursed lips, and a slightly concerned expression, i.e. where art thou, oh possibly perfect and much-needed male counterpart? What breasts I have are jutted out commendably, which is no small task given that I struggle to fill a 34B.

No one rushes up to offer their hand in gallant and complimentary awe, so I drop the pose and walk in. He must be running late.

I quickly size up the room. The twenty-or-so coffee enthusiasts present are either under thirty or over sixty. I pick a table in the corner, and sit down, pulling out my phone to check for texts. After a few minutes, I feel a shadow – a small one – hovering near my elbow.

An uncertain voice says, "Are you, umm, Izzy?" My exhilaration dips somewhere around my ankles, I turn to him, smile brightly and say, "Yep. And who are you?" Hope springs eternal.

"I'm Dan!" The man standing – or rather, stooping – before me has sparse, obviously dyed, dark brown hair, weighs about one hundred and thirty pounds soaking wet and fully clothed, sports facial wrinkling that makes Tommy Lee Jones look young for his age, and has a stuffed lamb in his hand with a bow around its neck. I am at a loss for words (which rarely happens, trust me). He hands me the lamb. I realize he has actually brought a gift that is more suitable for a three-year-old. Thoughts flash through my brain like lightning, the primary one being *this cannot be happening!*

The leprechaun pulls up a chair, and I try to control my breathing, which is erupting in nervous, tight pants. His lips move, but I hear nothing. I feel as if I am in a vacuum, sucked into a dark joke. I sneak glances all around to make sure no one knows me. Finally, I find my voice.

"Dan?! You don't look *anything* like your picture." I stare at him evenly, my lips clamped together. He should pick up on the fact that I am oh-so-irritated. The leprechaun grins. Even his teeth look old.

"Well, Izzy, I pulled a fast one on you." His grin widens and I see that several back teeth are capped in gold. "I have had a hard time meeting nice ladies as yourself when I put my own photo on my profile, but when I put the *new* one up, my message box got full overnight!" He cackles. I look away, because his teeth are beginning to bug me. In fact, everything about him is bugging me.

"Who is in the picture?" I ask innocently, hoping, at the very least, that it might be him at a younger age.

"It's my brother!" he cackles again and ends up coughing sputum into his hand, and I recognize a smoker's hack. His profile had specifically stated that he was a non-smoker. "About twenty-five years ago!" he adds. All but whacks his hand on his knee, as if to say, *Gee whiz! I done pulled one over on ya!*

I am so mad, I can almost feel smoke coming from my ears. I left my darling Mimi for *this*? I couldn't believe it.

"May I ask, umm, *Dan*, why you would think that women would be *okay with this*?"

He looks a little mystified. Men are so clueless about themselves. "My brother may be the nicer-looking one of us, but I am definitely the one with the spunky personality! I figured if I could attract a woman for a first date, after she talked to me a bit, she'd know I was somethin' special and forgive me for puttin' up that picture." He resisted cackling, for which I was grateful. I agitate in my chair.

"Did it ever occur to you, that decent women are really, *really* not into liars, and that it doesn't matter how great you think your personality is . . . that they would never trust you after something like this? Besides, looks *do* matter."

The leprechaun is disgruntled. "I thought women didn't care so much about looks. I know men do, but somewhere I read women were more interested in intelligence and conversation." He shrugs, and frowns at me. "No reason for you to be insulting!"

I can't help it, my lips curl into a grin. Intelligence? Spunky? Who uses the word *spunky*? Then I laugh outright. The situation strikes me as pathetically absurd. I muster up a bit of indignation and tell him what I think of his stupid ruse, and that his personality can never, in a million years, be classified as *spunky*. I grab my purse, my self-respect, and escape before I have to listen to more cackling.

CHAPTER 9

The Starbucks by my house on the way to work the next morning is packed, but I need the jolt of a three-banger, so I wait in the long line of cars snaking around the building. My head is killing me, and the dark circles under my eyes needed a double portion of under eye concealer to do any good at all. After meeting the leprechaun, I'd zoomed home to the kids, and after they'd turned in for the night I'd gotten back online. As usual, several potentials worth chatting with kept me up til the wee hours.

I smack the steering wheel in frustration. Vow to limit my nightly escapades. The tiny man hunter demon that sits on my shoulder shrieks with laughter.

"Good morning!" The cheery barista beams when it is finally my turn.

I hold my forehead and mmmph a reply. The barista, whom I know pretty well via regular drive-by-coffee-acquisitions, pinches her eyebrows together. "Izzy, are you okay? You look awful!" She quietly relays my order to a co-worker, because from long experience, she knows I need a three-shot latte this morning. I am appreciative of having to say as little as possible until after coffee is consumed.

"I'm okay, just not much sleep this week. Busy, y'know, with the kids, the job, everything." I try to smile at her but it feels more like a grimace. Even my cheeks hurt. I grope in my purse on the passenger seat, locate sunglasses, and put them on.

"Yeah, I can just imagine," she said, and adds, "plus it's not easy going out five nights a week, either!" She grins, because she knows my morning coffee orders are directly proportionate to my nocturnal meandering.

"Don't know how you have *time* to be a mom!" She slides a heat-protector on the cup and hands it to me from her perch in the window. "Have a great day, Izzy. Hope you feel better!"

I drive off to the office, thinking about what she said about not having time to be a mom. Wish she hadn't said that.

The Honda lands in my assigned parking spot at the *Sentinel* like a homing pigeon, and I wonder what the day will bring. One thing I really like about this job is its unpredictability. It has its flaws, but boring is not one of them. I don't even mind the tedious ride in the decrepit, ancient elevator this morning, and sail onto the second floor somewhat cheered, buoyed by three shots of espresso. Before I can seat myself at my desk, Jon Hoyt's angry face appears in front of mine and asks if I will talk to him about something.

Privately.

See? Never know what's going to happen at this job. However, I am not particularly fond of starting the day off with a mysterious and potentially conflict-laden conversation. Jon's desk is all the way on the other side of the sales floor, the classified side. An unspoken, but very real, boundary separates retail and classified departments. We normally don't have a lot to discuss with each other so there is no need for communication. Yet here was Jon, in retail territory. I am puzzled. Plus, I hardly know the guy.

I smile, and say, "Sure! What's this about, Jon?" He ignores me, turns and strides toward the currently empty conference room. Feeling like an errant puppy, I follow.

My co-workers on the retail side, busily sipping coffee and reading newspapers, cast questioning glances my way, and I shrug in response that I have no clue. They look at each other meaningfully, which irritates me to no end. I am so *not* fond of drama.

Jon opens the door and waits for me, which is polite, considering. I enter and sit at the conference table. He closes the door and sits across from me. He puts his elbows on the table, entwines his fingers, and immediately crushes my observation about the polite thing.

"I want to know what the *hell* you are doing talking to my client, Tom Burke! He told me you came by yesterday. That's *my* account."

I am momentarily confused. Quickly search my mind for a misunderstanding of the rules governing accounts and territories, and can come up with nothing that points to any wrongdoing on my part. "But Jon, I'm *retail*. I explained that to Tom. He mentioned you were his *classified* rep. I am not overstepping my bounds! In the retail department, we have been instructed to call on various automotive accounts and sell them retail stuff. Didn't you know that?"

He didn't.

I continue, "Since automotive accounts have not shown up in Main News, or Local News or Business lately, Phil felt we could resuscitate this business. Hey, if you want to talk to Phil, go ahead, but I am just doing what I was told."

I neglect to tell him I made an appointment with his client the following week. Money is money, and if Jon is mad because I might make a commission off this client, I certainly didn't care. I was pretty happy when the automotive accounts – which are responsible for the lion's share of advertising in the paper – were opened up to the retail department. I had no qualms about going after this business. In fact, since it was *new* business for me, it meant higher commissions. No way am I going down without a fight.

I lean forward, entwine my own fingers on the table, and look Jon directly in the eye. *Sentinel* salespeople have learned many sales techniques at mandatory workshops, mirroring body language being one of them. I smash my lips shut and wait.

Jon holds my gaze. After a few seconds, he smiles. I hold my tongue, knowing the one that talks next (as the saying goes), loses. Jon leans back in his chair, crosses his arms.

"Well, I'll talk to Phil." His eyes assess me. "Damn, you're *good*, kid," he says, pushes his chair back and leaves the room.

I watch his form recede and wonder what just happened. I think I won, but am not sure. He may have withdrawn the attack to regroup and strike from the rear.

CHAPTER 10

Phil is at his desk, chair turned so he can look out the second-story window in his corner office. His hands are tented, elbows resting on the arms of his chair. The phone, which normally rings incessantly, is quiet. In the neighboring office, I hear Birdie unpacking boxes, shoving books on the shelves, organizing drawers.

The phone startles Phil from his reverie, which I am betting is focused around his dream of retiring to a cabin in Montana, high above and far away from the rest of the civilized world. No annual quotas. No monthly reports. No irate clients or printing press issues. No budgets to churn out every year. Phil and I have discussed this often, a mutual dream.

I fidget at the door, which is open slightly, and wait for him to acknowledge that I can come in and chat. His hand gestures me in, and I sit in one of the two chairs in front of his desk as he takes the call. I smell a hint of Polo Blue, freshly inked newsprint, and a slight cigarette after-stench. Phil is having a tough time giving up smoking.

After a few minutes, he ends the call, focuses his attention on me. "What's up, Izzy?"

"Well, I have an, umm . . . issue, that I'd like to discuss with you." I cross my legs and pick a piece of lint off one pant leg.

Phil gives me his implacable face. "This going to take long, Izzy?"

"Nope," I respond.

He smiles. My meetings with Phil are rarely less than twenty minutes, and with the responsibility of an entire sales and production department, twenty minutes is a long time to spend with one person, unless the meeting is scheduled. This one is not.

Phil sighs, sits back in his chair, crosses his arms. "Go."

I lean forward, eager to be the first one to tell the tale. Before I start, he says, "By the way, Jon has already been here, so I know what this is about." My face crumples in mid-launch. Phil grins.

"Okay," I sigh, and regroup. "Phil, you know you can trust me with a valuable account right?" Phil looks up at the ceiling and clasps his hands behind his head, thinking. "I'll bite," he says.

"Look, I know Ardmore Chevrolet has a huge budget, and a really tight relationship with Jon, but didn't you tell us a couple weeks ago we should go after this business on the retail side? That we were missing opportunities? That if the business hadn't been in the retail sections of the newspaper in the last sixty days it was fair game?" Phil nodded. "I know I can pull more business out of this account, and just because Jon tends to guard his clients like a pit bull doesn't mean he is getting all he can out of them." Phil is still, quietly listening.

"I think Tom likes me. I think he would be okay with two reps as long as we were representing different advertising approaches to him, and I think I deserve a shot even if this might upset Jon. I have an appointment with Tom next week, by the way."

Phil's eyebrows shoot up to the ceiling and he leans forward. "You do?"

"Yes, and he saw me as a walk-in, with no appointment, yesterday." Phil shakes his head, amazed. "I have never known Tom to see someone sponta-neously like that. That's a big win, Izzy." I allow myself a humble smile, and watch my foot jiggle the patent leather high heel at the end of the crossed leg.

Phil continues, "Jon was pretty upset, you know. I am uncomfortable with two reps on a huge account like this, where there is a long history of satisfaction with the same rep." My shoulders slump. "However . . ."

I sit up straight again. Optimism reborn.

"In light of the fact that he saw you immediately, and that his budget hasn't bumped up in a couple of years, I will let you have a go at him. I'll tell Jon. That it?"

I nod energetically, grinning like an idiot. "Thanks, Phil! You'll be happy about this."

"I hope so," Phil says, turning toward his computer, my signal to exit.

Hurrying back to my desk, I scan the room for Winston. Where the heck is the Pod-King? I must tell him about this. We will fist-bump and talk about it for weeks. It is not often that retail wins part of an account from the classified team. I assume he is already out of the office calling on clients.

I decide to wait for him, and begin checking through the proofs on my desk, piling them in Lonnie's inbox to send back to production. My cell rings, and I recognize the number of my neighbor, Annie.

I answer with a brisk, "What's up?"

"Hi, Izzy, sorry to bother you, but . . . umm . . . some weird guy is outside asking to see you. He says he knows you and wants to come in and wait until you get home, that it is important that he talk to you. I am like – seriously? Izzy, is this one of your one-night-wonders? And if so, how do I get rid of him? He is totally creeping me out."

I am mortified. It is ten in the morning and someone wants to squat in my neighbor's house and wait for me? All day? I feel a lump of dread form squarely in the pit of my stomach.

"Man, Annie, I am so sorry! Did he happen to give a name?"

She thinks a moment. "Jacob, I think."

Quickly sifting through, my memory spotlights the man from a couple nights ago that was ridiculously angry on the phone when I told him I did not want to go out again.

"Okay, okay . . . Annie, sit tight, and whatever you do, don't let him in."

"All well and good to say that Izzy, but what if he doesn't want to go? He seems more than a little irritated, and is sitting on my front steps."

"Sitting?"

"Yep," Annie says.

Bizarre. "Annie, just tell him that I am out on calls right now, and won't be home till after six or so. I don't think I told him I have any kids, so I sure don't want him hanging around to watch them come home from school. I don't think they would let him in, but they might." Annie agrees. I sigh and wonder what to do. My heartbeat is erratic.

"Okay, Izzy, I'll tell him you are unavailable and see if he'll go quietly, but in the meantime maybe you could call the cops and at least make a report or get them to drive by here or something. At least alert them to a possible disturbance by a strange guy."

I agree to do this, ask her to let me know what happens, and we hang up. What a jerk! I turn to the computer on my desk, fingers flying, and quickly locate his number on our exchanged messages on the Findamatch site.

A deep voice booms by my shoulder. "Gotta love a woman that looks for guys online while she supposed to be working. Is that a dating site?"

I swivel, startled, my face turning bright red. Jon Hoyt is standing beside my desk, his arms crossed, a lopsided grin on his face.

I open my mouth to explain.

"Jon, it's not what it seems . . . I, ahh, I *really* don't get on these sites at work, it's just that a situation has arisen . . ." the words are tumbling out awkwardly and Jon's grin is growing larger. I give up, frustrated. Jon's remarks aren't helping. The lump in my stomach grows legs.

"So, Jon, *whatever* . . . it's kind of a mess that would take a while to explain. Did you need something?"

He nods and widens his stance. "Phil has emailed me about Tom Burke, and I guess I have no choice but to back off on this one. If you don't mind, would you keep me in the loop? He is a great guy, and a good friend of mine. I have tried to sell him on retail in the past but he has no interest, at least that is what he said at the time. More power to you if you can get him to do it."

Jon shrugs, tilts his head, pushes a hand toward me. "Friends?"

I smile, relieved. "Friends," I say, and clasp his hand. As he walks away, I try (but fail) to ignore the broad shoulders and snug fit of his pants. Then my stomach lump reasserts itself and I remember I am in the midst of a crisis.

I dial Jacob's number, cautioning myself to speak softly and kindly as if there has been a simple misunderstanding. No use causing him to go nuts on me. What if he's a psychopath?

"Hey, Izzy," he says.

"Jaaa-cob! Hello there. How are you doing today?"

"Good, but I need to talk to you. It's important. I came over to see you personally, because I knew you wouldn't let me come over if I asked you on the phone. I kind of thought, for some reason, you might be home today. Guess I was wrong." His voice is devoid of emotion, and I proceed slowly, trying to remember all those TV shows where detectives talked people out of suicide or off ledges and things. *What did their voices sound like?* Use that voice, don't get upset, Izzy, *don't!*

"Okay, well, I am willing to talk with you, but I am so-o-o busy right now, I am wondering if we could discuss this over the phone?" I hear a beep and look at my phone, Annie is trying to get through. "Wait, Jacob, hold that thought I'll be right back!" I say brightly, through clenched teeth, and switch over to the other call. I silently thank God that he doesn't know where I work, and that I have turned off the geo-locator on my phone.

"Izzy!" Annie's voice is close to panic.

"Here, I'm here, Annie. Jacob's on the other line holding. What's going on now?"

"Well, he left my house. I'm looking out the window right now, kind of carefully so he will not notice, and I see him driving away. But he yelled something about you I couldn't understand as he walked away. Then he walked back to my front door, and said he'd be back, you wouldn't get away with it – whatever *it* is – and you'd better be ready. Izzy, it felt like a threat to me. I think you need to call the cops."

The lump in my stomach now has arms as well as legs, and both are flailing wildly. I think I need some water. And maybe a mega-dose of Xanax.

"Thanks, Annie, first I'm going to try to talk some sense into the man. Then I'll call the cops if I can't settle him down some. Do me a favor, keep an eye out for the kids and make sure they get in without incident, and call me when they do in case I'm busy with clients, okay?"

"You got it, Izzy. Be careful with this guy. Call me if you need me to do anything."

I clicked back over to Jacob. "Hey, sorry, had to get that. So as I was saying – "

"Yeah, as you were *saying*, you were going to ditch me again, like the other night. I'll talk to you on the phone as long as you like, but seriously, Izzy, I *need to see you in person again*."

"Jacob, I appreciate that you want me to see you, I really do, but I feel that we would be better off as friends and not potential matches, and I am hoping you will respect this." His breathing is labored, and somehow I feel the warmth of it in my ear. I am about to faint. I look around the sales floor, and am glad most of the reps have already left. No one is close enough to hear the conversation, and I am grateful. I clutch my stomach and wonder how I am going to extricate myself from this situation without getting shot or tortured or something.

Jacob continues, "I respect it. I do. But you didn't even give me a chance! All I am asking for is a second chance. Your next-door neighbor didn't understand, and *you* don't understand. I am not the man you think I am . . ."

Yeah, I think to myself, you are a perfect candidate for lifetime therapy. Or jail. I know exactly the kind of man you are. I married a couple of them. Three, actually.

"I know there is a woman out there for you that is *perfect* for you," I purr, using the voice I reserve for the most recalcitrant. "I am simply not that woman. I am sure you have lots to offer the right woman (I hate myself for sucking up like this, but desperation has its own rules) and it is just a matter of time until you meet her. Why waste time with me? She might be the very next one you meet on Findamatch."

I hold my breath. Please God, let this man believe all the stuff I just threw up against the wall.

He sighs. "You may be right, Izzy." My stomach unlumps a bit. With a shaky voice, he says, "It's just that . . . you look so much like my ex-wife . . . that it kind of threw me. Hit a lot of my buttons, but seemed like fate, somehow. Déjà vu. Wanted to talk, *really* talk for a while. We just got divorced a few months ago, and . . . I'm just so *angry*, and messed up and . . ." Jacob chokes up and, to my utter consternation, starts sobbing. I am thinking, who sobs on the phone to someone after only one date and one veiled threat on a neighbor's doorstep?

My stomach is almost de-lumped and I feel a crisis is past. The poor man is just trying to get over his ex and the resulting fallout, I suppose, of a nasty divorce. Rule number one: never date a man who has been divorced less than a year. Never. I think with Jacob I sailed blithely over this rule and rushed to meet him in the heat of phone-flirting. Not the best idea. Really, really stupid idea.

"Jacob," I say gently, not wanting to interrupt his soggy ruminations, but still, I have work to do. I glance at my watch. Almost noon and I haven't made one client connection. "Jacob, I am terribly sorry about your pain. Really. And I know you have a good friend you can talk to about this. Do you? Do you have a phone number of a friend you can call right now?" He sobs affirmatively. "I'd suggest you call him or her, right now, okay? And I wish you the best. Oh, and by the way, I am going to be inaccessible for a while, working on a story. It will probably take months. Have to limit my contacts for a while, it's a safety issue. You understand."

Big, fat lie, but if he figures out I work for a newspaper, at least it is plausible. Not the best I could have come up with, but I figure in his depressed state, he is only half-listening anyway. I am hoping he mainly internalized *inaccessible.*

I say good-bye and end the call, wiping sweat off my face. My next phone call is to Annie. Then I Google and enter into my phone the direct line for the local police.

Just in case.

CHAPTER 11

After the incident with Jacob, my stomach feels like I've taken one gut punch too many. My head is screaming and I dig in my purse for ibuprofen, locate and toss back a couple, wash them down with cold coffee.

In an effort to head off a decidedly downward emotional spiral, I tackle a few of the more mundane administrative tasks I routinely procrastinate because I hate them. If I am spiraling downward emotionally, I might as well take advantage of it and do something I hate on purpose.

I push up from my desk, still a little shaky. Lonnie, my assistant, is not coming in until the afternoon, so I have plenty to do before I leave the office to visit clients. In short order, I hit the mailroom, the receptionist's desk, the billing department and the human resources department. After running all over the building, I return to the pod and pick up several ad proofs which I need to discuss with the art department before they are emailed to the client for final approval and released to the pressroom.

I scoop them up in my arms and stride down linoleum alley by Darlene's desk, the break room, various computer terminals dedicated to Photoshop stuff, and skid to a stop in front of the production supervisor's office.

Missy, the production supervisor, is in charge of the art department, and basically everything and anyone involved with output and pagination of advertising with editorial in the *Sentinel*. I am a little in awe of her. She diplomatically manages her staff, multiple deadlines, unanticipated problems, and editorial and sales department coordination seamlessly.

Since I have been unable to clone her personality and replace mine, I routinely solicit her help with production issues when Lonnie is not around.

Missy looks up from a desk piled high with copy and proofs.

"Hey, Izzy! What's up?"

"Not much. How about you? Got time to help me out?"

She looks past me, thinking. "Depends. Business or personal?"

I sit in an aging, padded, leatherette chair in front of her desk in the tiny office. There is a window behind her, but it is yellow and impenetrable and about seventy-five years old. The casing and sill around it have been painted so many times the window is sealed shut. Her office walls mirror those of the conference room – white cinder block thick with paint – but Missy's walls are warmed with pictures of her children, friends and staff. Her desk is indeterminate gray-or-tan metal with wood veneer on top. A magenta dahlia from Darlene's yard squats in a vase on one corner. Her chair squeaks on the linoleum as she wheels forward.

I lift up the pile of proofs in my lap. "These are all wrong. I am sure whatever artist worked on them meant well, but my instructions were not clearly understood, I guess. Do you think you might put me with Jessica? She's used to my ads. I am approaching press deadline this afternoon, and need to talk to someone in person to explain the changes."

Missy sighs, stretches her arms over her desk and waggles her hands. I relinquish the unwieldy pile of newsprint and wait while she sorts through. Missy and I have been through this scenario countless times. For some reason neither of us understand, my communication with the art team is dubious at best, and offensive at worst. I still, after eleven years, have no clue why I am not greeted with the same exuberance as some of my peers when I ask for help with an ad. Maybe I wear the wrong cologne, or my breath offends. Who knows?

"Well, Izzy . . . ." she begins, as she lifts page after page, noting the corrections. "Seems like those girls could handle this without you sitting with them, but – "

"Seems that way, but never happens, right?" I tease, but we both know it's mostly true. My written instructions are often misunderstood. Or ignored completely.

"Missy, these have to be proofed out correctly. We've had too many errors on the last ones." Missy nods, hands me the pile and stands.

"Okay, Iz. Let's go! Gotta keep the clients happy. Advertising sales is what keeps us going! Without you guys there would *be* no *Chatbrook Springs Sentinel!*"

I'd heard this line about a thousand times before. Both the editorial and production departments routinely dump out this line as we are creaking upward or downward in the ancient elevator in uncomfortable silence. A polite cough behind a hand. A clearing of the throat, then, "We sure *appreciate* you guys! All that work you're doing is really, um *appreciated!*"

Mostly this comes from editorial staff that work in hushed cubes, pecking away at their keyboards in full *inky wretch* mode.

No matter what is said in elevators, with a few exceptions, it is blatantly obvious that editorial types categorize the sales department as a necessary evil. Conversation topics with salespeople are limited to weather, sports, or movies. Certainly not relevant topics such as politics, education or ecological concerns. Salespeople, from the editorial team's point of view, tend to be woefully under-educated and outrageously overpaid.

We, the salespeople of the *Sentinel*, enjoy hearty guffaws about this and continue to enjoy our hefty and well-deserved commission checks with nary a guilty thought.

I have always thought it would be good to have a few transparent meetings with the different departments so we might understand each other, and therefore develop a better working relationship. And then I laugh myself silly, because, kind of like world peace, never going to happen.

I follow Missy into the production area, where several women are reading newspapers, chatting, drinking coffee and studying their computer screens. Piles of ad proofs adorn each desk.

"Morning, ladies!" Missy chirps. Hands pause in mid-air. Chatter ceases. Eyes land on me, and maybe it's my imagination, but each face seems to stiffen.

I really don't like this part of my job. I mean, who wants to enter an arena where one is left emotionally bleeding on the floor in mere seconds? Missy's presence provides a handy force field of protection.

"Izzy here has these . . ." she lifts the pile of proofs, "ad corrections to be made, ya'll. They are priority, and she needs to sit with someone. Who is available?"

I hear muted grumbles and see arms crossing in seated choreography all over the room. Silence blankets the department. I move closer to Missy.

Long seconds later, a hand waves from a corner cubicle. "Missy! I'll do it!" I shift away from Missy and breathe a sigh of relief.

Somewhere along the line I had managed to win over Jessica. I slither through each terminal station back to her shadowy corner cubicle filled with photos of various angelic beings and several dogs. I slip into the extra chair beside her. Her desk lamp gently illuminates her workspace with a cozy glow.

CHAPTER 12

After a quick lunch at a downtown deli, I am looking forward to three meetings I have scheduled that afternoon. My heels click briskly on the sidewalk. It is so hot the sidewalks seem to be floating, a heat mirage that recurs in the hundred-plus degree heat that shrivels much of Georgia into early autumn.

I gingerly test the front seat of my Honda – which has baked in the hot sun all morning – sit, lift my hair off the nape of my neck. The air conditioner blasts hot air on my face. I quickly lower the windows to let the heat escape until the car cools down. My phone vibrates. I look at the number, which is masked by the word *private*.

"Izzy?" An unfamiliar male voice, deep and guttural. I answer in the affirmative, trying to place the voice.

I hear the clearing of a throat and a shuffle of papers. I visualize him at his desk.

"This is Birdie," he smiles into the phone.

I wince, and respond, "Oh, hey, Birdie!" I turn up the corners of my mouth so I will sound somewhat enthusiastic.

"Izzy, I am schedulin' meetings with salespeople, and the ride-a-longs. I am free this afternoon. Mind if a ride with you today?"

I quickly run through a list of excuses, decide none of them are plausible. I already have three meetings set up, and come to the only decision possible.

"Oh no, no, Birdie, I don't mind, that would be great! Just great! Want to meet me in the parking lot?"

"Well, actually, do you mind picking me up in front of the building? And I haven't had lunch yet, can we run by somewhere and grab a bite to eat first?"

I glance at the clock on my dashboard, see that I have a little time to spare. "Sure. When will you be downstairs?"

"Ten minutes," he grunts, and ends the call.

The words that dance through my mind are not words one should entertain regarding upper management. *Pick him up in front of the building?* In spite of the fact there are no parking meters available and busy traffic is hurtling by? Wait *ten minutes* before picking him up? What am I supposed to do in the car, plan the dinner menu for my kids? Which actually, I realize, is not a bad idea and is exactly what I do. I also work on my attitude, which at that moment is dark and negative and profane around the edges. Does this man have no sense of courtesy? He can't walk two minutes to the parking lot?

After exactly eight minutes, I pull out of the parking lot into traffic and slide into the far lane in preparation to circle the *Sentinel* building and arrive at the front door exactly as Birdie appears. As I approach, no Birdie. I huff and circle again. No Birdie. My phone chirps and I glance at a text. Birdie says he is running late, will grab a bite of lunch on his own and meet me later. I am so irritated I nearly throw my phone on the floor, but don't, since the last time I did that it cost me three hundred dollars for a replacement.

I sigh, pull back into the parking lot, text him a response and give him an address. He texts that he will meet me there, and we can take his car to the next appointments. I fantasize for a moment that I should text back how insensitive he is to be so disrespectful of others' schedules. The reality, as a single parent and the lone provider for my household, is that a text like this would be a really bad idea.

The obligatory cheerful response drips from my fingertips in a return text. Then I dial my first appointment, for which I am now running behind, and let them know I am on my way. Then I fantasize about throwing my phone on the floor.

CHAPTER 13

Jon Hoyt

Jon orders another martini for himself and a beer for his client. They are having lunch at a restaurant in the River's Edge District, talking about the next trip to Chicago to watch the Cubs play. Jon made it a point to take clients to lunch at least once a month. Today's lunch happens to be with Tom Burke, the General Manager of Ardmore Chevrolet. Jon wanted to square things with Tom in case Izzy's approach had ruffled some feathers. After the meal, the men relax over coffee.

"So Tom, something I want to talk to you about . . . ." Jon begins.

Tom puts down his coffee mug, pats his stomach appreciatively and leans back in his chair. He is a little tipsy from two beers, and indulgent. "Okay, shoot. Something serious?"

"Depends." Jon says. "As you know, I am all about keeping you guys happy." Jon smiles his trademark lopsided grin.

Tom laughs. "We all know that, Jon."

Jon knows Tom is well aware of the contingent of automotive power brokers that Jon courts regularly, including owners and general managers of various automotive dealerships in the area.

"What do you want me to do? Talk to someone for you? Get you an 'in' somewhere?" Tom smiles broadly.

"Well, maybe sometime, but that's not the reason I bring this up . . . what I wanted to talk about was the rep that visited you the other day."

Tom's eyes light up briefly. "Izzy?" Jon nodded. Tom continued, "Man, she is gorgeous!"

Jon resists rolling his eyes.

"How old is she, anyway?"

"Tom, dude – you are married," Jon reminds him.

Tom laughs. "Oh, I know, I know. Fun to play a little, though. Besides, she was cool. I liked her. We have an appointment next week."

Jon masks his surprise. Yeah?" he said. "That okay with you? Having two reps from the *Sentinel*?"

Tom nods, thinking. "Well," he said, "what's the harm? I see you about once a week. How often am I going to see her? I really don't have a lot of time outside the office, but if she is discreet, buys me lunch once in a while, maybe gives me a little attention in my office when the door is closed . . . ." his eyes crinkle in amusement.

Jon does not smile.

"I think," Jon says, "you should consider dropping that idea." He chuckles, and continues, "This isn't one of the automotive-bimbo-sales chicks that hang around dealerships, Tom. So if you are just wanting a hot woman around, she'll probably get irritating after a while, because my feeling is that she is not gonna be receptive to that. Just a heads up."

Jon stirs cream into his freshly refilled coffee cup thoughtfully. This was a new side to Tom Burke, and it concerned him. He didn't think Izzy understood how some of the car guys ate women like her for lunch. He felt underneath the confident façade she was vulnerable to men like Tom. Something about her seemed almost needy.

"Just kiddin', Jon," Tom says.

Jon knew better, but didn't say anything.

"Kidding," Tom emphasizes when Jon doesn't respond. "It's fine. All good. I'll see how she works out and what she comes up with, and if I have any issues with her, I'll let you know. Okay?"

Jon nods, satisfied. He signals the waiter over, pays the tab, finishes his coffee. The two men shake hands and part ways.

Jon watches Tom walk to his car. He doesn't know whether to warn Izzy, or just let things play out.

CHAPTER 14

Izzy

St. Michael's Healthcare System is a vast, sprawling complex east of downtown. At its center is an intimidating, twenty-story hospital orbited by clinics and various peripheral facilities bracketed by manicured shrubs, flowerbeds and parking lots.

I pull the Honda into a parking lot punctuated by pansies. When it becomes obvious all the parking slots are taken, I squeak out an exasperated semi-expletive, and drive the perimeter a few times, waiting for one to open up.

My hands are sticky on the steering wheel. Questions nervously pound my mind. Will Birdie make a decent impression? What if he doesn't like my presentation? What are his expectations of me? Why do I care, exactly?

This client in particular needs to respect him. To *like* him.

It had taken me over a year to get Nellie, the Communications Director of St. Michael's, to free up more advertising dollars for the *Sentinel*. She definitely holds the purse strings to one of the more hefty budgets on my account list – over a million a year. My commissions would dive significantly if she diverted those funds to, for instance, healthcare-specific internet sites, or broadcast venues. My mission with Nellie is simple: keep her happy, show her results, stay connected about the value of our product, stay firmly rooted in her ad budget.

I swivel my head in both directions. Birdie has not yet landed. I dig in my purse for makeup bag, tilt the visor down, expose the mirror and touch up lipstick, blush and perfume. As I stow the makeup bag and pick up a few printed pieces to show Nellie, Birdie leans down, raps on the window, his grin super-sized through the glass. I jump in surprise and almost hit my head on the liner. Did he mean to sneak up on me?

I hastily get everything together and step out.

"Hi! How was your lunch?" I smile at him, tilting sunglasses from the top of my head to my face. Birdie apparently has not learned the two-foot personal space rule, and instead of moving a healthy pace away, moves closer. I can smell the cigar he must've puffed after a hurried lunch.

"Good!" he says. His tanned face creases into a thousand fissures, an after-result, I suppose, of an acne-scarred childhood. "How was yours?"

Careful, Izzy, you know you want to say a few choice words but, umm . . . no. "Oh fine," I respond, and promptly change the subject.

"This client is one of my bigger accounts, so I am glad you are able to be with me today. She doesn't have a lot of time, so I don't see her as much as I should, probably, but –"

"Why not?" Birdie interrupts. "You just have to be *aggressive*, and get in the door! When a client says no, they don't really mean *no*," he grins, the sun glinting off teeth as white as bleached porcelain. Which, coincidentally, is probably what they are.

"So, what's this account worth?"

My mouth hangs open in mid-nicety. This is the kind of information for which a new manager knocks gently at the door instead of breaking it down. Besides, he should already have this information. I stutter, "Umm, a lot. One of my larger accounts. I am assuming you have an account list and recap of monthly revenues?"

He assesses my face, registering faint disapproval. "When I ask a question, I usually get an answer, not a lecture."

I glance at my watch. "Gotta go, Birdie. We're late."

To his credit, he lets this go, and opens the door for me on our way to the elevator. We ride up silently. Birdie's hands are clasped behind his back. I sense his resentment, but I will deal with it later. My mind is focused on the account. I have several advertising opportunities for her that will fit her market niche, and am hoping to increase her allotted print advertising dollars over the next couple of months. I decide, during the last few seconds of the elevator's ascent to the administrative offices on the top floor, to prep Birdie.

I clear my throat. "Umm . . . Birdie?" He turns his head toward me. "Just wanted to ask if I might take the lead on this . . . or do you have a different agenda?" I nod at the bundle of promotional materials in my arms. "These are opportunities I have researched for her, and I wanted to make a presentation today. Any thoughts?" He regards me coolly as the elevator dings that we have just passed the thirteenth floor.

"It'll be all right," he says in dismissal, and strides off the elevator as the doors open with a metallic whisper. This does not do much for my confidence level. I indicate the direction of Nellie's office and invite him to follow with a nod of my head.

We enter the communication department's suite of offices where I check in with the receptionist. She smiles and presses a button that triggers a muted buzz somewhere deep within the labyrinthine offices and invites us to take a seat. A few minutes later, a forty-ish, bubbly redhead in a dark green business suit bursts out of her office and walks down the hallway toward us.

Birdie lights up when he sees her. He stands, raking her length with his eyes.

Nellie doesn't notice, but I do. She greets us with a welcoming smile and extends a hand to Birdie, which he takes in both of his and mumbles something that I cannot hear. She nods her acknowledgment, removes her hand with some effort, and glances at me. After she bustles us into her office, she waves us toward a round, gleaming conference table in the corner, and turns to me.

"Izzy! So nice to see you! Been a while. How are you?"

"Great, Nellie. How's life been on the top floor of St. Michael's?"

"Absolutely crazy!" She laughs and holds her hands palms up, one on each side. "I don't know how I do this, but somehow I do. Today is deadline for our in-house newsletter and the quarterly magazine we do for the mailing list. I'm glad I could squeeze you in!"

"Me, too. I've got some good opportunities to show you, but first, I wanted to introduce you to Birdie." I indicate him with a sweep of my hand, not that this was necessary, but because I felt he expected some kind of fanfare. He nods, blinds her with his teeth, and reaches for her hand. Again.

"I've heard so much about you!" He glances at me. I return the glance quizzically. If he'd heard a lot about her, it hadn't been from me. "From, um, Izzy, here . . ." he says, as if I were a faithful but unnecessary pet.

My brows knit together. So now I realize he's not only inappropriate, but also a liar when it serves his purpose.

"I'm doin' visits with the sales staff. Want to meet the *important* people, y'know, the ones that pay the bills!" Then Birdie throws his head back and laughs, still holding Nellie's hand. She tugs it free, and smiles a thin, tight-lipped smile.

I plop my pile on the conference table, and we sit. Nellie is rubbing her hand self-consciously, and I am about to deftly switch topics when Birdie decides to continue chomping on the foot in his mouth.

"So," Birdie begins. My heart chugs a little faster. My hands, which are underneath the table in my lap, clench. "What do you have to say about your relationship with the *Sentinel*? Is it workin' for ya? If not, we'll sure figure out why." Another blazing grin splits his face. He leans forward, places both elbows on the table, tents his hands, and waits for her response. The smells of cigar and cheap cologne sail in tandem across the table.

I am thinking, already, how to square things with Nellie later. He must've skipped *Diplomatic Small Talk 101* that most salespeople internalize before being let loose in the field. I am wondering if upper management even checked this guy's resume.

Nellie, ever the professional, responds, "Well, ahh, Birdie, is it?" He nods. She tilts her head toward me and slants her eyes in my direction. "Izzy is doing a great job for me. I feel her presentations and customer service skills are excellent. She makes doing business with the newspaper easy, and shows me the results. She constantly updates me with studies that show the bottom line, which I, of course, instantly forward to my Board of Directors to justify my budget with you. No complaints. How about you? How did you come to be sales manager at the *Sentinel?*" Her tone is slightly punishing.

Birdie folds his arms across his chest, clearly irritated. I can tell he is used to being in charge. I am beyond worried, closing in on mortified.

"Sweetie," he says, "I have been in management since before you were born." He smiles slightly, but his eyes do not. "I came to the newspaper by way of earnin' it." He presses thick lips together, and I rush to fill the uneasy silence.

"Nellie, ready to look over those opportunities I told you about?" She nods, relieved. I spread out multiple materials describing new sections and special magazines the *Sentinel* will be producing that will appeal to a healthcare demographic, and we become absorbed in technical details. Birdie taps his fingers, wiggles his legs, agitated. We ignore him.

After twenty minutes, and a firm commitment from Nellie to be involved, we both rise in preparation to part. Birdie slaps his hands on the table and pushes himself up from his chair. "Good to meet ya, Nellie! You just give me a call if Izzy isn't takin' care of things, y'hear?" And just when I think things could not get any worse, he winks at her.

Mortification is now official. After he shakes hands with Nellie (again), I hang behind a bit, and glance at Nellie's face, silently communicating my regrets. She smiles, winks at me and rolls her eyes. My laugh flaps silently behind clenched teeth.

I trot to catch up with Birdie, who is striding toward the elevator with all the self-confidence and assurance of an absolute ass.

We walk silently side by side and pause at the parking lot. To say that I am conflicted is an understatement. I sigh, and force out, "Well, how'd you think that went?"

He looks at me appraisingly, turns up the corners of mouth without showing teeth, "Fine. Who's next? Wanna take your car?" I thought he'd mentioned we would take *his* car. I nod in the direction of my car, juggle my purse and materials into a more manageable bundle and slide my sunglasses down off my head. "Let's go," Birdie says.

The rest of the day I hover between anxious nausea and outright shock, but fortunately, the remaining appointments were not with women. Men didn't seem to mind Birdie's, borderline-sexist, crude commentary. They'd snorted in laughter right along with him. I felt like an unwelcome fly on the wall, and had ticked off the minutes until the meetings were finished.

By the end of the afternoon, as I am taking Birdie back to his car at St. Michael's, my female antennae are definitely aquiver. My eyes slice toward his profile. His hand is tapping the dashboard, his other slapping out a rhythm on his legs. He seems to be in constant motion. He feels my glance, turns his head toward me. His eyes are a lifeless ice-blue. I can see gray roots where his color is starting to grow out.

No doubt about it, there *is* something kind of appealing about him, in a sleazy, dark Marlon Brando sort of way. But the guy is seriously stuck in another era. The one where women are supposed to be pretty ornaments that are seen, not heard. And apparently, the one where women must listen to disgusting jokes and feel greedy male eyes on their bosoms.

If the situation were not so ridiculous, I would laugh it off. But he is my boss, so I'm not laughing about anything. I'm just worried.

Really, really worried.

I glide to a stop next to his car. "Here you go, Birdie. Glad we got to do this today." This is an outright lie, but one sows seeds where one can. "Do you want to get together later in the week to discuss anything?"

Birdie winks at me with an expression that might have been cute, say, in 1952. He pushes himself out of the car, spins around and claps both hands on the roof so hard I bounce in my seat. He lowers his head, his hands still placed firmly on the roof. His eyes are inches from mine.

"You bet, sweetheart. We have lots to talk about. Lookin' forward to it. I'll be in touch." With that, he straightens his tie, pulls his shirt cuffs down, turns and strides to his car, trailing his signature aroma.

I am confused by his comment. Lots to talk about? What does that mean? The lack of sexual innuendo in my conversation? That I need to wink more? Wear shorter skirts? Push-up bras?

I skid out of the parking lot, tires squealing. The squeal is quite inadvertent, but my Honda can get serious traction when I'm mad. A quick look in the rear-view mirror reflects Birdie watching my departure, arms crossed, legs apart.

CHAPTER 15

Jon Hoyt

The gleaming black Volvo sedan pulls into the garage, the door humming smoothly into place behind it with a thud. Jon Hoyt tilts his head back against the headrest, and puts a hand over his eyes. The two drinks he'd had at lunch with Tom Burke were taking a toll, and he wishes he'd had more of an appetite.

He sits there a minute hoping the spinning will subside. His eyes lift to survey the garage, and his thoughts run to, as always, his wife, Marie.

Marie, who had spiraled long and hard to her eventual death due to breast cancer. She'd died in his arms, a tiny, skeletal whisper of herself wearing a pink bandana to cover her baldness. She'd smiled a weak smile at him before she died, her eyes leaking tears; an image he would never forget. After two years, he still struggles to push the scene out of his mind.

Think about something else, Jon. He sighs deeply and fobs open the trunk to gather groceries he'd purchased on his way home.

The once-immaculate bungalow he'd shared with his wife of twenty-two years was untended and lonely, now, except for Marie's cats.

The dust on the countertops puff up in little clouds as Jon enters with multiple plastic bags hanging off his arms. He kicks the door shut behind him, elbows piles of unwashed dishes aside, and puts the bags on the kitchen counter. Five scruffy cats run to welcome him, and he stoops to pet them. *Blasted cats.* He cannot bring himself to give them away. Not yet. His wife had adored these cats. He thinks he might keep them, but he is not sure and does not want to think about it. They are a little company, at least.

He stands in the kitchen after the groceries are put away, plastic sacks stashed by the cat boxes for easy cat-waste disposal. He assesses the smudged tile floor, the countertop covered by four days' worth of dishes, and his mood. Decides his mood doesn't warrant an hour of cleaning.

Jon steps over the felines gathered around his feet, grabs a beer from the fridge and carefully avoids the empty beer bottles and various take-out cartons scattered on the floor. He walks into the den, twists the cap off the beer, and settles into his favorite chair.

Originally maroon, the recliner had been claimed by cat hair, and now is best described as dusky rose. When Marie was alive, she periodically scraped the cat hair off their favorite lounge spots, but Jon simply doesn't care. Sometimes in the office, under the fluorescent light, he sees that his pants are covered with cat hair.

He guzzles the beer, picks up the remote and points it at the screen. He revisits his day and decides a stronger alcoholic beverage is in order. He'd been upset about Phil's decision to give Izzy part of his account, and wonders if she'd get others, too. Has enough trouble making ends meet as it is. Still paying off Marie's medical bills.

He thinks about the years of work he has put into that account: building the client relationship, planning dinners and trips and dropping by with special gifts. *It takes a long time to become necessary to a client, to become a trusted friend rather than a faceless vendor.*

Jon snorts, pushes off his chair and strides into the kitchen to grab the bottle of Grey Goose vodka he keeps in the freezer. *Screw life,* he thinks. *Screw everything.* He tilts back the half-empty bottle, takes a deep swallow, eases his head back into an upright position and wipes his mouth.

Holding the bottle aloft he proclaims, "Life will look a lot better in about five minutes!" His laughter holds a hard edge. He tilts the bottle again, and downs the remainder. He spins around to return to the den, loses his balance and falls, hard. The Grey Goose bottle explodes on the tile and heavy shards of glass fly in all directions. Prostrate on the floor, Jon opens his eyes, but the ceiling is spinning. He squeezes his eyes shut, and launches an impressive volley of profanity. Jon's head aches where it hit the floor. Suddenly he is so dizzy he can't move. He yells again, louder.

His neighbors, an elderly couple, are weeding their flowerbed and planting petunias when they hear the commotion. The husband glances at his wife. She nods toward the house, and he quickly runs to Jon's front door. He knocks, waits several minutes on the front steps.

"Jon? You in there? What's going on?" The doorknob turns in his hand easily, unlocked. "Jon!" His straw hat bobs as his head whips around to survey the rooms he passes through. "Jon!" he calls again.

He walks the length of the house and back again. Stops at the kitchen, located toward the front of the house. His nose wrinkles in disgust at the stench and piles of trash. "You in there?"

He listens a brief moment. Sobbing? His eyes pick out a pant leg, then a socked foot amidst the debris. Broken glass slivers the floor, nestled in crumpled envelopes or between empty beer bottles. He steps around the kitchen's center island and finds Jon in a fetal position, holding his head, eyes tight shut. The neighbor bends and lays a reassuring hand on Jon, then begins to gather shards of glass.

His wife steps in quietly behind him, her eyes filling with tears. She joins her husband on the floor beside Jon, and says, "It's going to be okay, Jon. We're right next door. We are going to look in on you from time to time, all right?" Jon ponders the kind face, belches loudly, and closes his eyes. They help him into his bedroom, give him aspirin and a big bottle of water; tell him they'll check on him later. Then they spend the next two hours cleaning his kitchen.

The cats all pile on the bed and begin purring and kneading Jon's inert form. Eventually they give up on dinner, engage in thorough kitty-baths, and curl into five furry, sleeping balls around Jon, two on one side and three on the other.

CHAPTER 16

Izzy

I hear the kids pull into the driveway, walk to the window and pull aside the curtain. The kids' car is parked in the driveway with the windows down. Strange. Maybe they have finally decided to air it out. The heady onion aroma in that car from fast food purchases would gag a camel. I let the curtain drop, and return to the kitchen. They'll be glad Mom is home early.

Mimi is the first to bounce in the door, and plunks her backpack on the kitchen table in one smooth, practiced move. Chad and Peter are close behind.

Mimi sees me first, and her face lights up. She begins her typical non-stop, adolescent monologue, which is fine with the boys, I notice. They seem distracted. Chad mumbles something about a nap and heads to his room. I watch him trudge upstairs as I listen to Mimi, puzzled. Peter, who has opened the refrigerator searching for something to eat, locates the key lime pie and stuffs a piece in his mouth.

"No basketball practice today?"

"Uhh . . . yeah, Coach said we needed a day off, so I hung out with Chad until Mimi was finished."

"That's weird. Isn't your huge game just two days away?" Peter shrugs, grabs the milk and closes the refrigerator. Opens a cabinet, locates a glass and fills it.

"Ever heard of using a fork for the pie?"

"Hungry," Peter mumbles through a partially-consumed mouthful, and downs the entire glass of milk in one gulp.

"Apparently," I respond, and lean back against the kitchen counter, arms crossed, watching him. He gives me a look. "Gonna watch TV for a while before homework, okay Mom?" he says, and leaves the kitchen before I can answer.

"Guess so," I say to myself, staring at the doorway through which he'd just disappeared. I vaguely wonder what is going on with the boys, but I need to fix dinner, and push this thought aside. Mimi and I pull out her homework, and I leave her at the kitchen table busily working on a science project that is due in a couple of weeks. I wash my hands, take out the pork chops I plan to bake for dinner.

With one hand I locate the cutting board, with the other I sift through the utensil drawer, a haphazard collection of knives, wooden spoons, spatulas and God knows what else. Everything gets thrown in there.

As I trim fat off pork chops, my mind wanders to what life would be like in a good marriage. To a thoughtful, kind man that would teach my sons man-stuff. A man that would give me some breathing room, at least with the bills and the yard. Sure, we have to be in love, but experience has taught me if practical things aren't taken care of – like, um, actually holding and keeping a job, paying the bills, being responsible about life in general – the *love* just kind of . . . dies. As Darlene had once wisely stated: "Izzy, your picker is broken."

Since my kids' dads are not exactly hands-on, the parenting falls to me. My mind creeps toward memories of ex-husbands who eventually exhibited scary things like physical abuse, out-of-control rage, sexual addiction, affairs. Memories of courtroom battles, custody arrangements, threats, hostile encounters bombard me like seagulls at the beach. I quickly push them into a mental compartment, and lock it. Someday, maybe they'll stay there.

And someday, maybe my picker will be fixed.

The dating sites are helping me with my choices, I tell myself, wondering how long I'd been standing at the kitchen counter, lost in thought, clutching a kitchen knife. Not exactly smart to lose focus with a knife in my hand.

I place the knife gently on the counter. The pork chops are now fat-free, well, except for the actual pork, and ready to go in the baking dish. I rinse my hands and dry them. Rotate to the baking dish drawer, bend, select. Mimi is head-down, scribbling notes for her project, at the table. I smile at her. She smiles back.

Dark green with fluted edges. A nice baking dish. I don't like to cook, but who doesn't love good presentation? I plop the pork into the dish and admire the rich color as a backdrop to raw pork.

I don't want to entirely give up on snagging a good man. But the Jacob situation is freaking me out. Gotta be more careful about handing out my home address, where I work, or getting picked up by a new guy at either place.

Afternoon sun streams through the kitchen window, backlighting Mimi, suffusing her hair with an angelic glow. I want to take a picture but concentrate on the fleeting, lovely moment instead. Pictures never quite capture stuff like this, anyway.

I grab a can of mushroom soup out of the cabinet and douse the pork chops. Okay, so I'm not exactly Martha Stewart. The oven door closes with a clank. I set the timer and clap my hands together. Any attempt at cooking on my part is worthy of a small round of applause.

I tiptoe into the den and see that Peter is asleep, gently snoring, one leg over the back of the couch, his arms splayed over his head. I stand over him, picturing him as a three-year-old, and carefully finger his gold, closely-cropped, curls. Mimi is still busy with her project, and Chad is napping in his room.

Great time for a Findamatch check. I back out of the den quietly, and race upstairs to log in for an hour or so before dinner.

CHAPTER 17

Chad and Peter

Chad and Peter's car creeps quietly across the street. Mimi is attending a Beta Club meeting after school and they had to hang out and wait a while before she'd be ready to go home. Peter, the designated driver, pulls the car around the back of the church out of sight and parks.

Peter reclines the front seat. Chad is sprawled across the back seat with his feet propped up in the open window. Both are smoking pot. Both are fanning the smoke out. Mimi would wrinkle her nose and say something the minute she got in the car, they knew.

Chad takes a long drag off a tightly rolled joint. "Hey bro, it's all right. It's just pot – it's legal now, in California, you know."

Peter glances over his shoulder to the back seat where his brother is obviously enjoying the hazy retreat from reality.

"Yeah, sure. But what are we going to say to Mimi? She'll smell it. I don't even know if she knows what pot smells like, but she sure as hell is going to know that something stinks." Peter is holding the marijuana cigarette tentatively, obviously uninitiated, taking tiny puffs. His forehead is beaded with sweat. His basketball coach would kick him off the team if he found out, but he loves his brother and wants to think that 'just pot' is okay.

"So what are we going to say to Mimi again?" Peter rolls the joint between his thumb and index finger. He turns the mirror to look at his face. The whites of his eyes are pink with clusters of red veins.

Chad, his joint now a nub, tosses it out the window.

"We're going to tell her we wanted to try smoking, and bought really cheap cigarettes, and since they smelled so bad we threw them away. Got it?" He giggles and closes his eyes. The familiar floating sensation is taking over.

Peter says, "Right. And you think she'll believe that?"

Chad doesn't answer. He lay in the back seat with a grin on his face and one hand over his eyes and giggles. Peter decides since he is driving, he doesn't need to partake of an entire joint, so he stubs it out and throws it out the window toward the tall weeds by the parking lot.

"We gotta go. It's about time for Mimi's meeting to be finished." His brother is silent. Peter hands him his half-finished Coke. "Here, drink this. It has caffeine. It'll wake you up a little."

Chad manages to grasp the can and lifts it to his lips unsteadily. "Wow," Chad said, "that stuff was really potent. I am . . . so dizzy . . ."

"Man, you're an idiot," Peter says. "I don't know why I let you talk me into this stuff." He starts the car and pulls out of the parking lot. Neither of them notice the woman peering out of the window in the church's office.

Izzy

The sunrise is brilliant outside my bedroom window. I stretch and glance at my alarm, then out the window. What a gorgeous fall morning! As far as I know, I have absolutely nothing pressing going on at work. No meetings with Birdie, no proofs to edit, no meetings with clients that I am aware of. The day is a blank slate, and it feels good.

After I make sure the kids are fed, equipped, and mom-waved out the door, I run upstairs to finish getting ready for work. I am simultaneously brushing mineral makeup on my face and tugging a comb through my hair when my cell rings. I'd left it downstairs.

I once figured out how many trips I take up and down the stairs on an average day. Thirty-five, give or take. Could've saved myself a trip, but I had blown it by leaving the phone downstairs. I drop the comb and the makeup brush and run downstairs.

"Izzy? You up and about?" a familiar voice asks.

"Yesss . . ." I respond uncertainly.

"This is Patrick McAllister, from Windsor Academy? How are you this morning?" I feel his smile through the phone.

Patrick is headmaster of Windsor Academy, and would not personally call a parent without significant reason. "Fine," I say, "until now. What's up?"

He laughs. "Why is that response the *only* one I ever get when I call parents!"

"Because the only reason for a phone call from you is that our kids have messed up. So have mine? Messed up?"

"Actually, Izzy, they have. It's the boys."

My airway starts to close.

I choke out, "It is? What is it? I thought they seemed to be doing pretty well lately. Their grades are good. Their teachers are not emailing me every two seconds. Peter is a starter on the basketball team this year . . . Mimi's in Beta Club . . ." I am blathering and I know it, but when I am nervous I blather.

Patrick interrupts, kindly, "Izzy, I know you have unique challenges. I have seen this situation before. Boys in single-parent homes sometimes act out in different ways. Especially a single mom and an uninvolved dad. Nobody's fault. Just the way it is."

I murmur agreement, thinking how much worse it would be if their dad *was* around. There are exceptions to every rule. He continues, "I got a call yesterday at home from the church across the street. This person saw your boys in their car in the church parking lot after school, smoking. At first she thought it was no big deal, just cigarettes, and made a mental note to talk to me about enforcing private property stuff with the students, but she had seen them throw the butts in the grass, and ran out to check. Sure enough, it was pot. Sorry, Izzy."

A confusing mix of emotions holds my tongue.

Patrick continues, "I am going to talk to them after school today and confront them with their behavior. I'd like you to be there, Izzy."

We arrange a time and end the call. The house is silent, except for the sound of the dryer in the laundry room, and the muted tick-tock of an antique clock in the den.

My aloneness drapes my shoulders like a shroud. I should cry, I think, but am curiously unable. My steps up the stairs to finish getting ready for work are measured. Robotic.

I glance at the clock on my dresser and see I have twenty minutes to make it to work on time. I tuck the conversation into a corner of my mind until later that afternoon. Then I finish makeup and hair, throw on some jewelry, trot downstairs, gather my stuff, hop in my car and go to work.

Just like every other day.

The office is quiet when I arrive, and Winston is already at his desk, deeply immersed in today's newspaper. I have managed, on the drive to the office, to talk myself out of being overwhelmed. Pot isn't the worst thing in the world, and hopefully this is an isolated occurrence. But what disciplinary actions will the school implement? And what should my reaction be to the situation? I label these thoughts *think about later* and shove them to the back of my mind.

I quickly scan the sales floor. Most desks are populated with busy salespeople finalizing ads. The press deadline looms for the classified staff, and their assistants fidget at various cubicle intersections, ready to zip to production with approved proofs. After deadline passes, the sales floor will quickly empty.

I slip into my chair, drop my purse into the bottom drawer of my desk. I try not to sigh or show other outward signs of distress because Winston is hyper-intuitive and I do not want to talk about kid issues all morning.

He looks at me over the glasses on the tip of his nose, turns a page, picks up his coffee mug in a mock toast and says, "Hi, there. And how are we this fine morning?"

He slurps his coffee, then puts his mug on the coaster on his desk. His chair protests as he leans back, stretches, crosses his arms and raises bushy eyebrows in my direction. The familiar body language suggests he is open to pod-versation.

"Hi, Winston. Fine, good, how about you?" I busily scratch around on my desk, hoping he will not look too closely at the expression on my face, which I am sure is more stress-filled than not. For once, I do not have a funny story about a new guy or an interesting profile on Findamatch. And I am definitely *not* open to pod-versation.

"Busy day?" he asks.

"Yep. Kind of. Gonna grab coffee, you want some?" He didn't, so I walk down the hall toward Darlene's desk, which is conveniently on the way, where I plan to elicit much-needed female empathy.

I stop in front of her desk after helping myself to the disgusting – but free – office coffee. As I sip, I grimace in disgust.

Darlene's smile is like sunshine on a cloudy day.

"Hey!" she says. "How's it going, Izzy?"

Darlene reads my face even better than Winston, and since I am primed for a little compassion, I relax and drop the mask. Tiredness, anxiety, fear of the unknown, self-pity, you name it, it's painted all over my face.

Darlene's expression registers alarm. "What? What's happened?" I give her the short version about the boys, the pot, the call from the headmaster. Wait for her response, hoping for a glimmer of light in a situation I find incredibly bleak, even in spite of my pep talks to myself on the drive to work.

"Izzy, not so bad. It's caught early, right? You've not seen anything like this before?"

"No," I respond miserably, "but I *am* gone a lot. I figure they are grown enough to do their homework, get to practices and stuff on their own. If this has been going on frequently, I don't think I'd know."

Darlene withholds comment. She thinks I should not date so much, especially when I run out to meet men after the kids are asleep.

"I know. *I know* what you're thinking! And I *know* . . . that I have got to focus more on them. It's just that . . . we need a man around, *I need* a man around, and how am I going to find one if I don't get out there and look for one?"

Darlene fiddles with the largest dahlias I've ever seen in a pink vase on her desk. She has an enviable green thumb. The pictures she'd shown me of the lush flowerbeds around her house stir in me a latent yard envy. Her bouquets pop up everywhere around the office.

She responds, "More to life than the perfect man, Izzy. Your kids need *you*, not just your paycheck." She pauses, and continues, "I know you think they are grown, kind of – and independent. And no, I do not have kids of my own but I have watched my friends' families through the years. I have watched some heartbreaking divorces and the stuff that happens after. The kids take a hit but they are resilient and can bounce back, if they have even *one* stable, dependable parent."

I stand before her desk, mute. The implication weighs heavily upon me that I am not stable, or dependable. My head hangs down, my ears muffled with virtual cotton balls, because in my present state of mild hysteria, I cannot stand even the slightest hint of correction. She has pierced the core of my guilt, and I quickly push the hurt away.

"Yeah, I know. I'll handle it. I hear you. I'll feel better about this after the meeting with Patrick, the headmaster, today. By the way, how's your situation?" My expertise in deft-topic-switching never ceases to amaze. Especially when it appears I am being disapproved of.

She averts her eyes, lays her hands in her lap. Uh-oh.

"I vondered when you would get around to askink." I notice her accent thickening, fondly regard the planes of her face. "I finally got up the courage to confront him, and he did admit to meeting a 'friend' for coffee once in a while. I didn't press it further, because I vant to believe him, but the fact that he is attracted to someone else . . . well, it's so *hard*. He said it's a client. Apparently, he has been fighting the attraction for a while. She is comink on to him or somezhink. Anyway, I am trying hard not to let it affect me here at work."

"Wow. That is huge. I'm sorry Darlene . . . but at least he came clean, right? At least you know what's going on, it's out in the open and now you can deal with it? He is crazy about you, I know it."

She gives me a half-hearted smile and sighs. "Ja. The weird thing is that I *do* know it. I *know* ve have a good relationship, but we've only been married five years. How do I know there aren't more things stuffed in his past that I don't know about? How do I trust him now?"

My back is starting to ache from tension, and I shift my weight to the other foot and twist. I have been at Darlene's desk too long. I surreptitiously glance across the sales floor to the management offices and notice Birdie standing at his office door surveying his domain. His eyes meet mine. His expression is dour.

"Darlene, I gotta go. Talk soon, okay?" She lifts her face to me which now has slight, wet trails down each cheek, and nods. "Hang in, honey," I say, and give her a quick shoulder squeeze.

"Izzy, if you pray, this is the time you should pray. For me. I am not sure what to do."

I cannot remember the last time anyone asked me to pray for them. Lots of people pray *for* me, which I do not ask for, but kindly acknowledge. I am stumped for an answer. I nod, smile and dash to my desk before Birdie can approach us and join the conversation.

My coffee has devolved into cold sludge. I slide into my cubicle and tuck my mug on its coaster. When I look toward Birdie's office, I see he has disappeared, apparently back into the hole from whence he came. I am so relieved, I laugh a little, and Winston ears perk up.

"What are we laughing about, Iz?"

"Nothing," I say, "it's nothing, really. Just thinking about how to plan my day. Hey, by the way, have you had a ride-along with Birdie yet?"

He leans back in his chair, arches his back, stretches his arms out in either direction and clasps his hands together behind his head. "Yeah."

"And . . . .?" I open the straight-off-the-press newspaper and smooth down the pages, enjoying the fragrance. Something about the printing industry. It's true that one can develop an unnatural affinity for the printed page.

I stare at my coffee-sludge, wishing for more caffeine, but decide I'm not that desperate. Maybe a diet Coke.

"I am processing," Winston says.

"Processing?" I prod further, "What happened? How many clients did you see?"

His chair squeaks as he leans forward and brings his arms to rest on his desk. He pushes his glasses off his nose, and they bounce on his chest at the end of his lanyard, which is a cheery yellow today. "Three. I took him to see three of my major accounts. I had about ten minutes' notice to set it up. My clients were nice enough to let me drop by with him, but it was awkward, to say the least."

His voice has dropped to indecipherable. I lean forward, wondering if I should have my ears checked.

He continues, "I seriously think something may be going on with him."

My eyes narrow. "Yeah? What do you think?" It is probably unwise to get so deeply imbedded in this conversation. A conversation with Winston can take many long-winded twists and turns, but there are choice bits to be had amongst the chaff. However, I need to get to work, and Birdie may alight at any moment.

Winston squints his eyes at me dramatically. "I think the man may be in need of *serious* therapy. I took him to three major accounts, and at all three, he got the ball rolling with dirty jokes." He pauses and looks at me questioningly. "He do that in your ride-a-long?"

I let out a long, troubled whoosh of air. "Yep, he did. Not so much with Nellie, at St. Patrick's, but with the men we went to see afterwards . . . it was like a men's trash talk club or something. What was really annoying is that they laughed right along with him! How would I go back to them and even approach this situation? Should we bring it up to Phil? Do you think he knows?"

Winston shook his head. "I am positive he doesn't know. I think Birdie keeps that part of himself well-hidden from management."

I think about the conservative nature of the *Sentinel's* management, and wonder how Birdie could keep this hidden. It seemed to plop out easily enough, along with a string of profanity that would make a bartender blush. He could not possibly know that the *Sentinel's* owners discouraged that sort of thing. At least I thought they did. Maybe something had changed.

"Oh, man," I whisper to Winston, "how are we going to protect our clients from this guy?" I think a minute. "And what if he actually drives them away?" I stare worriedly into Winston's calm blue eyes. "Is this guy gonna cost us money? I cannot afford that!"

Winston's hand jumps from his desk to grasp his lanyard, and he presses it between his fingers. "If we want to keep our clients, I think we have some pretty serious tap-dancing ahead of us." He cocks his head thoughtfully, gazes at me.

"I think you need to stay out of his way. That's what I think, Izzy." Winston then places his glasses back on his nose, turns his chair and resumes reading his newspaper.

CHAPTER 18

Later that day, after shoving what I, at least, considered brilliant advertising ideas under several of my clients' noses, I pull into the parking lot of Windsor Academy.

I slump down in the seat of the Honda, wondering what the outcome of the meeting with Patrick will be. I dump the situation out of its tidy mental compartment and indulge a few moments of dumpster diving.

What if this pot thing has been going on for a long time with the boys? What if Patrick accuses me of being an unfit mother? What if this is just the tip of the iceberg? Then what? What if the boys get kicked out? What if they are already brain-damaged? What if – okay, this is futile, I tell myself.

I breathe deep cleansing breaths, like when I was giving birth to each of them.

I quickly slide from helpless thought-meandering to righteous indignation. Shouldering this kind of thing as a single parent is atrocious. Unfair and wrong.

Before I can slide all the way to self-pity, I dig around in my purse, locate lipstick, freshen up my face and fluff my hair. If I am headed for the muddy valley of despair, I might as well look good.

I arrive at the administrative counter in the school office, putting on my very best "glad to see you again!" smile, although, in truth, I never have time to bake cookies, buy gifts for teachers, volunteer at sports concessions and therefore know none of the people in the office. I would seriously be more involved, I would. Can't though, my life's too jammed with other stuff.

When an occasion arises where I must talk to the school's administrative staff, I do so with chronic uninvolvement-guilt that seems, at this moment, to be reflected in my posture. I straighten up, push my shoulders back and brightly ask for Patrick as if it's the most routine thing in the world.

A woman nods at me, points to his door, and says, "Go on in. Your boys are in there with Patrick. They have been waiting for you."

Now, in addition to uninvolvement-guilt, I add late-most-of-the-time guilt.

When I put my hand on the doorknob, I feel as if I am going to crack into a thousand tiny pieces, which would possibly land me in a mental hospital, with the happy consequence of postponing this meeting indefinitely. With a sigh, I turn the knob and push open the door.

Chad is sitting on a chair, one leg hung over the side, checking his phone for messages. Peter is sitting in a chair on the other side of the room, looking out a window that overlooks the parking lot, lost in thought. They both sneak a glance at me which I optimistically interpret as mute pleas for forgiveness. An empty chair is placed between the boys. My stomach is performing calisthenics, and my hand drifts to pat it involuntarily.

Patrick lifts from his chair and extends a hand over his desk. I wipe mine on my skirt, and clasp it.

"Hi, Izzy, glad you could make it! Have a seat." He waves toward the chair directly in front of his desk equidistant from each son.

He clears his throat, sits, pulls his chair closer to his desk, and tents his hands.

I have never been inside the headmaster's office at Windsor, and as he is pondering his first words, I sneak impressions. The desk is dark, big, expensive, and imposing. His brag wall boasts several diplomas from prestigious universities, and a few pictures of him shaking hands with celebrities. I notice that he is a veteran of Iraq. The credenza along the side of the room beside Chad has several nicely framed photos of Patrick with wife, Patrick with sons, Patrick at the beach with dog.

A well-adjusted, perfectly normal family. I feel tears threatening to fill my eyes and will them to evaporate. Where is a husband when I need one? What the heck do I know about raising boys?

♩

"Peter, Chad . . ." Patrick begins, and pauses, waiting for them to pay attention. I give them a warning look. They straighten. "We probably already know why we are here, but I'll reiterate for the record, okay?" The boys and I nod collectively.

"All right," Patrick says. "We have a pretty good relationship with the church across the street. They have been very tolerant of our kids using their parking lot, or maybe pulling pranks on each other in their parking lot – the typical funny stuff that goes on in a school of our size. As we have gotten bigger, that relationship has become strained. I don't guess I need to spell out that this latest incident," he pauses to look at both boys, "has tipped them over the edge."

My heart constricts and I feel a lump congeal in my throat, a particularly unpleasant sensation. I glare at the boys, their mental compartment fully disgorged and awaiting evisceration.

"So . . ." Patrick continues, "boys, I guess you realize that you were seen in the parking lot smoking pot. And before you say anything, here . . ." he points to a couple of smudged, wrinkled nubs on his desk with charred ends, "is the proof. The church's administrative assistant ran out to see what you threw out your car window the second you drove off. You're busted."

I sneak a peek at each son. Chad's expression is insolent, his chin lifted. He looks beyond Patrick instead of at him. Peter is staring intently first at Patrick, then me, then back to Patrick, his hands twisting in his lap. His face is reddening and he is holding back tears. He is the first to speak.

"Mr. McAllister, Mom . . ." he clears his throat, "I just want to say I am sorry. I am sick to death of feeling bad about this, about what it might mean with basketball, about . . ." he dashes a tear off his cheek with one hand and continues, " . . . well, about everything. Whatever I have to do to make it right, I will. And I promise, I *promise* . . . this is the first and last time I'll ever smoke pot. Honest to God!"

Patrick scrutinizes Peter's face thoughtfully, then turns to Chad. "What about you?" he says.

Chad focuses on Patrick's face, then mine. Eyes ablaze with indignation, repentance apparently the last thing on his mind.

"So we got caught smoking pot. So what?" He shrugs. "Everybody does it. They just don't get caught."

He nods his head toward Peter. "Yeah, the wimp here, he didn't want to do it, he only tried it because I asked him to." Patrick's head dips in acknowledgment. He glances at me. He rolls his chair forward, listening intently. I am quietly edging toward hysteria and wonder if and when I should speak.

"Commendable, Chad, for you to let your brother off the hook. I appreciate your honesty. Now, let's talk about what we should do about this. What are your thoughts, boys?"

Peter glances at his brother, then looks at the floor and crosses his arms. I can see the stress in his body language. Chad tilts his head back and looks at the ceiling, pulling his hands together in front of his chest, thinking. Patrick winks at me.

I am so relieved, I nearly faint.

Peter says, "What about community service?" His brother rolls his eyes but manages not to comment.

Patrick says, "What kind of community service, Peter?"

"Well," Peter looks at his brother, a mute plea for assistance. "Maybe, um . . . painting buildings or picking up trash in empty lots or something?" Chad lowers his head and puts a hand over his face.

"What's wrong with that idea, Chad?" Patrick says.

"Well," Chad lifts his face to Patrick's. "For starters, in this area there aren't any empty lots around here, and who would buy the paint if we painted buildings?"

"Good points. What do you think about that, Peter?"

Peter, my sweet-natured, rule-abiding child; says "I just wanted to throw some ideas out there, kind of get the ball rollin' . . ."

"Yeah, well, how about a few laps around the track, or extra study halls, or something like that?" Chad says.

"Do you think that is appropriate discipline for this, Chad?" Patrick asks.

Chad shrugs and looks at the floor. Neither boy is looking in my direction, which is a good thing, because I do not trust my response to them right now. My stomach has stopped churning, and I feel Patrick is going to go light on this first offense, but that doesn't mean that I don't have to do my own due diligence at home.

Both boys lapse into silence; one sullen, the other scared. Patrick allows the tension to linger as we group think the situation. I am amazed at his patience and insight.

Finally, Patrick says, "Boys, the good thing about this is that neither of you denied it. I am really proud of your honesty. The bad thing is that there must be some sort of consequence, so here is my idea: after hearing both perspectives, I feel you should both have a first-hand look at the aftermath of drug addiction. I have developed a relationship with some of the NA (Narcotics Anonymous) groups around the area, and they would be delighted to see you there."

Both boys are sitting up straight in their chairs now, paying rapt attention. I am trying to shrink into the tiniest bit of humanity I can manage.

Patrick scoots his chair back from his desk and pulls out the shallow, middle top drawer. He shuffles around, finds a blue half-sheet with a form on one side, slides the drawer shut and stands, sheet in hand. He walks around to me, hands me the sheet. I scan it briefly, noting an acknowledgment of NA meeting attendance with Windsor Academy's imprint at the bottom and a space for both Patrick and an NA representative to sign to assure attendance. I am weak with appreciation. His smile is encouraging.

"Okay, boys," Patrick says, standing in front of me, his hands clasped behind his back, looking alternately from one to the other. "Here's the deal. Peter, I know you are truly sorry this happened, and I believe it won't happen again, but I do want you to attend two meetings, and I need the signed sheet to prove it. Chad, your situation is a bit different. Your attitude is different. You know that, right?" Chad sighs and slides as far down in his chair as humanly possible.

Patrick continues, "Look, Chad, I know it's not fair your mom has to try to raise you guys on her own. I know it's been rough, and you can get really twisted up inside about things. But *drugs – any* drug – is not the answer. In fact, it makes everything – and I mean *everything* – worse. Which is why I want you to attend eight meetings. I think you need to hear some of the stories of these guys. And maybe you'll get a glimpse of what your life could be like if you don't get a handle on this now." He leans back on the front of his desk and crosses his arms across his chest, looking at both boys.

"Sound like a plan?" he says.

"Yeah," both boys respond, in unison. Peter is tearfully grateful, Chad is rolling his eyes.

Patrick directs a kind gaze toward me. "Okay, Izzy?" I nod in humble gratitude and let the tears spill. The boys cannot stand it when I cry, so they leave their seats, give me twin side-hugs, and mumble they'll see me at home, and leave.

Patrick nods a terse good-bye, watches them strap on their backpacks and walk out. His chair scrapes back. He stands and smiles at me, his hands on his hips.

"Sorry you are going through this, Izzy. Believe me, you are not the first." He lifts one hand off a hip and points at me emphatically. "Just know, I'm watching out for them, as all the male teachers here do for the kids that are in one-parent homes. There are so many! *Too* many." He drops the gesture, sighs, and shakes his head. His eyes lift to mine, and he continues, "They'll make it. They're good kids. Just need some tough consequences once in a while."

I snuffle at him. He leans across his desk to hand me a tissue. I wipe my face and stand, still shaky from the emotional drain. When he knows I have regained some of my composure, he smiles broadly. "Kinda scared them, huh?" I laugh. We shake hands, and I exit through a pristine, gleaming hallway lined with lockers.

My eyes fill with frustrated tears all the way to my car. Why couldn't I meet someone like Patrick? Why? I huff a couple exasperated huffs and turn up the radio. My foot stomps the accelerator.

CHAPTER 19

On my way home, the mascara I routinely pile on every morning has given up in the onslaught and dribbles in pools under my eyes. A glance in the rearview mirror reveals an overwrought, wet-faced, perplexed raccoon. Not particularly attractive.

My hands grip the steering wheel. Loud, throbbing music is not helping my mood. I switch it off, and swipe at the gobs of mascara, resulting in sticky, black fingers. Search in vain for a tissue, which most sane women keep tucked in the console or something, but obviously, I am not a sane woman. Especially at this moment.

My thoughts are frantic, like butterflies trapped in a jar. I remember Darlene telling me to pray for her, and think perhaps this is the time to explore this option. For both of us. Since I am alone, I decide to talk to God just like he is in the car.

"Um. God." Seriously, Izzy? I tell my brain to shut up, and forge ahead.

"God, if you are up there, I really need some help right now. And so does Darlene, my friend. Would you please fix Darlene's situation, ahh . . . with her husband . . . you probably already know about it. And for me, I don't have a clue what to do with my boys." I pause, a fresh stream of tears erupting like Old Faithful.

"I really, *really* need help raising them. If you could send a good man my way, it would be much appreciated. If not, then tell me what to do about this situation. I am so tired, God."

I stare straight ahead, hands still tightly affixed to the steering wheel. My mind stops churning. My eyes stop gushing. I feel I might get a response. Maybe a holy vision, or the sudden appearance of an angel on the side of the road, hitching a ride. Morgan Freeman's voice quoting scripture?

When none of that happens, I take a shaky breath, and laugh a little. My grip loosens on the wheel and my thoughts turn to the serious conversation that must take place at home. I am glad Mimi is spending the night with a friend, and the boys and I have the house to ourselves.

The computer screen springs to life. My desktop background, a photo of a man smitten, handing a bouquet of wildflowers to a laughing woman, is a haven of sorts. A reminder of romantic dreams instead of hideous nightmares. A place where the world is safe and fun. That love is within reach, and available to the hardy souls that pursue it.

Chad and Peter had been dissected, disemboweled and appropriately boundaried, and I am soooo ready for a happy place.

I think briefly about the pitiful attempt at prayer this afternoon. My eyes narrow. Could that have had something to do with the words that had flown out of my mouth? The three of us had spent forty-five minutes talking through the situation in the den. Peter had stared at me with anxious, wide eyes. Chad's expression had been nonchalant, careless.

By the time the conversation concluded, both sets of eyes had slitted to grudging respect.

Today's meeting with Patrick had convinced me that my habit of looking on the bright side of things and burying the darker side of things didn't always apply. Nothing like stark reality to wake a person up. Sons and drugs? No bright side.

For once, both Chad and Peter had been motivated to pay attention. The consequences to their actions were, well, costly. On the heels of Patrick's ultimatum, their respect felt good. When had I lost it? Had I ever had it? Where was that piece of me that deserves their respect?

I shrug. Time to move on. The happy place awaits. My fingers fly over the keys.

The tingle of delight I feel as I log in makes me shudder.

Findamatch is my cool, breezy oasis in the midst of the single-parent desert. There are other dating sites, but I have the best luck on Findamatch. I can discuss the pros and cons of various dating sites all night if someone asks me. The messages waiting for me blink *This. Could. Be. The. One.* Blink, blink.

I tilt my head back, throw my arms out and thank God, if there is one, for the bright spot at the end of this day. I look at my computer's time icon: ten-thirty. Think about my schedule tomorrow. Not much going on. I still have time to run out, have a quick first meeting, and be back by one or so. No problem to call in late if necessary.

As I read the first message, I actually giggle. Only Findamatch has the power to make this thirty-nine-year-old woman giggle. The attention makes me feel as if I could accomplish great things. Impossible things. Like running off into the night to meet a handsome, seductive stranger while two errant sons and one angel lay asleep upstairs is entirely justifiable.

CHAPTER 20

The line around my neighborhood Starbucks is longer than usual, and since I was up until two, my mood is unpleasant. Ten irritable minutes later, I pull up to the window.

Lydia, cocks her head at me, and says "Another late one, eh Iz? The usual for you? Or do you need a triple shot?" I am thinking I should frequent another Starbucks occasionally, and stifle an urge to snark out an inappropriate response.

"Hi," I manage, adjusting my sunglasses over bleary eyes. "Yeah, a triple. Great idea."

The barista smiles, winks, turns to give instructions to the busy morning crew. She leans on the windowsill, waiting for my order and by her expression I see that she wants to chat. I am thinking, chat? Chat? I cannot *chat* today! I will bite your head off! Please do not chat! I look down at my lap, pretend to dig in my purse, but she is having none of it.

"Izzy, I know it's none of my business, but . . ." I resist throwing my head back in despair. No one should start a conversation with that lead-in when the recipient has had just a few hours' sleep and is grappling with many flavors of guilt and self-pity besides. I look at her through my sunglasses, hoping they are dark enough to hide eyes throbbing with red-veined impatience.

She continues, " . . . I think you should ease up on those dating sites of yours. Don't you think – and I'm just suggesting, please don't take offense – that you might be overdoing it a bit?"

I am silent a few beats, then mutter a generic response. Unfortunately, she dances on.

"I do not mean to be rude, Iz . . . but I have been there. A single parent, looking for a guy and all that. It can become . . . almost an addiction . . . and the kids kind of get lost in the shuffle. Just sayin'."

She turns to get my coffee, and hands it to me. "Just a thought," she says. "Have a good one!"

I zoom off to work, piqued, of course, and stung by her remarks. I decide I will think about them later, and slurp my coffee.

The *Sentinel's* parking lot is full by the time I arrive, and I circle the lot looking for open spaces. Nada. I park on the street, which is unfortunate, because I'll have to feed the meter all morning. I step out into traffic and hurriedly close my door before I am smashed to a pulp on the steamy, sun-baked asphalt.

Un-pulped, I trot up the worn, granite steps to the entrance just as Birdie is headed out to lunch. He catches my eye and smiles. I return the smile, thinking, can my timing get any worse?

"Hey Izzy," he says. "Running late this morning?"

I feel a wave of panic.

Whatever.

A commission salesperson's schedule is *supposed* to be flexible. "Yes, unfortunately, didn't feel so good this morning. Better now."

He regards my face curiously. "What was wrong?"

My brow furrows. Do I tell him the truth?

No.

"Kind of stomach thing. It passed." I wait for him to move on. He doesn't.

"Headed to lunch?"

He nods. "Want to join me? We never have gotten that meeting . . ." His eyes assess mine, a dangerous gleam in them. Or maybe it's my imagination. Four hours of sleep mangles my ability to discern things correctly.

"No, no," I say, too quickly. "Got lots to do, especially since I lost the morning . . . you understand, right? Can we take a rain check on it?"

He gives me a long, speculative, look. The silence lasts several seconds. My mouth opens to fill the empty verbal space with an additional reason to delay the meeting, but he interrupts me.

"Izzy, you know you can't keep putting off the meeting with me forever. Let's do it in my office this afternoon. How's 3:30?"

I resist frustration, command my face to maintain a pleasant expression.

"Fine," I say, my mind racing to potential empty spots in my day when I could grab a nap.

Birdie nods and we go different directions.

The elevator creaks and groans as usual, on its ascent. I am disoriented and groggy. The doors slowly separate, and I sling my purse and bag of assorted miscellany over my shoulder, checking my cell as I walk to my desk. My headache, on a scale of one to ten, has escalated to an eight. I tilt my sunglasses to my face to shield them from fluorescent assault.

"Top of the mornin' to ya, Izzy!" chirps Watson, apparently refreshed from a full and satisfying night's sleep and a relatively guiltless existence. I glare at him and shove my purse and bag into a drawer with a bang.

He raises his eyebrows, his hand crawling slowly up his chest to his lanyard.

"Really? Another late one, huh?" he says, noting the sunglasses, massaging the lanyard relentlessly. I am beyond irritated by this remark, but I love Winston, so he gets a pass.

"Yeah. Nice guy, though." I give him a little half-smile that hopefully communicates my regrets that I am unable to be chatty and winsome this morning.

"No kidding? Tell me about him." Winston is always optimistic and interested. He worries about me, though.

I unfold my newspaper, forgoing the typical morning chat with Darlene and accompanying coffee-trek, because my morning schedule has completely unraveled, and besides it's not morning anymore anyway. I take off the sunglasses. Squeeze my eyes shut, then open them one at a time. "What are you still doing in the office? Don't you have calls today?" I slant my gaze to the corner offices, and note with relief that all of them are empty.

"Well," Winston intones, "our esteemed new manager required my presence this morning for a meeting." He waits expectantly, knowing I would be breathless to know what went on.

I am so tired, I cannot muster even the tiniest hint of breathless. Except maybe to talk about Cole, my latest late-night acquaintance. "And . . . ?" I murmur, quickly leafing through the newspaper.

"You first," Winston says, smiling. He leans forward attentively, and I can smell his subtle cologne. He sports a tan driving cap today, and a baby-blue bow tie. Winston's ensembles are chronically interesting, and somehow he manages to pull them off. His wife must help coordinate his wardrobe.

I am a little embarrassed by my own ensemble today, which includes a wrinkled, cream-colored blouse I tugged from the dirty clothes, a simple tweed skirt, and a somewhat fashionable – but woefully un-ironed tan, linen jacket. Somewhere I read that linen is *supposed* to be worn wrinkled, so I thought I might as well test this theory since I didn't have time to iron, anyway. In my mad dash out the door, I'd forgotten to grab earrings, completing the aura of non-put-togetherness. My ensemble matches my headache perfectly.

"Me first?"

"Not if you don't want to, Izzy; I can see you are very tired . . ." he says.

I smile. But the quest for the perfect man is a driving force, and overcomes exhaustion every time. I enjoy talking about it.

"Naah, I'm okay, just lack a few hours' sleep. I'll catch up tonight. I met a local man. His name's Cole – isn't that the coolest name? – and he works in broadcast sales, so we have a lot in common." I describe our quick midnight meeting at a local bar, and a brief list of physical attributes.

"Had you been talking for a while with this guy?" Winston asks.

"No, but we clicked right away."

"How long is *right away*?"

"Um . . . well maybe two hours," I disconnected my eyes from his.

"Two hours . . . as in, you met him last night on the web and then ran out to meet him?" I nodded, surprised at the scrutiny.

"Izzy . . ." Winston said, choosing his words carefully, "I have sat here, listening to you talk about your internet adventures for at least a couple of years now . . ." he gazes at me earnestly, his blue eyes intent, focused, his forehead furrowed with concern.

"Makes for interesting stories, and a lot of funny situations with the men that didn't quite measure up or whatever . . . but I think you should give it a rest once in a while. Get some perspective."

"Perspective? What do you mean?" I lean back in my chair and cross my arms over my chest, alternately looking at Winston and the elevator, worried that managers may trickle in at any time and wonder why I am at my desk and not out pounding on clients for more advertising. I am not prepared for this conversation. I am not even remotely interested, either.

My thoughts start to veer toward how to get Winston to shut up, a strange and unfamiliar veer. I am perplexed, I am tired, I am irritable and I am a single mom. A powder keg waiting to be lit. Winston better back off, I decide, and just like that, my mouth takes a relational suicide leap.

"What business is it of yours, anyway?" I snap. "I am not a ten-year old. I am fully aware of the choices I am making."

Winston, unperturbed, leans back in his chair and picks up his lanyard again. "Are you?" he asks, which infuriates me.

"YES!" I practically scream. Assistants hovering at their various stations trying not to listen swivel heads as one in my direction. Oh great, just what I need. An assistant-wide fall from grace. Sufficiently chagrined, I mumble an apology toward Winston, and make excuses.

"My point," says Winston sagely. "Izzy, this stuff is affecting your work, your attitude. It's affecting your kids, too, I think. At least from what you've told me about some of their latest stuff. I don't get in your face about things usually, do I?" He waits for my response.

I shake my head no.

"Okay then," he says and extends his arms out to each side. "What have I got to gain by confronting you about this? Nothing!" I look at the floor and wish this conversation was over.

"I don't think you have anyone in your life telling you this could be a problem, Izzy. I am just trying to help you see something on down the line that could happen, something really difficult, if you don't get control of this. I am all for internet dating – fun, and all that – but you seem to cling to it. Kind of, well . . . inappropriately."

"Okay, Winston," I say out of desperation, trying to stop this gush of honesty that is causing me to squirm in my seat. "Got it. I'll think about everything you said. Now, can we get out of my business and back to yours?" I give him a no-nonsense stare.

He shrugs. "I guess."

Good.

"So how was your meeting with Birdie?" My tone is conciliatory.

"Ugly."

"Ugly?"

"I guess I am in kind of an irritable mood, too," Winston says."The guy just rubs me the wrong way. Asked me questions that did not even apply to my job."

My eyes get wide. "What kind of questions?"

"Well, like what kind of women clients I had. How many were single, that kind of thing. I hedged answering those and made a joke of it. Then he asked me what the salespeople did for fun, where we went to drink, or entertain clients." Winston leans forward. His voice gets softer. I lean toward him, mutual conspirators whispering over the eight-inch vertical divider that slices our cubicle into three wedge-shaped workspaces. Lonnie, our assistant, is nowhere in sight. Probably chatting up the girls in production, who love to flirt with him.

"Told me to expect changes. That our quotas were going to be twenty-five percent higher now! He made a lot of jokes about quotas, which I found particularly offensive. Asked how old I was, and when I planned to retire. Gotta tell you, Iz . . . after all I've been through at this place . . . he may push me to retire early."

He picks up his glasses from his chest, places them on the end of his nose and turns his attention to the newspaper open to the comics on his desk. I am too stunned to reply. And I have a meeting with Birdie at 3:30. I feel dizzy.

"Man," I whisper. "Yeah," Winston murmurs, his finger holds his place on Doonesbury. "I think we're in big trouble."

"Why would they hire a guy like him? I mean, "I realize he was faithful to the *Sentinel* over the years, but whatever possessed them to hire someone with no – "

"Oh, and I forgot! This is important! He asked about *you.*"

"Me?" I squeak. My stomach, which is delicate this morning anyway, gives a heave of outright nausea. I clutch at it with both hands.

Winston's voice is so soft I can barely hear, so I cover my mouth in hopes that what little is in my stomach won't come up all over him, and lean forward to listen.

"He asked about the rumors he'd heard about your online dating, if they were true and if it is affecting your job performance."

"Oh. God."

I jump up and run to the bathroom, leaving Winston staring after me in mid-sentence. My stomach relieves itself of all content exactly one second after I shove open a stall door and center my mouth above the toilet bowl. After I wash my face with cool water, I sit on the floral bench conveniently placed in the tiny foyer in the ladies' room to think and allow my stomach to get back to normal.

What I do after hours isn't any of Birdie's business. I think about my performance. The track record I have with my clients. The ongoing success I'd experienced in meeting – and exceeding – quotas. What is there to complain about? Has someone started knifing me in the back at the office? Who? Why?

Then it occurs to me. Who has the most to gain by getting me out of the way?

Jon, of course! The guy that had actually confronted me about talking to his client. The guy who thought I was stealing advertising revenue from him. I decide I will approach him for a purposeful chat.

I slowly walk back to my desk and sit in my chair. I feel like death warmed over, and need something to calm my stomach. Winston is gathering up his paraphernalia in preparation for an afternoon of drive-by selling.

I know he is hovering. Winston is a great hoverer. I smile at him, signaling that I'm okay.

"I'm fine, Winston. I am really glad you told me about this. I actually have a meeting with him at 3:30 today. At least I am somewhat, um, prepared." I shrug, and plop into my chair with a bounce, which is unwise and makes my head pound.

Winston's expression is unreadable. "Tread carefully," he says, smiles thinly, and steps away from our cubicle toward the elevator.

Great, I think. How does one tread carefully around a snake?

CHAPTER 21

Birdie fires up his laptop and munches a bite of sandwich. He eats in huge, gaping mouthfuls, barely swallowing before attacking another. A napkin is stuffed into his collar. It drapes across his chest, dotted with crumbs and bits of olive.

It is difficult to watch.

Jon looks away before he loses his appetite, and wonders what the retail sales team is going through with this guy at the helm. An interesting development.

Jon is huddled in his usual corner toward the back of the café. Birdie has commandeered a four-top toward the entrance with a view of the street and the front entrance of the *Sentinel*. Jon picks up his vegetarian wrap and studies Birdie. He is pecking on the laptop between bites, and smirking every few minutes.

Jon takes a cautious bite of wrap, ensuring that tomatoes or avocados or bean sprouts did not land on his white dress shirt. He studies Birdie as he chews – like a climatologist watches a developing tornado – with the morbid fascination that precedes potential carnage.

He finishes his wrap, licks his fingers, wipes them carefully on a napkin. Guzzles the remainder of his fruit smoothie. Checks his calendar on his phone one last time to confirm his afternoon appointments.

Thank God this guy is not my boss and I do not have to sit down and actually get to know him. I do not have to pretend I want to say hello as I leave, or talk about the damn weather, or suck up in any way whatsoever. His exit will take him past Birdie's table, and he wonders if he might slant his eyes at an opportune moment to see what Birdie is pecking at.

He nods to the counter people that know him as a regular, and moves toward Birdie's table. Birdie glances at him quickly, then looks back at the screen.

The snub doesn't bother Jon at all.

Jon pushes his way through the crowded café toward the entrance, past the counter where people are waiting for their order. The combined smells of fresh coffee, hot Panini, and homemade soup are intoxicating. Jon hesitates before the counter, considers a Danish for dessert, decides against it, and moves on. He walks quietly behind the table where Birdie is seated, and squints at the screen.

He grins, feeling he has gained the upper hand in a yet-to-be-determined battle of sorts, and strides out the door. He wonders when and how he can use this interesting bit of information to his advantage.

CHAPTER 22

The car is stifling even though I have the air conditioning on full blast. My seat is fully reclined. I am trying to nap, but I cannot get my mind to stop. I am disgusted that I stayed out so late.

Winston is right. It *is* affecting me. Maybe not my work, not now – but eventually, and probably soon. I tip my head to the side to glance at the clock on the dashboard: five minutes until three o'clock. I have another fifteen minutes before I should drive back to the *Sentinel* and have the meeting with Birdie.

I could beg off – tell him I am not feeling well? My head swivels side to side. The speculative gaze on the steps was probably a veiled threat. No. I can't get out of the meeting. I lift my hand and watch it for a few seconds. It is noticeably shaky. C'mon Izzy. Feel better.

Ten minutes later, I back my car out of the shady downtown alley. Ten minutes after that, I am cocooned in the decrepit elevator, my heart beating wildly. I whip out a small mirror from my purse. My face is pale, but passable. The doors hiss open, and I death march to Birdie's office. Knock on the door.

I hear his chair scoot back, then the tread of steps on carpet. The door swings open. His smile is a double-decker row of tombstones.

"Right on time! Come in, come in!" He indicates a chair in front of his desk with a wave of his hand, closes the door. I feel like a mouse cornered by a tomcat.

"Hold on just a minute," he says, "need to send a couple of emails." He sits behind his desk and carefully tilts the screen. Whatever he is working on, he doesn't want me to see.

I cross my arms and wait. Quickly take in his office furnishings for a hint that might aid in ass-protection should the need arise. Why did this man provoke fear? Fear of what?

I study his profile, focused on his computer screen. His long, tan fingers pummeled the keyboard, a diamond ring winking from his right hand.

His bookshelves are filled with inspirational books by various self-made men: Donald Trump, Iacocca, Patton, JFK. There is one stiffly posed photograph of him beside what I assume is his wife. Bleached blonde, slightly heavy, overly made-up. No children's pictures, and I wonder if he and his wife have any. The paintings on the walls are mostly ocean scenes featuring sailboats of various vintage. His desk is immaculately ordered; all right angles and clean spaces. I sniff a hint of sweet tobacco in the air; cigar, not cigarettes. I look behind him, through the window, at the blue sky beyond and long for escape.

He sends his final email with a flourish, turns his chair from his computer to me, slaps both palms down loudly on his desk, and gives me his full attention.

"Now! Finally! We have our meeting."

I shrink in my chair. My legs cross themselves automatically. "Yep," I respond. My voice is subdued.

Birdie leans back in his chair, which squeaks like a well-worn saddle. His chair is huge, tufted, imposing, and the color of dried blood.

"So, tell me Izzy, how are things going in your territory? What clients are you having trouble with, if any? How can I help?" He tents his hands, cocks his head and rivets icy eyes on mine.

I am taken aback. He seems almost managerial. Hesitantly, I fill him in on my relationships with major accounts, my personal goals for these accounts, and steps I am taking to accomplish bringing in more revenue.

When I pause, he jumps in. "Izzy, I can't help but notice from the reports that your numbers are satisfactory, seems your quotas are all reachable, and your client relationships are intact. All good things."

His eyes narrow. "But not quite good enough."

My eyebrows knit together. "What?" I feel played. Why had I let my guard down? I soften my tone. "Why?"

He grins a big-bad-wolf smile. "I think you could use a little refresher course in old-fashioned conversation," he responds. "I couldn't help but notice how stiff you were out in the field on the ride-a-long we did together."

I am stumped for an answer. My mind quickly runs to the follow-up call with Nellie after their unfortunate meeting. Nellie had been troubled by his rudeness. Took me a while to convince her everything was going to be okay. Stiff? Me?

I blurt out, "Ahh . . . okay. So what do you think needs to be done?"

He leans forward, elbows on his desk, hands clasped. "I think you should let *me* take you out for a drink. Loosen up. I'd like to share a few techniques with you that worked for me when I was runnin' after new business."

I am so shocked that I am silent. He mistakes this for consideration of his offer.

"Izzy, you have a good reputation here. You've been meeting your quotas. But the buzz around is that you are so tired every day from that online dating thing of yours that you can't take care of your own work – that Lonnie does it all for you. I'm afraid if you don't take it down a notch, I'll have to say something to Phil about your, um, effectiveness."

He pauses, watching my face. I am cautiously stoic, my gaze steady. Underneath the façade I am struggling with rage.

He continues, "All the more reason for you to get together with me to talk about different approaches."

He winks and continues. "We'll get you loosened up, gal. You won't have time for online matchmaking if you play your cards right."

I remember Winston's admonition to *tread carefully*. My mind is a butter churn, forming dense globs of thought. One seems palatable.

I smile through my anger. "Sounds like a great idea." The smile broadens. I continue, "Let's get Phil involved. I'd like his input too."

Birdie's smile falters, then returns. "Sure, we can do that. But I think Phil's out of town on business next week."

"Oh, that's too bad," I say. My voice drips with syrupy sweetness. Fortunately, this idiot doesn't know me well enough to realize that my voice *never* actually drips with syrupy sweetness, and that he should possibly put himself on high alert.

"We'll have to put it off a bit then, won't we?" He turns and looks out his window, then back at me. His slender fingers fidget with each other.

"By the way," I continue, in a gentle voice, "what I do during non-business hours is personal. I will schedule a visit with Human Resources to discuss protocol about the things you have brought up, but offhand, I'd say this conversation is inappropriate."

With that, I stand shakily, turn, and walk out the door, pulling it shut behind me. Where had those words come from?

I walk the twenty or so paces to my desk from his office and fall into my chair. The sales floor, except for busy assistants at their desks, is mostly empty. Salespeople are still out on appointments with clients, a few starting to dribble in to close the day by turning ads in to production or finishing call reports.

I am finding it difficult to breathe. Birdie, I realize, is on a mission. And somehow, the mission seems to include hitting on me – or getting rid of me.

Either way, I'm screwed.

CHAPTER 23

I pull myself together and go find Darlene. After a whispered, intense conversation, we agree to meet at Raphael's at five-thirty.

I am nursing a glass of Silver Oak cabernet when she slips onto a stool next to me at the bar and gives me a tight hug. I can't help it, tears bubble up and dribble down each cheek.

"*Vertrauen in den Herrn mit deinem ganzen Herzen, und lehnen Sie sich nicht auf Ihr eigenes Verständnis; in all deinen wegen bestätigen ihn, und er leitet deine Wege,*" Darlene whispers in my ear, then translates: "Trust in the Lord with all your heart, and lean not to your own understanding. In all your ways acknowledge Him. He will direct your paths."

I pull back and regard her kind face tearfully, thanking her with my eyes. I do not really understand her fascination with the Bible, but I acknowledge the comfort the words bring. I give her a final quick squeeze and turn back to my particular source of solace this evening: a great cab. I am at a bit of a loss for words. I guess we both are, and the comfortable silence is reassuring.

After a few minutes, she says," Should I go first?" Her eyes search mine, and I nod. She continues, "Richard and I have had some really hard conversations, and have decided to attend counseling for couples kind of schtuck in . . . a situation."

My eyebrows lift. I turn to her in surprise, "Really? Wow, that is great, Darlene. I admire you for that, it's a big step. Good for you!"

She smiles, but her eyes are weary. "Ja, it's good, but it's going to be hard. Clearing the air is alvays hard. But at least it's forward progress. Also, ve have agreed that Richard will give up the client that is coming on to him so he vill not have to see her on a regular basis. So that's where I am, and I am content that Richard is serious about our marriage, and that's a big relief. That's the latest in a nutshell. So now, your turn. What's goinck on?"

I look past Darlene at the mirror-covered wall behind the bar, hundreds of bottles of liquid solace reflected in the ambient lighting. I sip my wine, considering what to say.

"Well?" Darlene persists, expectantly. The bartender trolls the length of the hand-carved mahogany bar: snatch, douse, rinse, put glass away. Repeat. An efficient, practiced move.

I sigh and set my wine glass on the bar. Clasp my hands in my lap.

"Darlene, remember when I told you I was worried about our new manager, Birdie?"

She nods.

I quickly relate story after story of Birdie's coarseness and lack of manners, particularly with my female clients. I fill her in on some of Winston's comments, swearing her to secrecy. Her eyes get rounder with each revelation.

I continue. "And that's not the worst of it! Somehow, he has heard about my online dating and has suggested I stop." A smile flirts with Darlene's mouth. I notice, and irritatedly snap, "It's none of his business! Besides, he also indicated he wanted to *take me out* to discuss sales techniques that might loosen me up."

Darlene's mouth drops open.

"You are kiddinck me! Vhat is wrong with him?"

"Exactly," I say, vindicated.

"This is real trouble, Izzy. I had heard rumors about him, but nothing like zis." She thinks a minute, her hand on her chin, eyes squinted, brows pulled together. "I don't know what you should do. I think vhatever you do, there is a trap."

"Right. It only happened this afternoon, but between then and now, I figure I have to walk a tightrope. If I tell Phil, he might not believe me. It'll be Birdie's word against mine. You know how upper management sticks together." Darlene nods. "If I stiff-arm Birdie, there'll be hell to pay – he is not the sort of guy that fights fair. I'll lose accounts, he'll increase my quotas until they are impossible to reach! My commissions will dry up, and, well . . . I don't even want to think about it."

"Seems to me you have already stiff-armed Birdie," Darlene says. "How do you think he is going to respond to what you said about taking his personal remarks to HR?"

I shrug, and say "It's the first thing that reasonably popped in my mind. Believe me, I was so shocked at what he suggested, I wasn't thinking straight. Maybe I should have played along, given myself some time to think about how to respond."

"Sometimes," Darlene said, "ve just don't have a clue what to do. That's when I pray, Izzy. I vill pray for you. This is a tough one."

I nod my head. "I am thinking I should go to Phil. My track record has earned me at least enough trust that he would listen, don't you think?" Darlene tilts her head, her honey-colored eyes bright. "But I am going to wait and see what shakes out from the meeting. Maybe Birdie will just pretend it never happened. Maybe he will take a hint, and clean up his act."

I reach for my wine. As it glides smoothly down my throat, I close my eyes. Wine this good is a prayer in its own right.

CHAPTER 24

As I pull into my driveway and push the garage door opener, I sigh in relief. Home. The kids' car is already tucked inside the garage, and I am looking forward to some quality time with them. I'm determined to stay off Findamatch tonight.

My eyes adjust to the gloom of the garage as I sit, thinking. A small, white piece of folded paper tucked under one of the windshield wipers snags my attention. Where the heck did that come from? Must be an advertisement.

I hop out of my car, walk to theirs, lift the wiper and slide out the wedged note. The paper pops and rustles as I unfold it.

Immediately, both the evening and my stomach unravel. The note, handwritten, says, "I see you like Raphael's. I do too. Still hoping we can have that conversation. Jacob"

This creep Jacob has been *following* me?

I hold the paper at arm's length with fingertips only, like it is infected. My first response is to tear it up into itty-bitty pieces and toss it in the trash. The more subjective part of my brain insists that I keep it as evidence, in case things turn nasty.

I pull out yet another mental compartment, tuck the note and fear inside, along with a promise to the subjective part of my brain to file a police report.

The next morning, Chad, Mimi, and Peter are almost enjoyable before they sail off to school. The decision to focus attention on them last night made a difference. I'd even insisted they turn off all computers and TV and join me around the dining room table after dinner to talk. What a concept.

We'd discussed school, sports activities, girlfriends, whatever. I'd supervised homework, assisted where I could. I'd enjoyed the feeling of my children around me. The only mar on the evening had been Chad's moodiness when I'd tried to chat him up. He'd finished his homework in silence and gone to bed early. I'd made a mental note to grab some alone time with him to find out what's going on.

I'd resisted the urge to log on to Findamatch.

Kind of.

Just a peek before I went to bed, that's all.

9

I pull into my Starbucks drive-through, hoping to tell Lydia about my family night and reassure her that my kids were doing just fine. The young girl at the window gives me a cheery greeting and asks for my order. I give it to her – two shots only today

"Where's Lydia this morning?" I ask as she waits for the inside crew to make my latte.

The young girl's eyes cloud with worry. "Lydia had a family emergency last night, I think someone died or was in a terrible accident."

"One of her kids?!" I shoot back.

"Yeah, maybe. I am not sure," she turns to retrieve my latte, slips a holder on it and re-emerges. Hands me the coffee. "Busy today without her. I don't know what actually happened. Have a good day!"

I drive to work, stunned. Why had I never thought to ask Lydia about *her* personal life? I hope with all my heart that she and her family are okay. Think about how self-involved I must seem. Something to think about.

Later.

I take the stairs two at a time and burst out of the doorway to the second floor, effectively beating the elevator and nearly mowing down Jon Hoyt in the process, who looks shaky this morning.

"Hey Jon, good morning! How are you today?" I smile brightly. Amazing what a good night's sleep does for a person.

"Hi, Izzy. Not so good. But I'll be okay. Sick the past couple of days, think I'm getting better, though." He moves to the elevator, and I remember I need to somehow discover if he is the one demonizing me in the office.

"Glad you're feeling better, Jon. By the way, do you have time for a chat later? Maybe at lunch today, or late afternoon?"

His face creases into a smile. "Yeah. What about?"

I smile flirtatiously and stick out a hip.

So shoot me. It's a habit.

"For me to know and you to find out!"

Jon laughs and says he'd be available later in the day.

We arrange a time to meet at the office. He disappears into the elevator, and I slide into my chair, the wheels rolling across the ugly industrial carpet, the force of my pounce knocking me into the far side of the cubicle. "Ouch!" I yelp, and Winston looks up from his newspaper.

"Looks like the Pod-Queen has some bounce in her step today."

"A little too much bounce it would appear!" I respond, rubbing my side.

"How's it going, Pod-King?"

"Great. And I see that we are in a fine mood this morning!" he beams.

I reflect on this statement and gauge my mood. I think he is right, and unfortunately is not usually the case. Feels good. "Yep. Fine mood. Feel good." I stare at my desk, then across the sales floor. The staff is slowly filtering in. Muted conversation floats around the room. The smell of coffee and sweet pastries trails a few entrants, wafting behind them as they wind toward their cubicles.

Assistants are busily handing out stacks of proofs to their assigned sales reps, exchanging morning pleasantries.The managers are huddled in Phil's office around his conference table, clearly visible through the floor-to-ceiling glass. I wonder what they are cooking up, grab my mug and prepare to zip back to the coffeemaker for my morning serving of sludge and Darlene.

Winston slides his chair closer and leans in my direction. I sense a whispered confidence coming, and lean in, our noses approximately eight inches apart. "Are we laying off the internet a bit, hm? Getting a little more sleep, maybe?" His eyes are playful.

I slide my chair back, somewhat – but not quite – irritated. "Yeah, yeah, Winston. Had a night off. So what?"

He turns his attention back to his newspaper and picks up his mug of coffee, sipping, smiling. "Just an observation, that's all."

I snort in response, and dash down the hall past Darlene, who waves and smiles, and stop in front of the clattering, industrial-strength coffeemaker. A fresh pot is brewing and several white-shirted, delicious-smelling men are standing around waiting. They widen the circle, inviting me in.

"Hey, Iz. How's it going today?" an older sales rep asks. I respond with the generic, accepted response that typically is a lie, but today is not. "Fine. Great!"

Another of the group teases, "Another late night? Who's your favorite pick today, Izzy?" Chuckles all around, knowing glances slide toward my face.

"Actually, gentlemen, last night I helped my kids with homework, fixed dinner, went to bed early."

"That's a first!" one of the men blurts, ungraciously.

I will the coffee to finish perking so I can fill my mug and escape. "Yeah?" I shoot back. "And how would you know?"

The men look at each other. One of them says, "Birdie! Your name comes up often. He seems to know your habits pretty well, somehow." The men stare at my face appraisingly. Shock registers in my eyes, and I nudge my expression toward neutral.

"Yeah, whatever, " I say dismissively, "Lot of people say things, but that doesn't mean they actually *know*." The coffee has finished filling the carafe, so I lift it and fill my cup; then hold the carafe aloft, in a gracious mid-air request that they extend their cups to be filled. After which, I hope they will take their small brains and inappropriate conclusions back to their cubicles.

As if on cue, one of them says, "Those late night hours include some with Birdie, Iz?" I can feel the blood rushing to my face.''Of course not! " I stalk back to my desk to ponder this new revelation.

I sit in my chair in the pod, my hands unfolding the newspaper. The scent of fresh ink is soothing. How in the world would something like that get started? It could not be further from the truth!

My thoughts careen toward Jon, but that doesn't make sense either. I don't get the feeling that he is that underhanded. Or is he? I take a sip of coffee and grimace. Inside the mug, floating around the sides, are small islands of coffee grounds. I glance at Winston, who is on the phone setting up client appointments. The meeting with Jon this afternoon will clarify things. I begin flipping through the paper, checking that my ads have run correctly. I graze the headlines to keep up with what's going on so I'll have something to discuss with clients this afternoon.

As I force more coffee down, I ponder Winston's comments. And Darlene's. And Lydia, from Starbucks. They are right, after all. My shoulders slide up, then down. I *do* spend too much time online, and not enough taking care of my kids and my job.

The tiny man hunter demon that camps out on my shoulder roars to life and screams something about the efficiency of dating sites, and the impossibility of finding a man without them. I tell the man hunter demon to shut up. It cackles its way to a pout, then disintegrates.

Winston, who has concluded his call, turns toward me, frowning. "What's up? Your mood has gone from great to weird in the space of thirty minutes. Everything okay?"

I sigh. Sometimes it feels like Winston and I are married. He reads my body language like no one else, except Darlene, perhaps. I figure it would not be a bad thing to tell him about the coffee group's comments.

"Well, don't know if I'm exactly okay in light of what I just heard." Winston gives me his full attention, picks up his lanyard and slides his fingers along its length thoughtfully.

I continue, "Have you – ahh – heard any rumors about Birdie and me?" Winston's eyes get large, he looks up at the ceiling for a moment, concentrating. Drops his lanyard, pulls up to his desk and leans on crossed arms toward me. "Nope. What are the rumors?"

I quickly give him the basics. He is perplexed. He stretches out his arms and clasps his hands behind his head as he leans back in his chair. It creaks in gentle reminder that a squirt of WD-40 would be nice.

"Izzy, remember when I told you to *tread carefully?*"

I nod.

"I think the guy is seriously motivated to shake things up. And you are not bowing down to him as he expects. Plus, you have brought up a kind of veiled threat with the HR thing." He brings his arms to his lap and sits up straight. "All I know is, you are experiencing a, uh, *situation.*"

I nod, miserable. Tears spring to my eyes. I sigh and slap them away.

Winston doesn't notice. "I don't exactly know how you are supposed to deal with it, but I'd start with Phil. I think he'd believe you." He pauses, looks down at his desk, then out a window on the far side of the room. Winston is wearing plaid suspenders today, a matching bow tie; a maroon lanyard and a heavily starched white shirt. I notice a straw hat, the kind worn by well-dressed men in the south to shield rapidly balding heads from a punishing sun, perched on his desk. He smells great, as always.

"Iz, you gotta cool it for a while with the online dating thing. For whatever reason, Birdie is watching you like a hawk." He smiles. "No pun intended."

I smile, the tension fading a little with the joke.

"I know you want to get married again, find a stepdad for your kids and all that . . . but you can't give this guy an excuse to turn on you. And it looks like he is out for blood."

I gaze at his earnest face a few moments, thinking how fortunate I am to have this concerned-uncle type of man in my life.

"I guess so," I mumble, disconcerted, wondering how I can get my head around business today.

"Well, " I say to Winston, "can't do anything about it right now. Gotta try to figure out my day. I've got a meeting with Jon later, to see if he is involved. " Winston's eyebrows shoot up to his hairline.

"Yeah? You think he is mad about you getting your foot in the door with Tom Burke?"

"Well, thought he was, but we worked it out, and I think he is fine with everything. But when all this stuff came up, got me thinking maybe he's the passive-agressive type. Just want to talk to him to see if something's underneath the surface. Probably not. "

My shoulders shrug. I turn my attention to my computer.

"Hang in, Izzy," he says, lifting the straw hat from its perch and neatly tilting it over one eye. "Temporary. It'll pass." He smiles, salutes me, and heads to the elevator.

"Yeah," I mutter to myself. "Hang in there, Izzy."

CHAPTER 25

Birdie Costanza

Birdie slams down the phone. His eyes squeeze into small, mean slits and his hand drifts to his chin. His chair squeaks as he rocks back and forth.

This is getting ridiculous. Trying to pin me down, make me fit the mold. Are they serious?As if I haven't been successful in my own business? He mmmphs in disgust, pushes himself up from his chair and strides the length of his office to think. Floor-length curtains are drawn around the glass walls, the only light from dim morning sunlight through a window and an accent lamp on his desk.

He stops in front of the window behind his desk, clasps his hands behind his back, studies the second-story view. Thrasher Avenue in Chatbrook Springs is a busy street, and cars are jammed up, jockeying for position. The windows in redbrick office buildings across the street stare back at him, blank eyes. People flow in and out of revolving doors. Ornate wrought-iron street lamps adorn the sidewalks. Nicely maturing, evenly-spaced pin oaks line each side of the street, a landscaping project thirty years ago. Concrete sidewalks buckle here and there from root systems vying for urban space.

His gaze lifts. Storm clouds are rolling in across the river from the east.

He rehashes the conversation with the director of human resources. In her sweet, southern way, the director had informed him that a complaint had been filed against him for sexual harrassment. That she was sure it had been a misunderstanding, but she needed to have a sit-down with him as soon as possible, and when might that be?

He'd told her he would get back to her, chatted innocuously a few minutes, and slammed down the phone after his best, most cloying phone farewell. He is sure Ms. Isabelle Lewis is at the bottom of this. Who else could it be? His mind spans the various meetings he'd had with the retail sales team over the past few weeks. He is clueless. Unless, wait! Was this somehow related to his sense of humor? His jokes? He thinks a minute, and smiles. Masculine crude is imbedded in the southern culture, but some people may not understand.

He laughs, relieved. Must be it. This will be easy to clear up. First, though, he needs to have a brief chat with Phil to mention it, downplay it. Then he will drift by the general manager's office and do the same thing. Lay the groundwork. Talk about how sensitive some of the female sales reps are. Piece of cake.

He picks up his laptop and sunglasses, steps out of his office and locks the door, thinking about lunch. His eyes fall on Izzy, busily working at her desk. They narrow. He'll make sure this gal puts up or shuts up. Definitely. He casually strolls to the elevator, nodding at Izzy as he passes her desk. She barely looks up. All the better. She won't even know what hit her.

His smile dazzles the receptionist on his way out.

CHAPTER 26

Izzy

I fly home as if my car has sprouted Honda-wings.

The freeway is nearly deserted midafternoon and I enjoy swooping in and out of various lanes unhindered. I pull into my garage, quickly exit the car into the house, run upstairs and nudge my computer awake. I have about an hour and a half until the kids come home from school. My heart ramps up as usual, in anticipation. I hope for several messages. Lord knows I need them.

The men's comments around the coffeemaker had forced me to internalize a litany of depressing implications, and I need my favorite happy place like a diabetic needs insulin. Clients would have to wait until I sort myself out a bit. To my profound and utter relief, there are four, blinking messages and three *winks*.I quickly delete the *winks*, open the first message, scan it, look at the photo and open his profile.

"Astute professional seeks lovely lady. Prefer a professional career woman who values independence, integrity and romance. I am tall, athletic, successful and motivated to fall in love. Like poetry, good books, long walks, full moons, sunsets and jazz. Good – not great – dancer, but I can hold my own. Really like kids, and have two teenage boys. I'm mature, but not dull. Optimistic, but not unrealistic. Sports-minded, but open to turning off the game. Educated, but not stuffy. Political, but not narrow-minded. The lady I am looking for is attractive, intelligent, a non-smoker; interested in outdoor activities and likes (or tolerates) dogs. Hopefully she will appreciate a great wine, and not mind if I open the door for her."

Uh-oh. I'm in trouble.

I quickly click back to his message, which says, "Dreamsicle (my online pen name), I read your profile and am really interested in meeting you! Love your pics and description of yourself. I see that you have an interesting career, and our interests seem to be similar. I think you are one of the loveliest women I have seen on Findamatch. Please don't break my heart before we meet! Say I can call! Let's talk and see where it goes. I'm out of the country on business in three weeks, and would love to meet you sooner than later. Let's start with talking on the phone, what do you say?" Signed, "Anxiously, Brad."

The tension leaves my neck and back as I melt into a romantic puddle. Too good to be true, I tell myself. Then my perky optimism reasserts, tells me anything's possible to those who persevere. No guts, no glory, right? I click back to his profile and scroll through his photos, which include his dog and kids.

My flying fingers message him that yes, call, let's talk, I'm flattered, oh so flattered, and I give him my phone number. The adrenaline rush shivers through me. I sigh, reluctantly log off. Better head back to work before the kids get home and catch me. I stare at Brad's photo again for a few seconds. I put two fingers to my lips, then plant them on his. The other three messagers will have to wait, but I assure them silently that I'll message back as soon as possible.

I stand and stretch, then walk to the bath off my bedroom to freshen up before going back to work. The kids should be arriving home from school any minute.

At the edges of my mind, a detail hovers. I concentrate briefly, then remember – my meeting with Jon! Four o'clock! I text my assistant, Lonnie and ask him to relay a message to Jon that I am running behind. As I swipe mascara on my eyelashes, I realize the stress has vanished.

I marvel at the power of Findamatch to give me an instant boost. Perhaps, as others tell me, it will eventually be my undoing, but for now it's my best friend in the world. I pencil in the outline of my lips, then fill with color. Wink at my reflection in the mirror, and run downstairs, through the kitchen, out the door to the garage where my trusty chariot awaits.

A neatly folded square of white paper under the driver's side windshield wiper startles me. Was that there before I left the parking lot at work? Yes? No? Did I overlook it? If not, *how did he get into my locked garage*? My stomach knots immediately. I grab the note and throw it into my purse. Think about it later, I tell myself. I press open the garage door, back out, accelerate.

Lonnie greets me as I step the two paces to my desk from the elevator, his expression strained. I see by the height of the pile on his desk that he has quite a lot to do.

"Hi, Lonnie – need me to take some of my stuff and do it myself?"

He smiles gratefully, fingers through the pile and carefully pulls out several proofs.

"Oh my gosh, it would be such a help, Iz, thanks!" He hands me the small stack, which I look over quickly and lay on my desk.

"Jon around? Did he get my message?"

"Yeah," Lonnie says, one hand on the phone and the other inking corrections on a proof. "He seemed a little irritated that you're late. He's in the conference room."

"Thanks," I throw behind my back as I streak through the cubicles, wishing I had time for a new cup of tar-pit coffee, then realize this thought is ridiculous and hadn't my afternoon been screwed up enough? I throw open the conference room door and see Jon tapping his fingers on the conference table, waiting. The clock behind him on the wall indicates I'm twenty minutes late. "Jon, so so sorry – stuff came up." I trail off apologetically.

He nods, waving a hand that effectively erases my apology.

"So, I'm here. What's this about?" His voice is curt.

I sit. Not exactly prepared, but willing. I decide to start with the coffeemaker conversation. "I wanted to talk to you about something I heard this morning from some of the retail sales guys."

"Okay. Need more to go on." He sits back in his chair and crosses his arms over his chest.

"Of course, Jon, I am going to elaborate."

"Great," Jon says. "Now we're getting somewhere."

I resist the urge to frown. "I guess you realize that Birdie, the new manager, is kind of intent on getting to know us, and our account lists, really quickly." Jon nods.

"Well, almost all the retail team has been on ride-a-longs with him, and I've been hearing some stuff that concerns me about what has been discussed." I pause to study his facial reaction. He shifts in his chair, clearly puzzled.

"Yeah? What in the world would that have to do with me? This is all retail stuff. I've got a different manager, in case you hadn't noticed. Probably don't know anything that would help you figure out whatever it is you are trying to figure out. Which remains a complete mystery, by the way."

Our eyes lock, and I am momentarily stumped for what to say next. Okay, so I'm late and he's irritated. Fine. But is there a need to be a jerk? I mentally wave bye-bye to my diplomatic approach as it flies out the window.

"Jon, for gosh sakes, there is no need to be so mean! I am just trying to lay groundwork to ask a question!"

"Then, Izzy, I suggest you *ask the question*. I have work to do, and I've been sitting here for," he glances at his watch, "twenty-five minutes so far."

"Yeah, well I've got stuff to do too! I don't have time for this, this – rumor mill drama crap either!"

Jon's face registers surprise, he uncrosses his arms and leans forward. "What rumor mill drama crap?"

"Someone's been saying that Birdie and I are involved! I need to get to the bottom of this! It's . . . it's . . . SO not true, and I am disgusted that it's going around."

The surprise on his face muddles, then clarifies. "You mean, you think I am involved in this somehow?" My gaze is steady. I cross my arms, saying nothing.

Jon throws up his arms angrily, "You have *got* to be kidding! I don't get involved in that type of stuff! Never have, never will. Quite frankly, I am *insulted* that you think I would have anything to do with it." He pushes off his chair, his hands clenched into fists at his sides, his face reddening.

"Wait, Jon," my tone conciliatory. "I know I am not the most subtle person in the world – "

Jon settles his lips into a thin line. "So I've heard."

"But I thought that you might be really angry about the Tom Burke thing, and that maybe it was your way of adding injury to insult . . ." The words sound preposterous, even as they tumble out of my mouth. I shut it.

Jon, to his credit, does not storm out of the room in an angry fit, but stands his ground, staring at me incredulously. I do not look up, feeling the full brunt of my clumsy conflict resolution skills. I hear Jon's chair scrape back as he sits.

My eyes, which are glued to the floor, see his feet situate themselves an even eighteen inches from each other on the floor. His elbows perch on his knees as he leans toward me.

"I can promise you, Izzy, that I am not that kind of person. I know you don't know me well, but you can count on me to *never* do something like that." His voice is firm. "If I thought you were involved with your manager, I'd keep it to myself. Not my concern. Unless, of course, it starts to affect some of my accounts that you have a piece of."

I look into his face, startled by this comment. His expression is neutral, his eyes guarded. "I can promise you I am not – would not – *ever*," I sputter into unintelligibility, hardly believing I am defending myself against unfounded suspicions.

I am also thinking now would be a great time for a two-week vacation, if I could afford it. I stare alternately at the floor, and Jon's face, at a loss.

Jon stands. "I think this meeting is over," he announces. I stand as well.

"Jon," I say, squirming, "I really am sorry if I've offended you. Just thought I should ask you directly – right away – instead of letting my mind run down rabbit trails, getting mad, and *then* approaching you. I am kind of emotional over this. I think you can understand, right?"

He searches my face, seems satisfied, and nods.

"Okay, well, let's just put it away. Never happened. If you are dating Birdie, not my business." He grins.

"I'm *not*." I grin back. "He's way too old for me, and besides, he is married!"

"He is?" Jon asks, surprised. "Coulda fooled me!"

"Why do you say that?"

"Y'know, I've been here over twenty years, and I pretty much know what goes on all the time. I understand how management thinks and how to play the game with production. And editorial, too, for that matter. People may think I'm stupid when I play dumb, but I'm not. It's pretty smart to keep your head down and your mouth shut around here. While I am sitting at my desk in the afternoons turning in ads and fighting with production and sucking up to my assistant so I can get her to do what needs to be done, I am also observing what the hell goes on around here. It's *ridiculous* what goes on. And I just keep it to myself until – God forbid – something happens where I have to drag out some of the information I've stashed to protect my job. But one thing I know – that guy Birdie doesn't *act* married. And he doesn't wear a ring, either."

"I saw a picture in his office with a blonde woman about his age. Looked like a husband-wife shot to me."

He shrugs. "Maybe so. But a lot of married guys don't act married. Just the way it is. It's too bad, too." He turns his wrist to look at his watch – a beauty, a Rolex, Explorer Series, I think – and indicates he needs to leave. Then he blows my mind by saying, "What do you say we have coffee sometime, and you can tell me how that internet dating thing works?"

I stand there, hoping my mouth has not dropped to the floor. I couldn't have been more surprised. If he'd suddenly taken a swing at me, that I could understand. But a coffee date? I stutter that maybe I'd kind of, sort of, like that. Sometime.

He smiles. "Good. I'll be in touch. Take care, Izzy." I watch wordlessly as he leaves the conference room.

CHAPTER 27

On the way home, I suddenly remember the note I'd thrown in my purse before my meeting with Jon, and fish around for it, swerving a bit out of my lane, which inspires several drivers to do mean things.

Finally, my hand lands on a hard, small square. I retrieve it, determined not to open it until I reach a red light, and place it in one of the console cubbyholes. A few minutes later, I come to a full stop at a red light, and unfold the note. My stomach gurgles. Not only am I dreading reading the note, I'm hungry as well. I look forward to throwing something into my mouth when I get home. The paper is crisp, new. It unfolds easily. The words shout at me.

ALREADY LOOKING FOR NEW PROSPECTS, IZZY? HOW MANY DO YOU NEED? DON'T YOU HAVE TO GET TO BED EARLIER THAN THAT TO GO TO WORK? DOES THIS MEAN WE AREN'T GOING TO HAVE THAT CONVERSATION?

I crumple the note in horror. He'd been in my house? Watching me? How was this possible? Could he have seen me through a window? No, I realize quickly. My computer desk is in a windowless hallway on the second floor. Even when I take my laptop to the den, at night the blinds are closed. He'd have to be in the house to see me. The light turns green.

The rest of the drive home is a blur. My feelings are a ghastly mess. I manage to glue a smile on my face before I greet the kids. After dinner and homework, I will call the police. No more procrastinating.

Chad and Peter are at the kitchen table, books open. I hear Mimi's TV upstairs in her room. I quickly hug each son, which results in irritated looks and half-hearted attempts to pull away, but I don't care. I hug them every day whether they like it or not.

"So what's up guys? How was school?" I glance over their notebooks. "What homework are you working on?"

"Got those NA meetings tonight," Chad says. "Last one for Peter, but I still have to go. Six. More. Times," he says, his voice dripping with sarcasm.

"Yeah? Good. I am one hundred percent behind Patrick, as you know." I sit and look from face to face, arms folded on the table, leaning toward them. "So give me your impressions from the NA meeting. And turn off the music! I will never know how you can study with that stuff banging around!"

They exchange glances, and smile. Peter gets up, turns off the thumping music, and returns to his seat. I recognize the conspiratorial look between them. It is resignation mixed with reluctance when Mom wants to sort out stuff. They hate that. They also hate it when Mom tells them to turn off the music.

I wait with ears, eyes and body language poised alertly in their direction.

After a few seconds, Peter puts down his pen, places hands in his lap and looks at me. "Only one meeting, Mom. So kinda hard to tell – but my impression is that these guys have gone through some amazing, terrible things because they are using. Don't want to go there. Ever." He glances at his brother, then continues. "Chad knows it, I know it. I'm done."

I smile at him encouragingly, reach out and pat his hand. "Hope so, honey. Chad? What do you think after the first meeting?"

He sighs heavily, throws one arm over the back of the chair, and leans his head back, staring at the ceiling.

"So stupid," he says. "Pot is not a serious drug. It's approved in several states for um, sick people. It doesn't lead to *harder* drugs." His fingers carve air quotes.

"Going to these meetings is not going to change my mind." He is still staring at the ceiling, indicative, I think, of inner turmoil. When Chad does not look me in the eye, I know from experience something's going on. I think about how to respond. Wish I'd been a psychology major type of person, with a calm and introspective demeanor, but no, I had to be a bull-in-a-china-shop, Type A personality. Not real helpful where teenage boys are concerned.

I take a deep breath and dive in.

"I'd keep an open mind, Chad. I know you think pot is okay, but the point is, *it's illegal*. Period. Right now you've been given a pass from Patrick McAllister, but the cops will not be so forgiving. You may think you are able to do life 'high' but you're *not*."

I stop before my emotions escalate. I have so many issues fighting for attention that the tidy compartments in my brain are threatening to unlock themselves and dump out in a torrent of tears all over my kitchen table.

"Chad, you are an incredible kid with a bright future! But this pot thing – it's going to damage you. Please pay attention to what these guys say in the meetings. You can learn from them. You do not have to go down the road they have. Okay? Just listen. Be open. Promise?"

His eyes glaze over, but he nods his head in agreement, then resumes his homework. Peter takes this as his cue also, and picks up his pen. I take out the meat I've thawed for dinner from the refrigerator.

"I'm going to change and check on Mimi. I'll start dinner in a few, okay?" Heads nod.

I run up the stairs, at the top of which sits my laptop, taunting me. The pull is unmistakeable. I glance toward Mimi's room and see her partially open door and one sock-clad foot. Red and yellow stripes. Hear her clattering away on her laptop. I stand hesitantly before mine. "Mom! That you? Can you come here a minute?"

I pull out of my laptop's orbit, walk down the hallway to her room and push open the door. "Hi, honey. How was school?" Her bed, all pink and purple ruffles, indents in a whoosh as I sit. She minimizes her screen.

"Some of my friends are going to Starbucks. Can Chad and Peter drop me on their way to that meeting?"

"Which friends? And is your homework done, *and* you have not eaten dinner." Mimi scrunches her face as she thinks about this.

"No homework tonight. I'll eat dinner fast, and it's Katelynn and Stacey." I nod, familiar with these kids, but make a note to check with their mothers anyway, to see if this is okay with them.

"Let me make a call or two. Otherwise, if you eat first, I have no problem with it as long as Chad and Peter can bring you home after." She nods. "Dinner in twenty minutes." No acknowledgment, she is already back online.

After the dishes are rinsed and stashed in the dishwasher, I stand on the front porch and watch the kids leave. They wave. I wave back. The heavy bass line of the music they are fond of recedes in volume and disappears altogether when they turn the corner. Inside the house, my cell blurts out Rascal Flatt's "Life is a Highway," and I run to answer it.

"Is this the lovely woman on Findamatch that calls herself Dreamsicle?'"

My face flushes with pleasure. I am such a sucker for a good line. "Oh! Hey Brad! Glad you called. What's up?"

I drift out in a haze of romantic fantasy to the small deck off my kitchen, sit, and participate in the introductory ritual that is oh-so-familiar. By this time, I have polished my approach to perfection. I ask the carefully calculated questions, respond with equal parts flirtatiousness and evasiveness, and manage to extract enough information to figure out if I should go forward. After thirty minutes, he asks to meet somewhere. Perfect timing, with the kids gone for at least another hour and a half, so of course I throw caution to the wind (again) and tell him yes. We decide on a bar halfway between his location and mine and end the call.

I guess the police report, and the rest of my messages on Findamatch will have to wait until tomorrow. I fly upstairs to find the perfect outfit for a first impression jittery with excitement.

CHAPTER 28

Birdie Costanza

"That should do it!"

Birdie regards his bogus profile with pride. After a few weeks of subtly asking around on the pretext of getting to know the sales staff better, he'd managed to elicit quite a bit of information about Izzy. Hadn't really been too difficult to come up with a profile he figured she'd respond to. These dating sites are really like shooting fish in a barrel. So easy. Too easy.

He glances around the den and down the hallway to make sure his wife is still asleep. Her intrusiveness is distracting. Tonight she had plaintively asked him to come to bed with her, even though she knows the question is pointless. He'd decided a few years ago to leave the marriage emotionally. She is a stupid woman, he'd rationalized. He'd lost all respect for her.

Even though he'd left their bedroom to sleep in the guest room pleading a lack of sleep due to her tossing around and snoring at night, she still granted him sex frequently. The perfect relationship as far as he is concerned. Free housekeeping, laundry and meals. Sex on demand, which is not often, but still. Comes in handy.

In return, his wife doesn't have to work, enjoys a liberal financial budget and can go any damn place she pleases, including another bed if someone will have her. He doubts it. Doesn't care.

He stands, stretches, and lets his gaze wander the room. The house was an extravagant purchase, but a good investment. Even though the market had bottomed out recently, he believes the investment will pay off in time. Faded, expensive, oriental rugs cover the floor, wall hangings chronicle the travels he and his wife have made over the years. Gently lit original oils cover the walls. A spotlighted fountain gurgles on the back patio. Wisteria drapes the arch that beckons to the pool beyond. His wife had spared no expense decorating.

"All this. Wasted on a dimwit of a woman." He berates himself again for not divorcing years ago. She is past sixty now. He'd just have to put up with her. Don't want the trouble and expense of a divorce, setting up spousal support, splitting assets. He shrugs. Things are fine. They live separate lives.

His thoughts return to Isabelle Lewis. The first sight of her that day on the stairs had caused him a few sleepless nights. He is determined to lure her, convince her to see him. He can be a very patient men. After he earns her trust, which he undoubtedly will; he'll teach her a few things. For starters, a little respect. She cannot possibly realize the implications of her actions. He can't blame her, really.

She doesn't know the job with the *Sentinel* is merely a cover for more ambitious pursuits – chief among them a nice little pharmaceutical business on the side. Nope. That gorgeous, tight-assed, big-blue-eyed gal has no idea who she is messin' with. She'd learn. Real soon.

He licks his lips at the thought, then smiles, his teeth tiny beacons in the darkness. He really loved a challenge. Especially if a hot woman is involved.

Izzy

The night is a clear, stark black. Stars prick the sky in tiny, brilliant points of light. It's so clear a galaxy splotch is hazily identifiable, Brad had said, pointing as we lingered by my car. I'd tilted my head back, marveling.

It's getting a little cooler, I'd said, and he'd graciously draped his arm around me and kissed me on the cheek. My thoughts run round and round in my head, chasing their fluffy tails. My heartbeat is still elevated, my mind lost in a sea of storybook endings.

I pull the Honda into my driveway and wait patiently as the garage door strains open. The house is dark. Good, kids are still gone. They'll never know. Adrenaline surges break over me like waves cresting the beach. Brad had been an astonishing surprise. Great-looking, polite, intelligent, gainfully employed. I float into the house.

The clock on the wall in the foyer chirps ten p.m. I wonder momentarily about the kids, but feel sure the boys have hung around Starbucks to pick up Mimi and should be home shortly. I can't be stressed about anything right now. My thoughts at this moment are Brad. Mmmmm. Brad. I like the sound of it. Strong.

I sigh happily. We'd parted with a hug. He whispered in my ear that he'd call later in the week. I can still feel the chills that streaked up and down my spine as his breath tickled my ear. I want to lay on my bed and re-live the evening in my mind, but need to change quickly into pajama pants and a T-shirt before the kids come home and wonder where I have been.

I run upstairs and almost, but not quite, pass my computer before going into my bedroom to change. One tiny minute won't matter. I sit. I'd logged onto Findamatch so often that it nearly logs itself in. One blinking message awaits me. I click on it half-heartedly, as Brad has overtaken my thoughts, but the habit has a strong pull. I scan the message.

It takes my breath away.

"Dreamsicle: As I search for the perfect woman, I am always hopeful my search will yield that one woman – the one for me – that will fulfill my dreams, help me achieve the goals we will set together, fill the void in my life. The one awesome woman for which I will gladly buy flowers, write love poems, become a fool. The one to which I will give my heart – forever. I have to admit, Dreamsicle, that I was on the verge of giving up on Findamatch, having searched in vain for months, but then I found you. As far as I am concerned, there is no one that even comes close to you. Your eyes, your hair, your smile. I am completely enraptured. The things you shared in your profile, a perfect match for mine. My option with Findamatch expires soon, and you will disappear. Please say you'll meet me. I do not want to be aggressive, or too forward, but I am very serious when I say you have captured my heart with your profile. Meet me. Please. Read my profile. See if you do not think we might be perfect for each other.

If you agree, I will be waiting for you at Raphael's Piano Bar in River's Edge downtown. It's my favorite place, and I hope you like it. Eight this Saturday night. If you don't show, I'll take that as a no. Until then, Dreaming of you."

I sit in my chair, staring at the screen, stunned. Never had a message on Findamatch so captivated me. Why now? Brad is great!

Shaken, I remember the kids are not yet home, and run into my bedroom, throw off clothes in a pile in the corner, throw on pj's, run downstairs and rummage in my purse for my phone. No missed calls. My heart skips a few beats as I quickly press the number for each, then text. Eventually, Peter responds. "Hey, mom."

Hey mom?

"*Where are you!*" I resist yelling, but not by much.

"Still waiting for Mimi at Starbucks."

"What? Why are you *waiting* for her? She was supposed to stay there!"

"Nope. Not here." Boys are so infuriatingly terse. After a night floating on clouds of romantic delusions, I am free-falling back to reality with a resounding thud.

"Are her friends there?"

"What friends?" Peter responds. "We dropped her off, but no one came out to meet her. She went into Starbucks by herself."

Agitation beats against my ribs like a wild bird in a cage. In the jostle of plans, going over homework with the kids and dinner, I'd not called to check out things with Mimi's friends' parents.

"Okay, Peter, stay there. I'm going to make some calls. I'll get back to you –

and call me when Mimi shows up."

I call both sets of parents and to my consternation, both girls had not gone anywhere tonight. I am now officially hysterical, and when I am hysterical I do not think straight. I collapse downstairs in the den in a helpless heap, holding back tears of frustration. Where is she? She is twelve, for Pete's sake! I try to organize my thoughts. My hands are shaking, and my stomach, as usual, is a roiling mess. When did life become so complicated? I think hard for a minute, and decide her laptop may hold a key. Didn't I secretly save her passwords somewhere?

I run to my desk, where I keep my private stuff locked in a drawer away from the kids, locate the key and unlock the drawer. Various papers fly out and scatter themselves in square zigs and zags on the tan pile carpeting. After a few minutes, I hold up a crumpled piece of notebook paper upon which I'd hastily scrawled various passwords without Mimi knowing, and gasp out a frenzied version of the Hallelujah Chorus. Maybe I can find a few clues.

I enter her room and marvel at how neat and tidy it is. Had I noticed this before? Doesn't seem like it had always been neat and tidy. When had she started cleaning up her room? Her laptop is on her nightstand, charging. I pluck it up and sit amidst stuffed animals piled halfway down the length of her bed. Quickly log on to Facebook, where she spends most of her time, at least as far as I know. Do I really know that? Oh God, help me find her.

Facebook page seems fine, contains the usual assortments of innocuous posts and family news from twelve-year-olds. Checking private messages, I quickly realize that Mimi has been messaged by people I do not know, and quite a lot of boys. Alarms bells go off in my head. Hadn't I watched a program a few weeks ago about predators on Facebook posing as young boys, but are actually pedophiles cruising for victims? My heart is beating so hard it literally feels as if it will erupt from my chest. My hands are trembling, and I can barely control them to open message after message on Mimi's Facebook. I feel sick.

I open one that seems slightly off, and talks about meeting at Starbucks. After reading it, I am convinced this is the person she has met, and click on his Facebook profile. And of course, it is set to "Private," so I can get very little information. I jot down his name, his school, any information that is readily available, which isn't much, but at least it's something.

I quickly Google his name in White Pages, and several names pop up. They are in the vicinity, which is encouraging to me. It's possible he is not a predator, but a clandestine, age-appropriate boyfriend. I clutch at any shred of hope before I descend into a black hole of worry.

The phone rings. I just about jump out of my skin. "Hey," I bark into the cell.

"Mom!" It's Mimi. I am so relieved, I nearly fall to the floor. My hand has inadvertantly drifted to still the wild beating of my heart. "Mom, I'm okay. So sorry, I didn't mean to stay out so late . . ."

Tears streak down my face. "Mimi, it's nearly eleven! Where have you been? I was about to call the police! And who the heck is – " I stop myself before I reveal that I can log onto her computer. Don't want to give up the mom-vantage.

"Who is who?" Mimi says, puzzled.

"Never mind!" I snap. "You and the boys get home. Now! And I expect a full explanation."

"Yes ma'am." Mimi gets very polite when she realizes I am going over the edge. "Will do, Mom. We're on our way home right now."

I click off, wondering how much more a person is supposed to take. Is life ever going to get easier? I carefully place Mimi's laptop back where it was, re-connect it to the charger and smooth out her comforter where I'd been sitting.

CHAPTER 29

My bed had never looked more inviting.

I step out of a long, hot shower feeling somewhat restored. The private discussion with Mimi in her room, away from the boys' inquisitive ears, had left me thoroughly shaken. Tears streaming down her face, she'd confessed to meeting a boy that night that she'd been messaging on Facebook for some time, someone she had never met.

Indignant, she'd shouted that I did it all the time. I could not disagree, of course, and realized my ploy to hide my dating activities was lame, at best. My defense to her was that she is *twelve* and I am nearly three decades older, wiser and more experienced. To which she had sarcastically quipped, "Oh. So that's why we have had *three* fathers so far."

No good answer to that one either, but it hurt, and I had bitten my lip so hard it nearly bled. I plied her with more rules, wondering at the same time how I would enforce them if I was not around; grounded her for two weeks and left the room, taking her computer with me. Maybe a week or two without it will give her food for thought.

I left her cell, which is an older model and does not allow her to log on to Facebook. I didn't want to be completely heartless. She'd be texting her friends for hours, I knew.

I fall into bed, and my mind refuses to stop churning. I turn off the light, close my eyes, but my brain is stuck on replay. Birdie and his expectations, Jon's coffee invitation, Brad, my son's recent drug explorations, Mimi's surprising Starbucks episode tonight. Plus making a living, paying the bills – pretty basic, time-consuming responsibilities in themselves. Try as I might, I cannot get my mind to shut up. I toss back the comforter, pad downstairs for a cup of chamomile tea.

I will not, *not*, I repeat to myself sternly, log on to Findamatch. I hurry past the computer without a single glance.

As I am microwaving water for my tea, I decide to step onto the deck. The night air is cool. Thanks to neighborhood planners, there are no street lights to disrupt the full moon's incandescence. I can clearly discern my struggling rose bushes, barberry bushes and crepe myrtles against the privacy fence that surrounds my back yard.

A breeze whistles through the tall, slender pines around the perimeter of my property causing moonshadows to dance across the deck. A train's haunting whistle calls in the distance, echoes, and fades away. Its chug is reassuring. A reminder of the relative simplicity of times past. My sigh is deep and long. Maybe I should watch a Hallmark movie. Those *always* put me to sleep.

The beep inside signals my water is ready for the teabag and I return to my kitchen, drop the bag in the tea, add honey, and step back out. I curl into a padded wicker chair and pull my legs up against my chest. I glance up at darkened windows, secure in the knowledge that each child is in his/her respective bed.

In light of Mimi's escapade tonight, I am overwhelmingly grateful for the early discovery, and wonder how many single parents have struggled through the same scenarios as I have the past few days. I feel a symbiotic connection to each of them, sitting on my deck in the light of the silvery moon. A fellowship of suffering. A comedy of errors.

The tea is soothing, and delicious. It is so quiet, I can hear each individual night-sound. The crickets chirping, the frogs croaking. The twigs snapping.

My head whips around. Twigs snapping?

Just outside the fence. What is that sound? A racoon or fox going through the trash?

A crunch. A brush of a bush against the fence. A snap of branches. Then another. I sit perfectly still, tea aloft in one hand, listening. The sound repeats, then a crunch of steps upon acorns the squirrels have been scrabbling over. I turn toward the gate, desperately hoping it is locked. Metal grates upon metal, the sound of the lock being tried, but it holds through several attempts. Whoever it is had to push through some overgrown bushes to get to the gate. My mind balks at the thought of an intruder.

I breathe a silent sigh of relief that the gate is locked. The footsteps recede, and I hear them go through the front yard and around to the other side of the house. The steps stop at the fence, which has no opening on that side, and I feel someone peering through the slats.

Fortunately, I am nearly invisible in the moonlight, curled into my chair. I am afraid to move, and my mind claws toward the realization that it is probably Jacob and I have not given a police report priority, so, ohmigod, now what?

Good idea. Doesn't God hear silent prayers? I realize it would serve me right if He doesn't listen, but I do it anyway because I am desperate and praying, as far as I can tell, is what desperate people do. I close my eyes and think a heartfelt prayer as loud as I can.

I hear steady breathing through the fence, and will my heart to stop beating violently because I swear it is so loud it might give me away. *Now is the time to get a dog.* As usual, a good idea too late, but I mentally add it to my list of things to do when I am not busy being terrified.

Trying to breathe silently is becoming impossible, and I do not know how much longer I can continue. My legs are cramping but I dare not move.

The minutes drag by, the shadows in the yard shifting like elongated ghosts, taunting me with their movement. The night, like me, seems to be holding its breath. The crunch of footsteps begins anew, receding steadily. They shuffle through the lawn, then scrape pavement and, finally, disappear.

A few minutes later, a motor rumbles to life a few houses away. I heave a noisy breath, swing my legs out of the chair and massage them. I am positive it is *his* car, and run inside my house to the front windows to see if I might catch a glimpse of the vehicle, but it is no use. The car must be parked too far away for me to identify it.

I begin to tremble violently. After a few minutes of meltdown, I give myself another lecture. Dog or no dog, it's up to me.

I walk upstairs, grab my cell, check on the kids; walk back downstairs, check all the locks on the windows and doors, and call the police. Yes, there was an intruder, yes I have an idea of who it might be, no I do not need you to come out, yes I would like to request a restraining order, yes I will come to the station tomorrow to verify.

A perfectly miserable ending to a perfectly miserable day. Except for Brad. A tired smile tugs at one corner of my mouth, and after I make the police report over the phone, I drag my weary butt upstairs, locate two Tylenol PM tablets, and do my best to forget this day.

Except for Brad.

CHAPTER 30

"Aaaah, a three-shot latte morning, I see," winks Lydia, who I am overjoyed to see is back at the window.

"Lydia! I am so glad to see you! I heard you had some trouble lately," I trail off, hoping she will not consider this intrusive. She smiles warmly, shrugs her shoulders, quickly relays my order inside, then turns back to me.

"No, no, it's fine. Remember I told you I am a single parent? Like you?" I nod, glancing at the line of cars behind me. She continues, unperturbed. "My son was implicated in a hit-and-run," reaches back to retrieve my latte, which I am in dire need of, and continues, "not him, as it turns out. It was touch and go there for a while. Things are okay, now though." I take the cup from her hand, my eyes wide.

"How do you do it?" my tone vulnerable, transparent. Self-confidence erased somewhere between Birdie and apparent stalker.

She squints her eyes at me, assessing her answer. "God," she states firmly. "Without Him, I'd be a basket case, and my kids would probably be in jail." She smiles. "How do *you* do it?"

My head rocks back and forth. "No clue. I just know I need a three-shot today. Without it, I might as well go back home to bed."

The barista laughs. "Izzy, you are a trip. It's hard, being a single parent, but it's not a death sentence. We'll make it. I'll pray for you if you pray for me." Her eyes are friendly. I do not know how to respond, so I smile at her, toast her with my latte, and speed away, toward the office, and hopefully, some sort of peace. It's all I can do to pray for myself, and I do not think that is going very well, so why would I commit to pray for someone else?

Exactly.

I carry my latte, my purse and my all-purpose bag of miscellaneous what-ifs up the stairs and into the elevator, which happens to be crammed today with a group of students about to embark on a tour of our facility. I carefully balance my coffee above their heads, and am relieved when the second floor bell rings. As I wait for the doors to slowly wheeze open, one of the blessed little critters' heads bumps my coffee which promptly empties itself down the front of my jacket.

Perfect.

I smilingly acknowledge an apology (not from the kid – from the tour guide), struggle through the throng, out the doors and to my desk. Throw the now-empty cup in the trash. Cannot believe I must settle for the *Sentinel's* sludge-maker coffee. Again. I stare at the light brown dribble down the front of my linen jacket, remove it, and am relieved that the rest of my ensemble seems to have been spared.

Winston graces me by flipping his glasses neatly off his nose to dangle at the end of his lanyard. Brown leather today.

He silently takes in the stained jacket on the back of my chair, and the disgruntled look on my face. "Day not starting out too good, hm?"

I pull my chair up to my desk, turn and smile at him. "No big deal. Bunch of kids on a tour bumped my coffee over on me."

Winston nods. "Kids can be irritating. Should be on leashes," he quips, which makes me laugh. "So what's going on with you lately?"

I quickly consider how to answer, and decide Winston is a good enough friend that he can be trusted with the truth. Well, partial truth. I do not think he would be able to handle the whole enchilada.

"Well," I begin, "I had a weird day yesterday, actually." I pull out the bottom drawer, bang my purse into it, slam it shut, lean toward Winston with my arms crossed on the desk, and continue, "You probably won't believe this, but – "

All hell breaks loose across the wide linoleum aisle in the classified department, and our conversation is abruptly snipped.

"Whoa! What's going on over there," I say. Never one to run from a commotion, I bound from my chair to take a closer look. Winston turns his chair around, puts his hands behind his head, and leans back, watching.

"Out of the way! Get back! Give him some room!" I hear the classified manager shout as I draw closer. Elbowing through sales reps and assistants forming a tight knot around someone, I burst out at the front of the group. Jon Hoyt is laying on the floor, quite pale, and breathing rapidly. "So dizzy . . . dizzy," he keeps repeating.

People are standing around helplessly, and I figure it can't hurt if I insert myself since Jon and I have become bosom buddies lately. I kneel beside him.

"Someone bring me a wet towel or something!" I yell, and see a couple people sprint in the direction of the bathrooms. Jon is sweating profusely, murmuring incoherently. "And a bottle of water!" I add, sensing dehydration. Someone hands me bottled water, and I carefully tip up Jon's head and put the bottle to his lips. "Drink, Jon. It'll make you feel better. Have you eaten this morning?" He manages to take in a few gulps and then forcefully lays his head back down on the floor. "Dizzy," he says again.

"Jon, have you eaten today?" I ply. He shakes his head back and forth. I glance around the group peering anxiously at Jon and ask for crackers or a candy bar. The wet towel is handed to me and I wipe Jon's face, which is now drenched with perspiration. He is close to passing out, and mercifully I hear sirens in the distance.

"Just a few minutes now, Jon. Help is on the way. Hang in there," I whisper. He smiles the barest of smiles. "Give him some room," I say to the group who I am sure are wondering what the heck I am doing on their side of the building. "Just back away a bit so he can get some air."

They back away, and a few return to their cubicles, feeling the crisis is past. The classified manager and I sit with Jon, who is still extremely pale and now trembling. Someone hands a candy bar to the classified manager, who hands it to me. I lift Jon's head and beseech him to eat a small bite. He is beyond responding.

The paramedics explode from the elevator with great pomp in full hazard gear, paramedic vests and official-looking medical kits, wheel a collapsible cot towards us, and prepare their patient for transport. In the meantime, Lonnie has alerted the entire office that Jon is nearly dead, and more people are gathering. Assistants and production staff who have crept in from the back to find out what the ruckus is about, wring their hands and share concerned expressions.

I am crying a little. Jon is still non-responsive. The paramedics lift him with a one-two-three, practiced move and lay him on the cot. I shove the uneaten candy bar in his pocket as they strap him in, efficiently roll to the elevator, and disappear.

I find myself alone on the floor, in classified territory, wondering how to get back to . . . what was it I had been doing?

Winston strolls up, taps me on the shoulder and offers a hand, which I accept and lifts me to my feet. "Quite an exciting morning! Never knew you were such a nurturing type, Iz."

I never knew I was, either.

CHAPTER 31

Jon Hoyt

He orients slowly, as if emerging from a pile of memory foam. His limbs feel heavy and clumsy. His mouth is dry as the Sahara Desert, his lips cracked. Words tumble over his tongue, but all that emerges are dismal croaks.

Jon opens his eyes. First the right one, then the left. The whiteness nearly blinds him and he closes them again. He recognizes the bleep-bleeps that accompany a hospital stay. Eases his head to the right two inches and locates the IV strapped to his arm.

His thoughts are mushy. The meds that had knocked him out are wearing off. He more often than not longed for full unconsciousness anyway lately, so he buzzes for more meds. No matter how hard he tries to remember what happened, he cannot summon an orderly thought. He sighs, gazes around the room, and waits for the meds.

Later that afternoon, someone enters Jon's room. He can tell the person is not part of the medical staff because the typical smell of antiseptic is replaced by a clean, masculine scent.

"Jon?" a voice gently intones. He tries and fails to force his eyelids apart. "Jon? Came by to see how you are doin', buddy."

Familiar voice, but from where? Just can't focus. Just. Can't. Focus. Too tired.

"Jon," the person behind the voice picks up his hand. "I'm here for support. This is Phil, from work. I know we don't get into each other's personal lives all that much, but I can see you are struggling. *Really* struggling, and I understand. I'm going to leave now, because you are so medicated I don't know if you can hear what I'm saying, but I want you to know I'd like to help. I'll be back when you are a little more alert." He feels a small, hard shape being deposited in his hand and his fingers being closed around it.

The warmth of the man's hand recedes from his own as it is returned to the bed. Footsteps backtrack out of the room and down the hallway. *Help me?* The words dangle like ripe fruit as he slips back into a medicated, dreamless sleep.

Izzy

The afternoon passes in a pleasant mix of client phone conversations, setting up meetings, and finalizing proofs. Lonnie and I catch up on equal parts gossip and business, and I am reminded to be grateful for his assistance at work, especially since my personal life has slammed dangerously toward crisis-mode on several fronts lately. I am careful not to reveal too many details, as Lonnie tends to cast a wide net with his mouth, but since we are becoming friends, it is hard. It is nice to experience someone so interested in the details of my life, even if he is almost twenty years my junior.

Mid-afternoon, Phil stops by my desk. My mind quickly ramps through my business performance and decides there is no reason for a tongue-lashing. I smile and say, "Hi, Phil? How's it going today?"

He plants his feet and clasps his hands behind his back. "Good, Izzy, just fine. How are you?" I respond with the typical pleasantries, and wait.

He fidgets, looks up at the ceiling, then at me. "I have an unusual request for you to consider, Izzy."

My eyebrows rise, curious. "O-kaay . . . and what might that be?" Phil glances around, spots a vacant chair, and pulls up beside me.

His voice is lowered."Looks like Jon needs a week or two off, and I am looking for someone to take care of his accounts in the interim. Since you already have a relationship with one of his biggest accounts – Tom Burke at Ardmore – I thought you might be a good candidate. Get your foot in the door to sell the automotive guys some retail as well," he finished, the carrot brandished in front of my nose.

This is all I need, with everything else that's going on, but how can I say no? It really is a wonderful stroke of luck, and could result in some decent money coming my way. Besides, for Phil to ask this of me indicates a lot of trust, which I appreciate. All this zings through my mind in about five seconds, and I respond, "Sure, Phil. I'll be glad to help out. Got an account list I can work from?" He nods. Leans toward me, his expression serious.

"Izzy, we've got a situation with Jon. I have a feeling he is a full-blown alcoholic, or on the verge of becoming one. I do not want this information to go any further, understood?" I nod, my heart racing.

"Oh, no! Phil, Jon has always been the biggest producer for classified. Surely this is a temporary setback."

Phil shakes his head wearily. "Think it's been comin' on for a couple years, Izzy, ever since his wife died. His manager's been keeping me in the loop, and he's been going downhill for a while. I am by no means thinking of terminating him, nothing like that. I just think he needs help right now, and maybe for a few months. So when you commit to this, you need to understand that it may be longer than a few weeks." He studies my face. I am trying to figure out where this particular Phil has been hiding the eleven years I have been in his employ.

This Phil is kind and understanding and patient. I like this Phil *much* better than the one that castigates us in sales meetings a few times a month. I nod, and tell him I understand, and add, "I'm going to carve out some time to go visit Jon myself today or tomorrow."

He stands, nods. "Good. That'll be great, Izzy. He needs all the support he can get right now. I'll get the account list to you this afternoon." He walks toward his office, hesitates, turns back to me. "And thanks, by the way. "

I smile at him. Phil, the marshmallow. Who knew?

CHAPTER 32

The police station, located just a few blocks from the *Sentinel* building, sits squat and foreboding as I pull up and park. Twin flags – USA and Georgia – flap in the breeze atop metal flagpoles situated in front of the building. Pansies line each side of a sidewalk ending in double glass doors upon which is etched, in bold caps, "CHATBROOK SPRINGS POLICE DEPARTMENT." The pansies are an attempt to soften encounters with the police, I suppose. The pansies are not brightening my mood, but I think it's cute that someone tried.

I push open the double doors and locate what appears to be an information window. Like most state agencies, the floor is coated with cheap, gray-flecked linoleum and the walls are painted mental-institution beige.The chairs in the waiting area are metal frame with stingy vinyl padding that matches the walls. A montage of black and white photos chronicle the succession of police chiefs since 1947.

Lovely.

I sigh and approach the window. "Hi, there," I hesitate. The clerk, who looks bored and cranky, slides the window open and snaps, "Yes?"

"I was told to come and meet, um," I fish in my purse for my notepad bearing the name, "Detective Faraday, to fill out a request for a restraining order."

"Okay, have a seat," she grunts and closes the window with a bang.

Doesn't she realize my tax dollars pay her salary? Doesn't that earn me a little courtesy? I sit and wait. Pull out my cell and see that it's almost six p.m.

I quickly text, to which the kids respond that things are fine, so I slip the phone back in my purse, cross my arms, and wait. When six-thirty rolls around, I am understandably irritable. I approach the clerk's window. I stand there, fidget for a few seconds, which she ignores. I rap sharply on the window. She slides it back. "What?"

"Where's the detective? I need to get going. I was told this was routine and wouldn't take long."

She smirks. "Yeah, they all say that. " With effort, she pushes her substantial bulk off the chair and disappears. I return to the waiting area, trying to control the unsavory verbiage rolling through my mind in her direction. Finally, a middle-aged man with a tired face and an even tireder shirt and tie steps out and beckons me.

"Ms. Lewis?" He is carrying a folder to which is affixed a note. His head bobs down at the note, then at me. When I rise, he flips the folder open, and his eyes briefly graze the contents. He snaps it closed and tucks it under one arm, extending the other toward me. His clasp is strong.

He leads me to his tiny office, which contains a metal desk and two chairs exactly like the ones I'd been sitting on, and indicates that I take a seat.

He seats himself behind his desk, ruffles through a few papers, pulls one out, clicks his computer, scans it briefly, then gives me his full attention. "So you need a restraining order? Want to tell me why?" He folds his arms on his desk, leans toward me, listening.

"I think it's all detailed in the police report," I respond, wondering why I have to go through this again.

"Yeah, but we always get more details with the second, third or fourth time. So what happened?"

I slump in my chair, resigned. "Okay. Fine." My frustration slips out in a sigh. "I met this guy – Jacob – on a dating site. We went out once, and I decided not to go out again. He, apparently was not okay with that." I explain the incident with my neighbor, where Jacob had shown up and waited on her front porch, and the hostile phone call the morning after our date. I describe the unpleasant scene when Jacob's car had been towed.

"Hostile? How do you mean?" the detective is jotting notes on a pad as I talk. I relay the conversation, and he nods. "Okay, so the guy is less than courteous, kind of upset, going through a divorce, but you decide to go out with him anyway. You let a perfect stranger pick you up in *his* car, at your house, so now he knows exactly where you live. Got it. What else?"

Feeling a little defensive, because I am getting the sense this guy is cataloging me under 'idiot', I say, "For starters, he's left notes on my property."

I unzip the pocket where the notes are stashed in my purse, retrieve them, push them into his outstretched hands. He quickly unfolds the notes and begins reading.

"One of them I found on my car, under the windshield wiper in my *locked* garage, one was placed on my windshield while I was having a drink with a friend downtown."

Detective Faraday lays down his pad, sits back in his chair and crosses his arms over his chest. "Ever heard of the Craigslist Killer?"

I resist rolling my eyes, keeping them focused on the floor.

He continues, "Ms. Lewis, do you have any idea how many times this sort of thing happens? And it's mostly an online dating thing. Meeting a perfect stranger, with no friends to recommend this person, no idea of actual history – and you wonder why you are in a threatening situation?" He shakes his head in amazement leans forward, gazing into my eyes. "I would strongly recommend you utilize a different method to date. *Strongly*." He picks up his pen and resumes writing.

I squirm in my chair and wait.

He calls in the cranky woman from the information window, tells her to begin the processes for a restraining order. She glances at me, takes his notes, and exits. Detective Faraday entwines his fingers, thinking. "Ms. Lewis, I will need you to email us a detailed description of this man. We'll run a search on his plates and get the make of his car, if he has given you his real name. I am going to have a patrolman on duty in your neighborhood for the next week to see if we might catch him in the act of trespassing in any way. But a restraining order is simply a statement on file that he cannot come within three hundred feet of you or your property, and has to be enforced. If you see him, or think he is near, like last night around your fence," he hands me his card, "call me immediately and we'll get a car out there." He rises and extends his hand. I rise, extend mine. As we shake, his eyes bore into mine. "Get a new habit, Ms. Lewis. Have a good night."

By the time I punch my garage door opener, it is eight-thirty. I am so glad it's Friday I cannot put my gratitude into words. The week has completely wiped me out, both physically and emotionally. All I want to do is crawl into bed.

As I enter through the kitchen door, I hear the TV in the den, see a son asleep on the couch. I move through the kitchen to the hallway and check upstairs. Mimi is speed-pecking on her laptop with her door open. A good sign. Her door has been closed too much lately.

"Hi," I yell, "sorry so late! Everything okay? Did you get dinner?" A chorus of assents floats back to me from various parts of the house. I sigh in relief. Maybe tonight there will be no crisis to manage.

CHAPTER 33

Birdie Costanza

His smile widens as he types in responses to the woman that had just responded to his online profile on Findamatch. He licks his lips, stares out the window and lifts his hands from the keyboard in mid-paragraph, thinking. How should he proceed? The woman has indicated she will not be able to meet on Saturday, and they should at least have a phone conversation or two before arranging a meeting. He doesn't want to blow this. He is sure Izzy will recognize his voice and his scheme might disintegrate. He places supple fingers on the keys and continues typing.

"Dreamsicle, where is your sense of adventure? No sense wasting time, is there? We are both mature adults. I assure you, you will be surprised by my appearance." Birdie stops for a chuckle over that one. The omission of 'pleasantly' an overt choice.

"If Saturday will not work, I offer one last invitation: Raphael's, next week, Tuesday night, eight p.m. In the meantime, what else would you like to know about me?" He could play this game all day. At least as long as his wife is out of the house shopping, or whatever it is she did on Saturdays. He walks into the kitchen for a Stella Artois, pours it into a frosted mug and returns to the computer.

Come on, honey. Come to papa.

Izzy

All day Saturday I think about the man that has invited me to Raphael's. On one hand, I'd love to take him up on the 'adventure' aspect of the meeting, on the other hand, everyone in the world is telling me to stop taking risks online. However, who doesn't love a little mystery?

Logging off, I determine to stay off Findamatch for the time being. I have a lot of housework to catch up on. I push away the unpleasant sensation of rejection attached to the fact that Brad has not followed up on our meeting. I'm not fond of initiating contact, and though tempted to call or text him, I don't. My online style more closely resembles the deer stand approach: wait 'til you see the whites of their eyes before pulling the trigger. So far, it's proved very successful. Not the quality, exactly, but the quantity had definitely been impressive.

I shrug, pull out my vacuum cleaner from the closet, and re-route my frustration to the carpeting. There is an *endless* selection of men online. Not the end of the world if I don't hear from Brad. The vacuum roars across the carpet, shoved by an aggressive arm.

As the vacuum greedily sucks up stuff from my floor that shouldn't be there, I apply the same principle to my thoughts. Have I have been so single-minded about finding someone that the Findamatch thing is becoming obssessive?

Detective Faraday's words ring loud and clear in my head. Find another method to date, he'd said. I shake my head, and file his statement under *give serious thought later.*

Vacuum. Do laundry. Be a normal person with three kids and a house to look after. Pretend nothing weird is happening. I brush past the kitchen table, vacuum accommodatingly rolling along, and my eyes fall to the envelope that contains the restraining order that I'll take to the Registrar's office tomorrow to file.

Doesn't a restraining order indicate a problem? Is the online dating thing entirely stupid? Who else has these issues? All I hear from people that date online are *success* stories. Maybe they keep the hinky stuff to themselves.

I unplug the vacuum and re-plug into an outlet in the den, and turn it off. Then I run upstairs, collect laundry from each bedroom in a laundry basket, carefully lug it downstairs, staggering under the weight. I then plop the entire basket upside down in the laundry room and sort into whites, colors, towels. I heave a huge load into the washer, pour in detergent and swirl the start knob.

Next, I dig into the morning dishes and work until the kitchen is tidied up. Not exactly sparkling, but orderly. One kid is with her dad this weekend, the others are at a ballgame so I have an unusual few hours to myself.

Wiping my hands on a towel, I walk into the laundry room and shove the washed load into the dryer and heave another into the washer.

"There!" I congratulate myself. "Caught up." As a woman, it does feel good to get this stuff done. As a single mom, it feels endless and exhausting.

I run upstairs to throw on something other than pajama pants and a T-shirt. I'd promised to visit Jon in the hospital, and this is the designated day.

An hour later, I am navigating miles of disinfected hallway, my nose wrinkling in disgust. The smell is overpowering. I locate Jon's room, and knock on the door. "Come on in, everyone else has!" Jon's voice is strong, clear and irritable. I step in.

"I take it you've had a lot of company?"

His eyes smile. His mouth twitches with humor. "Yeah. But it's been real nice. Kinda outta small talk, though." He sits up, re-arranges the pillows behind his back, then leans against them. "Hey, I heard you were the one that took care of me when I was on the floor." I nod and shrug. He stretches an arm to the table beside his bed, picks up a small dark form. The candy bar I'd stuffed in his pocket. "You responsible for this?"

I smile, and nod. "You were supposed to eat it for energy, but you passed out before I could get it into your mouth."

Jon's face gentled. "I saved it. Reminded me that people can be really kind." His eyes rise to mine."Want to thank you for that," he says brusquely.

"Anybody would have done it, Jon, I just happened to be there." He contemplates this, his face assessing mine as I assess his. He looks great. His color has returned, he's shaved recently; his eyes and words are clear. "So what happened, anyway?"

Jon drops his head and studies the metal table by his bed, which holds a segmented, plastic rectangle with gelatinous wads in various shapes, colors, and sizes. A small carton of milk with a plastic straw jutting from the spout squats beside it, plus a box of tissues and a vase of dahlias. Obviously, Darlene and Richard had been by.

"Well, Izzy, not an excuse, but it's been really hard the past couple of years since Marie died. A stiff drink to numb the pain turned into two or three. A steady diet of vodka is not so helpful."

I suspected as much, but didn't say anything.

"Doctors and nurses tell me I gotta stop. I mean *really* lay it down. They said if they hadn't gotten an IV in me and pumped me full of meds, I could have – well, I wouldn't be here, I'll just put it that way."

"Sorry, Jon. That's really tough."

He nods glumly. "So, I'm layin' here tryin' to figure out how I'm going to do stuff without beer and vodka. They tell me maybe I can have a beer once in a while, but I don't know yet if that's a good idea."

"Maybe you could use some help? A support group or something?"

Jon gazes at me intently.

"Well, actually, Phil is pushing a group on me. I'm thinking about it."

I blink. "Phil?"

"Yeah," Jon responds. "Phil's apparently had the same problem, been sober about ten years now."

I am astonished. I'd never heard even a hint about this. My regard for Phil catapults into the stratosphere. "No kidding? I never knew that!"

"Nope. He doesn't like to talk about it. But he is like a huntin' dog when it comes to helping people. He can sniff out the ones that are sinking. He'd talked to me before, but I wouldn't listen. Took a trip in an ambulance and almost dyin' to wake me up."

For some reason this resonates so deeply, I fall silent.

He grins. "We never did have that coffee date to talk about your online dating stuff."

I grin back. "Yeah, well that's not goin' so well right now. Long story."

"I'm gettin' outta here in a few days. Let's shoot for a date to get together. I am gonna need some activity to keep my mind off drinking, y'know?"

I nod. "Sure, Jon. We can get together. I promise. You just get better, take care of yourself."

"Phil's commanded me to take two weeks off. No arguments." Jon shrugged. "I'll be lookin' for some company, for sure. I hear you'll be takin' care of my accounts. I'd like to prep you on them a little, okay?"

I nod. We set a date to get together, and part company. I cannot get his comment out of my head. "Took a trip in an ambulance and almost dyin' to wake me up." My life is so out of control I am wondering what it will take to get it back on track. I would like to avoid an ambulance and "almost dyin'" if possible.

CHAPTER 34

Izzy

Later that evening, I am waiting on the kids to arrive home when my hands start an argument with my head. My head is doing a pretty good job of resisting Findamatch, but my hands are about to rip off my arms and float upstairs to my computer by themselves.

My hands win. I sigh and walk upstairs. My fingers literally fly over the keyboard. When the heck had my hands developed a mind of their own?

I reluctantly notice four blinking "You've Got a Message!" icons and feel the pleasurable surge of adrenaline. Maybe this has become a bigger problem than I am allowing myself to realize. Chuckling, I tell myself that it is impossible to become addicted to online dating.

I see Brad is back in the picture. He lost my card with all my information, he'd love to see me again, needs me to call. The next one is a new guy, and after scanning, I drag the message to the trash icon at the bottom of the web page. Yuk. The third one goes straight in the trash as well. The fourth one is the guy pounding on me to meet him at Raphael's, appealing again to my adventurous spirit. His compliments fill a quarter of the page. Like a soothing whirlpool relieves aching muscles, they swirl over me.

This man intrigues me. At least what he has *written* intrigues me. His photos are kind of artsy, profiles with dramatic lighting and I cannot exactly tell how old he is, or even if he is good-looking. But I want to meet him anyway, because I want to believe I live up to his impressive commentary about me. I want to believe a man delights in me, finds me irresistible and fulfilling. That my father had been wrong about me. That I wasn't a failure, or a disappointment. Something to push away.

Everything he has written is pushing my buttons so hard I am finding it difficult to turn him down.

The kids burst in downstairs, yelling for Mom, so before logging off, I quickly make up my mind. I respond with one word: "Okay."

Twenty minutes away, in an exclusive area of Chatbrook overlooking the Savannah River, an overly whitened smile gleams through the darkness. He logs off Findamatch.

"Gotcha!" he says.

9

Monday passes in a frenzy of activity, and I am relieved that my mind is occupied. I do not have one minute to think about, let alone analyze, my tangle of situations.

When I arrive at the office, I find a list of Jon's accounts that need action immediately, so I hit the streets early, leaving Winston with a puzzled expression on his face. He is dutifully pressing his lanyard between nervous fingers as he watches me, his newspaper spread out in front of him on his desk. I wave a quick good-bye and hop in the elevator.

Later in the day, as I pull up to the fourth dealership in a row, I think about the managers I have met at each dealership. Each was expecting Jon, and each expresses regret that he has had a health issue, and each seems fine with my temporary stand-in status. So far, so good.

My final stop, Ardmore Chevrolet, is a relief since I know Tom and have already met with him once. I stride to the greeting desk sensing the end of the day is imminent, which makes me insanely happy.

The receptionist buzzes his office. When he does not answer, she announces over the intercom that Tom has a visitor, and would he please call the receptionist? Her phone rings immediately. She listens intently, her eyes smiling at me as she listens. He is in the Service Department, wherever that is.

I give her a disconcerted look, and she responds by giving me directions, indicating he is waiting for me there. I am thinking, who meets to talk about advertising in the Service Department?

I walk across what feels like miles of pavement, past hundreds of bright, shiny cars parked in crisp rows, down a well-manicured, landscaped hill with a pond, across a large driveway to a large glass door marked "SERVICE" in large block letters. I pause in front of the door to catch my breath. On the hill beyond, a duck family waddles single-file toward the pond, a comical sidebar to the more serious business of selling automobiles. I tug open the heavy door to the Service Department.

A gaggle of mechanics underneath cars suspended on hydraulic lifts stop what they are doing, stare, then continue working. No one seems to be obviously in charge, so I approach a man standing underneath one of the cars, hoping the lift will not suddenly collapse the weight of its vehicular tonnage.

"Tom around?" I ask. "He told me to find him back here, have you seen him?"

The mechanic chuckles, points to the back of the service building where a double door is standing open, toward a man on a golf cart intently studying his cell phone.

"There he is. Just like he always is, every Monday. You're sure not Jon, are you?" His eyes rake up, then down.

I smile at him, ignore the rude stare, and walk through the mechanics, wishing I'd worn pants. Golf cart?

I approach Tom, who rakes my frame with a glance up, then down. This is getting ridiculous. I cross my arms. Pants, I remind myself. Pants next time.

He says "Got your camera?"

I feel my brow furrow. Camera?

Before I can respond, Tom says, "Jon didn't tell you to bring a camera?"

I shake my head a bewildered *no*.

"I assume you are here in his place, right?"

I nod. "He's had some health issues, he'll be available in a few weeks and I was asked to take care of his accounts. We're supposed to get together to go over things, but . . ."

Tom waves me off. "Okay, hop on." He pats the space beside him. "I'll give you a little tour, and tell you what we usually do." We zip off and I hold on for dear life. To my skirt, which is blowing up at intervals, and my balance, which is precarious. Tumbling off a wildly veering golf cart in front of the GM of a huge Chevrolet dealership would do nothing to enhance my professional image. Especially if my skirt flaps up over my face.

"We are approaching the pre-owned vehicle area," Tom points in the direction of an acre-sized sea of cars, "and Jon usually spends an hour or so taking pictures of them for the ad. Here's the list." He hands me a sheet of paper with VIN (vehicle identification numbers) on it, and makes and models of each car. It might as well be a sheet written in Arabic, as far as I'm concerned.

"Jon takes pictures of a list of cars I provide him for the ad." I quickly scan the hideously long list, and squeak out, "Every week?" Tom glances sideways at me, careful to keep the golf cart aligned in the tight asphalt aisles between the vehicles.

"Yep. Sure does. So I guess you'll be needing to go pick up a camera and come back? Today?" I nod, wondering how I am going to fit my own clients in this week, and Jon's stuff, too.

"Great! Okay, so when you come back this afternoon, just grab the golf cart, hop on, find the cars out here somewhere," he waves a hand vaguely over the pre-owned vehicle inventory, "and get 'em shot. If you need to pull them out of the line, the keys are in the main building, just match 'em to the VIN number and tell the girls back there that you are with the *Sentinel*. After you've taken the pictures, and returned the keys, come find me." He waves in the other direction of the twenty-acre property, "We'll talk about ad copy. I'll be over there, probably. Okay?" I nod and smile. He dips his head, backs up the golf cart, and floors it back to the main building.

I discreetly hold down my skirt, and clutch the small, vinyl seat underneath me. Why aren't there grab bars in these things? I make a mental note to run home, grab my digital camera, and change to pants before my return. I also silently excoriate Phil, who painted this as a way to increase my ad revenue and left out a few tiny, insignificant details. Like the hours it's going to take looking up VIN numbers and locating specific cars.

This is slave labor for Jon. Period.

I tell myself I am fortunate to have a job. I tell myself this all the way back to the dealership's main building, through clenched teeth and wind whistling through my hair.

CHAPTER 35

After shooting cars all afternoon, I drag myself back into the pod, arms loaded with notes I'd made and the previous week's ads marked with corrections.

"Man! You look like someone ran you over with a truck!" remarked Lonnie, who was in his pod-spot like a good and faithful assistant should be, doing his thing.

I am so grateful to hear a concerned voice, that I would hug him if my arms weren't full. I drop the pile with a thump onto my desk.

"Yeah, well, I've earned it. I spent the day riding around on a golf cart, taking pictures of cars, looking up *VIN* numbers. Before today, I didn't even know what a VIN number was!" Lonnie gapes at me.

"Really? Why not?" he says, and resumes busily marking up ad copy.

"I don't know!" I snap. "Just didn't! My knowledge of cars stops at the entrance to the service department and the nice people that tell me they'll take care of everything. That's it."

Lonnie smiles, reaches to answer his phone, mutters into it, hangs up. "Well, I heard you'd be helping Jon out, and wondered about that. He's in an entirely different department. Can't quite figure that out. But you wanted a piece of that automotive business, right?" He grins widely.

I do not grin back. I am exhausted, and my irritation level is peaking.

"Yeah, sure, but I didn't know I was getting myself into this. What a lot of crazy stuff Jon has to do to keep those car guys happy."

At that moment, Winston emerges from the elevator. He has on a tan trench coat, tasseled, cordovan loafers, a driving beret, Oakley sunglasses. He smiles at Lonnie and me, then walks to the rack to hang up his coat.

"How we doing this fine afternoon?" he says as he sits in the remaining pod-space. "How's it goin', Pod-God?" he says, smiling at Lonnie. Then turning to me, "and our lovely Pod-Queen?"

We both respond with appropriate Pod-King responses. Lonnie is busy, and disappears with a stack of proofs toward production. I am too tired to be appreciative that I do not have to deal with production today. I gaze at the pile on my desk. Correction. No way am I going to get out of talking to production. Probably be here 'til midnight, and Lonnie is not one to volunteer for overtime.

Winston is settled in, returning phone calls, checking email. After a few minutes, he notices the huge pile on my desk. He nods at it, then looks at my face. "That all yours?" he asks, referring to the huge amount of work the pile represents.

"Noo-ooo, Winston, it happens to be Jon's."

Winston raises his chin and stares at the ceiling, thinking. "You must be the lucky recipient of his accounts while he's off. Correct?"

"Correct." I sag in my chair. I'd grab coffee, but I cannot stand the idea of end-of-day sludge. The thought of tackling the work before me without coffee plunges me into further depression.

"I'm really light today. Hand some of it over," Winston reaches an arm across the pod.

Smiling at him, I respond, "So great of you to offer, but it would take me longer to explain it than to just do it. Thanks, though." The arm withdraws and he cocks his head at me. His hand drifts up to caress his chin. "So look on the bright side, Iz."

"And what might that be, Pod-King?"

He grins wickedly. His fingers drop to his lanyard. "It'll keep you off the internet for a while. Maybe you'll be so tired, you'll stay *home* the next two weeks." He gives me a thumbs-up and a goofy expression

I don't appreciate it. I stick my tongue out at him.

Chuckling, he rises and walks toward production. Winston has no problem with production. Those girls all love him. Another depressing thought, since it's a well-known fact that they *hate* me.

I sort through the impossible pile, and stack them according to priority. Grab layout paper and a marker and start making annotations. An hour of steady work later, a tall shadow falls across my desk. I glance up from the tedious copy in irritation. I have a little trouble focusing since I have been working with impossibly tiny disclaimer copy for the past few minutes.

"Birdie! Hi, there. Umm, need me for something?"

"Loaded question, Izzy!" He smiles, as if he has just uttered the funniest thing in the world.

I grin, because I am probably supposed to, but silently wonder if this guy ever has a clue. About anything.

"Well, I'm kinda loaded up here, as you can see," I say, in an effort to persuade him to return to wherever it was he'd come from.

"I see that," he says. He steps closer and looks over my shoulder. The smell of cheap cologne plus the fact that his face is positioned about three inches from mine combine to make me terribly uncomfortable. I back my chair up. "What is this?" he asks.

"It's Jon Hoyt's stuff. Phil asked me to take his accounts while he's off. About two weeks. I thought you'd know about it already."

"No, I didn't," he responds, miffed. "When did this conversation happen?"

"Yesterday. You want me to get Phil?"

Birdie stares at me intently. "No. It's fine. Just wondering when you will have time to take care of your own accounts."

"Looks like a lot of overtime, I guess," I say, shrugging. "No big deal." This is a lie, but I want to appear the dedicated employee, and am always looking for ways to chalk up brownie points. The long-suffering Izzy. She deserves a raise. And a promotion.

Birdie continues, "Guess you won't have time for those late night meetings I've heard so much about?" The evil grin splits his face.

I resist puking.

"Yeah, probably have to limit that stuff, for sure!" Ha, ha, very funny Birdie. Now fly away. I stare at him pointedly, willing him to leave by my silence. I feel my arms cross themselves involuntarily, which he notices. What is it about this guy? His mere presence puts me on the defensive.

"Well, I can see you're busy," he says.

Then follows up with an ingratiating, "Can I help in any way?"

As if. What the heck does Birdie know about ad production? With syrupy sweetness that thoroughly disgusts me with myself, I respond, "Thanks Birdie, for the kind offer. I got it," and return to busily sculpting ad copy and rough drafts to give production.

He nods and leaves. I heave a sigh of relief, and return to the task of getting Jon's ads ready for production, which causes my tension to escalate again. Maybe Lonnie will consider staying late to help me. I come up with the idea that *Lonnie* take all those car pictures and drive the golf cart through rows and rows of cars and decide I will bring him an unexpected and generous gift tomorrow, wait a day or two, then ask him if he will do this until Jon gets back. This idea brightens my outlook considerably.

Although I'd been in touch with Mimi, Chad, and Peter throughout the evening and they'd assured me all was well, I feel a shiver of premonition as I pull into the garage. I shake it off, blaming it on extreme exhaustion and irritation. The ads had taken longer than I'd anticipated to mark up and turn in, and the conversation with production had been unpleasant.

Missy, the production supervisor – normally my advocate and buffer – had already gone home for the night, and talking to the women about the ad corrections was left to me. Fortunately, the night crew arrived in the middle of one of the more cranky episodes. The woman had angrily clocked out and left me standing in mid-sentence, holding wrinkled, marked-up, and apparently confusing ad copy. A kind, older woman on the night crew named Marcy walked over to me and put her hand out.

"I'll take it, Izzy," she smiled. "Come right over here and explain it to me," she said, nodding in the direction of her workspace. My over-stimulated emotions and under-stimulated affirmation quotients hugged her tightly and thanked her about fifty times. She laughed, and dragged over a chair for me to sit on. A bright spot in a long, bleak evening.

I sit in my car a minute, adjusting to the darkness of the garage. My eyes land on the kids' car tucked in already, and I know they are inside the house, either asleep or going that direction, because I'd talked to them on the way home. I shake off the feeling that something is wrong, get out of the car, start up the stairs to the kitchen, reconsider and click on the overhead light in the garage to sniff around.

Brightness illuminates the area. Rakes, loppers, an air pump, and various gadgetry cling to a pegboard nailed to one wall; an aging lawnmower sits in a far corner with its best friend, the gas trimmer. Metal shelving climbs the back wall, loaded with fairly common family paraphernalia. My eyes scan the cement floor and the kids' car, searching for signs of inappropriate activity.

I smell old grass, a little oil that has leaked from one of the cars, gas, paint thinner. Typical garage smells. My heels striking the cement garage floor in the middle of the night remind me of old Law and Order episodes, where Eames and Goren discover a body in the garage, draped halfway out of a car, drenched in blood. I should stop watching those shows.

Then I see it.

Not tonight, my mind screams. Tonight? After this horribly long day? My stomach clenches in fear. A tightly folded, small, white square mocks me from the windshield.

What time is it, anyway, I mutter to myself as I cautiously approach the car, lift the windshield wiper, and hold the small square gingerly between thumb and forefinger. I grab my phone from my purse with my free hand and click the screen on. Almost midnight. Self-pity, despair, and several other emotions that I have no energy to identify zip through me at warp speed. I turn off the garage light and climb the three stairs into the kitchen, firmly locking the door behind me. The note sails through the air and lands on the kitchen table. I scroll quickly through my contacts to find Detective Faraday. His phone rings several times, and finally, a groggy voice answers. "Yeah?" Cough. "What?!"

"Detective Faraday?" I whisper.

"You got him. What's up?" I picture him wiping his eyes and focusing on a clock by his bed. Maybe a lovely wife by his side, sleeping. I feel awful for interrupting him at home.

"I got another note," my voice is hushed, and has begun to warble. I am whispering because I don't want to alarm the kids, but the stress has rushed to every extremity and overtaken my vocal cords. I cannot stop shaking.

Detective Faraday is instantly alert. "Okay, umm, Izzy, right?" I shake my head, realize someone on the other end of a phone call cannot see a head shake, and murmur "Yes."

"All right, I'm going to call and get a patrol car out there immediately. What does the note say? By the way, we have analyzed fingerprints on the note, and it is definitely the man you indicated, so he is not using an alias. That's good news, because it means he's not trying to hide, and it's probably not pre-meditated. Probably just a reaction to a personal crisis. Which, unfortunately, you seem to be triggering."

"So what should I do?" I whisper.

"Read me the note, Izzy," he says, calmly.

"It was on my kids' car." I feel tears forming. One trails slowly down my cheek. I slap it away.

"Oh, man," Detective Faraday whooshes out a long sigh. "You weren't home, then? But your kids were?"

"Yeah, and I'm pretty sure the garage was locked. They know they are supposed to shut the garage door when they get home, no matter what."

"Izzy, is there a window in your garage?"

I think a minute. Yes! There is one in the small storage room at the back of the garage, one we never use. "Well, yes, there is one in a storage room, but – "

"Is it locked?" he barks. I start to cry.

"I don't know! Why is this happening?"

"Go check, Izzy, right now. Keep me on the phone while you do it. Take a flashlight or a bat or something with you. I'll wait." The implication hits me that he wants me to find a *weapon* before I go check the window. Seriously? This *cannot* be happening to me. I quietly enter my son's room and pluck up the bat that is leaning against their bookshelf. They stir, but do not wake.

"Okay," I whisper. "Got a bat. Heading for the garage."

"I'm with you, Izzy. Be careful." His voice is reassuring and I am thinking how grateful I am for our police force. Funny. I am grateful now, but just let me get a speeding ticket.

I enter the garage, and tiptoe toward the closed storage room door, my heart beating violently. I hold the bat in my right hand and turn the knob slowly with my left. The darkened room emerges bit by bit as the door creaks open. Light from the garage spills into the room, illuminating old cans of paint, a broken lamp, basketballs, a football, boxes. I push the door open further, and see the window, which is located high on the wall, shards of cobwebs hanging from the edges.

I lift the bat in pre-strike position as I push the door all the way open. I hear Detective Faraday's breathing on the phone. "What's happening, Izzy?" he says, causing me to nearly jump out of my skin.

I locate the string that turns on the lone light bulb in the room, and pull. The forty-watt bulb creates an eerie glow. To my utter and profound relief, the room appears empty. "I am in the storage room. It's empty." I lean the bat against one of the boxes and look around.

"How often are you in that room, Izzy?"

"Rarely. It's for stuff we don't have room for. Kind of forget sometimes, that it's here."

"Okay," he says, "go to the window and check the lock."

My nose wrinkles in disgust. "Okay," I say and move aside two squashed storage boxes. Looking around, I locate something to stand on, and reach up to check the latch. Push up on the window, which holds. Try again, and it reluctantly slides open. "It's not locked," I say, miserably.

"Lock it," Detective Faraday says. "Don't worry about it, Izzy, we'll get him. He is trespassing, and in violation of the restraining order. Just make sure you lock the door to the garage from the kitchen. Most people don't, you know. Not a good idea."

I nod, my heart slowing down somewhat, then say, "What happens now?" My bleary eyes fall on the two squashed boxes, realizing that he must have used them for steps after pushing himself through the window. I shove the boxes away from the window with a vicious kick.

"Well, what happens now is that we still have to catch him in the act. Anything you say in court, he can refute, and then we have nothing."

"What about the notes? Don't they have his fingerprints all over them?"

"Yes, but he's only in violation of a restraining order. Have you filed it yet?"

I sigh, "Didn't have time today. Do it first thing tomorrow."

"Good. We can't arrest him unless that's in place. Right now, I'll file a police report. We're building a case against him with multiple police reports, but so far nothing has been stolen, no harm has been done, so our hands are kind of tied."

My body screams for rest, and my mind wrestles with frustration. "So I'm *helpless*? How am I supposed to deal with this?"

"Go to bed, Izzy. Take sleeping pills if you have them. He's not going to try anything else tonight, and I'll have a patrol car stationed outside your house the rest of the night. Make sure everything is locked, and leave all your outside lights on."

"Okay. Thanks, Detective Faraday. Sorry, it's been a long day, and I come home to this! I am not in the best shape right now."

"I understand," he says kindly. "This will all be over soon, don't worry. He doesn't seem like he's escalating or violent. More of a nuisance than anything. By the way, we never did get to the note, what's it say?"

With one last look at the storage room, I exit and close the door. Make a mental note to call a locksmith tomorrow to put a lock on it. My heels strike the cement floor in the garage, then ring hollowly on the hardwood floors in my kitchen as I enter.

"Okay, here's what it says: HI IZZY. IT'S ME AGAIN. STILL LOOKING FOR A TIME TO GET TOGETHER. I WAITED FOR YOU OUTSIDE THE SENTINEL BUILDING THIS AFTERNOON, BUT YOU NEVER CAME OUT. I HAD A NICE CHAT WITH YOUR BOSS, BIRDIE. SEEMS LIKE A GREAT GUY. MESSAGE ME ON FINDAMATCH. ONE EVENING OF COFFEE, IZZY, THAT'S ALL I ASK. EVEN YOUR BOSS THINKS IT'S A REASONABLE REQUEST."

CHAPTER 36

After an incredibly hectic morning, I am finally coming up for air, and start to think about lunch when the phone on my desk rings. I snatch it up. "Izzy."

"Hi, Izzy, how's it going?"

It's Jon. Thank God. I'm beginning to think the only calls I get lately are direct lines to hell.

"Hi, Jon! Hey, I've been meaning to call to see when we could get together – "

"Yeah, that's why I'm calling. Do you want to meet somewhere? A coffee shop, like Starbucks?"

We make arrangements to meet later in the day and hang up. I find myself really looking forward to it, and even smile. Strange. My mind meanders to Brad, who has asked me out again. This makes me smile as well. Things aren't all bad.

Lonnie slips into his seat and picks up the phone to dial. Before he can complete the process, I signal that I'm caught up, he doesn't have to worry about my stuff today. He nods, smiles, and completes the call. The sales floor is nearly empty, the sales team having long exited the building in search of increasingly elusive advertising dollars. I gaze at my neat, orderly desktop and sigh the satisfied, relieved sigh that accompanies finishing an arduous task. I'm looking forward to a lunch break, then I have to try to make some progress on my own accounts instead of Jon's.

I pick up my purse and study the shiny new iPad the *Sentinel* had recently bestowed upon me. All our promotional materials have been stored and I can simply whisk out the iPad to show any product we might be presenting, plus I can input the order at that moment, instead of calling my assistant in fit of hysteria trying to meet production deadlines getting last-minute ads in. I am admiring my iPad when Birdie approaches. I freeze a grin on my face and lift my eyes to his. "Hey there, Birdie."

He smiles, and, as usual, his eyes do not. His icy, flat gaze scrapes up and down my form, which seems habitual whenever he is talking with women. I suppress a shudder.

"Hi, Izzy. Just wanted you to know, I've received end of the month sales reports, and your numbers look good."

I nod. "Thanks. Glad you approve."

His eyes squint, as if he's remembering something, then open wide. "Oh, yes! I remember now what I wanted to mention, your friend, Jacob, was waiting for you yesterday after work. He stopped several people, asking if you were here." I try to keep my expression neutral. My throat squeezes shut.

He continues, "I told him what I knew, which was not much as you don't keep me in the loop on your day." His eyes are stony as he waits for a response.

I am unable to formulate words for a few seconds, and squeak past the clenched throat, "Aaah, Jacob. Well, first of all, he is not a friend. He is more like an unfortunate acquaintance."

"Then why the hell was he standin' outside the newspaper building askin' everybody in sight where you were?"

"I am not sure, but it won't happen again," I say, before the terror of the night before creeps into my expression. I do not trust Birdie enough to dump the whole story. Somehow I feel this would be like hurling clumps of mud at a huge fan that would spew back in my face. I long for Detective Faraday to magically appear between us as a shield. Pun unintended.

"It better not. I have a feeling this is one of your online guys, and would definitely fall into the category of *affecting your work*. If you think this kind of thing is gonna go unnoticed, missy, then you better think again. I am on pretty good terms with the director of human resources now, y'know." He smirks and crosses his arms over a light blue shirt and a tie adorned with tiny, grinning, porpoises. The crevices on his dark face grow deeper as his smile widens. I stare at his teeth with morbid fascination.

I avert my gaze and slump in my chair. He nods at me in dismissal, and leaves.

"Hi, Izzy," the hostess smiles, "you here to meet someone tonight?"

I nod affirmatively, and say, "Yes, there should be someone waiting for *Dreamsicle.*" I smile a secret smile.

Her eyes light up. "Oh!" She waves in the direction of the bar, which is relatively empty during a weeknight. "The gentleman around the corner, sitting at the bar, mentioned he'd be looking for *Dreamsicle.*" She gives me a conspiratorial glance. Her secret, too, her expression says. What happens in Raphael's, stays in Raphael's.

I force some distance from the day. What a jerk Birdie had been! I am tired, but also looking forward to meeting the mystery man who will take me away from it all. The romantic rush of endorphins is already kicking in, and my mind has neatly compartmentalized the twin threats of Jacob and Birdie. I will deal with them later.

I arrange my lips in a slight pout, fluff my hair and walk to the bar, my eyes communicating confusion and helplessness, a combination most men find irresistible. My eyes adjust slowly to the darkness, and the tantalizing aroma of flamed steaks and fruity drinks tickles my nose. The jazz pianist in the corner is playing "Til There Was You," and a few people are quietly conversing on stools around the black Steinway.

How did this guy know Raphael's was my favorite place in Chatbrook? And what the heck am I doing meeting a man for the sheer *risk* of it, anyway? Don't I have enough on my plate? My jumpy nerves feel like someone is poking me with a Taser.

There is just one man at the bar, and he is sitting in the darkest corner, apparently expecting no one. I gaze around the room, looking for the mystery man. I decide to order a drink, and sit at the bar. Maybe he's in the men's room. The bartender smiles, then says, "What'll it be, Izzy?"

"I think, a pinot tonight. Do you have Bearboat?"

"Yep." He plucks a bottle from the shelves behind the bar, deftly uncorks, and pours. "Give it a sec, Izzy." I nod and wait. Turning the stool around, I scan the bar in case the mystery man appears. After a few minutes, I swirl and sniff, then sip. Heaven in a glass.

The man in the corner, who is within my peripheral field of vision, gets off the stool and starts toward me. As he emerges from the dark corner, like a movie scene in slow motion, recognition hits.

I clench the stem of the wine glass like a security blanket and lift it to my mouth. He gets closer, and to my utter amazement, pulls out a stool and sits beside me at the bar. I still feel the sting of his words from the office. The stench of his cologne curls up my nose. He must have freshened it up. I cannot stand to look at him. "Hi," he says.

I am silent.

"Understandable that you are upset, Izzy. We need to clear the air, I think."

I turn my head toward him. My voice is a snarl. "While I think that's true, Birdie, I am waiting for someone. So can we talk about this at the office?"

Twin rows of perfect teeth blaze through the dim lighting. "Nope. We're gonna talk about it right now. Who you waiting for, by the way?" The creases around his mouth deepen.

"My business. We've had this discussion."

His grin does not diminish by a single kilowatt. "Yeah. We have. But we have so much more to discuss, Dreamsicle."

The dread starts at my toes and slithers the entire vertical length of my body. My brain, a hiccup or two behind the dread, snags the realization I've been had. An impromptu prayer pops into my head before I can argue with myself that it never works

I turn to him, my tongue loosed, mad as hell. "You? *You?* What are you thinking? This breaks every privacy law ever legislated, for Pete's sake! This is – this is – *unspeakable!"*

Birdie's smile falters, then disappears. His eyes, in the murky light, are reptilian. Unblinking. His lips press close to my ear, and he whispers, "For Chrissakes, you treat me like a leper. It's going to stop. *Now."*

My hand still clenches the stem of the wine glass. I am afraid I will break it, so I consciously unwrap my fingers, nestle the globe instead, and drink. My mind is spinning furiously. I do not know how to react. Doesn't this fall under the realm of predatory? How does one go about proving it? What if one's predator happens to be responsible for your paycheck?

Suddenly, as if my impromptu prayer had been answered immediately, I hear the voice of an angel.

"Izzy? That you?" Detective Faraday stands before me, a trim, forty-five-ish, brunette woman at his side who I assume to be his wife. I have never been happier to see anyone in my entire life. I swivel my stool toward them, slide off, and stand. I resist the urge to throw my arms around his neck, sobbing with relief.

"Detective Faraday! How are you? So good to see you tonight!" My voice is forced and loud, but who cares? He looks at me strangely.

"Good, I'm good, Izzy." He puts an arm around the woman and extends the other toward her. "This is Marion, my wife. We do Raphael's about once a month. I guess you like it, too."

I murmur niceties to Marion, thinking how lovely it must be to have an actual, honest-to-God, normal marriage. At the same time, I hope I am adequately telegraphing my distress. Since I am turned away from Birdie, and do not seem inclined to introduce him, I feel certain that Detective Faraday has already sensed something amiss.

However, I quickly decide it might be good for him to know Birdie's name and why we are together. I turn toward Birdie, who is still seated on his stool, nursing a double shot of something the approximate color of urine.

"Detective Faraday," I emphasize his title on purpose, "this is Birdie Costanza, my Sales Manager." The men shake hands. Birdie's smile assaults the darkness. Detective Faraday's wife steps back a couple of inches.

"So how do you two know each other?" Birdie says.

Detective Faraday glances at me, uncertain as how to proceed. I jump in, seeing this as an opportunity to leverage the Jacob situation. "We met a few days ago, when I requested a *restraining order* on someone intent on bothering me." This said, I stared at him a few extra seconds.

"Would this be, um . . . that guy outside the office last night, what was his name?"

Detective Faraday inserted, "Jacob?"

Birdie bobbleheads up and down. "That's the one!"

"Jacob was waiting outside the office for you, Izzy?"

"Yeah, I hadn't gotten around to telling you about it."

Detective Faraday shakes his head, and pulls out a small notebook. Jots a note. "Gotta tell me whenever this guy pops up, so we can approach him."

I explain he'd not actually seen me, that I'd heard about it through Birdie.

His eyes blink toward Birdie's."And what did this guy say?"

Birdie shrugs it off and refers to my online dating as a 'joke' around the office and that Jacob is residual fallout of participating in stuff like that. Detective Faraday's eyes harden.

"This is not a 'joke' Mister, uh . . . Costanza, was it?"

Birdie nods. "Call me Birdie," he says with a brief flash of white.

"This man has trespassed on Izzy's property repeatedly," he pauses to glance at me, seeking approval to go on.

I nod.

He continues, "He's not just 'fallout' Birdie, he is a sick guy and we need to talk to him. Get him some help, or lock him up, one or the other." He reaches into an inside coat pocket and retrieves a business card, extending it to Birdie. "Call me immediately if he shows up around your offices again, okay?"

Birdie indicates he will.

"Well, gotta get going, we have a reservation and they're holding our table. Um, care to join us?"

I jump in immediately – too soon – which both Birdie and Detective Faraday notice, and decline. We share mutual nice-to-see-yous and they disappear into the restaurant, which is on the other side of the building.

When they are out of earshot, Birdie says, "You plan that?"

I shoot a glance upwards. "Nope. Didn't plan it."

He fidgets in his seat, and I get the feeling Detective Faraday made an impression. My hopes are short-lived.

In the next breath he says, "Look, Izzy, I know you've been avoiding me. Things are going to change. I set up this little scenario to prove that your online dating stuff is affecting your performance at work. You obviously are not careful, and the sickos you meet are starting to hang out around our building. So how do you think Phil will feel about that? What do you think he'll say when he realizes you had to get a *restraining order* on some guy you met online? What does that say about your judgment? Maybe you're fooling around with clients, too."

He shrugs, and continues, "Don't you have kids? Didn't I hear you had three? Aren't there laws that protect kids from unfit mothers?" he stares at my face intently.

I am numb by this point, and looking for an escape route. I finish my wine, and excuse myself to the ladies' room, hoping that I'll get some kind of epiphany on the toilet. I quickly text the kids on the way, confirm their activities, and tell them I'll be home in twenty minutes. I promise God if He will get me out of this mess, I'll be a better mother. I'll only get on Findamatch once a week. I'll start going to church. Clean my house more often. My pulse rate is off the charts, and I try deep breathing to calm down.

After washing my hands and freshening up, I feel a little better, and walk back to the bar with firm resolve. Resolve for what, I am not sure, but at least it has been resurrected.

I slide onto the stool. "Birdie, this has been an interesting little chat," (when in doubt, diminish the offender) "but I need to get home to my kids."

He smiles, and slides his fingers along my forearm. "Okay. For now, we'll put this on hold. But I want you to know, I've spent some time talking with Phil about you, and he is aware of the pending problems."

My eyebrows arrange themselves into stunned twin arches. *"What pending problems?"*

"Well, the Jacob problem, the online dating problem, the part about not meeting your sales quotas, those unsatisfied customers – those problems. All very serious." His voice is quiet, sinister.

My arm where he has touched it tingles, and I cannot wait to hop into the shower.

"But none of it is true!" I protest.

"Phil believes what I tell him. And so will that detective, if you think you might get him involved."

"What is it you want, anyway, Birdie? Why are you so intent on . . . intent on doing whatever it is you are doing? It makes no sense!"

"You've got to learn a little respect, Izzy. I'm in charge here. I'm in charge of your job, and at this point, possibly your reputation. What this means to you is that you do what I say. The fact that you met me like this – that alone is enough to cause serious trust issues. With Phil, with me, with clients . . ." His smile clearly communicates *no one messes with me and gets away with it.*

I feel sick to my stomach.

"But all is not lost, Izzy." He picks up my hand, and I jerk it away, incredulous. "If you play it my way, you'll meet and far exceed all your quotas. You'll be a shoo-in for Salesperson of the Year. Just play your cards right."

His eyebrows wiggle at me, and I almost throw up on him. Fortunately, my stomach asserts discretion.

He continues, "If you tell anyone about our little discussion, I'll spin it my way, so don't even bother. I'd suggest you carve out some time for me, Izzy. Purely business, of course." His eyes do a double rake.

I am so mortified, I cannot come up with a word to describe it.

Time has skidded to a stop, and my movements seem jerky. I feel faint. Birdie sees that I am wobbly, and puts out his arms to support me, but I push him away.

"No! Don't touch me!" I slide off the stool, grab my purse, and walk unsteadily toward the door, Birdie right behind me. On the stairs in the lobby, I stumble, and he quickly puts an arm around me.

"Izzy, just let me help you to your car, okay?"

I nod, unable to get it together and completely disgusted about it.

As we land on the sidewalk in tandem outside, I deeply gulp fresh air and feel somewhat restored. Disgusted, but restored. As fate would have it, Jon Hoyt walks by, skids to a halt in front of us, puts his hands on his hips.

"Hey! Izzy! What happened to you today? We were supposed to have a meeting at 4:30."

Birdie's arm is still attached to me, and I shrug it off. My face registers regret as I remember the meeting, which had totally slipped my mind while I was working on Jon's ads.

"Oh no! Jon, I'm so sorry, I totally forgot!" He gives me an appraising stare and then glances at Birdie.

"I can see that."

I turn and look at Birdie, then at Jon, and put two and two together quickly. "No! No, Jon, it's not what you think!"

"None of my business," he says. "See ya, Izzy. Birdie." Jon turns and walks away.

Birdie smiles in delight. "Now, that's what I call great timing! See what I mean, Izzy? Play it my way, or you'll regret it. I've enjoyed our little chat." He gives me a salute, flashes a wicked grin, and heads toward his car, whistling.

As I punch the car fob to my Honda and plop inside, my mind quickly proffers a tidy new compartment, and out of habit, I try to push and shove the evening's events inside.

Not happening. I can't seem to dredge up compartments big enough anymore.

CHAPTER 37

All the way home I berate myself, first with self-pity, then with self-flagellation. The flagellation is winning.

By the time I pull into my garage, my emotions are sufficiently and miserably flattened. How long is a person supposed to keep fighting with life, anyway? My eyes adjust to the gloom of the garage as I sit in the car, trying to control my deepening sense of fear. How did things get so messed up?

The house is quiet, dark. I guess the kids have decided to go to bed early for once, and my steps cause the flooring under the carpet to squeak as I check each bedroom. Mimi is on her computer in the middle of her mob of stuffed animals on her bed, Peter's still at his basketball game and Chad is snoring on the couch in the den. With a sigh of relief, I return to the kitchen and fix myself a quick bite.

In the stark kitchen light, holding a pickle in one hand and a turkey sandwich in the other, I feel crushingly alone. And anxious. Stupid. Scared. My teeth snap off half the pickle. It crunches and squirts juice down my hand, which I mop up with my napkin.

I rehearse the day in my mind, zipping through highlights. I'd filed the restraining order, finally, and am at least one step further toward resolving the issues with Jacob. Forgetting the meeting with Jon today had been a severe misstep, so I will make talking to him a priority tomorrow, especially since he thinks Birdie and I were together tonight. I throw the sandwich on my plate and drop my head in my hands.

I need desperately to try to talk to Phil and find out what Birdie has said to him, but what if he doesn't believe me? How can I prove the things Birdie said are vicious and pre-meditated attempts to control me? I'll come off sounding like a paranoid maniac.

Which, of course, is exactly what I am becoming.

I pick up my sandwich and rip off the corner with my teeth. Anger is beginning to churn through me, and it feels good, productive. My phone vibrates on the table.

"Izzy," I say, cautiously, my mouth full. My name comes out as *Itthhy*.

"Hey, Izzy, sorry to call so late, but my wife and I just got home and I wanted to touch base," Detective Faraday said.

My heart soared.

"Hi, Detective. Great! Touching base is good. Nice to meet your wife tonight."

He chuckled. "Yeah, she's a doll. Always patient when I run into someone I know from work, which, unfortunately, is nearly every time we go out. She's used to it. So, that guy you were with – is he really your sales manager?"

Taken aback by this question, my face arranges itself in a question mark, "Yes, um . . . why would I say that if it wasn't true?"

"Don't know." I can picture him shrugging. "A hunch. Something was off. If he's your sales manager, then I sure wouldn't want your job! His face seems familiar, but I couldn't quite figure out from where."

My mind is racing. Should I tell him about Birdie's threats? What could he do? He's already working on one problem-guy-situation for me, what will he think if I throw Birdie at him, too?

He must sense I'm not sure how to respond. "Izzy, I could tell by your face something was wrong. Wanna tell me what it was? That guy is off, somehow, my gut never lies. For starters, give me his full name and address if you've got it, I want to run him through our database."

"I'm not sure." My words are measured as my brain ponders how to position the situation with Birdie tonight. The truth might be a good thing.

Or not.

"I appreciate your call, I really do, but I need to work out some things on my own before I nail down any issues where he is concerned. Let me talk to some people tomorrow, then I'll call you. I think I can nip this in the bud. But yes, it was a bizarre situation. His full name is Birdie Costanza."

"Nip what in the bud?" he asks.

Oops. So much for discretion.

"The stupid situation that has evolved. I think you may be right, Detective, I need a new habit."

He laughs. "Oh, I see! This evening had something to do with the online dating stuff? Yep, need a new habit, Izzy." My expression is mournful as I wait for him to end the call. I appreciate him so much, but I am dying to jump into a shower and go to bed.

"Okay, well, just wanted to check on you. Call me if anything weird happens. We've still got patrol cars assigned to your street."

I agree to call, and thank him for his concern. Then I rinse my dishes, put them in the dishwasher and head upstairs where I sit at my computer and log on to Findamatch. Five messages tonight. I roll my eyes heavenward and thank whoever is up there. I needed something positive to happen. The long, hot shower can wait a few minutes.

I open the first one, happy for the first time today, then stew a moment. Didn't I just get completely blindsided tonight as a result of Findamatch? I resist reading the message, and quickly locate the message that had reduced me to a romantic fool but had turned out to be from Birdie. I drag the message to the trash bin, my face scrunched with the same disgust reserved for cockroaches. I click around on the site and find what I'd been looking for: Do you want to block this user? You bet I want to block this user. Forever. I hit *Yes* with a flourish of my wrist.

I archive his previous messages in case he tries it again, to check verbiage for similarity. But I don't really think he will try it again. Not after the nice detective had been so point-blank and friendly in Raphael's.

Opening the new message, I see it's from Brad, and smile. I had not had time today to message him back.

"Hey Izzy, where are you? Needed a dinner date tonight, but I guess I will have to wait until this weekend. Hope your week is going great! Looking forward to Saturday, hope you are too. Do you like sushi? Get back to me, Yours, Brad."

My smile has grown to cover half my face. A deep sigh rumbles out of me and I feel my body relaxing for the first time in two days. I feel protected by Chatbrook's finest, and complimented by Findamatch. Seeking additional validation like a pill head sniffs out narcotics, I click on the remaining four messages, trash two of them and read the others. Since I am so tired, I do not peruse their profiles, but their messages are affirming and fun and a nice end to the day.

I stand in the scalding shower, imagining Birdie's touch rolling off my body into the drain. Afterward, I want my favorite sleep shirt, and finally locate it in the laundry hamper. An oversize t-shirt with Georgia Peach emblazoned on the front. I slip it on. Five minutes later I'm dead to the world.

CHAPTER 38

Mimi and Peter

Mimi pushes open the living room window she'd left unlocked and hops quietly inside. It had taken forever for her mom to go to bed, but when she'd checked earlier, Mom was completely comatose. She knew her mom would not approve, but didn't she do the same thing? *Mom is so old-fashioned when it comes to me, but totally cool with it when it's about her.*

Mimi giggles to herself as she pads upstairs, slides out of her clothes and into PJs. She plans to fall asleep thinking of all the nice things the man who had picked her up a few blocks away had said to her.

The unfamiliar sound from downstairs awakens Peter, and he lay in bed a few minutes, listening. Hears furtive steps on the stairs and his sister's bedroom door opening and closing. He sighs, puts an arm over his forehead, and thinks about things going on in his family. Chad had laughed at him when he pled with him to stop smoking pot, and who knows what else he had gotten into lately. He'd skipped school today, and he didn't think his Mom knew about it. Now Mimi is getting weird.

Pushing an unruly blonde forelock off his face, he pushes out of bed and tiptoes down the hall to Mimi's room, knocking gently. He glances toward his mom's bedroom, hoping she'll stay asleep. She has enough on her mind. He tries to take some of the pressure off her, but isn't always able. He clutches his pajama pants, which are loose around the waist, and hikes them up.

"Mimi? Mimi?" he whispers. "Have you been outside?" Peter listens silently, hears the faucets in Mimi's bathroom switch off, hands being dried. Footsteps hasten toward the door.

"Peter?"

"Yeah, let me in!" The door eases open with a creak. Mimi's face bears slight traces of mascara, eyeliner and eye shadow. "Why in the world do you have makeup on at this time of night?"

Mimi hangs her head and digs a toe in the carpet. She wears candy-heart pajama pants and a T-shirt that says "I'm So HOT" in bright red letters with flames shooting from the word "HOT." She turns, walks the few steps to her bed, sits.

"I, umm, was out for a little while."

Peter stares at her. "Out? Where?" He eases the door shut behind him and walks closer to the bed.

Her face wrinkles into a scowl and she crosses her arms over her chest. The stuffed animals, carefully arranged on her bed, seem to be listening.

"OUT. Mom does it all the time. She just disappears at night, and I have no idea where she is or when she'll be home. So I thought I'd do it too!" She lifts a defiant chin.

Peter is astonished. Mimi is only twelve. He thinks about all the MTV she is fond of watching, and the dance moves he'd seen her practicing. "Mom is gonna kill you!"

"How's she gonna find out?" Mimi stares at him, her arms still crossed over her chest. "If you tell, I'll tell her I saw you making out with that girl in our car at school. As a matter of fact, I think you were doing more than making out . . ." she smiles. Peter's face registers shock.

"You . . . saw that?"

She nods.

"Mimi, that was a mistake. A really, really bad mistake. I shouldn't have gotten messed up with her, it's just that . . ."

"Yeah, yeah," Mimi says smugly, "I know all about her. She's supposed to be a real skank."

"Don't tell Mom," Peter says, "she's got a lot of pressure right now."

Mimi frowns and says, "She's ALWAYS got a lot of pressure! She is never home, doesn't do any housework, never cooks." Tears spills down her soft cheeks. "I'm tired of staying home! It's lonely and boring."

Peter nods. Since he is older, he understands things better than Mimi, but he can't deny her comments. He shrugs, "Mimi, she's doing the best she can right now. Just don't go out again without tellin' us where you are, okay? Who were you with, anyway?"

Mimi looks at the walls, then raises her eyes to the ceiling. Sitting on her bed amongst the tribe of stuffed animals, she looks like she is ten instead of nearly thirteen. "This man named Jacob. I met him when I was in the front yard one day. You and Chad had meetings at school or something."

"Jacob who? And how do you know he is a good guy? Mimi, that's crazy! You went off with a grown man?"

She shrugs. "Dad's never around. I just need someone to talk to, and he's been so nice to me. He's always bringin' me doughnuts and telling me I'm pretty. He's a nice guy, Peter. Please don't tell Mom. He wants to be her friend, too. He told me."

Peter drops his head into his hands, tired of carrying the responsibility for his sister and brother. So tired. And he doesn't want to bother Mom, she really is having a tough time right now. He'd overheard some disturbing phone calls. Not the least of which was that she had a stalker, he thought. Plus he knew she didn't get much help financially from his dad, or Mimi's dad, which made her have to work a lot. He tries to think what to do.

Peter grabs Mimi's shoulders firmly and turns her to face him. A few animals fall from the bed to the floor. They lie on their backs, sightless eyes staring at the ceiling.

"Mimi, this is important. You must promise to *never* see Jacob again. Do you understand? It's not right. He is not a relative, or a close friend, he's a STRANGER. We don't know him. And it's weird for you to go with him, or for him to want you to go with him. Do you promise?"

Mimi's eyes darken and she says, "At least he wants to be with me! At least he gives me attention, and makes me feel pretty!" She jerks out of Peter's grasp and flops, face down, into the menagerie on her bed. "Mmmkay, I promise!" she says, her voice muffled. "I won't tell Mom about the skank either, don't worry."

Peter reaches out to his sister, remembering her as a toddler. He pulls her into a big-brother bear hug. "Mimi, you are pretty and you are smart. We love you so much. Mom'll get it together soon, I promise." His chin rests atop her head, nestled into her hair. Anxiety plucks at his mind. He holds her tighter.

CHAPTER 39

Izzy

"Hi, guys!" The kids are in the kitchen looking reasonably prepared to go to school, and I, for once, had a good night's sleep and feel better. I am putting all emotional trauma on hold until I get to the office and talk to a few people. "Everyone have breakfast?" I reach for the cereal boxes on the top shelves of the kitchen cupboard, pull out a bowl for myself and fill it with flakes.

"Yeah, Mom, we got breakfast," Chad says. I turn and walk to the refrigerator, open it, pull out a jug of milk, pour it on my cereal, place it back in the refrigerator, and kick the door closed

"Good. How about homework? Everyone okay there?" I sit at the table and join them. My eyes assess each face. Peter and Mimi are subdued and quiet. Chad, the introvert, actually seems loquacious by comparison this morning.

"Okay, I take the silence as a good thing? That homework is not an issue?" Heads nod in unison. "So what's up today, everybody? Any plans after school?"

"Basketball practice," Peter says.

I nod, he usually stays late so this is a given. He catches a ride home with one of the team, and Chad drives Mimi home.

"Nothing but homework, Mom," Chad says, eyeing Mimi. "What's up for you, moron?" he asks Mimi.

She squints at him, making a face.

"Wait," Chad says, "I know! Facebook, Facebook and more Facebook, right?"

Mimi rolls her eyes and says, "Moron."

"Okay, well, I have a busy day, so text me if something is going on, okay? Let me hear from you," I grab my empty bowl, walk to the sink, rinse it and put it in the dishwasher. "Rinse your dishes and put them right here, okay," I say, pointing to the dishwasher where I'd just placed my bowl. They mumble assents.

I wave good-bye as they zoom down the street in the twelve-year-old Pontiac Bonneville that somehow keeps running in spite of 200,000-plus miles on the odometer. I am grateful that the kids seem to be okay. At least that's one worry I can cross off my list for now.

As I pass the mirror in the foyer, my eyes rest on my reflection. I've taken pains with my appearance today because I have some rather important discussions pending, and want to appear professional, maybe even intimidating.

My freshly washed, painstakingly flat ironed hair falls to my shoulders in a shiny sheaf. My eyes subtly scream *sexy, but innocent of all charges*, thanks to heavy-handed makeup, and my lips are a dusky, liquid rose. I'd picked out a gray, pin-striped pantsuit and added a creamy, silk blouse, four-inch, black platform heels, understated silver earrings and bracelet.

Pearls around my neck shyly accent the silk blouse. Nothing bespeaks sincerity of heart like pearls.

I'm determined to march into Phil's office and tell him everything. Then I'm determined to walk into Birdie's office and tell him to get the hell off my back. And if that doesn't work, I guess I'll have to start looking for another job; in which case, I am already dressed for the interview.

There's more than one way to skin a cat – uh – *buzzard*, I tell myself. As a last resort, I will pull in Detective Faraday, my personal Sir Galahad, to slay multiple dragons with his sword. I am not sure where my newfound energy is coming from, but I think it may have something to do with prayer.

As I'd touched my head to the pillow last night, just before the Tylenol PM slurred my thoughts toward la-la land, I'd muttered a very brief, but extremely heartfelt, prayer. This morning, I am just a teensy bit closer to believing there must be something to it. I am very surprised I am not slinking around in anxious defeat, devastated emotionally by last night's events. I am not only mysteriously energized, but militant and alert. Every nerve ending seems to have a tiny sword in its hand, poised and ready to strike.

I exit the kitchen, locking the door behind me and fob open the Honda, my eyes quickly scanning the garage for tightly folded white, mystery squares under windshield wipers. My new habit of locking everything in sight must be working.

I quickly back out of my garage, press the garage door opener, wait briefly to assure the door closes. A patrol car smoothly glide past my house. The patrolman nods at me. All is well, the nod says.

I speed off toward my morning latte, radio blaring. As I wait in line, I dig around in my purse for four bucks and change, sunglasses perched atop my head. I am two cars from the window. The Bluetooth asks me to take a call, and Brad's sexy voice floats into the car.

"Hey gorgeous! You up and about this morning? Thanks for giving me your phone number last night, I have no idea how I misplaced it!"

I pull up one car closer to the window, a goofy grin dominating my face. "Hi, Brad, I'm just pulling up to get a latte before heading to work. How are you this morning?" He responds with blessedly boring, normal niceties, confirms our date this weekend, and wishes me well.

When I pull up to the window with a goofy sigh, Lydia smiles brightly and says, "Hey Izzy! Where ya been? How's life? The usual?"

I nod, grateful that she is familiar with my order: a grande breve latte, double pump raspberry, extra hot. I quickly reconsider, and say, "Make that a triple shot this morning, okay?"

She winks. "Okay." She turns and quickly dispatches the order to an employee inside. "You look great, Izzy!"

I acknowledge the compliment. "Got sleep last night, for once. And I have some, uh . . . rather important stuff going on today."

Lydia's quick, intelligent, brown eyes graze my face. "Yeah?" She reaches to her right, slips a heat protector on the cup and extends it to me through the window. "Significant, huh?"

I nod, sipping the latte.

"I'll be praying for you, Izzy. Count on it." She waves the next car in as I scoot away.

That praying thing again. Seems to be a popular habit with people I like. Why hadn't I noticed this before?

Winston is calmly sipping coffee and thumbing through his newspaper when I land in the pod. Lonnie is circling the cubicles, distributing proofs to each salesperson. He nods and smiles at me over his pile of newsprint. The managers are clustered in Phil's office, laughing and talking, each clutching mugs of coffee. Sales reps populate each cube, and assistants flit to and fro like darting chickadees, awaiting instruction or chatting.

Darlene looks busy in the back, head down at her desk. She lifts her eyes briefly, having apparently felt mine, and waves at me. The conference room in the far left, back corner is empty. Jon Hoyt's desk, in the classified sales department located across the linoleum aisle, is still vacant. I think about re-scheduling our meeting, but that will have to wait for now. Today is specifically a Phil-and-Birdie day. Somehow I have got to begin the difficult process of untangling a huge mess. And I have no idea how to begin.

I notice Winston's perplexed expression. Since I am still standing, not sitting, he must be wondering why. I look down and realize I still have my coat on and my purse dangling from my shoulder.

Winston leans back in his chair and runs his fingers the length of the lanyard. "Good Morning! Looks like Pod-Queen has a lot on her mind today!"

I shake myself mentally and turn toward Winston. I pull the purse off my shoulder and close it in its drawer. Slide my arms out of my coat and drape it across the back of my chair. Sit. My whole body feels as taut as a violin string.

"Pod-King, you have no idea," I respond, smiling. "I am totally wired. Ready."

Winston cocks his head at me. Today, his dress shirt is pastel yellow. His tie sports a never-ending maze design in coordinated colors. The tie is apparently an attempt at three-dimensional whimsy, and is somewhat stressing me with visual overload. His glasses dangle from the lanyard, baby blue today, and his arms are crossed over his chest. His crisply starched khakis end at crossed ankles wearing socks that match the tie. He, or maybe his wife, must spend an hour each morning picking out stuff to wear.

"Ready for what?" he asks.

"I don't know if I can get through it all in five minutes. Just pray for me, will you?"

His expression reflects his surprise. "I will. Do I need a few more details first?"

I know he is pleasantly shocked, because in all the years we've worked together I have not once asked him to pray. Something is afoot that is out of the ordinary, the request says, and he knows it.

"Yeah, I guess. Pray for the meetings. I need to meet with Phil first, then Birdie." Winston's eyebrows launch themselves with mutual abandon.

"Yeah? Promise I get the whole story after the meetings?"

"Promise. But it'll take a drink after work to get through it. Let's just wait 'til things are kind of resolved, okay? Have no clue when that'll be, just know that things need to be resolved. Big time. Before I lose my mind."

He nods and seems to understand the seriousness of my situation. "Got it. I'm with you, Izzy. You've got my support, always, you know that."

I smile at him. "Yeah, I know. Thanks." I look around, realize I am without coffee. I wheel my chair backwards, push myself up and grab my coffee mug, which appears to need a thorough scrubbing. Instead of heading to the sludge-pot, I make a beeline for the ladies' to wash it out. When I push open the door, I nearly knock down Darlene, who is carrying a vase of dahlias.

"Whoa! In a hurry, Izzy?" she laughs, balancing her vase so the water does not spill.

I hold my mug out so that she can see the interior. "Eww! My gosh, Izzy, don't you ever wash that thing!"

"Hardly ever. What difference would it make? The coffee back there is mud, anyway," I tease. She wrinkles her nose in disgust.

"Ja, vell it might be mud but it'll taste worse if you don't vash that cup!" I snicker and sigh at the same time.

"So, how is it going, Izzy? Everyzhink good?" She sets her vase on the counter, crosses her arms and leans against a stall. We are the only ones in the ladies' room. I decide two prayer requests would probably be a good thing right now.

"No, everything is *not* good, and I haven't had time to bring you up to date. But I have to talk to Phil. And I have to get Birdie arrested . . . or fired . . . or *something!*" Darlene has the uncanny ability to get me to spill my guts, tears, and deepest forebodings at the drop of *eine Hut*.

"Ja? Oh no! What has happened?" She takes a step toward me and I warn her with my eyes. If she touches me, I will blubber all over her, and I cannot afford to blubber. She takes a step back. "Want to talk about it?"

"Yep, I'd love to talk about it, but things right now are totally out of control. I have to try to fix it. Right now." My jaw juts out in determination. I stride to the door, push it open, turn back toward her.

"Pray for me. Really hard today, okay Darlene?"

She nods, her expression concerned. "I vill, Iz. I vill. Let's get together soon and process."

I nod, glance at my mug, and continue on my way to fill it with a little sludgy initiative.

The coffee area is awash in white-shirted, tie-bedecked managers in a semi-circle, waiting for the final perk.

I'm in no mood for chit chat. Especially with a full complement of fresh managers.

As I get closer, I identify the men as Phil, Birdie, Milton from classified, and the classified telemarketing manager. I stop just outside the circle. I should make a run for it but they've already seen me and that would look weird. So I wait, my face studying the linoleum, hoping to avoid Birdie's eyes.

"Mornin' Izzy!" Birdie sings, his smile blazing like blanched bones at high noon. Obviously he is going to pretend nothing happened. And, as a bonus, he seems to have become my very best friend overnight. I mumble a response and look away, which, of course, appears as if I am being rude.

Phil gazes at me questioningly.

Milton, bless him, says, "Izzy, ready for coffee?" and pulls the carafe from the coffeemaker, which has obligingly perked its final perk. I obediently extend, and he pours.

I manage a few throwaway comments to the circle of men before I scamper back to my pod as fast as I can and lunge into the relative safety of my chair. It's now or never, Izzy, I tell myself. To live with this situation and pretend he did not threaten me last night is not an option. If I wait, it will only get worse.

Should I tell Detective Faraday first? I drop my head in my hands and try to think clearly, but fear has gripped my brain and I cannot summon rational thought. My landline rings and I peer at the number through my fingers. Blocked.

I cautiously pick up the phone. "Izzy, *Sentinel*."

"Izzy?" I roll my eyes and wonder why, when I routinely identify myself, does the caller invariably want to know if they have, in fact, called the right person. I suppose they must repeat my name to be absolutely sure.

"You got her. What's up? Who's calling, please?"

"Izzy, this is Mrs. Dubois, Chad's second-period teacher. I wanted to give you a quick call and see if you realized Chad has been absent a couple of days?"

My back whipsawed in the chair. "Absent? Are you sure?" Self-imposed denial. Sometimes it works.

"Oh yes, dear, quite sure. I checked with the receptionist and he's not been checked out. I also talked to a couple of his other teachers, and he was not in their classes either. Just thought you should know."

My hands feel ice-cold as all the blood in my body races to my thudding heart. "Yes, well, thank you for telling me. I'll figure this out right away." We say good-byes and I hang up, thoroughly shaken.

Phil walks by on his way back to his office, and stops by my desk. "Something going on, Izzy?" Like Winston, Phil has an uncanny sixth sense where I am concerned. I take a deep breath. Now or never. I straighten, and say, "Yes, Phil, there is. Do you have a few minutes?"

His eyes twinkle. "A *few* minutes? Izzy, you and I both know it is *never* a few minutes with you." He smiles and gestures with his hand to follow him into his office. I get up and trail him. Resolutely push my shoulders back and stick my chin in the air. A defensive body posture is important.

Phil closes the door after me and sits behind his desk. He pulls his chair up closely so that his elbows rest on top, and tents his fingers. His gaze is expectant. "Floor's yours, Izzy. You've got about twenty minutes. Go."

I'd rehearsed my speech all the way to work. The words do not come easily at first, but after a few sputters, they gush forth like Niagara Falls.

I tell Phil about the online match that had seemingly read my mind, and asked to meet at my favorite place. About my surprise when Birdie had stepped out of the shadows, and his references to the inappropriateness of my online dating. I tell him the personal critique that Birdie had lavished upon me unbidden, and the several attempts to matter-of-factly eject him from my personal affairs. Then I rehash the conversation of the night before, wincing at some of Phil's questions and inferences, and twenty minutes later, I close my mouth. I am a wreck. I have not started bawling, thankfully, but I am still a wreck.

"Jon called me last night, y'know," Phil says. Reaches for his mug and sips. How everyone seems to mainline the stuff all day long, I'll never know.

"He did?" I clench my hands in my lap. "What did he say?"

Phil put his mug down carefully on a coaster on his desk. I hear muted traffic sounds outside Phil's second-story windows, and a few sparrows warbling from the treetop branches visible through the window. The day is overcast, and dark gray clouds skitter across the sky.

"He's concerned about you. He called to tell me he'd seen you come out of Raphael's with Birdie last night, and it seemed strange. He did not want me to tell you that he called me." Phil shrugged. "But I think there's a point where everything needs to be dumped on the table. What he told me lines up with your story."

Phil continues, "I'll be honest, Izzy, Birdie has talked to me about some things that are very concerning. Not the least of which is some guy you met online has been waiting for you outside the office." He pauses and eyes my face.

"That guy is a total wacko!" I exclaim. "A very troubled individual. I even have a restraining order on him, because he's trespassed at my home. You can call Detective Faraday if you need proof."

"I get it, Izzy," Phil said. "But look at it from my perspective. I am truly upset that this guy seems to be a problem for you, but he *cannot* become a problem for the *Sentinel*. Your online stuff seems to be gathering predators. Not to mention, um, detective, did you say? Really?"

I nod, miserable. My eyes study the carpet.

"Birdie has a point in that it is affecting your work. You have been seriously distracted lately. Your sales numbers are pretty good, but I don't think they'll stay that way if things continue as they are."

I sit in front of Phil's desk, numb. Hadn't he heard me tell him all the crazy things Birdie had told me? The threats? The accusations? The bribe to make sure I am Salesperson of the Year if I *play it his way*? Maybe Birdie has more influence with Phil than I thought.

Phil fingers his mug, apparently thinking of taking another sip. Decides against it, and leans forward. "You've brought some pretty serious allegations against Birdie. What I want you to do is go see Human Resources, and fill out a report. Everything you've told me. I'll initial it, and we'll put it in his file. In the meantime, and until there is proof, business as usual."

"*Business as usual?*" I cough, my voice catching on the phrase. "How in the world do I do business as usual? The guy is – "

"The guy is my new *sales manager*, and he is innocent until proven guilty. In the meantime, what I want you to do is what I know you do very well – sell and service your accounts. And for the foreseeable future, Jon's accounts. Report to me. I'll tell Birdie that you are temporarily my responsibility until we sort some things out. Agreed?"

I nod, heartened that I will not report to Birdie, and resist the urge to leap into the air with a fist-pump. A minor victory, but an important one. Phil has not dismissed my comments as fabrications, and is even setting up some boundaries to protect me.

Phil nods assertively. "Okay, good. And one more thing." I lean forward in my chair, hands tightly wound around its mahogany arms. "Let's not let Birdie in on our little chat." His eyes assess mine, and I lock in. We are one. The mission has begun, and at least I feel Phil and I are on the same team.

CHAPTER 40

The walk back to my desk is almost buoyant. My feet barely touch the ground. I have an ally! As I roll my chair up to my desk, I notice the stack of proofs Lonnie has placed there is huge. My mind quickly rolls around to the day's schedule, thinking. I grab a note pad and pen and begin writing. Priority: Chad. Where the heck has he been if not at school? Second: Make appointment with Jon to explain things and bring him up to speed on what is happening with his accounts. Third: Darlene? What's going on with her? Fourth: Don't I need to make some calls on my own clients? I viciously scrawl over this line. Too much going on right now to try to work up some new business.

The morning passes in a pleasant mix of emailing proofs to Jon's clients, making corrections, and racing back and forth to production. The ads are running in Friday's paper, and the deadline is today, Wednesday, at four o'clock. I'd called Jon and he agreed to see me mid-afternoon, so I am forcing myself to deal with the production department in spite of their obvious reluctance to acknowledge anything I say. The saving grace is that the ads I am giving them to work on are Jon's, and they all adore him, so they view it as helping him, not me. On one of my trips back to my desk from production, Darlene waves at me to stop by.

She slices her eyes and leans forward, her voice hushed. "So vhat happened? I saw you in with Phil."

I shrug. "Not much. We are proceeding with typical HR reports, that kind of thing. I'll have time to go into more detail if we can get together outside the office." We set a time after work, and I suggest a place different from Raphael's. I don't know if I'll want to go back to Raphael's after what happened with Birdie. Creeps me out just to think about it.

"Okay," Darlene says, "and I vant you to know," her smile beams, "that Richard and I are doing great! The program that was recommended to us by my Pastor is amazink!"

"That is wonderful, Darlene," I reply, meaning it. "Good for you! I knew you would work things out. You are perfect for each other."

She studies my face for a minute. "Things aren't always what they seem on the outside. Ve all have our secrets, and that is where the trouble is. When the secrets get dumped into the open, things can begin to get better. That's what we are learning." I nod, not having a clue what she is talking about, but a soft, niggling voice at the back of my mind tells me to pay attention.

"Yeah? Well, glad it is working for you guys. Listen, I gotta get back to Jon's stuff. I never realized how much work that guy does! And those car guys – they are a different breed for sure! The general managers are makin' me work like a dog!"

Darlene smiles. "Ja, Richard has some auto accounts. They are tough. Picky. Are you getting along with them okay?"

I feel my face curl into a grimace. "Kind of. I am a little concerned that they mainly see my, um, female attributes and are not exactly focused on my expert marketing advice."

"Hm." Darlene's hand drifts up to her chin and stays there. The latest batch of dahlias on her desk are the colors of autumn, yellows and golds. Pinned to her cubicle divider is a plaque that says "Life is fragile. Handle with prayer." She continues, "Do you think, Izzy, that you may be teasing them a little, and they are responding to that?"

"What?" I frown at her, puzzled. "That's what women *do* in this business. Flirt. It gets business. It *keeps* business."

Darlene smiles and reaches out for my hands, which I resist pulling away. "No, Izzy, that's not what *all* women do in this business. And if you think about it, it's not a good way to keep business."

My brain pulls Darlene's comment in, then spits it out. I am not used to criticism, and especially when I seem to be meeting my quotas plus doing Jon's work as well. I should run back to my desk and keep my mouth shut, but of course, I don't.

Instead, I say, "Yeah? Well, if you think you can do a better job, just let Phil know, and I'll recommend you for my position!" With that, I turn on my heel and stride angrily back to my desk.

My chair bounces in protest as I land in it, still stung by the comment. Winston looks at me with a surprised expression, one hand holding his place on the comics and the other holding his coffee mug aloft. His brow furrows. I can never keep anything from Winston, so I take a deep breath and dive in with highlights. Just the highlights.

"Winston, I'm in deep this time."

"Again?" He smiles and winks.

I nod. "Yeah, but it's worse than you might think. I had a good meeting with Phil, though, so that's a good start to unraveling this mess."

"Mess? What mess?"

My landline rings. I answer and talk to one of Jon's clients as if he is the entire focus of my life, assure him he'd get a final proof immediately, and hang up. Winston is unperturbed. Pod-versation interruptions are a way of life on the sales floor, and it is an accepted fact that the client takes priority, always. We eventually pick up the threads of our conversations, as I do now. I place elbows on my desk and lean toward Winston.

"The mess that Birdie has caused. Or I have caused. Or . . . whatever." My gloom suddenly envelopes the pod. My face crumples before I can stop it.

"Oh, Izzy. There is no problem that cannot be solved. It's always darkest before the dawn, and all that." Winston leans in and whispers, "Birdie is a lawsuit waiting to happen, anyway. Maybe you are the one God picked out to expose him."

"Oh, great! That's all I need! To be a pariah for women's rights in the workplace. Yeah, I *need* all that hatred from my sales manager. Threatening insinuations can be extremely motivating." I give him a glare for good measure, then add, "My life is complicated enough!"

Winston leans back in his chair, crosses his arms. One hand slowly lifts to his lanyard, and his fingers begin their habitual caress. His eyes are studying the ceiling, as they always do when he is deep in thought.

Finally, I say, "What?! What's so interesting on the dang ceiling?"

He looks at me, and by his expression, I know that one of his epiphany moments is at hand. He cocks his head and says, "Izzy, you are a strong-willed, resourceful woman. Talented. A great mom. You've got a lot going for you. But it seems to happen over and over again . . ."

"What happens over and over again?"

His earnest blue eyes bore into mine. "I know it's hard for you to hear, but your relationships with men seem to kind of . . . implode . . . in one way or the other. Haven't you ever thought about that?"

I break our locked gaze and look at the floor. My arms cross themselves over my chest. I feel like an errant child, and I resent it. But I feel the ring of truth in his words, and I have been assessing my choices lately. Something has to change. I know, deep down, that if the same things were happening to someone else right now, I would be shocked. I would wonder what had gotten them to that place.

But Winston is prodding the single area that is a cherished escape for me. The men online that nurture me, accept me, want me. Never criticize or judge. Tell me I am pretty, desirable. Buy me dinner. Take me dancing. Some of them even tell me they love me. How could something that feels so good be wrong? Is it?

"Izzy? You still with us?"

I shake my head and smile at him. "Just thinking," I say, breathing out a deep sigh. "I'm tired of fighting, that's all. Tired of fighting trying to find a good husband, trying to meet sales goals, trying to get along with a sales manager I despise! Tired of being a single mom, for Pete's sake! How am I supposed to know how to raise kids – especially boys – without a dad?" Latent hysteria creeps into my voice.

Winston's eyes flash in concern. He stands and reaches over the pod divider to touch my shoulder.

"Izzy, I think it's time for you to give up. You can't do it on your own."

I am snuffling a little, and wipe the tears off my face. "Yeah, well I *am* on my own. What am I supposed to do? I can't *give up!*"

"You can," he says, his eyes gentle. "You can give it to God. He'll take it on, and as you pray – and I am praying for you, too, Izzy – you'll get a new perspective. He'll come in and give you wisdom to make the right choices. I can't explain how it happens. It's supernatural. Beyond our reasoning. But it works. It's real. And from what I can tell, you are quickly running out of options."

I am beyond irritated that Winston has picked this moment to evangelize me, but I am also beyond being able to help myself, apparently. Nothing is working. I am so worn out emotionally, that I do not know how much longer I can go on.

I lift my tear-stained face and say, "Sounds good, Winston, but it probably won't work for me. Kind of out of luck, here."

He smiles, and says "No luck to it. Just a simple acknowledgment of belief. Pick up a Bible. Start with the little book of First John."

I smile at him tiredly. "Maybe I will, Winston. My life could sure use a different direction right now."

Chad

Chad thinks about the crappy way his life seems to be going, and takes a pull off the joint. The nub nearly burns his fingers. He leans his head back against the rock high atop a bluff overlooking the Savannah River. His mom's office building is easily identifiable from his perch. He waves and snorts out a laugh.

"Yeah, Mom, what do you think of your son, now? Am I a loser, or what?" His sneakered foot slides off his perch, and he grabs random branches to prevent sliding down the bluff into the river. "Whoa!" He gazes at the five hundred-foot drop to the river through hazy eyes.

"Better hang on," He giggles, carefully releasing his grip on the flimsy bushes after re-positioning on the rocks.

"Stupid school," he announces to the vista spread before him. The Savannah snakes east and west. On his side of the river he could see the busy, refurbished heart of north Chatbrook; on the other, the River's Edge District, and Ardmore

Coliseum. A breathtaking view, but Chad is not seeing too clearly.

"Life sucks."

He brings the nub to his lips, but it has flickered out. He tosses it below, watching it drift down, down, down until it disappears into the rapid current.

"McAllister sucks, and that joint sucks." He laughs.

He studies the *Sentinel* building. "Hope she's not worryin' about me. Probably not, because she probably doesn't even know I'm missing yet!" He nudges his position into a full recline, and stretches his arms above his head.

The sun feels great on his face, and his problems are dizzily drifting away. No better feeling than getting high, and today someone had slipped him an Adderol as well. He enjoys a tingling undercurrent from the additive, like subtle electricity. His body is heavy, relaxed.

Would anyone really mind him taking a couple days off from school to get his head straight? Who would miss him? Chad closes his eyes. He isn't sure anybody really cares. Belatedly, he feels his foot slip off the rock that had been holding him in position.

By the time he reacts, gravity is pulling him toward the river at alarming speed. Branches, vines, rocks, clods of dirt elude his grasp as clumsy fingers rake for a handhold. He tumbles end over end and lands hard on a small ledge covered with thorny bushes fifty feet from the river's edge; a crumpled bit of humanity in baggy jeans, red converse tennis shoes, a Windsor Academy T-shirt and gray hoodie. Rocks and dirt flurry after him down the side of the cliff, bouncing off his inert form. Eventually, the landslide stops.

A lone, red tennis shoe, caught on a branch during the wild descent, sways above him in the breeze.

CHAPTER 41

Izzy

Chad's cell goes straight to voicemail for the eighth time in an hour.

The woman at the school office verified that Chad had not been in for two days, and I ask if she'll pull Peter out of class for me. She agrees, and I hear her scribble a note and give instructions to someone. Steps recede down the hallway. I picture rows of lockers on each side of the gleaming hallway and wonder which class Peter is in. She asks if I'd like to wait, or would I prefer Peter give me a call, and I think to myself, woman, if you were dying a thousand deaths because you do not know where your kid had been for two days, what would *you* do?

I wisely avoid going ballistic and tell her fine, have Peter call me. Give her my number.

As I dial Chad's number again a few minutes later, I see the school's phone number and quickly end my outgoing and pick up the incoming. "Peter?"

"Yeah, Mom, what's up?"

I am having trouble catching my breath. Fear does that to me. My mom radar is flying all over the place. "Hey, um . . . I am wondering if you know where Chad has been the last couple of days?"

"Uhhh . . ." Peter begins, then stops. Instead, he says, "Why are you panting?"

"So you do know! Tell me!"

He clears his throat. "Mom, I really *don't* know! I know he's not been at school, but he hasn't told me where he is! I didn't even see him last night, and this morning on the way to school he didn't say much. I guess he must've headed somewhere after the bell rang."

"Oh, God," I say, covering my face with my hand. I didn't mean it as a prayer, but maybe in an involuntary sort of way, it was.

"Wait, Mom," Peter says. "I think maybe I have a clue at least." I am silent, listening. He continues, "The other day he talked about needing some time to think, get his head straight."

My brow puckers. "Get his head straight? From what?"

"Well," my thoughtful son responds, "you know Chad, he's kinda deep, and he wanted to get perspective, he said. Perspective on . . . something. I forget what."

"Okay, perspective. Good. Now, son, think! Do you know *where* he might go to get this perspective?"

"Not really, mom, but I know he really loves the river. You know, the good memories we've had on the north side when we were watching the Fourth of July fireworks from Festival on the River? And the River Concert Series? Maybe that's where he went." He pauses. "I bet that's exactly where he is! I mean, how else would he go somewhere without my keys? The bus," he said excitedly, "the bus comes right by the school every thirty minutes, and I know it goes there."

I nod, thinking. "Okay, good Peter, let's start there. And if he shows up at school, call me. Immediately, okay?" He agrees, and we end the call.

I look at the pile on my desk, and decide Lonnie will have to pick up the slack for now. I run all over the office like a crazy woman, and finally find him leaning over one of the women in production, basking in the attention a forty-five-year-old, unhappily married woman gives a twenty-three-year-old, cute, buff, single, male. I resist screaming, and instead ask politely if he would step away with me a moment to talk.

He graces the woman with a charming, apologetic shrug of his shoulders. The woman glares at me briefly, then returns to her keyboard. To his credit, after I give him a quick rundown, his eyes darken with concern, and he agrees to take care of my ads the rest of the afternoon. I crush him in a hug of thanks and dash down the stairs to my car.

On the drive up the winding, narrow road to the Bluffs Office Complex, a rambling cluster of offices and scenic vista areas high atop the Savannah River, I call Detective Faraday in an attempt to calm down. My thoughts, to coin an appropriate phrase, have run amok.

So far I have a stalker, a boss who is possibly a jail-worthy pervert, and now, a missing child. Maybe he is not missing, I tell myself. *Maybe he is not missing*. I repeat it to myself about one hundred times on the way to the scenic overlook Peter suggested. My Bluetooth kicks in and asks me to take a call. *Yes*.

"Hi, Izzy," Detective Faraday's voice sighs through the air. I wonder how many other women run him ragged like this. Maybe he thinks I'm nuts. Maybe I am. I will think about this later.

"Hi, there. You have time to talk to me a minute?"

"Sure. What's up?" I hear the rustle of papers in the background, and voices over loudspeakers. The squawk of a police radio. Laughter from people in the background that apparently have no missing children. I think about the ugly chairs, and the institution-beige walls. I think about the unfriendly receptionist.

"It's Chad. He's my son. I think he may be missing."

The rustling of paper stops. "*May* be missing? What does that mean? When did you last see him?"

I carefully give him details, then wait. I know him well enough by now to know that he will quickly process the information and spew out a plan. He has a logical, well-ordered brain, which is the perfect antithesis to mine, and is why I force myself to be quiet and listen instead of dissolving into hysteria.

"All right. Where are you going right now?" I tell him. "Once you are up there, give me a call if you find anything. Otherwise, we can't do anything until it's been twenty-four hours. Your son saw him this morning, right?"

"Yes, and I saw him at breakfast. He seemed quiet, but nothing out of the ordinary."

"Well, kids this age do this stuff all the time. Worry their parents to death. I bet he'll be home after school. Anyway, I've got some information down, and I'll keep this out until I hear from you. Also, have your kids talk to their friends, or mutual acquaintances. Facebook? Do you have his log-ins? If so, check it out."

After I end the call, I floor my accelerator and don't slow down until I reach the top. I exit the car, my heart thumping wildly in my chest, fear constricting my throat. Memories of dragging lawn chairs to watch the fireworks wash over me. The kids had streaked all over the place in happy abandon on the grass, then settled in their chairs as fireworks split the night with color. I remember squeals of delight, the clap of little hands. I can almost smell smoke lingering in the air. Chad had been spellbound. "Mommy," he'd screamed, "it's so beautiful! I want to remember this night forever!"

I squeak out a little prayer, which comes off as more of a sob, and stride down the path to the overlook. My eyes scan the benches scattered around the area's perimeter. I stand smack in the middle and revolve in a circle. What I see: parking lot surrounded by maples brilliant with color, office buildings in the distance periodically disgorging an employee or two; the Savannah, roiling and churning, its banks straining at higher-than-typical levels, a trailhead; signs cautioning hikers that the trail is treacherous and steep. I walk toward the trailhead, the most logical place, I think, that my son might be in his current state of mind.

Decorative wrought iron borders cliff's edge, a subtle reminder to approach with care. My eyes scan each direction vertically and horizontally, then again. I take a deep breath, squint, and look again. Something catches my eye.

About halfway down a vertical drop of scraggly undergrowth and rocky outcroppings, I see a spot of red. It looks like a small flag someone planted on the side of the bank, a warning to turn back. My breath catches in my throat. If it's a shoe, I will have legitimate cause for a heart attack. Peter's favorite tennis shoes are red. I quickly dial Detective Faraday's number, and he says he'll join me and bring binoculars.

I sit on the overlook bench, my thoughts rising and falling with the energetic laps of the river.

9

Twenty minutes later I have tried Chad's number another ten times, and indulged in some rather strict soul-searching. When had I gotten so disconnected from my kids? Other parents didn't keep tabs on their kids 24/7, right? I checked in with them all day long with texts. Isn't that enough? I scrunch up my face and force myself to concentrate on Chad. Scenes play in my head like a movie on fast forward. Just like my life.

Chad's image in the scenes is blurred, small. He sits in a dark corner. His face is sullen and angry. I'd meant to sit down with him and talk a hundred times, but stuff always got in the way. Tears leak from my eyes. The scenes rushing through my mind slow to a snail's pace, and I see night after night of Chad on the couch, sleeping in front of the TV. I'd been glad that he didn't need me for something. But what if he'd been depressed? Or high? On who knows what? All I thought about was that at least *one* of the kids did not need my attention, thereby freeing me to clandestinely click away in my hunt for *The Yes*. Which, in my defense, did give me a small break from being responsible for *everything*.

God, I am so tired. Endlessly tired.

I lift my eyes to the river.

The panorama before me is actually quite beautiful. Chatbrook's charming skyline glints in the sun. Barges chug up and down the river. Speedboats whip by them. The sun is beginning its afternoon descent, and a few fluffy clouds dot the sky. The breeze lifts my hair. I wrap my arms around myself, feeling a chill though it is warm for October. If I'd focused on Chad like I was focusing now, he probably wouldn't be missing. *He is not missing!*

I scream silently at God, if there is a God, to find him.

A motor purrs into the parking lot and stops. The door opens and steps crunch toward me. I pat my hair into a semblance of order. I turn and watch him walk. He is on his cell, and carries binoculars. His trench coat flaps in the wind. I wonder if all detectives feel, because of TV cop shows, that they must wear trench coats or sacrifice credibility.

"Hi," he says simply, standing in front of me, scanning the view. "Nice view. Do you think your son comes here often?" He steps to the overlook. "Where's the red you talked about?"

I stand, walk to the edge, and point. He aims his binoculars, adjusts them. I am so close to him, I can hear his steady breathing. My heart double-beats in time to it. Finally, he lowers the binoculars. "It's a shoe, Izzy."

That's the last thing I remember.

CHAPTER 42

When my eyes flutter open, a beehive of activity surrounds me.

I lay on a bench, a trench coat bundled under my head as a pillow. A red strobe alerts me to the ambulance, parked on an incline a few feet away. I hear shouts, muffled, from the banks of the river. My foggy mind clears, and I leap from the bench.

Detective Faraday is barking orders into his phone. Police and emergency personnel are clustered around the overlook. Three of them hold a huge cable that disappears over the edge. Patrol cars fill the parking lot. A knot of stoic paramedics wait by a mobile cot on an aluminum frame, covered in crisp, white sheets. One of them notices me, and looks at Detective Faraday. "She's awake," he says.

Detective Faraday mumbles something into his phone, ends the call and strides toward where I am shakily standing. Gently seats me. "Sit, Izzy. You fainted."

I stare at him, mute, too afraid to ask the unthinkable.

"Chad's okay," he says.

The dam breaks. "Oh God Oh God Oh God," I say and cover my face. I wonder if tears have a cut-off valve. I never knew so many could come out of one person. I lift my eyes to his after a few moments of relief-sobbing.

"Do you know what happened?"

Detective Faraday nods.

"Yeah. Apparently he fell. He's kinda out of it, so we're gonna take him to emergency, get him checked out. You can ride in the ambulance." I heave a huge sigh of gratitude, and say "Thanks. For the pillow," I wave my hand toward the bench, which still holds the crumpled coat, "for everything," then burst into tears again.

Detective Faraday responds with a brusque, "Yeah, well, just the job," and awkwardly pats my arm. He continues, his voice softening, "Listen, after he gets to the hospital, you'll be met by a social worker that will ask you some questions. Be prepared. It's routine, but she'll want to know about your home life to kind of determine if he needs counseling, whatever, okay? Try not to be too emotional. They look for, um . . ." he picks his words carefully, "*signs* in a home." I nod, picking up on the warning, confused.

Signs? A social worker? Signs of what?

"Call me after he's home. Let me know what's going on. I'm still checking out some other things that you probably need to know about. For now, go take care of your boy." He nods toward the edge, where the disembodied voices are getting louder. "They're bringing him up now."

Never had I seen a more beautiful sight than my son, carefully tucked into a makeshift sling, being helped over the precipice by the police and handed to the paramedics. I cover him in hugs and kisses while the paramedics stand by patiently. One of them slaps tears off his face. Another is smiling. Chad's arm is in a sling, his face is covered with scratches that have bled, then dried. His hoodie is torn in several places, and his hair is matted with blood. His eyes are bleary.

"Mom," he says, and tears start at the corners of his eyes. "Mom, I'm sorry. Don't worry 'bout me, don't worry," he slurs.

The paramedics gently step in. "Ma'am, your son needs to be checked out. He's not able to tell us where he hurts right now. You can ride with us, but we need to go now, in case he has a head injury." I reluctantly release my hold on my son and follow the stretcher to the ambulance. I glance over my shoulder and watch Detective Faraday's tail lights disappear down the hill.

I turn my head to the river grinding its way west, into the sunset. The water ebbs and swells with laps of sun-kissed gold. The sky is an ethereal pink and blue. A few birds circle overhead. My eyes register the beauty, but it bounces away. My mind is a jumble of jagged edges.

A hand beckons me inside the ambulance.

After an hour of settling Chad in at the hospital, a bottle of water and two packages of Twix, I check in with my life. Lonnie assures me all is well on the home front, but my clients need some attention tomorrow. He says Jon's automotive clients are fine, have approved the final changes on their proofs, and are rather vocal in their appreciation of the new, female rep.

Peter and Mimi, who by this time are freaking out about where their mom is, gush with relief when I call. When I tell them what has happened, they are silent. I know the trauma will take some time to unpack, but I cannot think too far ahead. Automatic pilot seems to be operative, and I just do the next thing that presents itself. I assure them I'll be home soon, give them a few chores, talk about homework, tell them to lock all doors and stay home. Mimi grunts in disapproval, but knows better than to push it with a mom who is one hair's breadth away from insanity. I quickly call Jon Hoyt, apologize for missing another meeting, and schedule another. His voice is irritated, and I can't blame him.

Then the social worker walks in.

Probably not the best time.

I gaze at my son, breathing deeply into an oxygen mask on the single bed, covered in a hospital-issue, thin, white blanket that does nothing to ease the chill. He is hooked to an IV, which is forcing fluids. They have taken a tox screen, and are tallying results in a lab that is on-site, so I should know quickly what is in his system. I do *not* want to know what Chad has been taking. It is easier, sometimes, not to know. Things will probably work themselves out, anyway, I tell myself. Whatever it is will go away eventually, and things will be all right again.

"Mrs. Lewis?"

I feel like I am carrying a backpack loaded with bricks when I stand to greet the stranger who has entered the holy ground which contains my son, who, as it turns out, *was* indeed missing.

"Ms.," I correct her.

She extends her hand. "Thelma Wells."

I clasp her hand. She seems like a concerned neighbor that has dropped by to extend sympathy and ask if she should coordinate meals for us the next few days. But I have been prepared by my new best friend, the detective, who has insinuated government intervention if certain signs are present. I am cautious.

"Ms. Lewis," she continues, "I'm here merely as a service for the hospital – to see if you need anything, or if there is a way to help." She smiles brightly.

I say nothing, and fold my arms over my chest. My face is impassive as I wait to hear what more she has to say.

Her smile falters. "Um, so what happened?"

My head tilts questioningly. I am thinking, and why, exactly, is this any of your business?

"He fell," I state bluntly, and sit down. "This is not a good time, Thelma." She assures me with flaps of her well-endowed, chocolate arms that she knows her timing is unfortunate, but tells me in these situations it is best to talk quickly.

"Talk about what?" I stare at her, my mouth hard.

"Well, about what happened. We like to make sure we have the right information in our reports."

My eyes slit. She is on dangerous ground, and I am on the brink of insanity. A powder keg, and she is intent, apparently, on lighting the fuse.

"Information? Reports? What. The. Hell. *Are you talking about?*"

She stutters a bit, then continues, "Well, we have to fill out these reports. It's government mandated."

Oh. *That* helps. Just what I want to do right now. Please some freakin', intrusive, government agency.

"You have got to be kidding! My son has just been restored to me! He is injured! I am not talking to you right now! Go away!"

Instead of leaving, she pulls up a chair, and lowers her voice to a whisper. She smells pleasantly of talcum powder.

"Ms. Lewis, if you don't tell me what happened, I am required to report that you are uncooperative and argumentative. That will not be good for you. Better to just give me a few sentences about what happened."

To my utter consternation, my eyes fill with tears. I stumble through the story, she takes notes, nods at me apologetically, and leaves. I cannot imagine a worse job than the one she has. My son stirs. I approach the bed.

"Mom?" His eyes open and focus on my face. I smile at him and take his hand in mine. "Yep, right here, honey."

He sighs, then carefully rotates his head, taking in the IV, the medical trays, the testing equipment. "Guess you'll know what's going on pretty soon now."

My eyes widen."What do you mean?"

"What I've been taking." *Drugs.* He means *drugs,* my mind screams. I push aside the implications.

"Son," I say gently. "We'll work this out. We will. Just sleep."

"Mom, you just don't know, do you?" I stare at him intently, listening.

"I've been doin' this for a while. I know it's wrong, but it's a way I can feel . . . happy. Like there's nothing bad going on. Like we are a normal family."

I look away. I can't cry anymore. The tears have finally dried up inside me, leaving behind a vacant stare. Chad's hand squeezes mine, and he goes back to sleep.

CHAPTER 43

Hours later, lying in bed unable to sleep, my mind rehashes the day's events for the hundredth time. One would think the hamster in my brain would tire of the exercise wheel after a while. Tomorrow, I will have to down gallons of coffee in order to make it through. Probably a *four*-shot latte tomorrow morning. Lydia won't know what to say.

I twist my head to locate my phone and press the screen. Two forty-five a.m. Great.

Might as well get up, do the milk and cookies thing. I throw off the comforter and pad down the hallway, where my laptop sits, alertly blinking availability. I figure Findamatch would be a great comfort right now. Milk and cookies don't hold a candle to Findamatch.

I glance down the hallway, toward Chad's empty room. I am grateful he is safely cocooned in a hospital bed. Tomorrow, I've arranged with Phil to work a half-day, then take Chad home if all checks out. I had already contacted Patrick McAllister from Windsor Academy, and he'd been quietly supportive and told me he'd have Chad's assignments waiting for him as soon as he was ready to return to school.

The compartment in my mind reserved for Chad is quickly emptying, and tomorrow, I am supposing, it will be upturned and shaken vigorously. I push this thought aside. Right now I am grinning for the first time in two days, and it's all because of Findamatch.com.

I quickly log in and see five, blinking "You've Got a Message!" icons. My heart flutters. I am somewhat disgusted that I can feel anticipatory in my current crisis, but feel I've earned it. Not like I am drinking myself into oblivion. Not like I am having multiple affairs, or taking drugs. It's just a harmless trip down fantasy lane in the dark quiet of my hallway.

The adrenaline rush starts in my brain, tingles through my chest, then ends in a pleasurable, all-encompassing surge of endorphins. The feeling is nearly impossible to resist. I click on the first message.

"Dreamsicle, you have certainly picked out the right nickname, because after reading your profile and looking at your pictures, I feel you will make all my dreams come true . . . ." What a loser. I click on his profile anyway, just to look at his picture, which confirms my first impression. Ahh, no. He ends up in the virtual trash. I click on the next one.

"Dreamsicle, sounds like we should talk. We have a lot in common. I'm a sales rep by day, an actual person by night. After work, I morph into an interesting, fun guy instead of a numbers-driven, irritating drone. Can I get an amen? I see you're a rep, too. What do you sell? I see you have kids, me too. Love being a dad. Not fun being a single one, but hey, it is what it is. So read my profile. Let me know what you think. Reach out. Road Warrior"

I like this one, and click on his profile, where a great, sculpted face with an edgy, messy haircut looks at me with brown puppy eyes under thick, dark brows. His full-length shows him in professional attire, including sport coat and crisp, white shirt and khakis. I nearly wet myself. I wonder if responding to him in the wee hours of the morning will seem too forward?

Certainly not.

My response: "Road Warrior, you sound fun and interesting. I, too, morph into a semi-interesting person after work. I love being a mom, but wish I had more time to actually *be* a mom. So tell me about yourself, what do you sell? Where's home for you? All the typical, boring, get-it-out-of-the-way stuff. And more importantly, how current are your pics? Thought I'd beat you to it. I bet we could share war stories about how we've been burned in that area! Looking forward to hearing from you, Dreamsicle"

I read my response over a few times, and decide it is fine. Middle-of-the-road. Not too interested, not too uninterested. The flip side of the line about war stories should clearly communicate that he better match up to his pics. The leprechaun experience is still fresh. My palm drifts over my mouth to cover a yawn, and I reach toward the ceiling in a long stretch. The time icon on the laptop screen says four thirty a.m. Maybe I can catch a few extra minutes' sleep if I hurry. I glance at the still-blinking messages, and quickly click on each, not bothering to read the messages, and go straight to their pictures. After Road Warrior, they might as well be toothless, homeless old men.

I drag them all into the trash and go to bed. My mind spins at the prospect of talking to Road Warrior, and I smile myself to sleep, temporarily lulled by visions of nicely fitting, knife-creased khakis dancing in my head.

Maybe it will give me some relief from the jarring, repetitive, visual of my bloody, injured son being pulled over a cliff on the Savannah River.

The next morning is a blur of abbreviated explanations to Peter and Mimi, homework reminders, lunch-packing, ironing and throwing long-neglected laundry into the washer. I scramble around the kitchen after the kids leave for school, frantically wiping counters, trying to attain some sense of order since I'd effectively been on autopilot for the past few days and stuff is strewn everywhere.

Chad is still sleeping off the sedative, and I'd left a text on his phone, which is certainly the first thing his eyes will land on the minute they open. When had he traded the beloved stuffed puppy he used to sleep with for a cell phone? Not that long ago, actually, I smile to myself. I pause and take stock of the busy morning before me: re-schedule meeting with Jon, several meetings with my accounts, quick scan of Jon's proofs before they go to press, pick up Chad and his homework assignments from Windsor Academy, and . . . my mind sputters to a stall.

Birdie.

I glance at the time. Eight fifteen. Time to head out the door. I pour the last of the coffee into my travel mug, reluctantly foregoing Starbucks this morning in the interests of trying to be somewhere, anywhere, on time. I stop in front of the mirror in the foyer and assess my reflection.

I have on a cropped, mustard-yellow jacket over a tan and yellow jersey top with a cowl neck. Paired with a dark brown pencil skirt, dark brown hose and brown leather boots with fringe at the sides. I hastily search my mind to make sure I don't have another golf cart episode looming, assure myself this does not take place until next week, and decide the outfit is appropriate. My hair is behaving today, loosely swinging to my shoulders in a longish bob, bangs swept to one side.

I square my shoulders and hold my travel mug aloft in a mock salute to my image before I dash out the door.

CHAPTER 44

The minute I'm in my chair, Darlene appears at my elbow. I turn toward her, startled, tell her good morning, drop my purse in its drawer with a clunk.

"What's up?" My mind quickly runs a slideshow of all things Darlene.

She glances toward the managers' offices, which are empty this time of the day, due to the morning congregational around coffee brewing in the neutral zone between production and sales. This gives me a clue as to topic.

I sigh, wondering if my life will ever yield a boring series of non-events. A non-event-life is my goal from now on. Go to work. Go home. Raise kids. Clean house. That is all.

Darlene's mouth is moving, and I focus on her face.

"Izzy, I just vant to tell you quickly that Birdie is on fire this morning! I am not sure what is going on, but I heard your name mentioned when I walked past the coffee break area a few minutes ago." She has two dahlias in a vase in her hands, and places it on my desk. "For good luck," she says. "Vhen are we getting together?"

"Soon, Darlene. Very soon. I have lots going on." I shake my head and roll my eyes. "It's just beyond belief."

We make a date to meet after work at The Cup and Saucer, a familiar watering hole in the River's Edge District. As I watch her retreating back, I am not sure if knowing Birdie is on the warpath is a good thing or a bad thing. I probably would have retained my somewhat cheerful demeanor if I had not known, but on the other hand, knowing has put me on high alert. A defensive tension propels me forward.

I pick up the phone to call Jon. He answers on the third ring. "Hey Jon," I begin, and wait for a response, which is not forthcoming. I imagine the stony silence is accompanied by an equally stony expression.

"Jon, I need to explain . . . ."

"No need, Izzy. I'm pretty clear about what's going on."

My brow furrows. This was going to be harder than I thought. "No," I state sternly, "you really *don't* know, Jon. From last Tuesday night until today, my life has been pure hell, and things are not as they seem."

Jon snorts. "Really? Fill me in, please." The sarcasm rips through me like a knife.

I don't know why, exactly, but having Jon on my side is important.

"For one thing, Birdie is – " I screech to a verbal halt, thinking, how stupid can

I be? Management spot-checks these phones! This conversation might be recorded!"

"Birdie is what?" Jon says.

"Um, Jon, when can we reschedule our time to meet? I don't need to discuss these things on the phone, in person would be better."

"So, we are going to make a *third* appointment so I can be stood up again? Really?"

"Jon, I'm sorry, but there are actual reasons why I was not able to make it."

He pauses, then says, "Okay. One more time, but that's it. How about my house? Then if you stand me up, at least I won't have made a drive for nothing."

I agree to a time, then hang up. Lonnie is at his desk by now, eyeing me strangely.

"Sounds serious," he says, flipping through proofs, and handing me several. "These are going to press in thirty minutes. If you need changes, tell me now." I hurriedly glance through. Satisfied that they are correct, I hand them back to him after initialing with a red marker. "Thanks," he says. "Now, what's up?"

"Oh, just having trouble getting together with Jon to talk about his accounts, and he's getting a bit perturbed about it. That's all." I smile at him, then resume eyeing my to-do-list.

He puts his head down and whispers, "Incoming, twelve o-clock," and picks up his phone.

I look up and see Birdie barreling toward me, his mouth in a firm, hard line, effectively hiding the perpetual blaze of white teeth. I look up at him as if I haven't a care in the world. "Why, good morning, Birdie! And how are you this fine day?"

He stands beside the cube, arms crossed, legs apart. Militant.

"Don't know yet. Can I see you in my office?"

Fortunately, Winston slides into the pod at this most opportune of moments, sensing danger in the air. "Mornin' Izzy," he says, ignoring Birdie. "Remember, we have a meeting," he slides his gaze toward the empty conference room in the corner, "I reserved the conference room." Bless Winston, bless his pea-pickin' little heart, I chant, inwardly grinning ear-to-ear.

I give Birdie my most apologetic, hangdog expression, and say, "Birdie, can this wait? Winston and I have some things to discuss and we're on deadline . . ." I let the unspoken priority hang in the air. Printing deadlines always trump everything, and he knows it.

He glares at me and puts his hands on his hips.

"Okay. But I need to see you as soon as you are done. It's urgent." With that, he turns abruptly and strides to his office, slamming the door behind him.

"Brother," Winston exclaims, pulling off his driving beret and sunglasses and seating himself. "Looks like we need to have a meeting, right?"

I smile at him, my hand over my heart, which is beating wildly. "Right!" I laugh in relief, making sure Birdie is not peering out of his office. Grabbing my travel mug, which still holds a bit of coffee, I say, "Let's go!" Winston scoops up his fresh newspaper and follows me. We enter the conference room and shut the door.

"Hope this room isn't reserved by someone else," he quips.

"Yeah, no kidding. I thought Birdie's eyes were gonna bug out of his head when you said that! Perfect timing, Pod-King!"

Winston makes a courtly bow at the waist. "My pleasure, Pod-Queen." He straightens, pulls out a chair from under the conference table, sits. "Now, *what the heck is going on?*"

I figure it's time to dump my story. I don't need isolation and secrets, I need help and all the support I can get. I start at the beginning, including the counterfeit emails, the snarky comments around my desk, the off-color jokes and insinuations. When I get to the incident at Raphael's, his newspaper, which he has neatly unfolded in front of him, thinking we were simply going to waste thirty minutes before heading back to our desks, is forgotten. He leans forward eagerly.

"You have got to be kidding! *Then* what happened? I swear, Izzy, you should write a book!"

I gaze at him with sad eyes.

"Whatever, Winston. I have been through some rough stuff the past couple weeks, all because I have blinders on, I think. Well, you'll never believe it, but my detective . . . ."

"Detective?" he chokes out. "What detective? Have I missed something?" I sigh and quickly fill him in on the stalker, Jacob, and the restraining order; purposely omitting the Chad situation. Only so much a person can take at one time.

He flings his arms out wide as he throws himself against the back of his chair. "I can't believe you've been going through all this alone, Izzy." He regards me with eyes filled with concern. "I'm giving prayer for you more priority, that's a promise." He looks at the ceiling and crosses his arms. "So where were we, I mean, at Raphael's with Birdie?"

I continue, "He's threatening to lie about me to Phil – about work issues and my performance – if I don't *see things his way*. I have yet to know what that means, exactly, but at any rate, as he's really coming down hard, in walks my own personal guardian angel, Detective Faraday."

Winston's eyes shine with interest. "Maybe he is a guardian angel. Like me!" He laughs. "What timing!"

"Well, after that, it was all over. I could see Birdie backing off. Detective Faraday didn't trust him right away and could see I was not myself, so he's doing a little background on him right now, I think. After Detective Faraday and his wife left to have dinner, I started feeling nauseous, and Birdie helped me outside."

My eyes flash in anger. "Not that I wanted him to touch me!" Winston regarded me with regret, understanding. "I told him to get his hands off me, but I literally couldn't walk so he helped me down the steps onto the sidewalk. Guess who I ran into outside?"

Winston is barely breathing. "Who?"

"Jon."

Winston's forehead creases, mind spinning. "Jon?"

"*Hoyt*," I intone soberly. The implications hit Winston two seconds later. I watch his face unfurl from confusion to wide-eyed shock. "Oh no! Jon probably thought you and Birdie were, ahhh . . ."

I nod up and down slowly, my eyelids at half-mast, and cross my arms. "Yep."

Winston drops his head into his hands, his elbows resting on his knees. "This is killin' me, Izzy. I can't believe it." He lifts his face to mine. "What are you going to do?"

"Punt," I say, and push off the chair. "Thanks for the rescue today. You have no idea how much I appreciate it." I leave him staring after me, his lanyard, for once, untouched.

The morning creeps by like a senior citizen with a walker.

I perform the perfunctory tasks of touching base with clients, instructions to Lonnie, and a brief check-in with Darlene. I have texted Chad, and he responded he's groggy but among the living, so I pack up to head to the hospital, pick him up, take him home. The morning winds down, and my mind turns to the next steps I must take to gather Chad from the hospital and settle him at home.

Standing before the elevator lost in thought, I feel steps behind me, and with a sinking heart, realize it is probably Birdie. Not today, I whisper to myself, not today! He quietly stands behind me, waiting. I can smell the stink of his cigar-breath. I have no choice but to turn around.

"Birdie!" I give him my best pleasant surprise face.

He stands with his hands clasped behind him. "Izzy, I need you to come in my office. Right. Now." Inside, I crumple in defeat. Why hadn't I taken the stairs? Again, the stupid, ancient elevator thwarts a timely escape. When will I learn?

I mumble assent, and follow him to his office. He holds the door open for me, indicates with a stern point where I should sit, and closes the door behind us. I drop my purse, notebook and bag on the floor and sit, folding my hands in my lap. I resist the notion to extend my arms so he can hit me with a ruler or something.

He sits behind his desk, pulls his chair forward, plops his elbows on top of the desk and clasps his hands. His eyes, icy and penetrating, bore into mine. I respond with an icy stare of my own. I am a mother who has just had her son restored. Hear me roar.

"Phil has informed me you are now reporting to him." He waits for the effect this has on me. I do not react, but hold his gaze. When I do not respond, he continues, "I want to know why, Izzy. And I want to know *now*."

He rolls his chair back and the wheels squeak on the rug protector under the desk. The tufted, blood-red leather accentuates his red-veined, angry eyes. One of his hands strokes his chin as he watches me. I imagine a rattlesnake has the same expression right before it strikes.

My mind is on overdrive. The stress of Chad, Jon's accounts, dealing with Birdie, the stalker . . . all of it is about to push me over the edge. Foremost on my mind is my son, and no snake-from-hell is going to trap me in his office and keep me from him. I know I am on dangerous ground right now, and the next words may be fatal to my job, so I am quiet, which Birdie interprets as withholding.

He slaps his hands on the desk, palms down, and stands. "WHAT IS GOING ON?" he yells. I am so stunned, I nearly fall out of my chair. Does he really want other people to know he loses control like this? His voice drops to a sinister whisper. He leans toward me across the desk and says, "If you think I am not serious about what I said in Raphael's the other night, you are mistaken. Abide by my rules, or you'll find yourself without a job. Or worse."

I look at him with disgust. I just cannot take any more of this, and Chad is waiting for me. Deliberately, slowly, I pick up my purse, my bag, my notebook, and stand.

"I think, Birdie, that you should talk to HR about your concerns. At this point it is not only out of my hands, but I am not your responsibility now, either."

He is very still, watching. I feel the slightest tremor of fear. I shrug my purse into a better position on my shoulder.

"Don't think you can get away with this, Birdie." His eyes never leave mine. He tents his hands and leans back in his chair as I walk out the door. His smile is unnerving. My posture is braver than I feel, but I manage to propel myself out of his office.

Without a backward glance, I jerk open the door to the stairs and run down them as fast as I can, not stopping until I am locked into my Honda. My heart is beating so fast that I force myself to take deep breaths so I will not hyperventilate. The look on Birdie's face as I prepared to leave was truly memorable, and I chuckle at the thought. But not before I am well away from the *Sentinel* building and my breathing is back to normal.

Thirty minutes later I check Chad out and wheel him to the car in a wheelchair, which he finds hilarious. Twenty minutes after that we unload everything at home, and I settle him in his bed with juice, a muffin, and the promise of a serious conversation.

I push thoughts of Birdie's intimidation to the back of my mind, and concentrate on the blessing of getting Chad back in one piece. After all, I can only concentrate on one crisis at a time.

My laughter is brittle. When had that ever stopped them from coming all at once?

Later that afternoon, I tiptoe upstairs to check on my son. I knock softly on his door, and push it halfway open. Long shadows reach through the windows across his bed in the waning daylight. He sits at his desk, laptop open.

"Oh, hi, Mom." He closes the computer and turns to me expectantly. "Come on in. I slept for a while. Guess it's time to talk, huh?"

His eyes are clear and direct. I notice he's taken a shower. I'd been wondering if his disjointed attire and hazy demeanor had been a phase, but apparently, according to last night's tox screen, not. They'd found traces of marijuana and narcotics, but not in life-altering amounts.

"Yeah. Want to come to the den?"

He agrees and slowly walks behind me, favoring his injuries, downstairs to our cozy den. I sit in my favorite recliner, and he lowers himself carefully into a loveseat opposite. The antique clock on the wall ticks a steady metronome beat. I switch on the lamp on the accent table by the recliner.

Bookcases stuffed to capacity tuck against walls covered with framed family photos and random pieces of art. A cozy, welcoming atmosphere I'd carefully cultivated, and if someone entered my home, they would feel embraced by its warmth.

It mocks me now.

I gaze at Chad, the words bumping up against themselves awkwardly in my mind. "Your tox screen was troubling," I finally say.

Chad hangs his head. "Yeah. It would have been."

"How long?"

"A couple years."

I nod, inwardly stunned, but too exhausted by everything to respond with the shrieking that should accompany such a revelation. "Well, okay, wanna tell me why? How?"

He stumbles through a series of events that I'd downplayed in his life. The rejection from a couple of school events. The teachers that had underestimated him. His increasing fear that mom was unavailable. His dad's uninvolvement in his life. Our family's financial burdens. My late night meetings with guys.

I listen attentively. "How did you know when I was out? I was so careful not to wake you guys."

Chad shrugs. "Mom, you don't think we always *stay* asleep when you are gone, do you? We know you're out a lot. We all think about what would happen if you are away and something, well, what if someone got in? What would we do? We don't know where you are . . ." his voice trails off and his eyes rivet to the southwestern-themed area rug on the hardwood floor.

I am silent. My arms are crossed, which I note as defensiveness. I uncross them and wish I didn't think about stuff like that.

I sigh deeply. "Chad, you know I am really busy with work and trying to keep up with the house, getting you guys to your school events . . . online dating is really the most efficient way for me to meet men that, um, might be candidates for a man around here permanently." I sound lame, even to me.

He chuckles. "Yeah, right, Mom, whatever! So when you're gone, and Mimi has a nightmare and calls for you and you're not here, then me or Peter get to take care of her." He glares at me. "She needs *you*, Mom."

I feel a distinct burn in the pit of my stomach. And not only Mimi, but by implication, my sons as well, I think. I nod, and say, "I understand." Chad's eyes search mine.

"Do you? Do you really?"

I decide to switch gears. I'm supposed to be the one in control, not Chad. I take a deep breath.

"So, Chad, how serious is the drug thing? Are you going to need help getting off them? Because there is no option, you know. You can't just kind of . . . try drugs, play with them . . . without it becoming a bigger problem. We need to deal with it now."

"Depends," he says. "How serious is the online dating thing, Mom? Is it a bigger problem than you think? Are you gonna deal with it? I'll deal with mine if you deal with yours."

"It's not the same thing at all, Chad – "

"Oh yeah?" Chad sneers. "*Every night*, Mom. When's the last time you didn't go out? Except for when you just had to stay in for something with us or whatever, it's every, stinkin' night! I'd call that a *problem*!"

This conversation had not turned out as I wanted it to at all. The tables have turned, and I am sitting in the uncomfortable searchlight of my son's accusatory gaze. He needs some kind of deal, here, and I need to *man up. Woman up,* I correct myself. I need to *woman up.*

"Okay. If I make some changes, will you stay away from drugs?"

He looks down at the rug. "Yeah, I will. They're really not that fun anymore, anyway." His eyes lift to my face. "What are you gonna change?"

"How about if I agree to only go out on weekends?" Chad considers a minute, then nods. "That'd be better."

"Doesn't mean I am going to quit online dating, though," I quickly disclaim. "Not affecting you guys at all."

Chad rolls his eyes. "Sure, mom. And what if I just smoke a little pot on the side? Maybe just weekends? This conversation over?"

"It is if you're going to make some changes, son. You scared me to death! And Peter and Mimi, too! Please, if you're feeling scared, or something I'm doing bothers you, just come talk to me. I'll listen, I promise. And I also promise . . . to make more time for you. I'm sorry . . . so sorry honey, that I've been distracted. That I haven't noticed that your – " I quickly turn my face away and swipe at tears, at a loss as what to say next.

My arms open and Chad walks into them for a hug, a confused young man still needing his mom. *Really* needing his mom.

I had some schedule-shuffling to do. Something had to change.

After the hug, he mumbles he's going to go play video games. I watch his back recede up the stairs. His pajama pants are decorated with miniature Spongebobs. I run upstairs to toss on a T-shirt and jeans, intent on fully engaging with my household the rest of the day.

As I pass my laptop in the upstairs hallway, I snap it shut.

CHAPTER 45

"Top o' the mornin' to ya, Izzy!" Lydia smiles out the window as she hands me the latte. "How's it going?"

I push my sunglasses on top of my head, look at her, sip the coffee. "Not wonderful."

She tilts her head, concerned. "Kids?"

I nod affirmatively. "And other stuff, too. Complicated." I take another sip of coffee and glance in the rear-view at the twenty-odd cars lined up behind me. "Better go, I'm holdin' things up." I lift my latte in salute.

"Hang in there, Izzy!" she says as I drive off. Yeah, I mumble to myself, putting the coffee in my console cup holder. By a thread.

On the way to work, I turn off the news blaring from my radio. What am I supposed to do about Birdie? How am I going to be able to work in a hostile environment? Something has to give, and I am hoping it's not my job. I reach for the latte and take another sip. The freeway is crammed today and moving slow, so I have plenty of time to think. I push the thought of Birdie away and replace it with Chad. He'd been almost cheerful this morning before school, which of course, made me suspicious.

I'd told Peter and Mimi that we needed a family conference after school today, and they agreed. I am not looking forward to it, but it has to be done. By the time I pull into the parking lot, I am tense and irritable and hoping to avoid Birdie. Taking the stairs two at a time, I jerk open the door to the sales floor, and lo and behold, there he is right in front of me.

The Bird in all his thuggish glory. Diamond cufflinks. Perky pocket kerchief. Grin in place. Our conversation deftly buried under the compost heap of business as usual.

"Morning, Izzy!" His eyes dare me. I stare at him flatly, and walk to my desk. Not quite a full ignore, but close. He continues down the stairs. I sit at my desk and look around me, taking in the sights and smells and sounds. Assistants, as usual, are busily dropping piles of proofs on desks. Laughter erupts from the glass-walled office in the corner where Phil and Milton are exchanging pleasantries. Darlene waves at me from her desk at the back of the room, leaning forward over the dahlias to see me. A wisp of expensive men's cologne curls pleasantly under my nose from a nearby cubicle whose occupant has just arrived.

The hum of conversation, ringing phones, energetic steps up and down the wide linoleum hallway – all reassuring sounds. Normal sounds. God, what I'd give for normal! I feel tears and will them away. Compartmentalize, Izzy. You have work to do. Mouths to feed. Kids to raise. Falling apart is not an option.

Winston arrives, stands at the coat rack, shrugs out of his wool overcoat, and inserts it among the others. He then places his hat on the shelf on top of the rack, smiles at me, walks around to his spot in the pod.

"Morning, Pod-Queen! You're looking lovely today!" His demeanor changes abruptly. He leans forward, his voice dropping, "So how're things?"

I smile at him half-heartedly. "Mornin', Pod-King. Oh, you know, life goes on. It'll work out. Things are not good, really, but I am doing the best I can. One thing at a time, right?"

"Right!" he beams. I can tell the drama wore on him yesterday. Per our conversations over the years, I know he has enough drama in his own life without internalizing mine.

"Winston, can't thank you enough for yesterday." My head is down, perusing the fresh newspaper. The crisp, broadsheet pages rustle comfortingly as I turn them, scanning each.

"Never mind, Izzy," he says generously, "you've bailed me out on more than one occasion, too." I glance at him. He is opening his newspaper, flattening it with his thumb, then licking it to turn to his favorite section, Entertainment. The one with the comics and the crossword puzzle.

He sips coffee from a Jiffy Mart cup. "So how's the online dating going?" His eyes grow concerned, and he quickly adds, "If you have time lately, um, because of, ahh, you know . . . ." He shrugs apologetically.

I chuckle. "Yeah, well unfortunately, I always seem to be able to find time for that! It's going great, as a matter of fact, I met a guy who I think might have potential."

"Imagine that!" He smiles. "What ever happened to Brad? I think that is the last guy you told me about that had potential."

"Oh, he's still around," I say, flirtatiously, cutting my eyes at him. I am immediately dismayed. How can I think about men with several crises revolving around me? Any one of which could change my circumstances dramatically with a swift twist of fate. I grow quiet, thinking about how neatly I have compartmentalized my problems over the past years since the last divorce.

"I don't know, Winston, it just doesn't seem to be working anymore."

Winston's eyes snap from his newspaper to my face. "What doesn't seem to be working?"

"Life." I shrug, and pick up my ringing landline.

"Izzy, *Sentinel*."

"Hi, Izzy. Detective Faraday."

"Oh, Hi, Detective! How are you today?"

"Fine. Checking on Chad. How is he?"

"He's good. We've kind of processed, and I'm getting the kids together tonight to talk through stuff. He's been real honest with me about what's going on."

"Good, that's good, Izzy. Getting a kid his age to talk is an accomplishment. The single parent thing, well, that's tough on them. And you."

I am silent. He clears his throat and continues. "Okay, great, wanted an update, and also to let you know I've done some checking on your boss."

My eyes grow wide. "And?"

He continues, "And I found what appears to be an alias. Seems he went by Elias Comstock when he lived in St. Louis. He had a wholesale business that outsourced manufacturing to Columbia and Mexico." I hear papers rustle, and imagine him squinting at tiny lines of type. The rustling ends, and he says, "Name of the company was Cacciatore Manufacturing."

"Cacciatore?"

"Means "hunter" in Italian," Faraday explains.

I feel my eyebrows pull together. "Okay. So, is this important?"

"Yeah, could be." He pauses, and I picture him playing with stuff on his desk with his hands. I'd seen him do it. When he's thinking, he fondles things on his desk, like Winston's lanyard habit. "He's had a couple of arrests in St. Louis. Nothing that would stick, though. Also, and this should interest you, some misdemeanor sexual harassment charges. My best guess – in addition to his lack of polish where ladies are concerned – is that he's been involved in the drug trade. A wholesale business is a great cover for that kind of thing. I'm continuing to dig, but I'd appreciate it if you'd pay attention to any unusual travel activity on his part that's not related to the job."

"Wow. That would explain a lot. The threats, the aggression. That's kind of how I feel around him – like he's predatory."

"Yeah," he says, "I felt it too. I told you I had this radar thing goin' on. He kind of made it light up the night I met him. How's the stalker? Staying away like a good boy?"

"As far as I know. No notes, no calls. Maybe he's one problem I can forget about."

Detective Faraday chuckled. "Let's hope so. Not often that I run across a person going through all this stuff at the same time. Be alert where that guy is concerned. Don't let down on locking the doors, keeping the exterior lights on, all that, okay?"

I mumble assent, assessing the warmth that is coursing through me. What I wouldn't give to find a guy like Detective Faraday. I'd scoop him off the market so quick his head would spin.

A sigh escapes before I can reel it in.

He interprets this as discouragement, and responds, "Izzy, what you are going through is hard, but it'll be over. Don't forget, all problems can be solved. You'll find your way through this, and you'll come out on the other side a winner. You will, Izzy."

His kindness almost puts me over the slender edge to which I am clinging. Fortunately, Lonnie always keeps a box of tissues on his desk, and I reach over and snag one before a pond of snot and tears forms on my desk. I snuffle my thanks, say good-bye, and hang up.

Pathetic. Just pathetic.

I wipe my face with the mass of tissue, grab my purse and walk quickly to the ladies' room to repair the damage.

As I exit, I nearly crash into Jon. He stiffly acknowledges me.

"Jon! You're back!" Idiotic thing to say. I am perfectly aware that he's back.

"Yep. How're things going?" He stands, waiting, looking around the room instead of at me. A little reparation is definitely in order.

"Listen Jon, we need to talk as soon as possible. Instead of meeting at your house, how about lunch today? My treat."

He smiles thinly. "Okay, but my treat, because you've been taking care of my accounts."

I smile back and agree.

Promptly at 11:30, Jon fidgets at my desk, shifting from one leg to the other, as I wrap up a busy morning of contacting clients and making appointments. I feel like a juggler in my own personal circus, and I'm dropping balls all over the place. Unless I want to see my commissions sail out the window, I need to catch up on face-to-face time with my larger accounts.

I look up at Jon, who says with a grin, "Not gonna stand me up this time, Izzy. Ready?"

I run a hand through my hair and glance at my wrist. "Wow! Already lunch time! Yeah, I guess. Give me a minute." I reach in a drawer for my purse, slip my cell into it, stand, and push my chair under the desk.

"What a nag you are, Jon," I say, kidding.

"I've been told that before," he says. Extends a gracious hand toward the elevator. "After you."

Jon and I wait in front of the elevator while it rumbles up to the third floor, stops for an interminably long period of time, then rumbles down to the second with a thump. The doors slowly slide open, revealing, of course, who else? My best friend and nightmare, the Birdster. He barely looks at me and strides past us to his office, almost, but not quite, slamming the door behind him.

"Nice guy," Jon says, nodding toward Birdie.

"The best," I respond.

CHAPTER 46

The deli is semi-crowded, a comfortable crush of twenty-somethings that live and work in the artsy area around River's Edge, administrative types of all ages from various businesses that are housed downtown, and tie-and-suited financial types from investment firms or banks. Jon and I yell over the counter our preferences to the energetic sandwich-assemblers and snag and pay for them at counter's end, where another employee rings up the meal. I follow Jon to a four-top in a dark corner, somewhat removed from the fray. He sets down his tray, relieving it of content.

"So we can talk," he explains, indicating the table location. I nod, and unload my tray as well. He shoves out a hand for my tray, puts it on top of his, deposits both on a red cart, and returns.

I shrug out of my jacket and wrap it on the back of my chair. I look at him a little uncertainly. "Well, dig in," he says, and picks up his sandwich for a large bite. I follow suit, and for a minute, we both chew on what to say next.

"So," Jon begins, picking up the napkin in his lap and swiping his mouth, "you gonna fill me in? And by the way, I've had nothing but compliments about your work with my accounts." He looks at me expectantly. "Thanks."

I smile, and finish chewing my bite. "No problem," I say, and quickly napkin-dab, which transfers most of my lipstick to the napkin.

"They were nice guys. I didn't know you did so much legwork for those accounts! I couldn't believe everything they expected me to do. And you do it every, single week, right?"

Jon nods. "Yeah, but you get used to it after a while. And they know me so well, once in a while they'll help out, or run the same cars in the ad. There are shortcuts." He shrugs, picks up his sandwich for another bite, and eyes the fat dill pickle perched on the side of his plate. I tell him the golf cart story, and how I'd worn a skirt the day at Ardmore. He chuckles, and says, "Yeah, Tom told me about that. Said he enjoyed the short skirt."

I scowl at him, a hamster-scowl, cheeks stuffed with Swiss-and-turkey-on-rye. Jon throws his head back and laughs, nearly choking on a bite of sandwich.

When I've swallowed the huge mouthful, I remark, "Well, I for one, will not be pursuing your accounts. You can have those auto accounts. Way too much work."

Jon nods. "The automotive industry is tough, a marketing discipline that takes a while to understand. Plus, I don't think you know how car guys think.

Not the easiest guys in the world for a woman to work with, and they can get the wrong idea. A lot of women use their looks with those guys to get the budget. Kind of backfires on them, too."

My eyes scan his face. "What do you mean, backfires?"

"Makes 'em uncomfortable after a while. Especially married men – they either get the wrong idea and hit you up, or they act inappropriately, which eventually causes them to avoid you like the plague." He pauses to chew the sandwich, and takes a bite of pickle, trying not to spurt it all over himself and looks at me thoughtfully. "But I'm sure you know all that," he says.

His comments have pricked me, which I don't quite understand, and I wait patiently for him to continue. I'd never been called out on the way I approach male clients before. The lunch crowd is boisterous in the deli. Hungry, tray-bearing, customers walk by our table. The smells commingle in a stomach-satisfying potpourri as they pass.

He continues, "I had a few comments that were, um . . . not the kind of comments you want, Izzy, in a professional setting."

My eyebrows lift. "Really?" I lean back in my chair. "I don't think I did anything to – "

Jon interrupts. " I don't think you consciously did anything wrong, but they interpreted it that way. You might want to," he glances at my short skirt, "wear pants when you call on men. Maybe a longer skirt. And be careful . . . to edit your conversation. There's a line."

My eyes slide to the wall behind him and I bite into my sandwich, thinking. The words cut, but I don't feel he is being cruel. On the contrary, his honesty feels kind. Like we are on the same team. Jon is wrestling with the huge pickle and down to the last bite of his sandwich. He picks up another napkin from the tabletop and mops up pickle juice.

"Well, thanks, Jon. I just never really thought about it. Just kind of comes natural, you know . . . being single, I guess."

He smiles. "That's why I said something. If you are aware, you can head it off before it becomes a problem."

I nod assent. I'll have to give this revelation serious thought. Later.

For now, I need him to know about Birdie.

I clear my throat. "I really don't quite know where to begin about Birdie, but your comments kind of lead into it." His empty plate, pushed aside, bears two crumpled napkins, various sandwich and pickle remnants, and a plastic fork. He leans forward, placing his elbows carefully on the small table, folds his hands.

"Okay."

I wiggle in my chair, and organize my thoughts. "I knew I was in trouble when he rode with me to see my accounts initially," I say, figuring the beginning is as good a place to start as any.

"His primary routine to forge relationships is apparently dirty jokes, for one thing, especially around men."

Jon grunted acknowledgment. "Kinda figured that. Heard some stuff around the office."

"Well, I wrote it off, but it didn't stop. Then he talked to Lonnie, I think, and asked him a lot of inappropriate questions, mainly about my personal life, and – "

Jon interrupts, "You mean your online dating stories?" he said, smiling. "Izzy, that is common knowledge. You know that, right?"

I feel bright red spots form on each cheek. "I know people talk about it, but somehow I thought it was just, well, good-natured joking around!"

Jon shrugs. "Stuff gets blown out of proportion around a sales office, no question. Any office, for that matter." His eyes focus directly on mine. "You're a great-looking woman, Izzy. Somebody like Birdie? Well, any guy can size up his agenda. It's not all about sales quotas with him. I knew that in about two days, watchin' him. Everybody knows you've been on dating sites a lot, and yeah, your social life is kind of a joke around the office. So when I saw you with Birdie – "

"When you saw me with Birdie, you had the wrong idea!"

He studies his clasped hands and jiggles his fingers. "Yeah, to be honest, I did. Was irritated about it, too, because I had you pegged as a really nice woman."

I gasp," I *am* a nice woman!"

He looks at me and cocks his head. "I want to believe that, Izzy. I don't think you'd have helped me when I passed out a couple weeks ago if you weren't. I'm just trying to point out, that kind of situation will bite you." He crosses his arms over his chest and leans back. "Besides, I really don't know you very well, y'know. Maybe we can change that." He grins.

I sigh. "Oh great, Jon. Now *you* are hitting on me. Not helping!"

He laughs, and I make a face. Then I tell him as much as I can about what happened, starting at the point Birdie became intimidating in the office, his disguised online presence, and the threats. I throw in the detective for good measure, and tell him about Phil's support and the HR report about it that I had completed. After thirty minutes, my eyes glaze over, and I stop.

Jon's expression is kind. We don't speak for a few minutes. I become self-conscious. Have I dumped this information to the wrong person? Can he be trusted? Is he really a friend? Insecurity jabs at me.

Finally he says, "I'm sorry that you've been dealing with all this. I know you've got three kids at home, and you don't need this crap on top of everything else. It's hard enough just tryin' to make your quota every month."

I squint at him. I can almost see the wheels turning in his head. The more he processes, the more animated his expression becomes. "Birdie needs to be confronted! Does Phil know all this?"

I nod. "Yep, just told him. But Birdie got to him first. He doesn't know what to think."

Jon strokes his chin. "This is a tough situation. If I were Phil, I'd have to do some serious research. Look at the situation from different angles." He stops, heaves out a sigh. But I gotta admit, Izzy – "

"What?" I say, feeling rather warmly protected at this moment. Uh oh, Izzy, don't go there. You are vulnerable. Vulnerable and receiving-male-attention-that-feels-like-protection do not make good bedfellows. Don't say bed! Don't even *think* bed!

He continues, "I gotta tell you, that online dating stuff, it's *not* your friend. The jokes around the office kind of paint you as *woman-on-quest-for-her-man* and all that. From Phil's point of view, your reputation as a serial dater could color the situation with Birdie. Just sayin'. Somethin' to think about."

He glances uncertainly at the floor, unsure how I will receive this perspective. The ice in his Dr. Pepper has melted, making the drink an unappealing, watery tan. Underneath the glass, a wet circle sprouts; by-product of Georgia humidity.

My shoulders slump. "Yeah, I've heard that. I *hear* that. From everyone, lately. But it's hard, y'know?" I raise my eyes to his, a moment of truth pending. "It's an *escape* for me. After a hard day, some people like to drink, well I go to Findamatch.com. Doesn't seem anything but a distraction, but the more I think about it . . . maybe it is." I look over his shoulder, past people carrying trays of food, past wailing children sitting at tables with their parents, through the window to the street beyond. Think a minute about what I'd just said. "How else am I going to date? I don't have *time* to go to the gym, run marathons, join book clubs! Online dating is *efficient*. A great tool to meet guys. And I *have* met some great guys." I cross my arms. Then uncross them. "Just not *the* guy. Yet."

He nods. "Well, we all have our escape mechanisms, I guess. For me, it's about grief. It took many shapes and forms with me. Losing my wife was like getting kicked in the head. A concussion that took over my life. I drank to numb myself, and eventually it controlled me." He shrugs. "Probably still does. Working on it, though." He eyes the glass, picks it up, reconsiders and replaces it in the center of the watery circle.

My eyes probe his. I feel intimacy with another human being that is unusual.

Precious, even. I don't want it to end.

"Really? How did you, um, come to this awareness, or whatever?" I think a minute, and quickly say, "That day, in the office, when you-"

"That was it," he responds quickly. "That day, and some other things that happened. Took me a long time to realize what I was doing to myself. Phil helped me figure it out."

"You mentioned Phil before. So, did he get you in counseling or something?"

Jon smiles. "Better. He took me to this great recovery group. It was amazing to listen to other men who have gone through the same things, or worse." Jon shakes his head, threads his hands together behind his head and leans back. "Without those guys, I'd be in a rehab clinic for a long time, I think. It's cool what a simple support group will do."

His eyes slice to the right, then back at me. After a few seconds, he leans forward, plunges a hand into his pocket. When he pulls it out, it is holding a small metal object. With a smile, he extends it to me.

"Here, take this." Jon holds a well-worn, silver coin. I pluck it from his fingers and turn it over in my hands. On one side, it says *But whoever listens to Me will dwell safely, and will be secure, without fear of evil. Prov. 1:33*, and on the other *One day at a time.* "Phil put it in my hand at the hospital, and it's been a sort of touch point for me when I feel unsure of myself in this . . . well, new life I'm buildin' for myself." He shrugs, looks into my eyes. "Sounds like you need it more than me right now."

My hand closes around the coin. It feels warm. I am so grateful for this small kindness that I cannot speak. Jon seems to understand. He scrapes his chair back. "So, ready to get back to work?" I nod, put the coin in my pocket, and push off my chair, grabbing my coat.

As we walk in tandem back down Thrasher to the *Sentinel*, Jon assures me he'll keep our conversation private. "But be careful around Birdie," he says thoughtfully, "I'll poke around with the classified manager and Phil. I know all the managers have to tread lightly around potential sexual harassment stuff and Human Resources issues, but I think I can at least get impressions of what's going on. That's really great that Phil is taking you out from under Birdie's wing for a while."

I nod and roll my eyes. Jon grins.

"Can't help myself, his name invites ridicule, y'know?" He opens the door, and I hop up the three steps to the foyer and push the elevator button.

I groan when I see the elevator is stuck on the third floor. "Beat ya!" I throw the challenge over my shoulder, and run up the stairs.

CHAPTER 47

Izzy

I am buried in ad copy when my cell rings late that afternoon. I lift my head and take a breath, thinking about all I have accomplished today, which is a good thing but results in a ton of work to turn in before I can leave the office. I'd driven all over town meeting with clients and fortunately, they were receptive and interested in the new advertising opportunities I'd placed before them. Having Jon and Phil on my side has energized me. Getting back to a workday that is "normal" feels good.

But I still look at the phone as if it is going to bite me. I do not recognize the number. "Hi, this is Izzy . . . ?"

A brisk, warm voice responds. "Hey, Izzy, this is Thelma. From the hospital? How's Chad doing?"

I feel my forehead furrow, then clear. "Oh, yes, Thelma. Social Worker. Hi, how are you?"

"Good," she says. "Doing follow-up stuff today." She waits for me to fill in the blanks about Chad.

"Chad's good, as far as I can tell," I say, measuring my words. "We've had pretty serious discussions, and they will continue."

"Great," she says. "Opening up those lines of communication with teenagers is the most important thing. And how is he responding to the discussions?"

I am becoming resentful, as well as irritated that she is interrupting my work, and answer with a flash of what I'm feeling. "Fine. Are you going to tell me how and what to talk to my son about, Thelma? What's the purpose of this call, anyway?"

She sighs. "I know you find this difficult, but after talking with Chad at the hospital, and your other two kids, I really feel there are some issues you might want to process. The agency I work for has some suggestions. We run into these situations all the time, and there are ways to cope that are extremely helpful."

I resist screaming that it is absolutely none of her business, and wish I'd not agreed to the "phone interviews" with my kids that she'd requested. I have zipped past irritated and closing in on downright mad.

"Helpful? How about a *good marriage*! Now that would be helpful! Kind of tough doing this alone." Just when I thought it was safe to get back into the water. Instead, I am responding to a civil servant like a hysterical thirteen-year-old.

"I know," she murmurs sympathetically. "I know it is, believe me. And let me get to the point." She clears her throat.

"I'm on the edge of my chair."

She pauses, then plunges ahead. My tax dollars at work. "Izzy, my department, the Family Services Agency, suggests that you attend a recovery group where you might feel free to share your concerns with single parents committed to the same goal. Where you'd not feel so . . . alone."

I laugh in disbelief. "You have got to be kidding! When would I have time?"

"Okay, well, I had hoped it would not come to this," Thelma says, her voice sober. "It's not an option, Izzy. You are going to *have* to make time for it."

I am stunned into silence. Detective Faraday's words boomerang back to me: "They look for *signs*, Izzy." Signs of what, I wondered at the time, but awareness dawns. All I need now is for Jacob the Stalker to torch my house. Then life would be complete. I hurriedly retrieve the thought before God hears me.

I finally find my voice again, and sputter, "*Have* to make time for it? Is this some kind of mandate?"

"'Afraid so, Izzy. I wouldn't call it a mandate, exactly. More of a free pass to sanity."

"Free?" I squeak.

"Yes, free," Thelma says."This won't cost you a dime. The program is free. The recovery program for single parents is especially successful, and is split into genders. So you'll be talking about your struggles in a confidential environment with other women. Sharing issues as a single parent brings a lot of strength, Izzy. A lot of answers, too. This is a *good* thing."

I slump in my chair and put a hand over my face, covertly glancing around the sales floor to see if anyone is noticing my meltdown. They are not. At this time of day, if sales reps are not already gone, they are heads-down trying to meet a deadline, and the last thing they are interested in is someone else's phone conversation. "Well, I guess I have no choice, then," I whisper. "When is this thing supposed to start?"

"Day after tomorrow. It's a weekly group, and I know you'll thank me for this later." She gives me the address and time and I jot it all down on a sticky and stuff it into my purse. Maybe it'll get lost in there, and I'll have a good excuse not to go.

"Another thing, Isabelle," she pauses to select her words, "you'll be getting a follow-up visit sometime over the next couple of weeks. A spontaneous visit."

I do not trust myself to speak. And I certainly do not think she has earned the right to address me by my full name. I sit up straight in my chair, granite-faced.

"Your kids, as you probably are aware, are extremely concerned about how much you are away in the evenings. I assume you know this?" I remain silent. "Well, I am assuming you do. I am hoping, that when I talk to your kids again over the next few weeks, that this concern will be neutralized. Am I clear?"

"Very. Clear." My words are clipped. Like my wings. Who gave her the right?

"Okay. Good." Her voice brightens. "So I'll be looking forward to hearing about how the first meeting goes. Will you give me a call, and let me know how you like it?"

I assure her, with all the sarcasm I can muster, that I will be delighted to do just that. I savagely punch end call, put my phone on silent and toss it in my purse.

The pile on my desk seems to be multiplying. It will take another hour or so to clear before I can head home. How am I going to fit in a meeting every week?

I read somewhere if I repeat things over and over I will eventually believe them. It's only one night a week. It's only one night a week. It's only one night a week.

I repeat this several more times. Then I attack the pile on my desk.

After exactly sixty-seven minutes, I race in triumph down the linoleum highway to production, skid to a stop in front of Marcy's inbox, my friend on the night crew, and dump the whole pile. She startles, swivels from her computer screen, acknowledges my face, smiles and nods. I give her a quick hug, then race back to my desk to re-schedule the family conference for tomorrow night. Tonight, I need a good dose of Darlene. And a heart-healthy glass of wine or two.

"You are not serious!" Darlene's face is flushed, possibly from the martini. "Izzy, vat's next? I am so worried about you!" I laugh at that, because she has not heard but one tiny bit of what is going on.

"Oh, sweetie, there's more, but this state agency thing is killing me. I don't know what to think! I am a good mom, make a good income, don't sleep around, keep my kids relatively happy, right? Why is Social Services coming after *me*?" I pick up the glass of Bearboat Pinot and sip. It slides comfortingly down my throat and ends in a warm glow somewhere around my naval.

She ponders this question a few seconds, and ventures a guess, emboldened by vodka and three chubby, liquor-infused, olives. I'd picked an after-work-drink location right across the street from Raphael's, hoping that Birdie wouldn't hop in unexpectedly. At this point, the concerns I have about him have taken a back seat to concerns about my family. Being inspected by Social Services gets one's attention. If he steps in the door, he'd better not say one word to me.

"Do you zhink your kids have said somezhink . . . um, that would cause alarm?"

I shrug and study my wine. The globe is half-empty and lipstick imprints march around the edge. The Cup and Saucer is deserted tonight. Darlene and I practically have the place to ourselves. Dozens of patterned china saucers line the walls in a whimsical nod to the name of the restaurant. The hardwood floors are dark, substantial and, judging by the scars, well-trod. Café curtains, white lace with scallops at the bottom, hang from rods placed halfway up the windows. A red trolley rumbles by on the street outside, devoid of passengers but available just in case. I take a minute to consider Darlene's questions.

"I don't know. I am not sure what they look for, and maybe my kids brought up something on their list of no-no's." I shrug, pick the glass up by the stem. Though it's not quite empty, I signal the bartender for another. "All I know is I have this stupid recovery group to attend tomorrow."

Darlene's face creases into a smile. Her hand inches along the bar for mine. "Izzy, this may be a blessing in disguise! Sometimes we get so caught up in our own lives, we are not able to see clearly. I know for me, and for Richard too, we were shtuck. Really shtuck, until a friend told us about the group we are attendink."

I slide my hand away from hers as my second glass of wine arrives. I down the remainder of the first glass, hand it over, and begin the second. "Yeah? Well catch me up on that. How's the group going? And Richard is supportive?"

She nods vigorously, reaches for and sips her martini. "Oh, yes! He is so sad over what was happenink. What it was doing to me. He just, vell, who knows? He was weak. Nozhink actually happened . . . ." She shrugs. "At least I hope that's the truth. And we are working on our marriage. It's hard, because seeing the truth is always hard. But," she waves her martini glass for emphasis, "once the truth is out, then the healink starts. Secrets are like cancer." She sets her glass down with a clink on the varnished wood. "It's hard to dig deep, to find out the reason for things, but sometimes we have to."

I think about Jon's comment at lunch about escape mechanisms. What was it that I was trying to escape? Good question. I tuck the thought away quickly, and reach for my wine. "So the social worker's interference is my main problem right now. The other one, that ranks up there pretty close, is Birdie." I quickly recap the more substantial episodes, avoiding mention of Detective Faraday.

She puts both hands over her face, parts her fingers and looks through them. "I had no idea, Izzy. I just thought he was your basic run-of-the-mill scumbag." Her hands lower to her lap. "I really figured that he vould be gone pretty quickly. Did I ever tell you vhat it vas that Richard knew about him?" She takes a quick sip of her martini.

I shake my head.

"He said Birdie has a long string of sexual harassment charges. That's the rumor, anyway."

My expression hardens. "Would've been nice if management had checked out that little detail before hiring him." An angry gulp of wine gives me a coughing fit.

"So have you told Phil? About everyzhink you just told me?"

I nod and say, "Yeah, I reached out to Phil, and was pleasantly surprised that he, well, he seems to support me. But please, just keep this between us, okay? I have no clue how far Birdie is willing to go to keep me from exposing him. Don't know if he's approached others on the sales team, women, especially the younger, naive ones that might believe him?" I let out a slow breath. "I'll sure be glad when all this is behind me."

"You know me, Izzy," she says, smiling. "I'll be praying like crazy. Won't tell anyone but God."

I smile and down the last of my wine. We mutually acknowledge the time, re-wrap ourselves in coats and mufflers, murmur our good-byes, hug and part. I am less tense when I slide into the Honda, and ease onto the freeway. Knowing that Darlene and Winston are praying for me is comforting. It may be an exercise in futility, but it is still nice to know someone cares enough to do it on my behalf.

Jacob and Birdie

Jacob quickly slumps in his seat as Izzy exits The Cup and Saucer with her friend. His new buddy, Birdie, had told him Izzy's favorite bar was Raphael's, so he'd parked across the street every night this week to watch and wait. When she abruptly shows up two doors down from where he is parked, he panics.

When he'd been served the restraining order Izzy had filed, he'd torn it up into tiny pieces and tossed it in the trash. Proof that she is, indeed, on par with his ex-wife, even though he'd been willing to give her the benefit of the doubt. He remembers the phone conversations after they'd connected on Findamatch. He loves thinking about their time together and the phone conversations leading up to it. She'd been so warm and inviting on the phone.

His expression sours. The unfortunate series of events after the first date had scared her away. Why doesn't she give him another chance? At least talk to him? When his ex had divorced him, she'd gotten a restraining order, too, but he still found ways into the house. HIS house, not hers. Even though it had been awarded to her as part of the settlement.

Jacob's head shakes in disgust as he watches her unlock her car and get in. It is uncanny how strongly she resembles his ex. Just a few hours with her is all he asks. He needs to see a glimmer of appreciation in her eyes. Reassurance that he is a decent and honorable man.

Jacob watches Izzy drive off through slitted eyes. *I'll get you to listen, Izzy.* Restraining orders are just worthless pieces of paper. He slips a hand in his pocket to retrieve his cell. A voice answers after two rings. "Hello, um, is this Birdie?"

"Yes. Who's calling?"

"Jacob." The other end is silent.

"I've located Izzy, and am following her now," Jacob says as he maneuvers his car out of his parking space behind Izzy. "She doesn't remember my car, I'm sure, so she'll be unaware. Any last minute thoughts? About the plan, I mean?"

Birdie whispers, "No. I think our little Izzy-Belle will be much more . . . approachable . . . after this."

"As we've discussed," Jacob says, "all I ever wanted was a little uninterrupted time with her."

"I know, Jacob," Birdie reassures him. "Just remember your part of the deal. I was never involved in this. Right? We simply met outside the *Sentinel* building a few times."

"Absolutely. Thanks for your help with this, Birdie. It's only a few minutes of her time. Just so she'll understand . . . why it's so important that I speak with her."

"Yeah, I know. She needs your point of view, Jacob. It'll really help her to talk to you. I get it. Sometimes women need to be . . . aah, convinced . . . about what is in their best interests."

Birdie puffs on his cigar as he listens to Jacob's whining. What an incredible piece of luck that she just happened to have attracted this pitiful man. After he tries to break into her house to "talk" to her, he'll give the police an anonymous tip. A public scandal will corroborate everything he's been telling Phil.

"Be sure and call me once you're in," he adds. *I am almost there.* His expression is gleeful. *Maybe I can even find a way to get the incident covered in the Sentinel.* Phil will have no choice but to get rid of her, he considers, thoughtfully. Clouds of cigar smoke levitate around his desk.

If the idiot can't find a way into her house, my back-up plan is idiot-proof. Once she's fired and gone, I'll have a clear shot.

Birdie ends the call. Ultimately, his plan to move up is on track. But Izzy is a major obstacle. One he plans to shove out of the way.

CHAPTER 48

Izzy

It's eight-thirty when I pull up to my house. I slip into the kitchen, hoping to spy on the kids. My last call indicated they'd been busily completing homework and doing chores.

Right.

I'd like to believe it, but past experience proves my kids often say things that placate me and are not necessarily true. I *must* make time to be home with them more. My steps are hushed as I move through the house. Chad, as usual is snoozing on the recliner in front of the TV. I step over and shake him. He opens one eye, then the other, stretches and rubs his face. A feeling of relief washes over me. He is safe.

"Hi, Mom," he smiles. "Long day?"

I tousle his hair. "Yeah. How was yours?" I look into his face for signs of pinprick pupils, vacant stares, all the stuff they told me at the hospital to look for. He seems fine.

"It was okay. I aced my science test!"

"That is so cool, honey. Way to go!"

Chad smiles. I can tell by the way he moves he is still stiff and sore from his injuries.

"Kinda celebrity status at school now."

"Yeah? So your friends read the story in the paper?"

He rolls his eyes. "Right, mom. The paper. Uhh, no. Online. It made national news."

Great. Thelma should love that. Now the whole *world* thinks I'm a bad mother. My mind races to what Phil must think. I sigh, and say, "Family conference? Do you think you guys are still up to it? What are the other kids doing?"

"Mimi's on Facebook in her room, and Peter's still at practice. Let's do it tomorrow, like you said earlier." I tell him I have to attend a support group, fill him in on Thelma.

"Cool, Mom," he says. "I think that'll help you."

I look at him, stunned. "Help me with what?"

"With online dating." He shrugs. "No secret, Mom. We know you're looking for a guy 24/7. We want you to stop, because you're gone all the time." He crosses his arms and frowns. "*All the time*. Remember our deal."

I look away, because I know it's true. I'm not quite ready to acknowledge it, however.

"Well, maybe. It's only for six weeks, anyway."

"Like my thing that Mr. McAllister made me do, Mom. I thought I'd hate it, but I really like it. I may even keep goin'." He looks at me speculatively.

I hug him, and say, "That would be amazing, Chad. I'd love to see you do that."

He thinks a minute, and says, "Probably I wouldn't have done it unless someone had made me, Mom. Like you. Bet you would never go to a recovery group unless that woman had made you."

"That's right, I wouldn't. We'll see how it goes."

I pat his shoulder, go back into the kitchen and look for something to eat. I'm so busy most of the time, I forget to eat, and force myself to find something halfway healthy. I am scrounging in the refrigerator, when I hear the garage door pull up, then close. A few minutes later Peter walks in, slings his backpack and gym bag on the kitchen table. I quickly fix him a sandwich similar to the one I am preparing, and we sit and eat.

The man hunter demon that I have repeatedly fed and watered suddenly springs to life and hisses that I should wrap up the conversation and find some privacy for Findamatch. I struggle to be attentive to Peter's discussion of his day through the filter of my more primal instincts. As I strive to remain focused on my son, I experience a mini-revelation.

For a long time, I have forced disengagement from the kids as soon as possible after work so I can connect with Findamatch. Virtual possibilities have become more real, more affirming, more important. *Than my kids?* This thought is so utterly revolting that I nearly blurt out my revelation to Peter, but mom-sense kicks in.

Kids do *not* need to know everything that goes on in Mom's head.

This is called parental discretion.

I suddenly realize a huge compartment is about to burst open in my mind, an epiphany of sorts, and feel the sharp need to be alone. I give Peter a regretful look, and tell him I need to change out of my work clothes as an excuse for a hasty exit. Random meltdowns have become a way of life lately. No need for him to witness one.

I quickly walk upstairs to my bedroom, close the door and sit on the bed, waiting. I sense some kind of impending cataclysm, and squinch my face together in an attempt to attune. The man hunter demon is curiously silent, a withered caricature screeching no more. My mind becomes a jumble of blurred scenes. Like a slideshow, they focus one after another.

First, Peter. Responsible, diligent, vigilant Peter. Stress lines his face. Too young a face for such stress, I think. *Exactly*, a voice inside me answers. I recognize it as the same voice that told me my husband would deny me before that last, fateful therapist visit. That had been a shot in the dark, a bolt out of the blue . . . a fortune-cookie experience that I'd attributed to indigestion.

But after the final session, when my husband had uttered the impossible words that denied our marriage vows so permanently, I'd had to admit there was something to it. I listen with intent, watching the scenes unfold instead of discarding them as nonsense.

Mimi comes into focus, a small form amidst stuffed animals. Her computer is in her lap, fingers flying. She silently mouths something to the screen. She giggles in delight, like the young girl she is, and responds online. Who has made her smile? Who is she contacting?

Do you care? The voice inside me sounds like the flutter of a thousand butterfly wings, gossamer-light. *Does she think you care?*

The impressions are relentless. I see Chad, then Peter, then Mimi, then it starts over again. Mimi, a small ghost in her room tapping out silent messages. Peter, his face empty, anticipating another basketball game Mom would not be able to attend. Chad, clinging to the side of a cliff, yelling for me, his system sluggish with chemicals.

Birdie's leering face, followed quickly by Jacob's, which I barely remember and appears blurred, his hand repeatedly sliding a note under a windshield wiper. I hear the crunch of footsteps, the grating of the latch to the gate being tried. In rapid succession, images of men I'd met over the last two years march before my eyes interspersed with images of lonely, confused kids at home. Afternoons I'd raced home before the kids to log in to a dating site instead of calling on clients. The farce I'd become at the office. I beg silently for the images to stop, tears streaming down my cheeks.

What is the common theme, Izzy? The voice persists. *Think.* I wipe the tears off my cheeks and look around for a tissue. I pluck one out of the brightly-colored cube of Kleenex on my night stand, and blow my nose. *Concentrate.*

Time has ceased to exist. I scrunch my face, resolute. I do not know where this voice is coming from, but I have my suspicions. I concentrate hard, my eyes closed. Slowly, a seated form comes into focus. The image zooms in, and my face, starkly clear, fills the scene. My eyes are bright, focused; my cheeks flushed with excitement. I am embarrassed, almost repulsed, as I watch my own facial expressions; reactions to the men I am apparently messaging via Findamatch. The woman before me is extracting seductive words, flattering clichés, ardent compliments. Her body language disgusts me, her twisted lips dripping with lust. I am shocked at the wide chasm between self-perception and reality.

Finally, I have had enough. "Okay!" I whisper sharply. "I see it! I see it!"

Do you? What do you see?

I grab another tissue and blot my eyes. "The common thread," I tell the voice, feeling utterly ridiculous, "is that without a man I feel empty. Worthless. Without a man in my life, I cannot succeed at anything. Parenting, work . . . anything. So I *must* find one. It takes time. It takes great effort. It takes . . . it takes skill."

You are unable.

I cannot believe I am having this conversation, if it can be considered, actually, a conversation, and ask, "Unable? What does that mean?"

You are not the right kind of woman.

I fall silent. Surely this is a dream. A dream I am having, fully awake. I lean back on the bed and roll my head, aware of a stiff neck from holding the position so long, and prop myself with my arms.

Eventually, like a gentle caress, I somehow feel and hear these words:

You are chasing the wind.

I blink, astonished. Suddenly, the day I'd been served with divorce papers leaps to the front of my awareness. I had been devastated to find myself a single parent again, and had vowed that things would be different. That I would *not* live life alone, or raise my kids alone, no matter what. Nope, I was going to *find the right man whatever it took!*

I am painfully aware this approach had not exactly been working for me.

I feel my gut twist in a knot of anguish, shame and regret. The knot suddenly unties, and I feel different. Lighter, somehow.

Are you ready to give up, Izzy?

A beat or two passes. A light clicks on in my brain. Hadn't Winston asked me that? I'd pushed the question aside, and here it was again. Yes. Yes! I am ready to give up.

Run after Me. Chase Me. Catch Me. Delight in Me. The voice shimmers like a mirage, rises and falls in cascades like a waterfall, then disappears.

I concentrate as hard as I can, but the voice, the impressions, are gone. I am unaware of how long I had been sitting, transfixed. When I turn over my clenched fist, it holds a clump of sodden tissue.

I slowly orient to reality. A distant pounding hammers the edges of my mind. With a start, I realize someone is pounding on my bedroom door, which I had locked.

"Mom! Mom! Are you okay?" Peter's voice is agitated. I quickly push myself off the bed, swipe my face with the mass of tissue, and open the door, where my beautiful son stands, worried. I do not want him to worry about me. Ever again. I hope it's not too late to repair the damage I've done. I long to see a content, happy, smile on his face. On each child's face. Always.

I hug my son tightly. "Yeah, I think so, Peter. I think everything is very . . . okay." He eyes me strangely, and we walk downstairs.

After the kids are in bed, I pause in the hallway, staring at my computer. I sit, curious. I wonder if my perception will have changed after my *encounter* with . . . whatever it was. God, I guess. My desktop screen, which is a picture of my hypothetical perfect man handing a bouquet of flowers to a woman, seems trite now. Irritating. I quickly change the desktop image to reflect me and the kids, then log in to Findamatch. Three messages. One is from Sculpted Road Warrior-man, and I read:

"Dreamsicle:

I want to assure you my photo is current. I haven't gained a hundred pounds since it was taken, either. Smiley face. Sounds like we have a lot in common. I'm originally from South Carolina, so you'd have to put up with the accent. I've moved around a lot, and it's been quite the journey. Smiley face. I have two kids, girls. Their mom lives in South Carolina, and she visits when she can. I have custody of the kids. Long story. I am sane, make reasonable money, and have been single three years. Smiley face. I hope you'll consider me a contender for your affections, and give me a call. My number is (501) 555-2177. Would love to hear the voice that goes with that face. Road Warrior

I ponder the message, then click on his full profile and read the details of his preferences, goals, height, weight, eye color. I am strangely detached. Normally, I would write back immediately, my communication filled with flirtatious hooks and entendre, but I do not feel the familiar rush of adrenaline tonight that pulls me forward. The smiley faces throughout the message annoy me. My chin drifts into my palm. My eyes fall on a plaque Darlene had given me recently, which is placed on my desk.

"Denial is NOT a river in Egypt. *Principle One: Realize I'm not God; admit that I am powerless to control my tendency to do the wrong thing and that my life is unmanageable."*

I awkwardly bow my head. "God, I admit that my life is out of control. Unmanageable is an understatement! How did I get myself into this mess?" I wait a minute, half expecting a verbal response. When none comes, I continue,

"I realize I have been wrong. I see it now. I know you were talking to me in the bedroom." A huge sigh escapes me, and I realize I am tired. *So tired*, and sleep seems a much better option than communicating with men online. "I have been in denial, haven't I? I have not been seeing things too clearly. Thanks for helping me see, and I'll try to give up, whatever that means. Amen."

When I open my eyes, my computer has hibernated. I think this is an excellent idea, and do the same.

CHAPTER 49

The next morning is blessedly uneventful, and I am humming and sipping my latte on the trek to work during morning rush hour. Chad, Peter and Mimi had been in better moods than usual, and I fully attribute it to my decision to connect with them. A little focused attention goes a long way, I'm learning.

As I pull into the parking lot, I spy the homeless man who had thrown my quarter back in my face a few weeks ago. I dig around in my purse and come up with a five dollar bill. I stride purposefully toward him, and plant it in his hand. He stares at me suspiciously.

"You're welcome," I say, and cross the street to the ponderous turn-of-the-century double door entrance to the *Sentinel*. I avoid the elevator and take the stairs, wondering how the day will turn out, hoping fervently for boring. Boring is good. Boring is preferred, actually.

I pull back the door to the second floor, and smile at Donna, the receptionist, who as usual, is surrounded by a crowd catching up on the latest personal news. They turn and mouth good mornings and how ya doin' as one, then return to Donna's stream of unending information.

Winston has made it in, and is perched at his desk, newspaper already flattened into submission. A Starbucks cup is on his desk. I notice his white hair had been recently buzzed, and his goatee neatly trimmed. The ever-present lanyard that holds his reading glasses is a simple, gold chain, and he wears a starched yellow dress shirt and a tie featuring tans and blues upon which float several tiny, red images. I cannot see his socks, but I am positive they match everything. I dump my purse in my drawer and bounce into my chair. "Mornin' Pod-King!"

"Morning, Izzy." He turns his head in my direction, sips his coffee, smiles. "Doing well?" I nod, and open and smooth my newspaper.

"Yep. Doing great, actually. So what's up today?"

"Oh, the usual," Winston says. "Wars, rumors of wars, stock market decline, more government mandates." He shrugs. "You know."

I smile. Winston is a political conservative, and I am a vote-for-the-man-not-the-party person. A conversation headed in a political direction is a recipe for disaster. I change the subject.

"Sounds depressing. Any news on the home front?" My eyes rove around the sales floor to indicate my meaning.

Winston moves toward me, lowering his voice. Uh oh. "Birdie came in very early, which is unusual, so I wonder if something is up." He moves in a little closer. "He didn't look very happy, either." I am wondering when Birdie had taken over my every waking thought at work. I reluctantly pull the compartment in my mind labeled *Birdie* to the front of my brain.

"Great. I so look forward to the day when I. Don't. Care."

I throw an *I am so sick of all this Birdie crap* expression at Winston, then viciously clasp my latte, which promptly results in errant drips of coffee on my newspaper. I swipe them away.

Winston nods regretfully. "I know, Iz. I'm sorry."

"Nothin' for you to be sorry about. It's just something I have to deal with. I'm hoping things will come to a head soon, and maybe he'll be . . . well . . . gone." I take a sip of coffee, then set the cup on the desk and clasp my hands, studying his tie. "Winston, what are the red things on your tie?"

He looks down and smiles. "Sharks." He gazes at me with calm blue eyes, a sea of inscrutability behind them. I smile, and say, "Why are they red?"

"Color of blood," he says, and without cracking even a hint of a grin, turns back to his newspaper.

Birdie's office door abruptly opens, and his tanning-bed visage appears over a white, starched dress shirt and brilliant red tie. He catches my eye and motions me in.

"What a way to start the day!" I mutter. Winston leans back in his chair, slices his eyes toward Birdie's office, then back to me; flips his glasses off his nose, and begins to move his fingers up and down the lanyard.

"Hang in there, Izzy," he said. I'd heard that so many times lately I want to puke. I obediently join Birdie in his office. I flinch when he closes the door. Most *Sentinel* managers, in fact all of them, hold open-door meetings with salespeople.

"I have a problem, Izzy, and I need your input on how to deal with it," he says, eyeing my face. His expression is unreadable in the curtains-drawn gloom of his office. The effect leaves me off-balance. Since I now ostensibly report to Phil, I am not sure why my presence is required in this office.

"Okay, I'll bite. What's the problem?" Non-committal. Unconcerned.

He smiles. "Your friend Jacob is still hanging around, and it needs to stop. I've seen him several times, before you arrive at the office in the mornings, and also after work. I don't think you want Phil involved in this, so I thought we could come up with a way to handle it quietly."

A big gotcha. Why does he go out of his way to create impasses with me? Why can't he let things just . . . unravel? My brow furrows with concern.

"Birdie, you know the man is unbalanced, and that I have a restraining order in place. I don't know what else I can do. If you think I should approach him, then I certainly disagree with that strategy. That is what he wants!"

"Know this, Izzy, if Jacob manages to set one foot in this office lookin' for you, that will be grounds for immediate dismissal." I stare at him, alarm bells clanging loudly in my head. His smile blazes; a half-moon of tombstones.

"How in the world can I prevent that? That's security's job, not mine!"

He is unfazed. "I'm just tellin' ya, Izzy, this is serious. We can involve Phil if you like . . . ."

"No!" I interrupt, hastily. "He doesn't need to know the guy is continuing to harass. Let's keep him out of this if possible."

"Okay, well I just wanted you to know that I've checked the HR regulations, and 'harassment' or 'stalking' is defined as immediate grounds for dismissal. Just wanted to let you know. You can go on back to your desk now," he says, turning to his computer screen.

I sputter, "But, Birdie, surely that regulation means that no *employee* should stalk or harass. It can't be talking about a situation like mine!"

He turns and eyes me with contempt. "It is not all that clear actually, but it certainly can be interpreted both ways. Take care of it, or we'll have a significant problem on our hands. Have a good day, Izzy."

I leave his office in emotional disarray, which is perfect. It's my latest default position anyway. I am not unduly stressed, but on the other hand, am unduly stressed. A centipedal shiver crawls up my spine.

Winston turns from his newspaper-and-coffee time toward me. "Izzy! Your face is white as a sheet! What happened?"

I mumble that I do not want to talk about it, and he reluctantly drops the subject. I command my mind to calm itself. Think, Izzy. Think! What can be done about this? Did he mean that Jacob was outside *this morning*?" I cringe at the thought, and pull up Detective Faraday's number on my cell. Think about calling him, but I'm sure he doesn't want to talk to a hysterical female at this hour of the morning about a *what if.*

Lonnie approaches and lays a pile of proofs on my desk. "Mornin' Izzy. How's it goin'?" he says, oblivious to my personal edge-of-disaster situation. I tell him fine.

My desk – typically is a haven of sorts – suddenly seems sinister, foreboding. My eyes rake the room, ferreting out potential dark clouds.

As if on cue, an unfamiliar man walks into the sales department from the production department, obviously unsure of himself. He passes by Darlene, who eyes him. He stops in front of her desk. I see her ask if he'd like her help. I watch him tell her no. My stomach clenches as I realize – somehow know – this is the *dark cloud.*

He sees me at the same moment I figure this out, locks eyes with mine, and moves toward me. He seems to stutter-step a frame at a time, like stop-motion photography. I experience tunnel vision. My hands grip the edges of my desk.

Winston looks over the eight-inch cube divider at my face, follows my gaze, sees Jacob, then looks back at me, unaware of specifics, but pretty sure I am not experiencing boundless joy at the moment. I decide action – any action – is preferable to waiting out the inevitable, and leap from my desk hoping to deter an outright train wreck. I scurry toward him.

"Jacob," I say, forcing a smile, "is that you?"

His eyes are vacant. He has not shaved in a while and his beard is a stubbly gray. His hair looks unwashed. His eyes slit. "Yeah, it's me. Thought it was about time we talked. No restraining order is gonna force me to do anything!"

"Keep your voice down!" I hiss desperately, sensing several pairs of eyes watching. I take his arm, freeze a smile on my face, and steer him toward production, to the neutral zone that holds Missy's office, the coffee area and a few graphic designers. His breath is sour. How the heck did he get in? The doors are opened only by entering a personal employee code. I don't have time to think about it, and urge him on.

So focused am I on getting him off the sales floor and away from management, I fail to realize they will all be clustered around the coffeemaker at that hour, waiting for fresh coffee to take to their morning meeting. My heart sinks as I realize there is absolutely no way I can paint Jacob as a friendly acquaintance or a client. His appearance has raised eyebrows already. Plus, he apparently has rehearsed a speech that he intends me to hear. Publically.

Fortunately, I'd slipped my cell phone into my pocket when I realized my stalker had entered the building. I'd tapped the most recent number, Detective Faraday's; leaving the phone on speaker.

Jacob begins his speech as I propel him off the sales floor by declaring how unfair women have been to him all his life. I resign myself that this horrific scenario will simply play out however it plays out, and am at least comforted that I am surrounded by hundreds of co-workers. If he must make an actual approach, this is probably the safest place to be. His voice escalates as he realizes, that in my desperation to spirit him out of the building, I'm looking around at everyone and everything but him. We do the exact thing I am trying *not* to do – we draw an audience.

I placate. I beg. I cajole. But he will not be deterred. His robotic dissertation moves on to the notes, and he wonders if I appreciated how difficult it was to get into my garage. How did I think it made him feel when I didn't even have the courtesy to answer?

I sneak glances at the group loosely encircling us. A few snicker, but most are incredulous, or concerned. Some are capturing the moment with their phones. To blackmail me later, I am guessing. Phil is glaring at me, and Milton and the telemarketing manager look at me with astonished expressions. Birdie's smile, at the back of the group, covers half his face. I think this odd, and as Jacob continues his diatribe, my mind backflips to Birdie's earlier warning, which now seems a little too perfectly timed.

My thoughts are interrupted when Detective Faraday, bless him; followed by two of Chatbrook's finest, bursts onto the scene.

"Izzy!" he exclaims. "This him?" I nod. He tilts his head in Jacob's direction, and the two cops whip out handcuffs and shove a copy of the restraining order in his face. They forcibly move Jacob through the sales floor, make the unfortunate choice to take the elevator, and he shouts his angst toward me the entire five minutes it takes the cursed elevator to crawl to the second floor from the third. When the doors finally swoosh open, he meekly walks in, flanked by two cops, turns, and stares at me with throbbing, sorrowful eyes as the doors close. I almost, but not quite, feel sorry for him.

I stand there, mute, numb and sickened, the scene stuck on replay.

Detective Faraday quietly steps up to me, notebook and pen in hand. "Somewhere we can talk, so I can get details, Izzy?"

Phil, who has followed us to the elevator, says, "Conference room is open, you are welcome to use it."

Then to me he says, "Izzy, after the detective is finished, my office. Immediately. Got it?" Phil walks away, shaking his head, enters his office and closes the door with a bang. As I lead Detective Faraday to the conference room, I look back over my shoulder, and see Birdie watching us. He is standing by my desk in a wide stance, arms crossed over his chest, smiling. A light flashes through my dimwit brain. I give him the best hater-stare I can muster, and enter the conference room with the sound of his laughter ringing in my head.

I slowly thread my way through the cubicles with Detective Faraday after our meeting, walk him to the elevator, advise that he take the stairs, thank him, and tell him good-bye. Then I glance at Winston, who is looking at me in horror, as though I need immediate medical attention, which I probably do. I smile encouragingly, point to Phil's office and lift my hands by my sides, palms up. He understands, and clasps his hands together indicating that he will pray. Seeing his hands positioned in prayer takes me to my epiphany last night. I don't just hope now, I *know* there is something to prayer.

I glance across the floor to my desk, which is piled high with work. Lonnie glances at me and raises one palm as if to say, "What do you need me to do?" I smile at him weakly and wave my hand in a little circle. He nods, translating as, "Take care of what you can, I'll be back when I get back." A good assistant understands nebulous gestures as if they are complete sentences.

I approach the glass walls and lightly knock on the closed door. He beckons me in, and tells me to close the door. I do, trying to make as little noise as possible. I step to the chair in front of his desk softly, as if walking on eggshells. A sort of penance for my sin. I sit, clasp my hands in my lap, cross my ankles and look at the floor.

"So what happened out there today, Izzy? I am really looking forward to your explanation." He pins me to the chair with angry eyes. I look beyond him, out the windows and see blue sky, cotton candy clouds. A few hardy leaves still cling to the trees outside Phil's window. Little flags of orange and red flap at me in encouragement, like I've almost reached a finish line.

"Um . . . didn't I tell you about the stalker?"

Phil's expressions darkens. "No. *Birdie* told me about a stalker. I was hoping it was an exaggeration."

Phil pushes his reading glasses to the top of his balding head and rubs his eyes. His desk is cluttered with several piles in various states of completion. The small, round conference table behind me shoved into a corner of his office is covered with recent offerings from the marketing department. On it are boxes of pens marked with the *Sentinel* insignia, imprinted stress balls of various shapes and sizes, calendars featuring historical black and white *Sentinel* photos. In different circumstances, I would be picking out several goodies for my clients and driving to see them bearing gifts.

Not today.

"Okay, Izzy," Phil says, leaning back in his chair, crossing his arms over his chest. "Go."

I take a deep breath, and dive in, hoping Darlene is praying for me along with Winston. "First, let me apologize. I had no idea things would get so crazy." Phil waves his hands, indicating I should get to the story, and leans forward, his eyes intense, hard orbs.

"Okay, I met this guy on a dating site . . ." Phil sighs, and fidgets. I continue, "and we went out once. Just once! I knew something was off about him that night, and tried to encourage no further contact. The next morning he called, and got all bent out of shape that I would not go out again. And that is the honest truth, Phil! I did everything possible to get him off my back!"

"How was he on your back? What does that mean? I thought you just went out with him once."

"I did," I said, "but he continued to call. I blocked him from the site, so he could not message me. I told him on the phone I did not want to see him again. He doesn't have my email address. I thought that was the end of it, but he then started leaving notes for me at my house. He wasn't supposed to know where I live, but somehow he found out. After the second or third time those notes started showing up, I went to the police and filed a restraining order. The detective you met has been working on this, helping me know what to do."

Phil plants an elbow on his desk, drops his cheek onto his palm. The gold-rimmed glasses atop his pate are in direct line of the morning sun spilling in through the windows. Points of reflected light dance along the walls with every shake of his head.

"That is all well and good, Izzy, but I have a sales department to run. I'm not equipped to deal with irate ex-husbands, irate ex-dates, irate adult kids or whatever! The point here is," he pauses to slip his glasses off the top of his head to the bottom of his nose, lifts a sheaf of papers, scans it, and continues, "that this report from Birdie has a lot of incriminating statements in it. The time lost due to your online hobby is affecting your work, he says, and today . . ." Phil puts down the report, plants crossed arms on his desk and leans forward. "Today was just . . . unacceptable. Period."

I stare at the floor and shift in my seat, crossing my legs. My foot immediately begins to jiggle uncontrollably, a nervous habit. I cross my arms and look at him. "Phil, you don't know the whole story . . ." Tears well up in my eyes, and I stare at the floor, wishing the well would dry up. It is ridiculous how much I have been crying lately.

Phil rips the glasses off his face and tosses them onto his desk. "No, I guess I don't! Why don't you fill me in? I don't know what to believe anymore! First I have this . . ." he gestures angrily toward Birdie's report, "report that Birdie has filed with HR, and now I have actual proof – in the flesh – that he may be right! Not to mention that your allegations about Birdie are up for grabs. Who the heck knows if all *that* stuff is true?" He lifts his elbows off the desk and holds his arms out in a beseeching gesture. "As your friend, I'd like to believe you, but as your boss I have responsibility for the entire sales department, not just the queen of Findamatch.com!"

I push myself up in the chair, uncross and re-cross my legs. "How the heck did you know the name of the site?"

"Doesn't matter. Actually, I think everyone knows." He sighs, picks his glasses up, places them on top of his head. "You know I am fond of you Izzy. I do not want to be backed into a corner, but there are actual rules about this stuff! It's now a police matter. Out of my hands! I know you think your online dating thing is cute and fun and all that, but this is a *serious* situation. The guy could've had a gun! People might have gotten hurt, or killed! In your best interests, and the interests of the company, a temporary leave of absence is probably in order. Worst case scenario, termination."

The tears spill over, and my voice quivers. "But Phil, you know I need this job! My numbers are good. My clients are good. How could you . . . fire me . . . over something like this?"

Phil looks up, his voice gentled. "Izzy, I would never fire you. But regulations are regulations. Birdie brings up good points, if they are true; and I need to figure a way around it, but right now," he shrugs, and places his palm on the report, "I have some research to do. Don't know when I'll find the time to do it, either." He scans the top of his desk and sighs. "All I know is that this stuff with you has got be over. Immediately. And you . . ." he stares at me, "gotta focus on work. *Work*, Izzy. You cannot afford another incident like this one. Are we clear?"

I quickly make a decision. I look at Phil, my cheeks drying, my expression solemn. My voice has shed its quaver. "Phil, I know this is hard to hear, but I think, well . . . I think Birdie and Jacob planned this. Together."

CHAPTER 50

Thirty minutes later, I leave Phil's office, and when I reach to close the door behind me, he tells me to leave it open, and lifts his fist in a thumbs-up. I am grateful to leave on a positive note, and walk quickly back to my desk to survey the fallout from an entire morning of tending to the stalker incident. Lonnie is absent, but my desk is filled with proofs marked in red with questions for me. I scan the sales floor, which is largely deserted, and try my best to act nonchalant, as if nothing really happened, all forgotten, forgiven, and no, I was not up to sharing details. No.

I see a small hand waggling at the back of the sales floor, lean forward and identify its owner as Darlene. She'd apparently waited for me, because normally she was on her lunch break at this time. She hurries to my desk, pulls up a chair.

"So, how'd it go? Oh my gosh, Izzy! I cannot believe what happened! What did Phil say? I traded my lunch hour with Beth so I could wait for you!"

"Darlene," I say, marking proofs and dropping them on Lonnie's desk, hoping that we are still on track to meet the printing deadlines for these ads, "wanna go to lunch?"

Fifteen minutes later we are tucked inside the The Blue Plate Special, an out-of-the-way restaurant within walking distance of the office on West 15th. Darlene's face is solemn as I relate to her the short version of the Jacob debacle.

"But, Izzy," she says, thoughtfully, "wasn't there somezhink – I mean, some detail on his profile – that would haf tipped you off to his state of mind?"

I shrug, study my oval white plate holding today's $5.99 special: meatloaf and gravy, mashed potatoes, green beans. I stab my fork into the meatloaf and take a bite. It is actually quite good. Though possibly in the vast minority, I love a good southern meatloaf.

I chew, thinking, then swallow. "Yeah, you know Darlene, there probably was. But I don't think I could have recognized it before. I was just so into the game."

She cocks her head. "*Was*? Vhat does that mean?"

A grin tugs my mouth upward. "I had what I would describe as an *epiphany* last night." I load my fork with a mouthful of mashed potatoes and dump them in my mouth. They are smooth and butter-y.

She fiddles with her coleslaw, changes her mind, spoons bar-b-que beans into her mouth instead. "Interestink. Tell me!"

I put my fork down, take a sip of my sweet tea, set the glass down. As objectively as possible, I tell her what happened last night in my bedroom. By the time I am finished, her eyes are shining like freshly minted copper pennies.

"I am so certain, Izzy," she says, pausing to construct her words, "that zis is God's answer to prayer. Winston and I haf been praying for months. Richard, too. I have not felt the online thing was going well for you for quite a while, but did not know how to tell you."

I shake my head, laughing. "Oh, you told me! In countless, small ways. I might have acted like I didn't understand what you meant, but I did. I just didn't want to hear it. I especially didn't want to give up Findamatch."

"How vell I know. I knew it was bringing you the male attention you crave, and it felt good to go out on all those dates, but I was vorried about the effect it was having on you and your family. I never thought you'd end up with a stalker, but of course, now that I think about it, as much as you were dating, how could one not be a rotten apple? Maybe several rotten apples!"

My mind balks at the phrase *male attention you crave*, and I ask her what she means. She reaches for her tea, squeezes a lemon wedge into it, sips.

"It is – or was – very obvious to me from our conversations about datink, or the men you married, that you vere lacking the right kind of man in your life to help you figure things out from a male perspective. Maybe always, starting with your dad?" Her voice rises on the end as a question, and her eyebrows pop up as she waits for my response..

"Totally," I say, in agreement. "My dad was not into warm, fuzzy conversations with the kids. He made the money, mom took care of the house. My parents just thought I would figure stuff out on my own, but looking back, as a little girl I felt, well, kind of abandoned, maybe?" I look outside at people striding down the sidewalk in twos or threes. It's a beautiful, warm fall day but I feel a chill rush through me.

"That's probably why I enjoy online dating so much. It's a stress reliever, and instant validation with very little emotional investment. A steady stream of compliments. Romance at my fingertips. Potential dates. I *love* it."

She sticks her fork into the beans, coaxes a few on the fork, lifts to her mouth, chews, then washes it down with tea. "Yeah, I would imagine that stuff feels really good at first. All the sizzle of chemical attraction. Being wanted, with no expectation. No problems to work out, just a vonderful feeling of bliss. Of course, zis is a fantasy. Anyone can sustain romance at first. It's the commitment after the initial attraction that keeps it goink." She puts her fork down, picks her napkin up from her lap, wipes her mouth. "So is it an obsession, Izzy? Out of control?"

I think a minute. "Probably," I say, nodding, as if convincing myself. "Probably over the last year or so it has turned out that way, but after last night, I feel different. Detached. It's weird." I pause, considering. "I think back to the men I married, and think I said *yes* for the simple reason that they paid attention to me. *Any* attention from a man felt so good I wanted it to last, I guess. One after the other had this hideous secret that came flying out after a couple years. I was totally unprepared to deal with some of that stuff! I had no clue about any of it before it happened. Or maybe it was obvious, and I just couldn't see it, or didn't want to? Then I found myself, over and over, in a nasty divorce.

"And now, after last night, it's like a fog is lifting. I chose to ignore the hints that were there when I'd been dating them. I figured we could work things out, and minimized stuff that I should never have been okay with in the first place."

I mop up the last of the meatloaf and mashed potatoes, and with them, the conversation. "Oh, well. Better late than never, right?"

She laughs. "Sometimes God makes us work really hard through our stumbling blocks, and sometimes He blows our minds and simply takes them away. I think in your case, with one sveep of His hand," she lifts her arm in an attempt to illustrate a vast God-sweep, "He has removed your stumbling block – that craving for any man, if he vill give you *attention*."

She sees me wincing, and reaches across the table to lay her hand on mine. "Sorry, Izzy. I know it hurts. But it hurts good like a cut that has just been doused with alcohol, right?"

She continues, "It's nice that you are not bragging about how many men you've gone out with lately, or telling a bunch of stories about how cute the latest guy is. I couldn't even keep their names straight!"

I make a face at her. "That bad, huh?"

She nods, chewing, quickly asserts, "That bad."

We exit the restaurant, an easy camaraderie between us. I feel an imperceptible breach in our relationship has been mended, and tell her so.

"Ja, I agree," Darlene says, and continues. "It was gettink to the point that we were on entirely different paths, and I was getting a little tired of hearing about man after man. I knew it was all goink to go up in flames at some point. I guess, as of this morning, it has!"

"True," I say. "Phil's pretty upset, and Birdie, well I don't want you to repeat this, because I need to do a little detective work, but Birdie apparently put Jacob – the stalker guy – up to this!"

Darlene does not respond with the dropped jaw I am expecting. To my surprise, she is supportive of my theory, and says, "After all you've told me about him, I wouldn't doubt it, Izzy. It seemed so strange when that guy walked through the office this morning. For one thing, how the heck did he get in? Our security is really ratcheted down!"

"I think Birdie gave him his code. That's part of my research. Do you know who has the list of codes that are entered at each entrance to our building?"

"Ja. Operations. Talk to the operations manager. Or better yet, have Phil get the list."

"Great idea," I tell her, brightening at the thought of crossing another unpleasant task off my to-do list. "Phil has more clout, anyway, and they'll think he's checking up on an employee."

As we ride up to the second floor and prepare to part ways, she grips my arm, looks into my face, and says, "Izzy, I am so proud of you! You are on the home stretch. All these zhings you are goink through now? Puffs of smoke. They will vanish right before your eyes. Wait and see. Life is goink to get better."

As I step out of the elevator, I almost believe her.

Then Birdie's face spoils everything.

I wave to Darlene, who hurries to her desk, and try to sidestep Birdie, but he quietly moves in front of me. "Quite a scene this morning, Izzy," his gaze is mocking. My brow furrows, and I look at the floor. I figure when in doubt, close the mouth.

"Am I making myself clear, Ms. High and Mighty? Wait until you see the copy of the latest report I give Phil. It won't be flattering, I promise you that." I raise my face and stare at him.

"What do you *want*, Birdie?" I say, somewhat emboldened by my conversation with Darlene and the knowledge that Detective Faraday has my back. Which suddenly reminds me, he'd found a trail of illegal activity in Birdie's police file. My spine stiffens.

The evil grin makes an appearance. "I want you to disappear, Izzy. And I think my wish is coming true. Don't you?"

I return his grin with one of my own. The shadowy fear I feel in Birdie's presence has disintegrated. My confidence is returning, and the realization that Birdie's presence alone has been responsible for sucking it out of me the past few weeks sickens me. I feel anger zip up my gut, out my mouth.

"Yeah, well here's a news flash: I want you to disappear too. And guess what? It might happen. Just a heads-up. I am not your problem, Birdie; I am Phil's problem. So if you want to keep your job, I suggest you talk to Phil or HR instead of me, until the truth comes out." I glare at him. "Which should be any day now."

He laughs. "Good one, Izzy. I'm an *expert* at throwing people under the bus." He inclines his head toward the few salespeople that are still in the office instead of out calling on clients, heads down in cubicles fifty feet from us, oblivious to the unbelievable conversation taking place.

"My team is on track to have one of the most successful years in the history of the newspaper. Everyone except *you*, that is, which my report will show. Don't think I'll be going anywhere anytime soon."

I decide to end the discussion from hell, and say, "Always a pleasure, Bird. Keep me posted. I have work to do." His smile widens, and he yanks on each pristine, white cuff from under his sport coat, admiring the cufflinks. "Oh, I will. You can count on it."

I walk briskly to my desk, turn and sit. To my delight, I discover Phil has been watching the whole episode between Big Bird and me behind his glass walls. He steps out his office door, which had been partially open, and forcefully calls out Birdie's name.

The blazing grin falters. He pauses uncertainly, then strides toward Phil. The door to Phil's office closes, and the curtains around the glass walls close in a rush of fabric. A gush of relief flashes through me. What I wouldn't give to be a fly on the wall and hear *that* conversation! I figure this is as good a time as any to set up a meeting between Detective Faraday and Phil, and grab my cell.

CHAPTER 51

Piccolo is a great neighborhood restaurant and bar five minutes from my house, one I frequent periodically. Tonight I had agreed to meet Sculpted-Face-Edgy-Hair for a drink before the meeting Thelma had insisted I attend. Maybe it's a final act of defiance before I must suffer the indignity of a recovery meeting. Whatever it is, I'm looking forward to it.

I feel the Honda jerk against a curb, correct my angle, re-adjust, park, and run to the entrance, patting my hair into place on the way. I do not pause to look in my rear-view mirror to refresh my makeup, and it appears I am not going to make my patented Betty Boop entrance, either. Interesting.

I walk to the bar and plop onto a stool. I feel none of the endorphin surges and schoolgirl giggles that typically accompany these meetings, and in fact, am so relaxed that I don't care whether he shows or not. I need to get home to the kids, then to that silly recovery meeting at eight.

My eyes adjust to the bar's darkness. The decor could be grudgingly described as French Country. A somewhat clumsy attempt at impressionism hangs on the walls at various intervals, punctuated by wall sconce lighting. The bar has brass accents and wicker stools and a hook for purses or coats underneath. Plantation shutters adorn the windows.

Piccolo is touted for its great food and friendly staff, but more importantly, offers an excellent wine selection by the glass. I can live without sumptuous decor, but the wine list has to deliver. I order Markham Merlot, a good Napa red.

A brief shaft of light splits the dimness as the door opens, then shuts. The hostess minces to her station, asks if the man would like restaurant or bar, and he points toward me. I obligingly wave and smile. On a lust-worthy scale of one to ten, the guy rates at least a nine-and-a-half, and the hostess is understandably disappointed. She waves him into the bar.

I light up like a firefly, temporarily forgetting my new leaf that had just been turned over. This guy is gorgeous, and it is very hard for me to keep from salivating, let alone think straight. He gives me a side-hug and cheek-buss.

"Finally!" he beams at me. "You are every bit as pretty as your picture!" He looks around the room. "Nice place. What are you having?" I tell him. He orders a wine cooler. I forgive him for this immediately. Some things can be taught.

His drink arrives quickly, which is good since I am having trouble conversing due to stress, guilt, exhaustion or a combination of all three. He sips, swivels, wiggles his eyebrows, hand-mimes a cigar. "So, you come here often?"

Ha, ha, very cute. Groucho Marx.

"No," I respond," not really. They just have a great wine list." I wisely resist telling him I live right around the corner. "So what are your favorite places to go?"

He tips his glass, gulps down his drink in two swallows, orders another. My brows knit together. My newfound objectivity feels unfamiliar. I am adjusting on the fly. My typical fluttery-eyelashes, seductive comments, trilling laughter, woman-on-the-prowl behavior is inoperative at this moment, and I do not quite know how to engage without it.

Sculpted-Edgy clutches his drink. "I live in Glenwood. Y'know, up north of Chatbrook Springs?" I nod, remembering he'd had no address on his profile. "So I don't get to the Chatbrook city lights much, just to work, then it's a forty-five minute drive home, and," he shrugs, "gotta take care of the boys,."

"I understand completely," I say. "Kids kind of usurp a social life most of the time, don't they?"

He gazes at me through rapidly-lubing eyes. "I don't know what 'usurped' means. You're gonna hafto 'splain that one to me!" he laughs and downs his second wine cooler.

I push aside negative first impressions. "Usurp means to preclude." Too late, I realize that he probably won't know what that means either. "So I know you are a salesman. What do you sell? How's business lately for you? It's kinda tough for me out there."

Casual conversation. Getting to know each other. This comment should elicit a fire hydrant gush of information. Men love talking about what they do for a living.

He grins. "Now, that's kind of a *secret*."

A secret? Really?

"So, you CIA or something?"

He places his drink on the bar with a clunk, empty, and signals another. "Now, now," he says, patting my hand.

Patting my hand? I squint at him.

"Don't you worry your pretty little self about that. Let's just say I sell something that's absolutely necessary to our survival as a nation."

"Don't I get the least, tiny, little hint?" I prod, curious. If I am going to hammer the last nail in this guy's coffin, I want to go out in a blaze of glory. My man-tennae, once blunted by idiocy, are now on full alert. If he sells militia uniforms or something, I am outta here. He considers my question as he waits for his drink

"I guess I can give you a hint." He winks. "It has something to do with livestock-induced methane gas."

I blink. "You mean, the gas produced by cattle, um, manure? That was discussed as an energy source or whatever?"

He nods proudly. "Yep! We have a patent on a device that will revolutionize the energy industry! Just takin' a little while for some folks to catch the vision."

The hilariousness of meeting a man I met online that sells a device that will utilize cow farts for a living overwhelms me, and I try to stifle an inadvertent low-level snorting. Which turns into giggling, of course, that I am unable to stop. A series of guffaws is right around the corner, but I struggle to get hold of myself before this happens.

The bartender and Sculpted-Edgy look at me in consternation. The early dinner crowd is arriving, and as I wipe hilarity-tears off my cheeks, I decide an exit is imminent.

Which is sad because the guy's looks could stop traffic.

Oh well.

I slip off my stool, hoist my purse on my shoulder, tell him it's been lovely, really, meeting him, but my kids need me, I have work to do, and hope he has a nice drive back to Glenwood. He is pleasant enough, but I see question marks in his eyes. He'll have to fill in the blanks himself, because I am done. I motion the bartender to bring my bill, pay my tab. Give Sculpted-Edgy the obligatory nice-to-meet-you-goodbye-hug, and speed-walk to my Honda.

I manage to exit the parking lot before I give the situation the full benefit of an appropriate response, and roar with laughter all the way home.

I unlock the garage door to the kitchen with relief, glad I can cross *that* one off the list, and the fleeting thought occurs to me that I should consider taking a break from Findamatch. I immediately push it away. Like I said, fleeting.

I run upstairs to change, run back down to give mom-hugs all around and prepare a light dinner for the kids. They catch me up on their various activities, and I counter with a full explanation of why I have to go to a meeting tonight.

As one, they are supportive and excited. I am a little taken aback by such enthusiasm for my apparent need for recovery, but then again, I have been on a roller coaster ride the past few weeks unlike anything I'd ever known, so nothing surprises me at this point.

I am not sure how to dress. I decide on jeans, bulky sweater and boots. I drag lipstick over my mouth, fluff my hair with my hands and hop in my Honda, patting its dashboard affectionately. Who doesn't love a Honda? I plug in the address on my GPS, which takes me through west Chatbrook to Peachtree Road, left on Magnolia Lane, and eventually the programmed female voice suggests I take a sharp right. I do, because I have learned that disobeying the GPS is never a good idea. I jerk the Honda right, drive until I spot a group of whitewashed stucco office buildings.

I park, approach what appears to be the main entrance. To the side of the entrance is a free standing sign that says, "***There is strength in shared support. All welcome!***" I stand there, thinking about the events that had led to this point, and am overcome with a desire to get back in my car and go home. Where I belong. With my kids. I'll ignore the computer, promise, I say to myself.

Yeah, right, myself says back to me.

With a resigned sigh, I pull open the door. Fear of what will happen if I don't, according to Thelma-the-social-worker, trumps my reluctance to encounter the unknown.

A black woman, forty-ish, sitting behind a desk loaded with books and information, greets me merrily. "Hey, darlin'! You here for a meetin'?"

I stutter that I am, give her Thelma's card, and tell her my name.

"Oh, yes!" She says, clearly delighted. "I got a call from Thelma today! She said to watch for you!" She pulls a group of documents together and paper clips them. "Here you go. This'll explain why we do what we do. The meeting starts in five minutes, right down that hall." She points, then says, "After the large group, there will be small groups, some for men, some for women. You'll be in the love and relationship group, honey."

"Love and relationship?" I repeat, confused. "I thought this was a group for after divorce, for single woman, or . . ."

She laughs. "Oh, don't worry! Lotsa people are confused at first. We don't just have groups for the typical categories like chemical or alcohol addiction, we have groups for the stuff you don't hear much about. Like you, for instance." She regards me somberly, entwining her fingers on the small metal desk she is seated behind.

"Honey, you had no clue what you were doin' was called insanity – doin' the same thing over and over again and expecting a different result. Nobody does, when they first come here. What we do is open your eyes and let you see the *truth.*" She shuffles a few papers on her desk, locates one with adhesive, peel-off labels. "Will you fill out a nametag and wear it? Makes it easier for folks to get to know ya, that's all." She shoves it at me, along with a marker, and continues to beam like a lighthouse.

There is something warm and honest about her, and I like basking in her aura. I am reluctant to leave. I want to pull up a chair and get to know her better, but instead, I obediently fill out a nametag, peel it off, affix it to my sweater.

"Okay, um, thanks for the information." I wag the pile of papers she's given me.

"No problem, honey. You enjoy your meetin' now. Let me know how it goes. Stay a little afterward and let's talk some!"

I smile and walk down the hall. My first recovery group friend. I wonder if they are different from regular friends. I open the door she'd told me to, and walk into a comfortable room that in one corner holds a small group of musicians with drums, guitars, keyboard, amps; and in the other, a buffet of food being served by a few smiling men and women. The smell of chili wafts up my nose, and I sniff hot cornbread as well.

At the front of the room is a simple, wooden podium, with a large screen behind it. Along each side are several circular tables where people are seated, talking and eating. The room is huge, more like an auditorium; and chairs are set up in the center in neat rows. People chatter in clusters of six or eight around the perimeter.

I stand there, silently surveying the activity, not knowing how to act or what to do. I feel vulnerable. Alone. The man hunter demon suddenly roars to life and squeals that I should get out of there and back home, where I can visit with my *real* friends on Findamatch in the comfort of my own house. My face feels flushed, hot; my palms are sweating and I recognize the symptoms of acute anxiety. Just as I am about to bolt, a hand rests gently on my shoulder. "Izzy?"

I turn, look into a familiar face. "Jon! Hi!"

Jon's eyes crinkle as he grins. "Thought that was you. Welcome! I'm really glad you're here! This is the best group of people, ever!"

I smile wryly. "Well, I didn't actually decide to come on my own. It was the social worker assigned to my son that – let's see, how should I put this – *strongly suggested* that it would be in my best interests to attend."

We laugh. I am surprisingly comfortable with Jon, and flash back to our lunch. Revelations shared. Two survivors hoping for a strong emergence on the other side of the pain. I find myself wanting to tell him about my recent epiphany, but it is fresh yet, and I haven't fully sorted out the implications.

"What group are you headed to?" Jon asks.

"Um, I think the lady at the desk called it love and relationship?"

Jon nods. "Yeah, that's a great group. It's really a shame how many women get caught up in that. I thought of you Izzy, when I started coming to this program a few weeks ago, and saw the name of that group in our handout. I never thought in a million years you'd come. And here you are!"

I shrug. "Life happens. What can I say?" I do not want to go into a full explanation, and somehow feel that he will understand.

Jon smiles. "It does, that's a fact. Have you eaten?" I tell him I have, with the kids, earlier. "Okay, well if you want, they start with a two dollar meal that's really great every week, at seven o'clock. You can come if you want, or not. I usually do. Don't like to cook,." I grin at his reference to typical bachelor behavior.

"Just for the cats," I say.

"Yeah, cat food in a bowl. I can handle that." He chuckles.

"So what happens now?" I say.

"Well, this group is a Christian recovery group. It's like AA, or NA; but the Twelve Steps focus on the teaching of Christ in the Bible. So we start off with a few praise songs . . ."

"You mean like hymns?" I interrupt him, surprised.

"Well, kind of," he considers my face, "but not really. They are songs that honor God, but they are cool. Upbeat. Hand-clappin' stuff."

I am clearly unconvinced.

"You'll like it, Izzy, I promise. It's very uplifting and kind of washes the day away."

"I can certainly use that! I'm open to about anything right now, and besides, it appears I don't have a lot of choice in the matter."

He steers me to where he is sitting, and invites me to take a seat beside him. The lights come up, and a man steps to the podium and welcomes us. He congratulates the newcomers as if stepping through the door the first time is tantamount to winning an Olympic medal, and encourages us to keep coming back. Announcements are quickly relayed, and the lights dim. A hushed expectancy fills the room. I look around, and see people popping up from their seats all over the room, until everyone, including me, is standing.

The band starts to play an unfamiliar song, but it instantly appeals to me. People begin to clap to the beat, and I join in. Smiling faces around me belt out the song at the top of their lungs. I glance at Jon and smile. Some are closing their eyes, which I find puzzling, others are smiling, singing, watching the musicians. The beat is intoxicating. Fun. The words march across the screen behind the podium, and I ponder their meaning.

The lyrics sound vaguely Biblical. I am acutely aware of my deficit in this area. I sneak another glance at Jon, and see that he is singing as loudly as the others, clearly enjoying himself.

After a couple of songs, the lights are brought up and a different speaker steps to the podium, identifying himself as someone who struggles with sexual addiction. I bolt upright in my chair. So it IS an actual addiction! I'd never quite believed it when it tore apart my last marriage, but then again, I'd never really known much about addiction, period. The speaker shares a mind-numbing personal story of abuse and secrets and lies. I hang on every word, and when he is finished, the group gives him a standing ovation. He cries in gratitude as he leaves the podium, thanking God for setting him free.

I am not quite sure I belong here, but I am certainly riveted. Jon glances sideways toward me. I return his gaze, and smile.

The thought lingers that I still have time to dash out to my car and disappear.

The large group concludes, we are given directions to our small groups, and I tell Jon I'll see him after, if he's still around. He says he will be. I walk down a narrow hallway and stop in front of a small plaque that identifies the Love and Relationship Addiction group. The door is partially open, and I rest my hand on the doorknob, hesitant to go further. Why had I agreed to this? What am I doing? Panic floods my nervous system.

The door swings open, nearly knocking me off my feet. A wisp of a woman with Brillo-pad hair, merry eyes and an infectious smile opens the door.

"Hi, there!" she says, "Thought I sensed a deer-in-the-headlights moment! Come on in! We won't bite." She ushers me into a group of women of all ages seated in a circle of folding chairs. Their smiles are warmly inviting.

The leader closes the door, indicates we are ready to begin, and shares group guidelines geared to individual, uninterrupted sharing. She then invites us to introduce ourselves, and talk a little about what we struggle with. The closer it gets to my turn, the more uncomfortable I become.

"Hi, I'm Izzy," I say, imitating the other women's remarks. The group shouts back, "HI, IZZY!" I am stunned and embraced at the same time. I continue. "Uh, I am not sure what I believe, but I know something wild is going on in my life, and I think it's directly attributable to prayer." Smiles all around, heads nodding. "I struggle with . . . online dating. I, um . . . love it!"

A few snickers of understanding.

"It's cost me a lot, though, and I realize if I don't get a handle on why I feel compelled to . . ." my voice falters. The group waits, silently. My eyes dart around the circle. ". . . why I feel compelled to run off in the middle of the night to meet men, I could lose my kids. Or my job." My voice drops to a whisper on the last few words, and I am surprised I'd blurted this out.

Tears well up in my eyes. I see a box of tissue in the middle of the floor, and realize that its placement there is anything but random. I stand, pluck one out and sit back down, dabbing at my eyes. The women are staring at me expectantly, waiting for me to continue. I do not feel up to sharing details. "Anyway, that's it, thanks."

After an hour of listening to other women share how their lives had been eviscerated time and again by their clueless choices in men, I am an emotional wreck. Their experiences, so transparently shared, triggers an onset of images in my own life. Regret squeezes my heart so hard I feel nauseous. The leader of the group approaches me afterward, concerned.

"You all right, dear?" I look into her kind face, and mumble that no, I'm having a hard time. She smiles. "Lots of you girls have a hard time at first. It'll get easier. Until you are aware of the consequences of your choices, you are unaware that you need to forgive yourself to move forward. It was hard for me at first. Hurt like hell, if you'll excuse the expression." I laugh weakly, and think about Darlene. She is the only person I can think of that I'd heard this kind of stuff from. I am wondering if I can keep it up. It does hurt like hell, actually. My hand seeks the coin in my pocket and rubs it.

"C'mon," she says. "You look like you could use some juice, and a snack. Let's get you some nourishment. You don't have to figure everything out at once, don't worry. We try to take one day at a time. God will only give you as much as you can handle."

With that, she takes my arm, lifts me from my chair, and walks me to the refreshment table. I feel like a complete idiot. I point to a pitcher of apple juice, and a woman obligingly pours me a cup and hands it to me. I wander down the row of desserts, and pick out a cookie adorned with M&M's, thinking how much my kids love them. I take my cookie and juice to one of the circular tables, sit, dig my cell out of my purse and text the kids, who assure me they're fine. I quickly text back that I'll be home in the next few minutes and remind them to lock the doors and keep the exterior lights on.

Jon approaches, and says "This seat taken?" I smile at him and move my head right and left. "Savin' it for you, Jon."

His plate holds a slice of pie, two cookies, and a yellow square, which I assume is a lemon bar. He follows my gaze. "Gotta get the homemade goodies when I can," he says. One of the cookies disappears from his hand in two bites. "So what'd you think? How was your group?"

"I'm processing," I say, and take a small bite of cookie. Lift the juice, sip. "It was amazing, actually. I'm thinking about what to do with the information. Seems so random, doesn't it?"

Jon's forehead wrinkles, his eyes questioning. "Random? Why?"

"Well, why would all these people get together, and just spill their guts on the floor? And nobody says a word to them in the group, or pat their shoulder, nothing." I shrug, pick up the cookie, take another bite. "I admit, there was a lot of stuff I totally relate to, but how does this help?"

Jon grins. "I thought the exact same thing, Izzy, when I first came. It's kind of strange how it works. There is something incredibly therapeutic in sharing about stuff uninterrupted. I don't understand it either, but this I know: since I've been in a group, I feel less helpless. More hopeful. Like I am not alone in my battle."

"So you feel you are in a battle? With what, life?" I cock my head, waiting.

"Well, according to the Bible, life is a battle. There is good, and there is evil. Real, actual evil that tries to take us down, through whatever means we are vulnerable to. For me, it was drinking. The amounts of alcohol I consumed on a daily basis caused my mind to deceive me. I was not rational. I forgot what I was like before . . ." his voice falters. He looks at the wall a few seconds, then continues, "before Maria died. Still hard." His words are nearly unintelligible.

I touch his arm. "I know it is Jon, I can only imagine what you've gone through."

"Yeah," he says, "well, I can only imagine what *you've* gone through lately! Yours is fresh, mine is not." He looks into my face, searching. "And I know you haven't told me everything, not that you have to, of course. I just know there's more going on."

I sigh. Push the remainder of a cookie into my mouth, and chew. We are silent a few minutes. After I wash the cookie down with the last of the juice, I continue, "There is, but I've kind of given it over." His eyes encourage me to go on. "As Darlene says – and Winston, too – God is in charge. They have both been praying for me like crazy," I laugh. "Can't get away from it, so I have decided to give it a try."

Jon smiles. "Me too, Izzy. Looks like we are makin' the trip together." He extends his hand for me to clasp. "Friends?"

I extend mine, and it is enveloped in his stronger, larger one. "Friends," I declare, and smile.

CHAPTER 52

My bed feels inviting and warm as I pull the comforter up, plump the pillows. The meeting had been eye-opening, to say the least. To think that there are untold numbers of women, just like me, who want a relationship with a man so badly they will sacrifice time, effort, money – even their kids – to get it. Their faces, stories, swim in my mind as I drift to sleep. Chad, Mimi and Peter had pounced on me the second I entered the kitchen, wanting details. The primary word that comes to mind when I think about their expressions as I related what my group had been like, is *relief.*

Pure relief.

It had been a long time since I'd felt that close to my children. The realization is jarring. Something has begun in me, something pivotal.

Tossing and turning, sleep is hopeless. I stretch, toss back the comforter. Plod to the kitchen, grab a bottle of water and a couple of ibuprofen. The rooms downstairs are dark, and I listen intently, still spooked by the thought of Jacob, who is now out on bail awaiting a court date. I hear nothing but the slight creaking of the house settling, the whir of the heating unit as it revs up to whoosh air through the vents, the refrigerator humming. Comforting house sounds.

Satisfied, I walk upstairs. Warning flags flap uselessly in my mind as I sit at my computer and log in. I know it's a lousy idea, but habits die hard. Findamatch tells me I have six messages waiting. I feel a familiar stirring in my chest as I open each. A smile spreads across my face after each one, their complimentary remarks slaking a deep thirst in my soul. The desire I feel to contact them is palpable.

In a split second of what the group tonight called *sanity*, I drop my head and ask God to intervene.

At that moment, the security alarm I'd set before going to bed shrieks. I leap out of the chair like a scalded frog, and run to my bedroom, where my cell begins ringing. My hands are shaking as I pick it up and answer.

"This is Izzy," I say.

"Ms. Lewis, your alarm has signaled us that there may be an intruder. We've notified the police, who should be arriving in approximately three minutes. Are you okay?"

"Yes, yes . . . I think so! I need to check my kids' bedrooms . . ."

"Ms. Lewis, keep us on the line. Are you on a cell?" I assure them I am, and quietly walk out into the hallway toward my kids' rooms.

"I am walking to their rooms now," I whisper, and enter each room. Peter is up, dragging on his pants, and I tell him to stay with me as I check the other bedrooms. Chad is standing at his door with an anxious look on his face, and I tell him to fall in behind us as well. "Cops are on the way, kids. Stay with me. Let's check Mimi."

I open Mimi's door. The stuffed animal menagerie is on the floor, her bed rumpled. Her window is open, the curtains softly billowing. Her bathroom door is closed, and I assume that's where she is.

"Mimi!" I whisper. "I need you!" The fan in the bathroom abruptly ceases, and she opens the door. "Mom? What is it?" She steps out, her intense, blue eyes wide. Sun-streaked, blonde hair twists in unruly waves over her shoulders. I motion all the kids into her room, lock the door. We all plop on the bed as a unit, nervously clutching each other.

"The alarm went off. The police will be here any minute. We just need to stay together." I look at her open window, thinking. "Mimi, did you . . . ?"

Her hands fly to her face in embarrassment. She looks at me regretfully. "I think so, Mom. Oh gosh, I'm so sorry!"

I sigh in relief, not the least irritated that she'd opened the window, forgetting the alarm was on.

"It's okay, Mimi." I run my hands through my hair, take a deep breath. My mind zips back to the quick prayer. Not exactly the way I'd have chosen to interrupt the temptation.

"Okay, guys, back to bed now, but lock your doors, okay?" They agree, and leave. I hug Mimi, tell her to be more careful, and over my daughter's head my eyes fall to her desk, upon which sits her laptop, open to a Facebook profile with a familiar face.

I release her, and pad over to the laptop. "What's this?" I turn, look at her. She looks at the ceiling and crosses her arms. "Okay, so I stayed up too late! What's the big deal?"

"Well, for one thing, you'll be dead tired tomorrow." I peer at the profile, and to my horror, see that the belongs to my stalker, Jacob. I sit and quickly sift through her personal messages.

"MOM!" Mimi runs over, attempting to close the laptop but I push her away.

"What the heck are you doing!" I scroll through her messages, finding Jacob's communications to her, quickly scanning them. "Do you know who this guy is? My God, do you have any idea?!" Mimi stands beside me, furious.

"It's none of your business!" she screams. "I have my own life! He is a nice man, and he says nice things to me. He is kind of like a big brother. I like him."

I stare at her in disbelief. "You have two perfectly awesome big brothers!

This guy is . . . well, he's . . ." words fail me. I quickly log into her settings, and block him. Then I turn to my daughter, whom I have ignored for the better part of two years, and regard her silently. Sadly. Things have to change, I tell myself. Nothing is worth this. *Nothing.* I experience an unprecedented level of hatred for my actions.

I am devastated, but for the first time in a long time, I am hopeful, too.

I shut off her computer, rise from the chair, sit on her bed. "Mimi," I say, patting the bed beside me. "I need to talk to you."

This time the pansies that line the walk to the Chatbrook Springs Police Department entrance appear as tiny, smiling faces, instead of colorful thickets of paranoia. They seem to bob their heads at me in a cheery welcome as I run up the sidewalk to the meeting. I muscle open the door, enter, and stand once again before the ill-mannered woman at reception. A flash of recognition hits her eyes. She slides the window open. "Yes?"

"Here for the meeting with Detective Fara – " The window abruptly slides closed. Within seconds the door to her small office opens and she steps out.

"This way," she says. I follow her ample, swaying, backside down the same narrow hallway, but this time it reeks of lemony antiseptic. We pass the same dust-colored walls and the same bright posters advertising Bulldog Auditorium's latest theatre offering. She raps lightly on Detective Faraday's door, opens it, motions me in. I thank her, and she exits, closing the door behind her. Detective Faraday and Phil rise to greet me with handshakes. After being asked, I say yes, I would indeed like coffee, and Detective Faraday leaves to get it.

Phil and I sit on tired, matching metal-and-gray vinyl chairs next to each other in Faraday's tiny office. Phil sips coffee, and asks me what I hope to accomplish with this meeting.

"Information, that's all," I say, thinking about his reaction to the revelations he will hear in a matter of minutes. I am enjoying the hope of imminent vindication, but feel a tug of fear, its fingers reluctant to release me without a fight. What if he doesn't believe me?

Detective Faraday arrives, hands me coffee, a stirrer and two creamers. I mumble my thanks, and he sits behind his metal, civil-servant desk, folds his hands over each other.

"So, to what do I owe the honor of this occasion?" he asks, looking from Phil to me. Phil clears his throat, looks at me.

I clear my throat as well, sip coffee. "Detective, I think it's time for Phil, who is acting as my supervisor temporarily, to be in on things. Everything."

Faraday gives me a puzzled look. "I thought Birdie was your supervisor – ?"

I shake my head. "Phil's arranged to take that over until we sort things out. Birdie's mad about it, too."

Faraday nods, understanding. "So you've told Phil," he gives Phil an inclusive glance, "a little about what's going on?" I nod assent. "Yep. But not all."

Phil's face is a mask. He is listening intently, the only indication of inner turbulence a slight tapping of his fingers on the arm of his chair.

"All right, then. Phil, here we go." Faraday smiles at Phil. Phil does not smile back. He leans forward, sets his coffee cup on the desk, settles in his chair and folds his arms over his chest.

Faraday says, "My first question to you is this: did your HR department run a routine background check on Birdie before hiring him?"

Phil looks sheepish. "Ahh, no. Since we'd been friends and business associates for ten years or more, we felt it unnecessary."

Faraday holds Phil's gaze for a second, then says, "Probably not the best idea. For starters, Birdie has a record in St. Louis that includes a few question and answer sessions regarding drug trafficking. No arrests, but it's my understanding with a bit more evidence, it would have been a slam dunk." He stops to sip coffee, continues, "Izzy did not ask me to look into this man's affairs, but as she has had problems with a guy named," he pauses to pick up documents from a file folder open on his desk and study them, "Jacob Samuelson, I've been suggesting various protective actions and we have developed a professional relationship." I glance at him quickly, acknowledging the grace with which he edited the Chad incident from this conversation.

Phil looks at me, then at Faraday, crosses his legs and sighs.

"I ran into Izzy when I was out with my wife, at" he looks at me for confirmation, "Raphael's, right?" I nod. He continues, "She was with Birdie, whom I did not know at the time, I but assessed his body language as adversarial and hers as frightened. I knew Izzy well enough to read her expressions a little, and she was not herself. If anything, she was nervous and paranoid, which I thought unusual."

"Later that evening, I called her to make sure nothing was amiss, and she told me Birdie had threatened her after luring her to meet him at Raphael's by pretending to be someone else online. She thought she was meeting a date, not her boss." Faraday pauses as his fingers walk through the file, searching for something. He pulls out two pages and hands them to Phil.

"Here is the report. Read for yourself."

Phil's expression grows strained. By the time he reaches the bottom of the second page, anger flashes in his eyes, and he slams the report down on Faraday's desk with a thunk. He swivels in my direction.

"*Why*, Izzy? Why didn't you tell me this?"

"I couldn't Phil! Birdie had already laid groundwork against me, don't you see? He told me he had you wrapped around his little finger!" I am having a hard time controlling my emotions. "That you'd never *believe* me. He said he would fake my numbers to make my sales look like they're falling, all kinds of stuff. I hoped he'd cool off, but he hasn't and he's made my life miserable. Trust me, I thought about telling you all this, but had to think about the best way. Then when Jacob showed up at the office, it left me no choice. Obviously, you had to be in the loop, or all the lies Birdie implicated about me would be confirmed." I stop to take a sip of coffee, glance at Faraday, then back at Phil. "I really think he was in collusion with Jacob."

Phil stretches his arms out wide in supplication. "Why? What's the connection? How would he have met him?"

I let out a long breath. "I didn't want to have to tell you this, but the man has been waiting for me outside the building for quite a while. He's has approached several people, who blew him off, but Birdie stepped right up to the plate and told him all kinds of stuff about me."

Phil's eyebrows rise, his eyes wide. "Why would he do that? Did he know the guy from somewhere?"

I shake my head aggressively. "No! He simply saw an opportunity to undermine me. That's what I'm tryin' to tell you! That's why I brought you to meet Detective Faraday. I knew you wouldn't believe me!"

Faraday has leaned back in his chair, watching with interest, his eyes bouncing from my face to Phil's.

Phil's expression is pained, helpless. "How am I supposed to get at the truth, here? What if Birdie's seen the error of his ways, and this job is a new start for him? Maybe he thought this guy Jacob was a friend and that he was doing you a favor."

I think about Phil's compassion toward those enmeshed in addiction, a new side of him that I don't fully understand, but see how it could affect his reaction to this discussion. Complicating the issue is that he'd signed on to Birdie as a good choice for retail sales manager. He needs a way to extricate himself without damage to his reputation, and I don't blame him. Me? I just want Birdie off my back and Jacob in an institution or medicated, whatever works. And to live my life in peace. Boring. Boring is good.

I cross my arms, look at Phil, then Faraday, who remains silent. I continue, "I don't know, Phil. I guess it's up to you to find the truth here. I *know* the truth, or I wouldn't have dragged you to the police department at eight o'clock in the morning."

Detective Faraday decides he should step in as moderator. "Phil, I know since you've not been in on this from the beginning it's not easy to follow. I can assure you, Izzy has done everything by the book, has held firm under a lot of pressure. I don't feel right about this guy, Birdie." He picks up his coffee, drinks, then sets it on a leather, circular coaster imprinted with *Chatbrook PD / Protection 'round the clock* in gold.

"After talking with Izzy yesterday, I think she's got a point. You might want to ask for the security video from yesterday, and see if Jacob got in by punching in a code. You have a pad outside each door, right?"

Phil nods.

"Any problem getting that footage?"

He shakes his head no, and says, "I can get it. Not a problem."

Faraday continues, "As I see it, the guy has been manipulating Izzy because she is not comfortable with how he conducts business."

Phil's forehead furrows, his hand drifts to his chin.

"Izzy, want to tell him what you told me?" Faraday says.

I clear my throat. "Phil, on our ride-a-long, the primary way he tried to *connect* with my clients was obscenity, dirty jokes, inappropriate comments." I fill him in on examples. "When he tricked me into meeting him at Raphael's, he told me things were going to go his way, or I'd be out of a job. He has repeatedly asked me to go out with him so he could," I use the first two fingers of each hand to indicate air quotes, "loosen me up."

I pause, thinking how heavy the burden of carrying this with me every day to the office has been, feeling the load lighten as I speak. "I didn't want to tell you, really, because I knew you'd be upset and think I was paranoid, but as time went on and the threats grew more direct, I had to get you involved. And here we are."

Phil looks as if he'd been run over by a Mack truck. His face is drained of color, his eyes dark and staring. I can tell his mind is scrambling toward how to unravel a huge mess.

Faraday says, "I know it's a lot, Phil. This is my suggestion." He eyes Phil's face, gauging his reaction to the information-dump. "When you get the footage, if Jacob is on it, keying into an entrance, bring it to me, it'll be great evidence. Birdie can't get that footage can he?"

Phil's face hardens, and he says, "Not if I get it first. I don't think he's been an employee long enough for people to trust him. I'll go directly to the operations manager the moment I get back to the office and check into it."

Faraday rises, sensing the meeting needs to end. "Okay, great." He fishes in his desk for a card, hands it to Phil. "Call me with any information. Also, as I told Izzy, I'd like to know if he makes any international travel plans."

Phil nods. "You got it." To me, he says, "Izzy, I'm sorry you couldn't trust me enough to come to me with this, but I understand. I'm gonna think this through, and talk to my higher-ups. Could be between the footage, the identity code, and the information I've gotten here . . . may be enough to distance ourselves and approach him about finding other employment."

Faraday says, "Could be. But hold up on that until we talk, okay? I may need some help if an arrest is warranted."

Phil pushes his shoulders back, adjusts his tie. "Okay. I will. We done here?"

Faraday smiles and nods. "Thanks for coming in."

"No problem. Appreciate the time." He turns, inclines his head toward me, opens the door and strides out into the hallway. Faraday and I are silent as we listen to his footsteps recede down the hall.

I slump in my chair and rub my eyes. Faraday shuffles the papers back into what I assume is my file, sits. "I never figured this would get so . . . convoluted," I say, through my hands.

Faraday smiles. "Yeah, well, it's for the best. Birdie needs to be jerked around a little. Is that guy married?"

I nod in the affirmative.

"Man!" he says. "I sure wouldn't want to be his wife."

We say our goodbyes, and I resist hugging him. I am so glad to have Detective Faraday on my side that I can hardly speak. For the first time in a long while, I see a flash of light at the end of a very long and dark tunnel.

CHAPTER 53

Later that afternoon, Phil walks quietly to my desk, leans over my shoulder and asks if I have time to come to his office. In light of recent events, the slightest crook of his index finger and I'd come running. I hop up, throw my proofs to Lonnie, who gives me an irritated look, and follow Phil to his office. He waits by the door as I enter, then closes it.

He sits behind his desk, sighs, lifts his readers to the top of his head, rubs his eyes. Then he pulls his arms behind his head, interlaces his fingers, leans back.

"Okay, Izzy, here's what I've found out. This is just between you and me. Period."

I shake my head up and down, mute, my heart beating a thousand miles a minute. I glance toward Birdie's office.

Phil follows my gaze. "Don't worry, he's not here. I made sure he was out with one of the reps. Don't want him too bent out of shape over our meetings that don't include him."

He leans forward, picks up a couple of flash drives, hands one to me. "A copy for me to show Faraday, a copy for you to have. Hide it."

I look at him, and put the flash drive in my lap. "Okay. What's on it?"

"Obviously, Jacob, and he's punching a code into the security pad. No way he could have gotten in unless someone had given him the code. And we all know who's code it is." Phil slaps a frustrated hand on his desk. "How could I have missed this! He did such a good job of hiding who he really is!"

Unused to such transparent emotion from Phil, I am surprised. Instead of simply a quota-driven slave driver with no time for the staff except when goals are missed, I am seeing a man capable of righteous indignation and compassion.

"Phil, it could have happened to anybody."

He snorts. "Right. I've only been doing this twenty-five years. You'd think I would have picked up on *something*. Now we're in a mess that could have been prevented if only someone had done a simple background check."

"Yeah, and I could have prevented a lot of things if I'd looked ahead, too. A lot of this is my fault." I am mortified at the part I seem to have played. Image after image of nights spent on Findamatch roll over me.

Phil shrugs.

"We're human, Izzy. Can't foresee things. Hindsight, is – as they say – 20/20." He taps his fingers on his desk, brings his glasses to his nose, lifts a file and opens it. Jabs at a document inside, retracts it, hands it to me. "This is what I cannot believe!"

I take the proffered paper, quickly scan. A summary of Birdie's activities a decade ago, that Faraday had apparently emailed Phil. The report details purported drug trafficking, drug possession, possession with intent. I raise my gaze to Phil's, twin light bulbs in my eyes. "You ever notice how Birdie has intense mood swings? Goes from laughing to anger in a matter of minutes?"

Phil nods. "I have, yes."

"Follow me on this – do you think Birdie is still using?" As the words tumble out of me, my newly gained knowledge from my experience with Chad gains a foothold, drives a stake in my mind. "Seems like one of the first tip-offs of a user is mood swings. Another is pinpoint pupils. Another is irrational thought."

Phil takes his glasses off. "You think Birdie is high? As in, since he's been here?"

I shrug. "I don't doubt it. Would answer a lot of questions for me. His behavior is anything but normal, and he has trouble keeping himself under control. I'm not the only one that has noticed."

Phil says, "I've talked to the other salespeople he manages, Izzy. They've not indicated anything out of the ordinary. In fact, their figures are up, and I've attributed it to Birdie's leadership, so I don't think that – "

"No!" I interrupt fiercely. "They're *afraid* of him! There is something about him that puts everyone on edge, trust me. Dig a little deeper with them. You'll see."

Phil sighs. I extend the paper to him, which he slides into the file folder, and puts the folder in a desk drawer. "Okay, Izzy, so whatever happens, looks like we have a problem, and it's *not you*."

I smile, "Thank God for that!"

Phil smiles back, "Yes, thank God. Look, after I talk to Detective Faraday about this, let's get together and discuss how to move forward. I don't want to step on toes that don't need to be stepped on."

I nod. The political conundrum this is creating for him must be horrible.

He continues. "If he's actively using, then it's easy. He'll be dismissed. If he's not, and all we have is Jacob and the code, he may lie and say someone stole it from our database or whatever. So let's proceed with caution."

"You got it." My eyes graze his face, gentle. "Thanks, Phil, for how you are responding to this. You cannot imagine the relief I feel that I'm not losing my job!"

Phil taps his fingers on his desk, thinking, and mutters, "I'm just sorry I didn't catch on sooner, Izzy." He shakes his head, rolls his eyes. "We'll figure it out."

Switching gears, he says, "Heard you were at a meeting last night . . . ?" and smiles.

I am puzzled. "How did you know – "

"Jon told me the minute I got into the office. He's really into the program.

He couldn't wait to tell me about you. I couldn't go last night, but I am usually there, too, in the alcohol dependency group.

Feeling a distinct shift in our relationship, I say, "I thought we were supposed to keep all that confidential . . ."

Phil says, "Oh sure, but if I want to tell somebody about my struggle with alcoholism, I can. The confidentiality is for others. You don't want to tell other people about someone else's involvement in case they do not want others to know. Been sober eight years now." He smiles broadly. "It's a great feeling. I'll tell anybody that asks."

"That is awesome, Phil," I say, meaning it. "I never thought I had a problem, but apparently, the online dating is just a symptom of something deeper. I got so much out of my first night! Not sure where it's going to end up, but I am definitely looking forward to the next meeting."

He nods in understanding. "The first meeting is the hardest, when you actually admit to yourself – and others – that you have a problem. Then everything's easier after that. I was amazed how many guys had struggled with situations similar to mine, and that gave me hope. I wasn't such a bad guy after all. If they made it, then so could I." His eyes lock with mine. "And so can you. Probably see you there at some point."

Phil is head down already, pulling a pile toward him. He waves in dismissal. I return to my desk, glad it is nearly time to head home.

Lonnie trots in from the back and asks if I need anything. I hand him a pile of ads I'd meant to take back to production but hadn't. Winston has graced us with an appearance and stops at the coat rack near the elevator to hang up his coat. He makes his way to the pod.

"Hey, Pod-Queen!" he says, "how are things today?" He slides into his chair, takes off his sunglasses, places them carefully on his desk, lifts his reading glasses to the bridge of his nose.

I lean back in my chair, cross my arms. "Good, Pod-King. *Great*, actually." For the next few minutes, Winston and I laugh and joke about sundry and superficial things. We compare notes on sales quotas, client situations. Lonnie has agreed to take my ads to production (yay) and turn them in so I don't have to. Phil's wave as he exits down the stairs is returned in triplicate by our pod. The end of day tasks feel almost normal.

I swivel to grab my stuff in preparation to go home with a deep, satisfied sigh. Winston leans over the cubicle divide conspiratorially, and my heart beats a little faster. Oh *please* don't let there be a new drama unfolding, I silently beg God.

Lately this prayer thing has become a habit.

I lean in Winston's direction.

"Any new stuff on the Birdster?" Winston asks.

I scan the sales floor. Most of the salespeople have gone for the day, or are busily wrapping up. Birdie's office is closed, his door locked, so I figure he is still out on the call with one of the reps as Phil had indicated.

"Yeah. Between you and me, Birdie's wings are about to be clipped."

Winston's bushy, white eyebrows rise above concerned, pale blue eyes. "Really?" He leans in closer, his voice hushed. "What happened?"

"Can't tell you. I'd have to kill you."

Winston rolls his eyes. "Seriously, did something happen?"

"Yeah, it did. But I cannot give out details. Just really pray that the truth comes out. And that there are no repercussions for the *Sentinel*, or Phil."

His eyebrows rise another eighth of an inch. "Phil? He's involved now?"

I nod. "That's all I can say. Pretend I never said anything, okay?"

Winston sticks fingers in both ears and closes his eyes. "Hear nothing. See nothing."

The elevator door glides open with a slow screech and Birdie steps out. He stops to stretch. I watch him, thinking that he is probably worn out from all the new jokes he had to come up with for client bonding today. He sees me watching him, frowns, and strides toward his office. Unlocks the door noisily, enters, slams it behind him. I wonder what is so important in his office that he locks it every time he's gone for even a few minutes.

Winston sits in his chair, fingers running up and down his lanyard. I smile the teensy smile of the almost-liberated, pluck my purse from the drawer, slam the drawer shut. I wish Winston a nice evening, and walk to the elevator. As usual, its ponderous descent takes forever. I figure because it is old, it gets confused easily. I turn to the right. Walk to the stairs instead. My hand is on the doorknob when I hear, "Izzy, can you come see me for a minute?"

To his credit, Winston resists looking in my direction. Birdie's hyper-paranoid suspicions pounce at the slightest provocation, and I am grateful for Winston's discretion. I turn and tell him I must get home to my kids. Always a handy and believable excuse. And usually true.

He squints, which I'm guessing means he is *not* pleased; and walks to where I am. I can tell by his expression he didn't really think I'd decide to come in and talk to him, but I can also tell by his expression that he is determined to talk to me anyway. So I stand, waiting, my palm polishing the doorknob with perspiration.

His expression is menacing as he walks to me. One hand reaches over my head to lean against the wall, the other lands on his hip, effectively pinning me in the space. I smell the stink of cigar, and the sour breath of a liquid lunch. "If it isn't Ms. High and Mighty herself," he slurs. I have the presence of mind to check his eyes. His pupils are tiny dots.

"It appears we have ourselves a little situation." The word comes out as "sitch-ee-yay-shun." I notice his hands are trembling, another indicator.

"What situation, Birdie?" I respond, compassion creeping into my thoughts now that I understand the possible source of his strange behavior. He continues, "I have ways of findin' out stuff, sweetie," he says. "Word is that you dug up some of my past that I thought had been laid to rest a long time ago. Ten years ago, to be exact."

"We all have a past, Birdie," I said, my mind grasping at straws. How could he know? Who had told him? Does it matter? "I have a past. Everybody has a past. I didn't dig up anything, by the way." Nope. Faraday had done the digging. His eyes hold mine.

"I've been tryin' to give you some slack, Izzy, really have. But I can see you are one of those who just doesn't *listen!*" His voice rises on the last word. Winston glances at us. I am relieved he is still here. "I'm just sayin' watch your back," Birdie hisses through clenched teeth. "You don't know who you're messin' with." I feel pity mixed with a huge desire to get away from him. He pushes off the wall, crosses his arms, takes a step back and widens his stance, never taking his eyes from mine. I pull open the door, my hand slipping off the knob a little, and have to grab twice. As I run down the stairs, I hear him yell for Lonnie.

CHAPTER 54

All the way home I want to shoot myself.

Lonnie! Patient, dedicated, Lonnie. Steadfast employee. Energetic assistant. Traitor-at-large.

I pound the steering wheel in frustration. He was sitting there listening to my entire life, when I thought he was marking up proofs, taking care of his own business and ignoring mine! How could I be so stupid?

I walk into the house and head straight for the wine rack. I select a bottle of Clos du Val and uncork. The door to the deck squeaks as I open it and step out, waiting for the wine to breathe. The bushes and trees in my backyard have passed their fall color prime, and are quickly losing plumage. I step back in, pour the wine, sip, close my eyes for a silent savor moment, and return to the deck. The days are shorter now, and dusk tamps out what's left of the sunset.

I sit in the twilight, listening to the breeze rustling through the trees, watching the stars pop out one by one. The wine relaxes me. I study the vastness, picking out the North Star, the Big Dipper. Words catapult from my mouth to heaven. I ask God to forgive me for being an idiot. To do a miracle, and take the threats away.

I am silent, then, listening.

When I leave the deck, I feel something important has just taken place

An hour passes. Two. One sleepy eye pops open and stares at the clock. One o'clock in the morning. The pull to go to my computer is so strong, I feel as if I am wrestling with an adversary. I will myself to stay in bed, to sleep. I argue with the man hunter demon that hisses I am missing a great opportunity. Right now! Eventually I rise and tiptoe down the hall.

I stare at my computer.

Maybe this is what addiction feels like. No! No! The man hunter demon shrieks. This is good and necessary and you have earned it! You deserve a little fun! Remember how good it feels? Surely you remember!

I log on. Three blinking messages await me. The warm sensation I typically feel is absent, and the act of opening the messages feels forced.

After opening and reading the messages, instead of elation, I feel nausea hurtling through me like a fireball. I barely make it to the bathroom.

My insides heave into the commode as I hastily kneel, my knees imprinted by cold, hard tiles. My hair clings damply to the sides of my face, which hangs over the bowl, awaiting the second heave. My arms clutch the sides of the toilet as if this will steady the churning in my stomach.

"God, I promise, *promise* I will break this addiction. But I need your help. I can't do it by myself. Please help me!" Over the next several minutes, my stomach ceases its roiling, my head stops spinning and my eyes clear. I sit my back against the bathroom wall, push the hair out of my face, and feel the clamminess recede. I know with absolute assurance the episode was meant to pull me from self-destructive behavior. I'll do nearly anything to prevent nausea.

Only God would know that.

I carefully pad back to my bedroom, clutching my still-tender stomach. My screen-saver merrily rotates a photo of the kids and me laughing and hugging each other.

I get it, God, I get it. Sigh. *I get it.*

Birdie

Birdie sits, as usual, in a darkened den, the only light from the banker's lamp illuminating the laptop on his desk. His personal email tells him there had been several meetings between Izzy and Phil, one off-site this very morning. Lonnie had been true to his word. He is very appreciative of the pills Birdie supplies him, and is happy to return favor for favor.

Lonnie is a trusting, stupid fool. He thinks about how easy it is to manipulate people. Most of them are fools. Except, perhaps, Isabelle Lewis. He sighs, sips his scotch, and pushes off the leather couch.

He walks to a painting on the far side of the room.. His eyes trail over the scene: hunters celebrating their kill, an unfortunate deer hanging upside down, tethered to a branch, its lifeblood draining, the eyes wide and staring. The animal's tongue lolls to the ground. The hunters' faces are wreathed in smiles, their arms uplifted in jubilation. Inscribed on a small, oval plate centered at the bottom of the frame, is the title, "Predator and Prey." He never tires of the painting. Turning his head slightly left, he surveys the trophies on his wall. An eleven-point whitetail, an elk, a wolf. The wolf had been an accident in hunting camp, but had become his favorite. Something in the eyes.

He walks to his desk, opens a drawer, lifts a box of cigars and selects one. Snips off the end, lights, puffs determinedly. Smoke trails him like a vaporous snake as he walks back to the painting. His fingers grope in the dark for a small, hidden button, then press. The painting swings out to reveal a wall safe. He swirls the knob, opens the safe to check his stash, which includes a few pounds of weed, six ounces of cocaine, and assorted containers of prescription meds. He lifts a small, amber, cylinder and twists off the white cap. Extracts two pills. Removes the cigar, throws them into his mouth, washes them down with scotch. Replaces the cigar and sucks, hard. The safe is snicked shut with a metallic click. He pushes the painting back into place. Then he walks to his desk, turns off the banker's lamp and shuts his laptop.

His extra-large La-Z-Boy squeals as he contentedly pushes it all the way back and closes his eyes. The ember at the end of the cigar brightens, then wanes in the darkness.

CHAPTER 55

Izzy

The weather app on my phone insists that it is boot-and-sweater weather. I stand before my closet, considering, and pull out a long, fuzzy, sweater vest that I hope will pull together what I already have on. I shrug into it and stand before the full-length mirror in my bedroom. My hair is now past my shoulders, and cannot decide if it should flip up or curl under. A haircut needs scheduling immediately. The circles under my eyes are pronounced due to lack of sleep, but good concealer works miracles, and blush goes a long way.

I decide I'll do, even though, as usual, I have not had time to iron things and am a little rumpled. I assure myself no one will notice under the vest, and run downstairs to make sure the kids have everything they need for school.

"Nice boots, Mom." Mimi says, slurping instant oatmeal. Chad is stuffing books into his backpack, and Peter is texting. They look up at me and smile their good mornings.

"Hi, guys, anybody need anything today? We good?" Heads nod in unison. If I want actual information from teenagers, I'll have to dig for it. "What's happening after school?"

"Usual, Mom," Chad says, "picking up Mimi." His eyes slide to her face. "Right, kid?" She nods and scrapes up the last of her oatmeal, rises, puts her dish in the sink.

"How about you, Peter?" I open the refrigerator, considering my options for breakfast.

"Basketball, Mom. Always."

I nod, "Okay. When are you gonna be home?"

"Not sure," he says, hedging. I turn, notice Mimi looking at him, a smile on her face, hands on hips. My eyes slice from his to hers, a question in them.

Mimi laughs. "Yeah, Mom, he's not sure lately, because he's got a *girlfriend*!"

"Oh?" I look at Peter. "That right? Who?"

Peter mumbles the name of one of the cheerleaders, his cheeks reddening. I realize my kids have lives of their own, much of which I have been missing. A rush of appreciation zips through me like a spring shower. I really am changing. Perhaps it is not too late to start over with my kids.

"That's great, honey. Will you bring her over for dinner soon, so I can meet her?"

Peter gives me an astonished look. "Really? When would you have time? Um, I mean . . ."

I smile at him. "Things are different now. I'd love to meet her. I'll make the time, don't worry."

He smiles at me. Grabs his backpack, slings it over one shoulder. "Okay."

"By the way," I continue, "when's your next game?"

"Uh, tomorrow at six." His face pinches together. "Don't tell me you are actually thinking about coming?"

"Yep. Definitely. I am going to be there for more of your games."

The look he gives me is gratifying, and I feel I have just won a Mom-medal. Mimi and Chad are both standing very still, watching.

Peter is the first to break the spell. "Yeah, well that would be great, but I've heard it before." The three of them exit the kitchen, clomping down the stairs to the garage and their car.

I deserve that, I tell myself silently as I wave goodbye and watch their car back down the driveway into the street. I do, but I'll show you. I will.

Winston is well through coffee-and-newspaper time when I arrive at the top of the stairs, somewhat winded. I open the door cautiously, hoping Phil is in the coffee break area with the other managers. The coast seems clear, so I trot briskly to my desk, all business, quickly drop my purse in the drawer and shut it with a bang. Winston, not missing a beat, says "Made it this time, not to worry. Phil's in the back, and I haven't seen Birdie this morning." He does not look at me, his eyes locked on the newspaper, coffee at the ready in one hand. He turns his head toward me, sips his coffee. "Don't understand why commission salespeople have to be in their chairs at exactly eight-thirty anyway."

I smile. "Me neither. What's going on this morning?"

He thinks a minute. "Seems calm. No calamities that I know of. Yet."

I nod. "Well, I bet one will be coming along any minute now."

"Think so?" he asks, one hand drifting to the ever-present lanyard. His fingers work at it relentlessly, oblivious to the habit.

"Yep. I think so." I grin wickedly.

He leans over the divider, and whispers, "When, exactly?"

I lean toward him, nearly nose-to-nose. "Watch and see."

He leans back, indignant. "That doesn't tell me anything!"

I laugh. "Yeah, I know, but believe me, if you see the HR director wandering around up here, in and out of Phil's office, or Birdie flitting around, something's happening."

He responds, "Birdie is *always* on the warpath lately. What's going on with him, anyway?"

"A lot," I say. And leave it at that. I open my newspaper to Main News and smooth the pages with a practiced thumb slide. "Gotta get coffee, want any?"

Winston grimaces. "Kidding, right?"

I grin at him, and dash to the back, with a pit stop at Darlene's desk. "Hey! Morning, what's going on?"

She looks up from the stack of invoices she is concentrating on, places a ruler underneath the last entry, folds her arms on her desk, looks up at me, and smiles. "Not much, working. What's up?"

"Lots. Had an excellent meeting with the detective I told you about and Phil yesterday. Gotta keep it quiet though," I said, my voice dropping as I glance around.

"Ja?" Her face glows with interest. "Vat's the latest?"

I hold my hand out in a *halt* gesture. "That's all I can say for now."

She sighs. "I'll be so glad when life gets back to normal for you."

"Normal for me is changing, I think. In a good way." I give her a quick thumbs-up, and continue the next few paces to the coffeemaker. My nose twitches at the scent of male cologne, a hint that the managers have circled the wagons.

Several upper-tier professionals form a casual loop around the coffeemaker. As I approach, I see Birdie standing uncertainly behind the others, obviously outside the circle. This feels vindicating, somehow, and with a bounce in my step, I part the wagons.

A chorus of good mornings greet me, a few cups lift in salute. We banter about my accounts, which I find a refreshing alternative to bantering about my online activities. My self-confidence, which I had apparently misplaced, has been reborn. I feel a comforting camaraderie with this group today, and wonder when on earth it had slid off the rails.

We joke about each other's clients, and after a few minutes, one of the men lifts the fully perked pot to pour. I stick out my coffee mug, thank him, and turn to leave. Suddenly, Birdie steps toward me, his eyes blazing. "Leaving before even acknowledging my presence?"

I turn toward him, resigned. An uncomfortable silence descends on the group. I lift my steaming mug to my lips and sip.

"Good Morning, Birdie," I say, holding his gaze, and wait. His hands are trembling, his face pale. The pocket kerchief is hastily stuffed rather than carefully folded. He stares at the men now gazing at him with interest.

Birdie then makes the unwise decision to go public. "Izzy, here, has been participatin' in a campaign to get me busted," he declares. "She thinks she can do no wrong." His laughter is grating, hoarse. "So I have a record! It was ten years ago! Everybody has stuff in their past!" He sniffs several times. I look carefully at his eyes. The pupils are pinpoints. I am thinking, even though I despise this guy, he is about to walk down a path from which there is no recovery.

Then I quickly jump to an obvious correlation. Could Birdie benefit from recovery? The thought stuns me, and I realize certain things might be happening for a reason.

Phil glances at me, nods imperceptibly, and moves near Birdie, slipping an arm through his. "Let's take a walk, Birdie."

He reacts to Phil's touch like a poisonous snake has sunk its fangs into him. "No way! I know you and Izzy," he gestures toward me, "have been talkin' about how to take me out."

"Take you out?" Phil's eyes assess Birdie's as he massages his arm where Birdie had pushed it away. "What do you mean?"

Birdie retrieves the pocket kerchief and wipes his forehead, which had begun to glisten. "You guys have been having lots of meetings, Izzy's been avoiding me. You've taken full oversight of her responsibilities. What else am I supposed to think?"

I am aghast. How could he do this in front of the whole management team? Not to mention the production staff, which are standing in doorways, wondering what the ruckus is about.

Phil tries again to move the conversation to his office. Birdie takes this as a personal affront, and pushes Phil roughly. He then turns toward me, his eyes hard as marbles. "This is all your fault, you bitch! Couldn't just go along, could ya? I knew you were trouble the first time I ever set eyes on you." His voice has softened to a low growl. His hands are clenched into fists at his side. He slowly raises one arm, and I watch as if hypnotized, unbelieving. Birdie lunges toward me like a wild animal. I squeak and hop out of the way.

Things blur after that.

As I step away from what I perceive to be an attack, Birdie loses his balance and falls, taking my steaming mug of hot coffee down with him. The coffee splashes out and burns several managers, who yelp in surprise and pain. Out of the corner of my eye, I see Darlene running toward me. Lonnie, who had been in production, trots up the hall to see what's going on, and I see his eyes widen when he sees Birdie is the center of the commotion. He skulks back to production, head lowered.

Birdie rises from the floor like an angry Phoenix. "You know what I'm talking about, Izzy!" He dusts himself off, spreads his hands to the men around us in various states of coffee-splats and confusion. "Just ask Jacob Samuelson!"

Phil's head snaps to attention, he grabs Birdie's arm. "Okay, Birdie, let's go. Now!"

Birdie rips his arm from Phil. "No! You have a right to know what she's been up to! And it's not *selling*!"

My face is ashen. Sure, I've had my online exploits. Certainly it has affected my work somewhat if I've come in tired from staying out late. But not this! What must the other managers think? I look around, chagrined. Phil catches my eye and winks. I release the anxiety, take a deep breath, and summon a little courage.

"Birdie," I say, "whatever it is you're on, it's messing with your head. What the heck are you talking about?"

The other managers chuckle, which is exactly the reaction I'd hoped for. Birdie is so mad spittle is dribbling from the corners of his mouth as he spits out words. "Bitch!" He sniffs, grabs his handkerchief and wipes his mouth. "You've never wanted me here!"

My demeanor, which has become almost serene, surprises me. "Birdie, that just isn't true. All I ever wanted was you to do your job. Without crude comments and dirty jokes. Without trying to get me to go out with you. You're married, aren't you, Birdie?" And just like that, I destroy his credibility, and retain mine.

He lunges for me again, but this time, three managers grab his arms. Phil quickly calls Security, and indicates with a head slant I should return to my desk, that he'll take it from here. Then he smiles. I translate the smile as "We just got him handed to us gift-wrapped and tied with a bow."

I walk back to my desk nearly dancing with relief. I feel giddy, light-headed. Maybe the nightmare is over. Maybe I can enjoy the job I love again. Darlene is nervously flitting around her desk, worry in her eyes. I give her a brief recap, promise to talk to her at length about it in the near future.

Winston is standing in the middle of the aisle with his hands behind his back, anxiously chicken-necking. When he sees me, he raises one hand, I assure him I'm okay with my eyes, and he returns to his desk, where he knows he'll be informed in due time through pod-versation.

My desk, by this time, is covered with ads awaiting attention. I force myself to focus, call client after client, let them know their proofs are in their email inboxes, waiting for their review. After an hour of scurrying to meet deadlines, I feel somewhat caught up. My assistant is still absent, and I'm becoming irritated that he's not available to help me. I place both elbows on my desk and shove my chin into my hands, thinking about the relationship between Lonnie and Birdie. My mind chews on this for a while, and spits out the unsavory deduction that Lonnie might be involved in this mess.

I think about his demeanor lately, which has been choppy, abrupt. Very unlike him. Add to this the number of times I'd seen Lonnie exit Birdie's office, which had perplexed me. Assistants do not usually spend a lot of time in a sales manager's office. I feel my eyes grow wide at the dawning realization that Birdie had probably been *supplying* him in exchange for information about me.

I turn to Winston to disgorge this line of thought, then tell myself to keep my mouth shut. Some things are better left unsaid until I figure out what to do with them. Besides, I have no proof.

I have a hard time keeping my eyes off Phil's office. His door is closed, but the curtains are open. Birdie sits in a chair in front of Phil's desk. His chin rests on his chest, his back slumped.

The police arrive to escort Birdie to a waiting patrol car, where I am sure Detective Faraday is smiling to himself that his suspicions were correct, after all. As Birdie passes the pod, a policeman on either side of him, he gives me a look of pure contempt.

Winston is sitting quietly across the pod-divide, taking it all in. He glides his thumb and forefinger up and down the lanyard. I know he is watching the shifting expressions on my face and coming to his own conclusions. After Birdie has disappeared into the elevator, I close my eyes, bow my head. A deep breath causes my chest to rise, then fall.

"Izzy, it wasn't you." Winston's voice is soothing. "It wasn't ever about you. The guy has problems, really severe ones. He's medicating." My eyes pop open, and I turn my head toward him. "You knew?"

Winston nods. "I suspected. I didn't know for sure, but I've had experience with drug addicts. My daughter. My grandson."

My mouth drops. "Oh, Winston, I never knew!"

He shakes his head and smiles. "Don't have to know. I just try to keep it separate, that's all."

I gaze at him in understanding. My heartbeat is slowing, the adrenaline surges less urgent. "Me too. I call it compartmentalizing."

"Yeah," Winston said. "We all do that. Sometimes life gets so complicated, I just can't think about it all at once, so I have the personal stuff, the work stuff, kind of separated in my mind."

"Does that work for you?" I ask.

"Nah," Winston says. "It's just my small attempt at trying to keep it together."

I laugh. "Well, the past few weeks, I've discovered something really major about that, Winston."

His eyes light with interest. "And that is?"

"That I can't keep it all together. It's impossible. Without God, it's impossible."

"Never heard you say anything more true, Izzy," he said, turning his attention to his newspaper now that the crisis had left the building.

"So help me, that's the truth," he reiterates quietly.

Winston reads the paper a minute or two, then turns his head toward me as he flips the page.

"What do you think is going to happen to Birdie?" His eyes slide toward the corner office. Phil is turned away from his desk, looking out his windows. I follow Winston's gaze.

"I don't have a clue," I say, and nod my head in the same direction, "but you can bet Phil is figuring that out right now. This is a tough one for all concerned. Management has to think about the reputation of the newspaper. I wouldn't want the responsibility of spinning all this, that's for sure." I pick up my cell, see a couple of missed calls from the kids, realize I've worked right through lunch. Gratitude that the clouds over my life seem to be clearing spreads through me like warm sunshine.

"Winston, do you think I've earned an afternoon off? I think it'd be a good thing to be home when my kids come home."

Winston smiles, leans back in his chair, clasps his hands behind his head. "I most certainly do, Isabelle. I think that's an excellent plan." I grab my purse from the drawer, slam it shut, survey my desk for anything I might need to take home, decide there is nothing that cannot wait until tomorrow. I stop briefly by Phil's office and make sure he doesn't need me the rest of the day. He turns, rolls his chair up to his desk and pounds his desk with a fist.

"Well, we've sure gotten ourselves into a fine mess this time, haven't we, Izzy?"

Confused, I say, "Um, yeah, I guess, but I think the mess is resolving itself!"

Phil laughs. His fingers tap dance on his desk. "Maybe the mess is resolving for *you,* but my mess is just beginning." He studies his hands, then looks at me. "I'm so sorry, Izzy, that you've been dealing with this. I honestly had no idea."

"I know, Phil. I never once thought you did. I was frankly surprised that you hired him in the first place. Most of us were!"

Phil's eyebrow shoot up. "Really? The sales team had doubts from the beginning?" I nod emphatically. He continues, "Man, I wish I had better intuition about that stuff." He shrugs. "Not much I could do about it anyway, the final decision was made from higher up."

"I know, Phil. No worries."

He eyes my face. "We good?"

"We're good." I say, smiling. I turn to leave. Phil says, "And another thing – "

I take my hand off the door, turn back to him, waiting. He folds his arms across his chest. "I'm thinking about what's best for Birdie, too, not just the newspaper. You get what I'm sayin'?"

I consider the statement in light of the recent revelations about Phil's extra-curricular activities. "Yep. I totally get what you're saying, Phil."

CHAPTER 56

Two months later

Raphael's is packed, and I jostle through throngs of men and women celebrating the end of the week toward the bar. The crowd presses in, an amorphous, multi-headed, laughing mob. I can't seem to locate Darlene, but eventually her drink rises to the occasion.

A pink Cosmopolitan drifts through the mass, a small hand holding it high. Darlene is so short, her arm is lost among the throng and the drink seems to propel itself. I push an attractive, middle-aged man aside with an elbow, inching closer to the floating Cosmo. The man smiles at me, holding my eyes. I notice he is wearing a wedding ring, and give him a *go home to your wife* look. What is it with men, anyway?

The crowd swells around me, and I must move or get crushed. I swivel my head, bullseye the Cosmo, and scoot sideways toward it. After a few more exclamations of *excuse me* and *sorry*, I am in shouting distance of Darlene. She is peering in all directions, two heads shorter than those near her. I watch, laughing, as she struggles to bring her drink to her mouth, then lifts it again as people push and shove around her. She's stuck. She can't drink, she can't move, and she can't find me. I swoop to her side. She turns toward me with relief.

"There you are! Oh my gosh, I didn't know if I vould ever find you!" she shouts.

I shout back, "Next time wear your four-inch platforms if we come to Raphael's on a Thursday!" She nods and laughs. I grab her arm to steer. "I saw a table way in the back, away from the piano. That okay?" She nods, and we fight our way through the crowded bar. The entire place twinkles with Christmas lights and wreaths are hung on the windows. We turn left, push through a crush of people waiting for their reservations in the lobby, walk past a wall of windows blinking red, white, green.

We fall into chairs at the only vacant table available, gasping. The table holds a single, lit, red candle, its base adorned with holly.

"This was *your* idea, Izzy!" she pants.

"I know, I know, but I think I'm ready now. Besides, I have news worth celebrating!"

Darlene smiles, brings her drink to her lips, sets the glass on the table. "Ja, I think you are ready."

I regard her face fondly, grateful for her friendship. "I really love this place,"

I say, hugging myself, looking around. You know, I haven't been here since, well, since . . ."

"I know," Darlene says. "I've thought about that. You haven't come here since that awful night with Birdie."

I nod, remembering. A waiter appears. His eyes flash with recognition, and he gives me a flirtatious grin. "Well, if it isn't my favorite sales rep! The usual, Izzy? Where have you been, anyway? I've, um, missed you." His eyes drop to half-mast.

I stare at him a minute, then at Darlene. I am no longer the person I was, I realize. A light has been turned on inside me, and its warm glow seems to consistently expose the dark pull toward the wrong things. I am embarrassed by the way I used to tease the young man leering at me.

"I think tonight, I'll try a Cosmo, like hers," I say, nodding toward Darlene. "I've been busy with, um – "

"Priorities," Darlene finishes for me.

I look at her and smile. "Right."

As the waiter leaves to bring me my drink, Darlene studies me, says, "You *are* a different person now, Izzy. I can see it. Everyone can see it."

"Yeah?" I pause, cock my head, look into her eyes. "Well, I can feel it. Even with the waiter. Do you remember him?"

She laughs. "Oh, yes! I remember thinking you two had something goink on! And that he was way too young for you!"

I let out a deep sigh. "It makes me sick when I think about how blind I was. I thought flirting and being sexy was the way to *be* with men, professional or otherwise. It just always seemed to work."

"Doesn't work," Darlene says, flatly. "Tried to tell you that before, but you weren't ready to hear it. Not the kind of attention you want from men. Seriously."

"I know," I respond, my fingers playing with holly leaves around the candle. A few holly berries roll onto the tablecloth. I put my hands in my lap. "I know that now. I was skeptical about the recovery group thing, but hearing the other women talk about their issues has opened my eyes to mine. How my kids – or anyone, for that matter – could stand me, is a total mystery." The waiter silently delivers my Cosmo, and I take a tentative sip. My face curls into a grimace. Why did I wander away from wine? The Cosmo might as well be Pepto-Bismol. I push it away.

"I always knew that you would wake up. Under all your kidding and gushing about the latest man in your life I saw the woman you could be after you – well, after you balanced all that out. You were just confused, that's all. When things started to fall apart, you got help." She studies the candle. The flame bounces and flickers in her eyes. "That's all that really matters. Don't get too down on yourself."

I look at her. "Well, I got *desperate*, but I didn't go for help. It was forced upon me, thank God! I wonder if I'd ever have gone myself."

Darlene grins. "Who cares? You are where you are supposed to be, you've acknowledged God, you're starting to move in a different direction. It's awesome to vatch, Izzy, and I'm so proud of you!" She picks up her glass, drinks, continues. "Richard and I have completed the marriage counseling, by the way, and I must say, our marriage has never been better." She giggles. "Ve are like newlyweds again!" She slits her eyes, adds, "Including the bedroom!"

"Too much information, Darlene," I laugh in protest. "Remember, I'm a single woman!"

"Not for long, I'm bettink," she responds. "Usually, when I finally lay down my agenda and quit chasing after whatever it is I want; that's when I get it." She shakes her curls, pushes them off her face."How is Jon these days, anyway?"

"Jon is just a friend!" I say, surprised. "What makes you think that he and I are, um, anything else?"

She rolls her eyes. "I see the way you two look at each other. I see him hanging around vaiting for you to get off vork. Come on, Izzy."

"Friends. I'm not really dating right now. It's been hard, but I'm determined to break the hold Findamatch had on me. I had no idea."

Instantly, a pleasurable surge rushes through me like a Pavlovian response. I ignore it, knowing it will subside. In time, I hope it will disappear altogether. "I've got one more month to go before I allow myself to do it again. I don't think it's wrong, per se, but for me, it was an addiction, I am sure of it." I shrug. "So I'm taking a break from it."

"I think you should make it *permanent*, the break," Darlene says.

"Maybe," I say, thoughtfully. "But I don't think the online thing was the enemy. I think somewhere along the line my whole approach to life got screwed up. That if I didn't have a man around – *any* man, didn't matter – I was incomplete. I've thought about this a *lot*. The attention I got from Findamatch validated me. Made me feel loved. I needed male attention like I needed food. Maybe more. It was crazy! I was such an idiot."

Darlene folds her arms and gives me a serious look. "Izzy, you were not an idiot. You simply did not have the tools to choose wisely. You've told me a little about your childhood. It's kind of a classic psychological consequence. The dad in the home is there, but absent. He goes to work, he comes home, doesn't really connect with the family, leaves that to mom. Voila'! Little girl lost. Especially little girls that need lots of attention and affection, but didn't get it from their fathers. The little girls end up being big girls still running after daddy's attention." She shrugs. "Classic."

I nod, look down at the table, and mutter, "If it's so stinkin' classic, why didn't I see it?"

Darlene leans in conspiratorially. "You didn't vant to, of course! You were havink too much fun prowling for the next man! But the fun ends just about the same time the pain starts. Can't outrun the consequences. Just the way it is."

She picks up her drink, holds it high. "Let's toast! To better days ahead!"

I lift my glass toward hers, clink it. "To freedom! Onward! Upward!" She laughs, swings her glass higher, and we drink together. Well, I don't actually drink, I kind of nibble the edge of the glass because a Cosmo is disgusting.

Darlene folds her arms on the table, her face relaxing in a contented sigh. "So, vat are we celebrating? You said you had news."

I lean forward. "Well, for one thing, Jacob – the guy who stalked me – sent a message through his lawyer, apologizing. He's on probation, has done his community service, and is not a threat anymore. That's huge to me."

Darlene's eyes are shining. "That's awesome Izzy! Really somezhink to celebrate! I am so glad that is over for you. One down, one to go," she says, referring to Birdie.

"Actually," I say, "there's an interesting development with that situation."

Her eyes shimmer with interest. "Yes? I think the last thing you told me was about his sentencing for drug possession and trafficking. Did he go to jail? Or did he get probation?"

"He was out on bond for awhile, until sentencing, then a weird thing happened." I give up on the Cosmo and signal the waiter for a glass of wine, letting the suspense build. I waggle my eyebrows at Darlene.

"I can wait you out, Izzy. I know you are dying to tell me," Darlene says, her mouth a pert bow. She clasps her hands in her lap.

The waiter sets a glass of cabernet in front of me. "It's Clos du Val, Izzy. Your favorite," he sighs into my ear. I smile my thanks. He leaves, obviously disappointed by the lack of sexual innuendo in my response. I laugh, then lift and sip, a satisfied smile flitting across my face.

"Phil found this odd loophole that says when it's considered a first-time offense, the person can be remanded to the care of an approved individual."

"You're kidding! What is Phil up to?"

I feel the tears well up, spill. "Compassion. He's such an amazing person! I hated Birdie. *Totally* hated him. But watching Phil, well . . . let's just say I am willing . . . to be willing . . . to forgive."

"So what the heck is Phil doing with him?" Darlene stares at my face intently, her drink forgotten.

"That's the celebration part," I say, enjoying sharing something uplifting.

"He's got Birdie in a recovery group for drug addiction!"

She laughs, delighted. "Oh my goodness! That Phil, he is somezhink!"

"It's all taught me huge lessons, that's for sure." I stare out the window toward the street, watching the quaint, red trolley rumble by. The trolley is decked out in Christmas lights and wears wreaths front and back. A Santa hat tips precariously on one corner, and I wonder how it stays up there. A few specks of snow drift down, then more. The breeze catches the flakes, propels them erratically as they descend. People on the sidewalk look up laughing, hands or tongues extended. Snow in Chatbrook is quite the event.

"What's that, Iz?" It strikes me that it had been a long time since we'd gotten together without a crisis or two hanging over us. Also, sadly, I realize that most of our previous conversations had been dominated by my need to talk about the men in my life.

"Well," I continue, "for one thing, I've come to the conclusion a lot of my decisions have *not* been based on reality." I think a minute, formulating the thoughts that have recently started to coalesce, but hadn't been spoken aloud. "I created this Pollyanna world. Remember those books?"

Darlene nods. "The ones where the young girl played "The Glad Game," right?"

I shake my head. "She always looked on the bright side, no matter what, even though her situation was, well . . . not hopeless, but pretty bad. After I read those books, I adopted her attitude. To the point that it minimized my ability to see reality."

Darlene gazes at me uncertainly.

"Okay, well, somehow I got the idea if I just would put a positive spin on a relationship or a situation, that would make everything turn out okay. Of course, it didn't. I would accept stuff I should have *run* from. I only looked at the positive, and pushed aside the negative."

Darlene's eyes narrow. She lifts her Cosmo, drinks, thinking. Nods in understanding. "Ja, I can see. I remember some of our conversations about the men you dated where you just glossed over certain issues. I thought at the time, uh oh, she might vant to look a little closer at those issues."

"Between the happy face I tried to wear all the time and the daddy thing goin' on – " I sigh deeply. "I was a pretty scary woman."

I pick up the wine, sip. Notes of blackberry and chocolate slide sumptuously down my throat. I silently tell the wine I am sorry I was unfaithful, and promise I'll never stray again.

I continue, "The past few months have taught me no one is beyond help. If my eyes can be opened and I can change, so can anyone else." My laughter is half-hearted. "I was absolutely clueless! And I did the same dumb stuff over and over again!"

Darlene's soft gaze is filled with empathy. "No kiddink. If I think I have it all figured out, that is when I need the most help. I never thought my marriage would get to the point it did. It was a *crisis* that made us seek out a counselor. We were *desperate*. Prayer, too. I think prayer led us to the right things."

"That's another thing," I say in response to her comment. "Prayer. I never gave prayer a thought at all! God was a figment of people's imagination as far as I was concerned." I shrug. "But now, everything is different. Everything."

She tips her glass toward me. "To God!" Our glasses clink.

"So you going to church anywhere, Izzy?"

I shake my head no. "One thing at a time, right?"

She smiles.

"Jon's invited me to his, and I'm thinking about it."

"Just friends, huh, Izzy? I think you have been so confused about men that you can't even recognize a good one when he slaps you in the face." She grins, then edges across the table and whispers. "Just so you know, a good one is slapping you in the face! And you don't even have to dig him up online."

"If he *is* interested, I sure don't recognize the signs. Where's the excitement, the romance? What should I be feeling? What are the correct things to think about? I'm learning all that stuff in my group, and I'm quite frankly, terrified I'll make another mistake. I don't think I've *ever* dated the way it should be done."

Darlene smiles, and says, "Give yourself some time, Izzy. Working on yourself, recognizing what in *you* has been attracting the wrong type of men, that's more important right now. And you are having a hard time forgivink yourself, I think." She signals the waiter to bring menus. "Besides, you can still enjoy Jon's company until you are more sure of yourself. Nothing wrong with being friends."

I am warmed by her encouragement. And she's right. I should work on myself and not think about attracting a guy right now. A romantic relationship is the last thing I need. Forgive myself? Another revelation.

I stare upward at an impressive montage of antique molded tiles and watch the ceiling fan lazily move the air. Our candle's flicker-cadence exactly matches that of the ceiling fan.

"I still struggle, y'know."

Darlene turns from watching the snow cover the sidewalk and street with delicate lace patterns. "You do? With what?"

I sigh. "Wanting that old rush – the rush that comes when a new guy gives me all the attention. Just bein' honest. The thrill of the hunt. I know it's not good to want that, but it felt *incredible*. In a way, it restored my confidence after my last marriage. Made me happy. Gave me energy."

"I understand," she says. "All that feels really good, I don't disagree. But it can be a counterfeit of the real thing. If it has potential, the initial chemical attraction develops into something deeper. Something with roots and stability, that gives you a deep knowing that *this* person is the one you want to do life with. There is such a . . . *peace* about it! Her head tilts as she thinks. Her arms cross. "The initial excitement – the romance – doesn't go away, exactly, it just evolves."

She laughs. "You may not think that sounds so excitink, but there's *deep* contentment in it. For instance, even when Richard and I were having problems, I somehow knew we were going to be okay. I can't explain it, exactly."

She continues. "I think you were in love with the chemical rush of first meetings. And with the online stuff, you were in total control, or at least you thought you were." She leans her elbows on the table, looks out the window. My eyes follow hers. The snow is magical. "So you did it over and over again. But if a relationship is the right one, you aren't in control. It just develops a life of its own. And it feels *perfect*. It's not a struggle." She shrugs, reaches for her glass. "Common sense has to kick in at some point. You cannot just make stuff happen."

I roll my eyes. "Common sense is a buzz kill."

"Right," she says, smiling.

I am comfortable, and it's a new feeling. Though Raphael's is full of available men tonight, I am more interested in chatting with my girlfriend than prowling the bar. This is a miracle.

My reverie is interrupted by Darlene's chuckle. "Vell, vell, vell. Look who's walked in." Her grin is filled with mischief. "Just when you least expect it . . ." She turns her head toward me, picks up her glass in salute.

I follow her gaze down the hall, and see Jon Hoyt in the foyer. His eyes are searching, and eventually land on us. Darlene waves him over. I give her a look. She laughs. Jon's hands busily shed gloves as he walks. His hair glistens with melting snow, and his overcoat is dusted with the stuff. He stops at our table, shaking snow out of his hair. Jon smells like Christmas.

"Hi, ladies," he says, looking directly at me. His hand drops to the back of the empty chair beside me. "This seat taken?"

Darlene's expression is a study in restraint. I am hoping she will pull herself together. Had she told him we were going to be here? My hand gravitates to the coin in my pocket.

I grin at him, and pat the chair. "Savin' it for you, Jon."

ρ

AFTERWORD

This story has been floating around in my head for years.

After years of pursuing a thriving, healthy relationship with disastrous results, I was stunned when I realized I needed to work less on running after a relationship and more on becoming the right kind of woman. My wake-up call was loud and long. So were the consequences of my choices.

Looking back over my relationships with men after spending a few years in a recovery group for codependency, I was sick about some of my choices, but delighted that the blinders were being ripped off my eyes. Eventually, I became more objective, less needy. I was able to stick to a list of non-negotiables when I dated someone.

To be clear, the book is *pure fiction*, not an autobiography. My grown kids have asked me which one of Izzy's kids they are, and I tell them not a single one. They laugh and don't believe me, but it's true. The story is based on a compilation of facts and observances; the characters are a composite of people I've met, worked with, shared a glass of wine with. Maybe Izzy is a little bit like me. Maybe she's a little bit like all of us.

Do you have a similar story? I'd love you to guest post about it on my blog. Feel free to drop me a line at **www.KerryPeresta.com**.

IF YOU, OR SOMEONE YOU KNOW, IS HAVING DIFFICULTY EXTRICATING THEMSELVES FROM UNHEALTHY BEHAVIORS OR RELATIONSHIPS, HERE ARE SOME HELPFUL RESOURCES:

Boundaries: When to Say Yes and How to Say No to Take Control of Your Life, Dr. Henry Cloud and Dr. John Townsend, Zondervan, 2004

Safe People and How to Find Relationships That are Good for You and Avoid Those That Aren't, Dr. Henry Cloud and Dr. John Townsend, Zondervan, 1996

How to Get A Date Worth Keeping
Dr. Henry Cloud, Zondervan, 2005

Life's Healing Choices
John Baker, Simon and Schuster, 2013